MW00807340

The
Mistress and
the Key

Also by Ben Mezrich

The
Mistress and
the Key

BEN
MEZRICH

GRAND
CENTRAL

NEW YORK BOSTON

The events and characters in this book are fictitious. Certain real locations and historical public figures are mentioned, but all other characters and events described in the book are totally imaginary.

Copyright © 2024 by Ben Mezrich

Cover design by Flamur Tonuzi Design. Cover image of face/running man by Hayden Verry /Arcangel; clock tower by Getty Images. Cover copyright © 2024 by Hachette Book Group, Inc.

Hachette Book Group supports the right to free expression and the value of copyright. The purpose of copyright is to encourage writers and artists to produce the creative works that enrich our culture.

The scanning, uploading, and distribution of this book without permission is a theft of the author's intellectual property. If you would like permission to use material from the book (other than for review purposes), please contact permissions@hbgusa.com. Thank you for your support of the author's rights.

Grand Central Publishing
Hachette Book Group
1290 Avenue of the Americas, New York, NY 10104
grandcentralpublishing.com
@grandcentralpub

First Edition: October 2024

Grand Central Publishing is a division of Hachette Book Group, Inc. The Grand Central Publishing name and logo is a registered trademark of Hachette Book Group, Inc.

The publisher is not responsible for websites (or their content) that are not owned by the publisher.

The Hachette Speakers Bureau provides a wide range of authors for speaking events. To find out more, go to hachettespeakersbureau.com or email HachetteSpeakers@hbgusa.com.

Grand Central Publishing books may be purchased in bulk for business, educational, or promotional use. For information, please contact your local bookseller or the Hachette Book Group Special Markets Department at special.markets@hbgusa.com.

Library of Congress Cataloging-in-Publication Data has been applied for.

ISBNs: 978-1-5387-5467-2 (hardcover), 978-1-5387-6910-2 (large type), 978-1-5387-5468-9 (ebook)

Printed in the United States of America

LSC-C

Printing 1, 2024

For my dad, my scientific advisor; and my mom, my first reader
And for Tonya, Asher, and Arya, who are always up for a grand adventure

The
Mistress and
the Key

CHAPTER ONE

Living the dream.

Jeff Pokowski, forty-six and built like a fire hydrant, cursed to himself as he furiously dabbed at the coffee stain spreading across the middle of his flannel shirt while simultaneously navigating his oversized pickup truck down a mostly desolate stretch of the Schuylkill Expressway. The coffee wasn't his fault; the damn night-shift kid at the twenty-four-hour gas station near his house in Glenside—the sort of working-class suburb that lately felt more working than class—was either perpetually stoned or stupid, more likely a combination of both. He'd overfilled Pokowski's order again, taxing the structural integrity of the disposable cup and its plastic cover, which had obviously been designed by someone equally stoned or equally stupid. Then again, Pokowski had a growing suspicion that most people he met, worked with, or was related to were incompetent.

In most lines of work, that didn't matter much: A keyboard warrior at some accounting company screws up, someone's paycheck is late; a kid at a gas station overfills a coffee cup, maybe he ruins someone's morning. But in Pokowski's profession—construction—lack of attention had a tendency to domino. Measure a beam wrong or put a few screws out of place, ten moves later, you got a building collapsing on the nightly news.

Which was why it wasn't completely unusual for him to be

1

spiriting his truck down the Schuylkill at four thirty a.m. on a Tuesday. He was the head site manager—what they used to call a foreman—on Apex Development's newest project, a twenty-six-story mixed-use office tower and retail monolith squatting near City Hall. As such, he'd enjoyed plenty of face-to-face time with the pimply teenager working the midnight-to-five at the Citgo station by the ramp to the expressway.

Still, today's call had been more annoying than most. As Pokowski continued attacking the coffee stain, which was now roughly the shape of Texas and still spreading, he tossed a glance at his phone on the passenger seat.

Six automated calls, actually, beginning around two a.m., from the worksite's security panel. Not quite a misplaced beam or an errant screw but, according to the calls, at least one of the proximity alarms at the site had been going off for nearly three hours now. Neither of the two overnight security guards had called in from location or reset the password. Worse, neither of the bozos—Ted Passatore, a sliver of a kid who'd busted out of cop school six months ago, and Lucas Balloux, a Canadian working his way through some sort of grad school at the city college—had answered their cells when Pokowski had tried them. He'd finally given up and crawled out of bed, nearly overturning Annie, his wife, in the process. She had a habit of sleeping with one of her legs draped over the lower half of Pokowski's body, which had seemed sexy for the first seven years of their marriage, but now felt more albatross than swan.

Thirteen years in, she'd barely stirred as he'd gotten dressed in the dark. Pokowski hadn't been overly concerned; no doubt, the two security guards had wandered off their posts for an unregistered break. For Teddy, it would be par for the course; the kid had been kicked out of cop school for a laundry list of minor indiscretions, and he was a frequent visitor to many of Philadelphia's after-hours bars. If the job market hadn't gotten so tight in the previous couple of years, Pokowski never would have hired him. But Teddy had come with a license to carry and a promise that he would do his best to reform. Pokowski had always been a sucker for screwups begging for a second chance.

Lucas was more of a surprise; the guy spoke four languages and brought philosophy textbooks with him to his shift. But Pokowski knew how boring it could get on a worksite during those hours after midnight, when the streets went dead save for the late-night bar hoppers, the odd and ambling flocks of homeless, and the ever-present scurry of oversize sidewalk rats.

Whatever the reason for the lack of response, Pokowski had had no choice but to drag his ass down to Center City. Ten minutes more and his Ford was now slithering through narrow streets, a densely packed span of modern and old, lined on either side by gentrified rental apartments and ritzy retail stores with glass façades and imposing front steps. These were not the eighteenth-century row houses he'd have passed in Old City, or the colorful awnings, diverse eateries, and dive bars he'd find in South Philly. Here, the cars parked on the curbs were mostly black, fancy, and foreign. He made his final turn onto Seventh Street and immediately saw a familiar gap in the urban sprawl—a high chain-link fence, running the length of a football field, that outlined his worksite.

His heart beat a little harder as he parked his truck alongside the fence. There was something thrilling about a site at this stage in the development phase. Even though an office building wasn't exactly the Taj Mahal, the idea that soon something huge and permanent would rise out of the scar of dirt on the other side of the fence, changing the landscape of the city for perhaps centuries to come, was a heady thing to contemplate.

But the feeling was short-lived. As he stepped out of his truck and onto the sidewalk it was hard not to notice that behind the fence there was a palpable lack of dinosaurs—no diggers or excavators or dump trucks, just a long stretch of churned-up dirt lit by various lanterns hanging from orange extension cords.

The dinosaurs had been pulled off the job four days ago—barely a week into the initial foundation dig—and Pokowski couldn't even hazard a guess as to when they would be back.

He grimaced as he moved along the sidewalk toward the entrance gate a dozen yards down the fence. Of course, he'd had worksites shuttered many times before; no matter how much preparation went in before groundbreaking, issues could always pop up. Sewer problems, electrical complications, even the rare sinkhole that somehow eluded the geological surveys and sonar flyovers, which could translate to weeks of overtime as the teams of engineers figured out a workaround—but there was almost always a workaround. Once, on a project just south of Center City, Pokowski had been on a site that had ground to a stop when a shovel team had uncovered a dead body; that had been a headache and a half, once Philly PD had gotten involved and turned the whole damn place into a crime scene. Pokowski could imagine that plenty of champagne flowed around Apex Development's head offices when the ME determined the man had OD'd on fentanyl, negating the need for a homicide investigation or a lengthy trial, and the police tape had come down almost as quickly as it had gone up.

But Pokowski knew this situation wasn't going to be anywhere near as simple to solve. This particular stoppage had nothing to do with sinkholes or dead junkies. Hell, this headache was the sort of thing that could only happen in a handful of places, a rarified list of geographical locations. Center City, Philadelphia, just happened to be one of them.

He reached the gate and drew a key from his belt, but then he realized the lock was already open. Damn—not only had the two idiots left their posts, they hadn't secured the site on their way out. Anyone could have wandered in. With Pokowski's luck, a herd of homeless might have already set up a camp by the port-a-potties, and he'd need a court order before he'd get any help from the local PD to get them rousted. He shook his head in anger as he pushed through the gate, and into the wide-open dirt field of his worksite.

A glance toward the village of blue portable lavatories, in the nearest corner of the wide, rectangular field, set his mind a little at ease. But it wasn't really the port-a-potties that captured his attention as he let the gate shut behind him; his thoughts instinctively followed the makeshift path that ran down the center of the vast site, lit by a string of lanterns hanging from fence posts that had been driven into the thick, upturned dirt.

Thirty feet in, the dimly lit path ended in what looked to be a dark indentation in the dirt; he'd been there the morning that the shovel crew had dug through the four feet of topsoil—and had seen the looks on their faces when the lower ridge of their excavator's scoop had clanged against something that damn well wasn't supposed to be there.

He made short work of the dimly lit path, his workboots thudding against the packed dirt as he went. He slowed as he reached the lip of the decline, then lowered himself to the top rung of the short ladder his crew had set up when they'd first realized what they'd found.

The sound his boots made when they hit the flattened-out ground beneath the ladder was decidedly different; even though there was still a thin layer of topsoil, it was obvious that beneath the dirt was something hard, a layer of stone. At first, his crew had assumed it was natural, a bit of limestone that the geological survey had missed or an underground boulder that was angled just right to have confused the sonar. But then Pokowski had given his guys the go-ahead to start scraping away the dirt—and he'd seen, along with the rest of them, that there was nothing natural about what they had found.

The surface beneath this area of their dig site was indeed stone, but not a single, sheer layer, like he would have expected. It was made up of what appeared to be small, polished individual stones, that had been cobbled together with some sort of mortar he was not familiar with. Breaking protocol, Pokowski had been curious enough to turn one of his drill teams loose on a section of the mortared stones; when they'd suddenly broken through to some sort of underground cavern, Pokowski had realized they'd found something well beyond his pay grade.

Then again, a cobbled-up cavern that wasn't supposed to be there, on its own, probably wouldn't have been enough to shut down a worksite that was conservatively costing Apex three hundred thousand dollars a day. But then Pokowski's geological engineers had climbed down through the hole his drill team had cut into the stones, then come back up with wide eyes and gaping jaws—and Pokowski knew his life was about to get complicated.

Eight hours later, an entire battalion of PhDs from the city's Historical Heritage Foundation had been trampling through his worksite, sporting notebooks and digital cameras, looking like kids on Christmas morning.

Now, standing at the edge of the cobblestones, Pokowski peered through the darkened opening, which his crew had carved into a shape resembling a manhole and outfitted with a steel-runged ladder. He shook his head again. Twenty years on the job, he'd never had a stoppage caused by an archeological find. Although he himself hadn't been down into the hole—the Heritage wonks had made it exceedingly clear that nobody was to set foot in what was now the property of the City of Philadelphia—he'd been told that it was going to make national news when the HHF finally released their findings, and photos, to the media.

As he stood there, in the dim light of the lanterns, and looked at that inviting, gaping manhole—Pokowski had to admit he was a little curious. He wondered if Teddy and Lucas had maybe gotten a little curious themselves. Had a few drinks at one of the after-hours places then stumbled back, setting off the proximity alarms, and climbed down to take a look.

Pokowski leaned his head down toward the opening and listened. He didn't hear anyone mucking about down there, but that didn't really mean anything. From the amount of time the HHF folks had spent down the bottom of that ladder, he was pretty sure whatever was there was more extensive than a single cobblestone cavern.

He rubbed his jaw, then decided he might as well check it out. He was, after all, head site manager. A mouthful like that had to come with some level of discretion, didn't it?

He heaved himself over the edge and started down the ladder.

It wasn't until Pokowski stepped off the last rung that he realized the floor of the cavern was made of the same cobblestone as the ceiling, now a good eight feet above his head. It took him a moment to find the switch for the string of electric torches his engineers had strung in random twists along the walls. As the dim orange light flickered through the space, Pokowski saw immediately that whoever had constructed the cavern had been skilled, careful, and precise. The walls had been mortared together with very few gaps, and the handful of wooden beams and cross boarded rafters that held the ceiling up had been lacquered in some sort of preservative. Even after being sealed up for an incredible length of time, they had barely warped, certainly not enough to have given the structural engineers who had first climbed down here any real concerns about the place caving in.

It was a strange feeling, stepping forward into a place that had been sealed up for what the HHF wonks figured were more than two and a half centuries. When someone had last strolled across these stones, names like Washington and Jefferson weren't simply embedded on street signs or splashed through the pages of history books. This place *was* history. Even in Philadelphia, finding a perfectly preserved structure from the Revolutionary War era was nearly unheard of. The last thing the HHF could compare the discovery to was when a demolition of a bank building on Fifty-Third Street had revealed a vault dating back to the turn of the twentieth century, still containing three saddle bags filled with banknotes.

One step forward into the cavern, and Pokowski could tell that the HHF had stumbled onto something much more exciting than a money-filled vault.

The walls on either side of him were lined with wooden shelves, the wood held together by the same shiny preservative that coated the main beams. The lowest shelves were mainly taken up by books—thick volumes, many with gilded covers that might have been lined with silver and gold. He couldn't quite make out the titles in the dim lighting, but he wasn't interested enough in the reading material of the time to take a closer look. More interesting were the items on the higher shelves. Glass jars, beakers, and test tubes, interspersed with devices that looked like old-fashioned scales, oil lamps, and mechanical objects he couldn't begin to identify. He recognized gears and hand cranks, but could not imagine what the various machines were used for, or what they were doing in this underground cavern—

His thoughts paused as he heard a noise from directly ahead—some sort of shuffling sound, perhaps workboots against the cobbled floor. He peered forward and saw that the cavern he was in curved to the right, into what appeared to be a narrow hallway.

"Lucas? Teddy? You morons down here?"

Maybe he was being a little harsh, but he knew how much trouble he himself would get into if the HHF figured out that he had been poking around in their sandbox. Lucas and Teddy were looking at a quick firing, possibly even a citation for trespassing.

To Pokowski's surprise, there was no answer from up ahead. He took a breath, tasting musty air, and started forward. Four steps, and he'd crossed the cavern and entered the hallway, which ran several more yards, then turned a sharp corner into what looked like an open space, maybe twice as big as the one he had just come from. As he reached the threshold, he noticed that the room was significantly darker than the one he had just moved through. Though the electric torches continued along the walls on either side, it appeared that a number of the bulbs toward the far end of the room had either blown out or been unscrewed.

As he crossed into the large space, it took a moment for his eyes to adjust. There were more shelves on either side, piled high with more devices, and he got the immediate feeling that this was some sort of laboratory. He hadn't been a great student in middle school and he didn't know much about Revolutionary times. Muskets and cannons and crap like that; did they even have scientists yet? Wasn't it an era still dominated by things like witchcraft and astrology?

He took another step forward, searching ahead for the two security guards. Beyond the shelves, he began to see more objects he couldn't identify: more mechanical-looking machines, some quite large, with gears and levers and sporting hand cranks and foot pedals. But his attention quickly shifted from the devices to three much more recognizable objects at the very far end of the room. *Three heavy wooden chairs, facing him.* One more step deeper into the darkened space—then he realized the chairs on the ends were occupied.

He immediately recognized Lucas, on the chair to the far left. The young grad student turned security guard was sitting straight up against the wood, his wide shoulders back and his arms resting on the chair's thick armrests. He was in his uniform, which looked starched and clean, and the badge on his shirt glinted in the sparse light. But above his collar, his face looked—wrong. His blue eyes were open, wide, as was his mouth. But even from a distance, Pokowski could see that his skin was abnormally pale. Almost white, like porcelain.

Pokowski's gaze shifted to the other occupied chair. Even with the uniform, it took Pokowski an extra second to recognize Teddy. The kid was also upright against the wood, arms against the armrests. But where Lucas's face was abnormally white, Teddy's face was—

"Christ," Pokowski gasped, stumbling backward. Before he could turn and run, something moved toward him incredibly fast. He felt an arm twist around his neck and then he lost his footing. The arm tightened around his throat, cutting off his blood supply, and for a moment the room darkened. He felt himself being dragged forward, his 180-pound frame nothing more than a bag of feathers.

A moment later, he was shoved backward into the empty seat between the two security guards. His arms were yanked behind his back, twisted at an odd and excruciating angle, then bound together at the wrists by something that felt like wire. He struggled, but he was pinned to the chair by his arms, and even the most minor motion caused the wires to dig into his skin.

The figure came around in front of him. It was a man, indeterminate age, thin, angular, with high, bony cheekbones. The man's skin was almost translucent, and his blond hair was thinning and perfectly cut; it appeared the effort of dragging Pokowski across the underground chamber hadn't displaced a single strand.

The man straightened the sleeves of his impeccably cut, sky-blue suit, then cocked his head to one side. "Mr. Pokowski?"

Pokowski looked at the man, bewildered. His arms were killing him, and his chest was heaving against the coffee stain painting the plaid of his shirt.

"Your colleagues were kind enough to inform me that you'd be stopping by, when they were unable to check in."

Pokowski swallowed, feeling the bruises rising around his throat from the man's obviously practiced chokehold. "Who are you?"

"Not really relevant. It's much more important who you are. You see, your colleagues were unable to provide me with the information that I need. Not for lack of trying—they were quite agreeable chaps—after a fashion."

Pokowski glanced toward Lucas, to his right. The Canadian wasn't moving, and his skin seemed even more glassy and pale up close. Pokowski shifted to his left, toward Teddy—but stopped himself before his gaze settled on the poor kid's face.

"Stay with me," the thin man in the suit continued. "As I said, I need information. It's really quite simple. Two days ago, an engraving made its way to a pawnshop not three blocks from your worksite. This engraving was very intriguing to my employers."

The man reached into his suit jacket and removed a photograph. Pokowski squinted to get a better look. It was black-and-white, a picture of a picture—the engraving, he assumed. It showed two men in some sort of workshop. On a table between the men were two objects; even in a photograph of an engraving, the objects were easily recognizable.

A kite. And a key.

At least one of the men in the photo was also familiar, maybe both. But Pokowski was finding it hard to concentrate on something he might have learned about in seventh grade, while tied to a chair between two dead bodies.

"I don't know anything about that," he finally murmured.

"No, I wouldn't expect you would."

The man put the photograph back into his jacket.

"I spent some quality time with the owner of the pawnshop, but unfortunately the man wasn't helpful at all. Not entirely his fault; an octogenarian, half-blind. He couldn't give me much to go on as to the identity of the individual who had sold him the engraving. But he had confirmed that the seller had in his possession a number of remarkable items that might be of similar appeal to my benefactors."

The man turned, casting a gaze over the shelves loaded with artifacts behind him.

"A minor bit of detective work brought me here, to this... place. A mid-eighteenth-century laboratory accidentally unearthed by your excavators, just a few miles from the old man and his pawnshop. Seemed like a likely place to start, don't you think?"

The man's eyes settled on an odd, rather large piece of equipment standing next to the shelf; it was some sort of machine, made mostly of wood, about four feet high. The base was an oversized pedestal, on top of which sat a round glass ball, the size and shape of a fishbowl. The ball sat on a cushion of what appeared to be rough felt; above it, a complex system of gears connected to a pair of pulleys, which ran all the way down to the ground, where Pokowski noticed an oversized foot pedal. Next to the pedal, a pair of what appeared to be long metal needles ran from the machine to a series of glass panels, which were hanging by strings from a strange copper rack. On the other side of the panels was another long needle, attached to a length of thin copper wire.

"It's quite an exquisite piece, don't you think? According to my employers, who were intrigued by the photos I forwarded them before you arrived, it's an electrostatic generator, attached to a series of modified Leyden jars. Circa 1750. It was a marvel of the time period."

The man stepped toward the machine and returned holding the long needle. The copper wire snaked out behind him as he approached Pokowski's chair. Pokowski noticed that the base of the needle where the man gripped it tightly was covered in some sort of dark rubber.

"Though it seems rudimentary today, this device represented a groundbreaking advancement in man's mastery of his environment. Static electricity was generated, and then captured, through conduction into glass batteries. You wouldn't think so from looking at it, but this device is capable of generating ten times the voltage of your average commercial electrical socket."

He held the needle in front of him, turning it in his hand.

"At the time, it was used mostly for parlor tricks. 'Electrical fire,' they called it, scientific advancement in the form of a magician's act. In the court of Louis XIV, a hundred and eighty soldiers standing in a line, holding hands, were made to jump into the air from a single, small charge. Game birds were regularly killed and cooked, for audiences in the dozens. Giant sparks lit up darkened theaters, to grandiose applause."

The man seemed to smirk, as he turned the tip of the needle toward Pokowski.

"Trivial applications of such a powerful invention, in my opinion. But it's not the brush that creates great art; it's the hand that holds it."

Pokowski stared at that needle, hanging just a few feet in front of where he was pinned to the chair. He felt his throat constricting.

"What do you want from me?" he pleaded. "I don't know anything about any pawnshop."

"But you do know who might have had access to this place. You could give me a list of names, likely threads to follow. Access to employee files, current addresses."

"I'll tell you anything you want," Pokowski blurted, still staring at that needle.

The man paused. But the smirk remained, as he lifted a foot and placed it on the pedal at the base of the electrostatic device. He gave it a single pump, and Pokowski's gaze shot to the glass ball, which had begun to spin.

There was a sizzling sound, and Pokowski felt the hair on his arms rise. Suddenly the man was moving forward, the needle shifting toward Pokowski's face.

"Wait," Pokowski said. "I said I'll tell you everything!"

"I'm sure you will," the man said, but the needle kept moving closer.

Pokowski squirmed against the chair. His arms fought against the wire, which dug into his wrists. He arched back, but the needle was now only inches from his face. He turned his head to the side. Despite himself, he was looking right at Teddy, and now he couldn't avoid seeing the poor kid's face. Unlike Lucas's, the kid's skin was bright red, a color that reminded Pokowski of a boiled lobster, or maybe the way the sun might look, in an hour or two, when the first flecks of dawn woke the city above this damn cavern, or laboratory, or tomb. Bright red, even more so than the kid's rigid, open mouth. But Teddy's skin wasn't the worst part. The worst part—*his eyes*.

Teddy's eyes were no longer in their sockets. They were hanging, lifeless, down against his cheeks, from the burned, tangled cords of his optic nerves.

Pokowski started to scream, but the needle was already arcing toward his chin. A second later, his entire world went white.

CHAPTER TWO

Two hours later and three hundred miles north, Special Agent Zack Lindwell leaned against the cool stone of one of a half dozen Corinthian columns framing a side courtyard of the Massachusetts State House—one of the most imposing buildings in the Commonwealth, situated near the peak of Beacon Hill, across from the bucolic calm of the iron-gated Boston Commons. Zack breathed in the crisp early-morning air; his chest still felt tight, a sensation that he tried his best to ignore.

It didn't do him any good to dwell on what he had experienced not twenty hours earlier. When he blinked, he was still lying on the deck of a 225-year-old sailing ship, his entire body paralyzed as he slowly suffocated from a paralytic poison that had been injected into his arm by a killer with long sable hair and high heels. He shook his head and tried to focus on the present, but he couldn't go a minute without those thoughts creeping back in. Still, it wasn't going to do him any good to dwell on what might have happened, what almost happened—*what didn't happen.*

Because he had, indeed, survived, and the moment on the sailing ship hadn't been the end of an investigation: *It was the beginning.* Which was why he was standing in this courtyard, beneath the shadow of the State House's famous gilded dome, an address he had visited numerous times in his capacity as the head of the Art Crimes Division of the FBI's Boston Field Office.

Although the two-story red brick façade of what was likely Charles Bulfinch's crowning accomplishment was an impressive example of the Federal style, it wasn't the architecture that had drawn Zack to this address again and again over the years. He had come for the art—paintings, sculptures, rare artifacts—inside the marbled halls crisscrossing the nineteenth-century seat of local government. The State House had one of the oldest public collections in the country, with over three hundred works dating back to the Revolutionary Era, and it had many times been a target for thieves both opportunistic and sophisticated.

In the 1970s, a band of criminals had attempted to make away with the Abraham Lincoln portrait in the Doric Hall, the former main entrance to the building that was now mostly a museum; they had nearly made it to the grand ceremonial front doors, reserved for visiting presidents and foreign heads of state, when a passing state trooper had noticed their getaway van parked down Beacon Street.

A decade and a half later, a page from the 1629 Massachusetts Bay Company Charter was successfully taken from the basement of the main building in a brazen, daytime heist; luckily, the artifact was recovered seven months later, by accident, in a raid on a local drug dealer's home—the priceless piece of history found just sitting in a cardboard box, next to used needles and other drug paraphernalia.

Nearly every decade since, attempts had been made on the various portraits and sculptures dating back to the late eighteenth century. Zack himself had investigated two such incidents: He'd recovered a bust of George Washington that had been pilfered from a third-floor conference room by someone in the State House cleaning service, as well as a drawer full of Revere silverware that had disappeared after a governor's dinner not six years before.

Zack could still remember the chills he'd felt seeing the sweeping initials—*P.R.*—carved into the spoons and knives when he'd intercepted and cracked open a packing crate on the cargo belt at Logan International, just minutes before it was about to be loaded onto a flight leaving for Europe. The silverware had not been anywhere near as valuable as the missing page from the Massachusetts Bay Charter, but the near disappearance of something as lowly as a fork, crafted by one of the most famous figures in American history, had reminded Zack of why he'd chosen to dedicate his adult life to chasing art thieves. That piece of silverware was more than its simple, artfully molded curves; it was a—however small— piece in the chain of human creativity, and its value went beyond whatever it might bring at auction or in whatever black market bazaar it might have eventually ended up in.

It wasn't merely the thought of a valuable artifact being stolen that disturbed Zack to his core; he knew, better than most, that the vast majority of stolen art was never recovered. Only 5 percent of works taken from museums, private collections, or public spaces such as the State House was ever seen again, which meant that a theft of a famous painting or sculpture, or even a fork signed by Paul Revere, wasn't just an ordinary crime, like a bank robbery or a mugging; it was an offense against history itself.

Zack pushed off the stone column and stepped forward into the courtyard, wearing a grim look that had nothing to do with his weakened physical state. The place was deserted, not only because of the early hour but because it was ostensibly still a crime scene, one that had nothing to do with stolen silverware. There were six police cruisers parked a dozen yards behind him along Beacon, and at least ten officers were still milling about inside the building and beneath the scaffolding that rose up along Bowdoin Street, on the other side of the golden dome.

A crime scene, though it wasn't even entirely clear that any crime had actually occurred, at least anywhere near the courtyard where Zack was standing. He'd listened to the chatter on the police band in his car as he drove over from the hospital, where he'd been kept for observation since he'd been taken from the sailing ship, now docked in the Charlestown Navy Yard. It was obvious that the officers on the scene were running blind. The initial incident that had brought the lights and sirens—a gunshot reported by neighbors a few blocks away, at the corner of Mt. Vernon Street and Acorn—had begun the confusion; instead of shell casings and bullet holes, the officers had found the remains of a shattered gas lamp and evidence of the strangest caliber of ammunition any of them had ever seen. Not a bullet, but a lead musket ball that had apparently been fired by a Revolutionary Era pistol, shattered pieces of which were still strewn about the cobbled street corner.

In quick succession, the reports of the musket shot had been coupled with an even more alarming call: An elderly woman in a third-floor apartment directly across Bowdoin Street from the back of the State House had been washing her hair at around four a.m., when she was certain she'd seen someone fall off the side of the building—from right below the edge of the golden dome.

The officers had indeed found blood, but no body, on the stones of a courtyard similar to the one where Zack stood; forensic teams had been going over the area for many hours now, with little results.

An antique musket fired at a streetlamp in a quiet corner of Beacon Hill and a jumper from the dome atop the State House might not have brought a dozen cops and a full forensic team to the State House steps. It certainly wouldn't have warranted a visit from an FBI agent. But after what Zack had seen over the past two days, he didn't fault the Boston Police Department for reacting zealously to the incoming reports. A dead body tied to a chair at the Encore casino in Everett, then two more corpses found lying prone in a warehouse in South Boston, followed by incidents at three major historical landmarks spread across the city: the Bunker Hill Monument, the Boston Tea Party Museum, and finally, the USS *Constitution*, the famous former warship and floating museum. Zack himself had been assaulted there while trying to protect the two prime suspects linking all the crime scenes together. It was as complex a case as he'd ever encountered. And all of it was somehow linked to the biggest unsolved art heist in history.

Zack shook his head as he took another step into the courtyard, then focused his gaze on the object that dominated the center of the stone space ahead of him. Not a painting, certainly not one of the eleven paintings that had been lifted from the Gardner Museum over thirty years before and never recovered—Zack had spent the previous two days shadowing the BPD as they stumbled from crime scene to crime scene, chasing hints that the missing artwork might finally surface. The object in front of him wasn't stolen art at all; it was a *bell*. Not just any bell, but a perfectly crafted replica of the Liberty Bell, one of fifty that had been sent to each and every state as part of a fundraising project back in the 1950s. Crafted to the exact specifications of the actual Liberty Bell, which was still housed near the tower in the Pennsylvania State House in Philadelphia, the 280-pound bronze instrument had originally sat prominently near the front entrance to the Massachusetts State House. But after the terrorist attacks of 9/11, the replica bell had been relegated to this side courtyard, where it had gone mostly unnoticed in the ensuing decades.

Certainly, nobody had tried to steal the hefty object, and under normal circumstances Zack would have had little reason to care about a replica bell with little appeal to the sort of thieves he'd made his career apprehending. But these weren't normal circumstances, and Zack might have found himself in this same spot, in the shadow of the golden dome, even if the BPD hadn't gotten calls of fired muskets and falling bodies.

He took another step—then paused, noticing immediately that something was wrong. The bell, he knew, was supposed to be a perfect replica of the original bell, down to the consistency of the bronze used in the mold and the mathematical curve of its sides; but he also knew that one aspect of the original was not supposed to have been copied. And yet here—

"It's cracked," he heard himself say, out loud, because it made no sense.

The crack ran right up the middle of the bell from its bottom edge, exactly as he'd remembered seeing in photos. He had no way of knowing how long the crack had been there, or if it was some-how related to the events of the night before. Could something like that have happened naturally, the result of age, or faulty design, or the difficult Boston weather? Surely, someone would have noticed such a thing, and reported it to the State House staff—something Zack would be able to check when he returned to his office.

He continued forward again, until he was right in front of the Bell, which seemed even larger up close. Then he slowly lowered himself to his knees. The motion hurt—his body still felt stiff from his brush with the paralytic, but his curiosity consumed him, mak-ing it hard to think about anything else. He lowered his head until he could look under the bottom lip of the bell—

And there it was, hanging as if it had been designed specifically for the job, the bronze clapper. He knew he should have gone back to his car for evidence gloves, but he couldn't control himself. He carefully reached up into the bell and found where the clapper was fastened to a hook at its center, then gently removed the object and brought it out from under the curved sides of the instrument.

It was heavy and thick, at least a foot long. The surface was smooth but looked very old, much older than the replica in front of him. He placed it delicately on the stone floor of the courtyard and then turned it to the side. There, clearly written across the bronze:

"Proclaim Liberty."

Zack breathed hard, his cheeks warming. So he *had* seen it right; lying there on the deck of the USS *Constitution*, in the mayhem around him—he'd seen that same clapper, lying in a box that appeared to have been made of gold, sporting that same broken phrase: *Proclaim Liberty*.

"You gotta be kidding me," a guttural voice suddenly broke from behind Zack in the courtyard.

Zack didn't need to turn around to know it was Marsh, the burly, pug-nosed detective who had been leading the case for the BPD since the first body had been found. Marsh's voice had a tinge of violence to it, which seemed even more grating at such an early hour. Zack figured he should cut the man some slack; they had both been going straight for a long time, with little to show for their efforts. What had begun for Zack as an investigation into those long-lost paintings had morphed into a tour of the city's historic landmarks, always on the heels of the pair of fugitives who seemed to be leaving so much mayhem in their wake.

Marsh thought the fugitives—a young woman with a troubled past, and an ex-con who favored denim and had just matriculated from a five-year stint at MCI-Shirley for a series of bank jobs—had left a trail of dead bodies across his city and was angry enough by now that any trace of the perpetually suffering police grunt's objectivity had long since evaporated. But Zack had already begun seeing the case through a much more nuanced lens, even before the young woman had saved his life on the deck of the *Constitution*.

"What, they took time off from their killing spree to try and steal a bell?" Marsh grunted.

Zack shook his head. He didn't believe Hailey Gordon and Nick Patterson had killed anyone; they had been intimately involved with the stolen artwork from the Gardner, but the trail of bodies had been the work of the people chasing them. Hailey and Nick might have been thieves, or thief-adjacent, but they weren't killers. He also knew Marsh wasn't the sort of cop who got nuance.

"They didn't come here to steal the bell," Zack said, his back still to the detective. "Just to ring it."

Zack could feel Marsh staring at him, but he didn't say more. He didn't know what he could have said, certainly nothing that would have made sense to the detective. He hadn't made sense of it to himself yet. He took the bronze clapper in his hands and slowly rose to his feet.

Marsh looked at the thing in his hands, and the rolls of his thick, jowly face hunched together. "That some sort of evidence?"

Zack didn't answer. He wasn't sure. The bell, the clapper— they were somehow connected to whatever Hailey and Nick were after. Pieces in a puzzle, brushstrokes of a painting still unrevealed.

Without a word, Zack moved across the courtyard, passing the confused detective. Marsh was a blunt instrument; he wasn't the type to care about the bigger picture. His goal was to bludgeon his way to an arrest. For Zack, an arrest was almost always besides the point. He hadn't dedicated his life to solving art crimes to catch criminals.

For Zack, it was *always* about the bigger picture. Recovering art before it was lost forever, restoring the links in the chain of human creativity before it was irrevocably broken.

He had gotten involved in this case because of the missing Gardner paintings, but he was certain the puzzle in front of him, the painting waiting for his brush strokes, was something even more valuable, and more important, than solving the biggest art heist in history.

CHAPTER THREE

The needle was at least three inches long, glistening steel that flashed even in the dim light of the windowless storage room. Small bore, tapered to a frighteningly sharp point, trailing a dangling twist of antiseptic thread that spun behind like the string and ribbons of a kite caught in a turbulent wind. The needle hovered for a moment above the bare skin of Nick Patterson's shoulder, held not unmenacingly between the rubber-gloved fingers of a trash-can-shaped man with a thicket of dark, curly hair and five days of scruff. Then it descended in a sudden, vicious arc.

"Ouch," Nick spat.

The man grinned, as he began suturing the four-inch wound that ran from Nick's upper delt almost to the bottom ridge of his trapezius.

"I told you this would hurt you way more than it would hurt me. Next time try and have them shoot you in the leg. Lots more skin to work with."

Hailey Gordon winced as much from the man's thick Boston accent as from watching his work with the needle. She was only a few feet away, perched on a metal stool she'd found in a corner of the cramped space. The man with the needle sat on a similar stool; only Nick was enjoying the first-class accommodations of a half-reclined dental chair, its dark green vinyl bristling with chrome knobs and levers. There was even a spit sink next to him, which was now filled with bloody gauze and used medical tape.

"Your bedside manner leaves a lot to be desired," Nick grunted, as the needle went back and forth through his skin, slowly sealing up the wound.

"That's why I became a dentist and not a doctor. Everyone assumes we're sadists. Hell, it would be a disappointment if I didn't act like an asshole."

"Not much risk of that," Nick said.

"Hey, nobody's tried to put a bullet in *me*. You've been outside, what, two weeks? And already someone's been using you for target practice."

After a quick glance at Nick's six-foot-two frame sprawled out on the dental chair, Hailey winced again. Nick had been bruised and battered over the past two days to a point that would have broken most men; the bullet that had grazed his shoulder was only the most visible of his injuries, the one that had needed immediate attention. His head was wrapped with a strip of bandage, and one of his ribs was at least bruised, possibly cracked. Under better circumstances, she'd be checking him in to a hospital right now, not listening to the dropped consonants and overblown vowels of a "stitchman," as Nick had referred to him, in a basement storage room beneath a dental office tucked into a nondescript alley in Dorchester. One of the few stretches of the south side of the city that had somehow avoided gentrification, which made it a relatively safe place. Or safe enough, Nick had told her, when he'd finally agreed to deal with his shoulder before continuing down the rabbit hole.

Hailey was pretty sure that even for Nick, their hunt for answers was no longer just about money. At first, sure, they had both been after a quick and easy score. He had been trying to fence the stolen

Gardner art, eleven paintings worth half a billion dollars that his associates had tucked away in a warehouse in Southie, not more than a few blocks from where they were now. She had stumbled into the scheme while running from casino security after card-counting her way through the Encore's blackjack pit. And she had gone along for the ride because it had seemed like the right thing to do. Well, maybe not "right" in the mainstream, philosophical sense of the word, but as someone who'd been on her own since the age of twelve, living under a fake name in a carefully constructed false reality, she didn't exactly function within the traditional conceptions of morality.

But compared to Nick, she was a choir girl; she pulled off cons, but he was *actually* a con, an ex-con, recently released from prison and right back to the same playground that had landed him behind bars in the first place. The only surprising thing about Nick had been what had happened after their easy score had fallen apart, after their attempts to sell the stolen artwork had led them into a mystery spiraling backward 250 years, a trail of dead bodies piling up behind them as they chased that secret down Boston's Freedom Trail with trained killers on their heels.

As Hailey had grown more determined to find answers to what was really going on—what was valuable enough that it had inspired the Gardner theft, a series of murders across the city, and, in some ways, the historical events that had led to the Revolutionary War itself—Nick had been the one suddenly along for the ride. He could have left her on her own multiple times, which might have been the smart thing to do, but he seemed equally determined to see this through. Maybe he still had his eyes on the value of what they were seeking—incalculable wealth, world-changing power—but Hailey believed that Nick was as much in this for her as he was for whatever score they could get.

Which meant she now felt a sense of responsibility beyond whatever other feelings were building inside her. As they'd made their way out of Beacon Hill the night before, weaving between the gas lamps and the early-morning joggers that skirted along the edges of the Commons, Nick had started to flag behind—and Hailey had immediately suggested a stop at the nearest emergency room. But Nick had been against the idea; they were probably the two most sought-after fugitives in the city, and there would certainly be police officers wandering the halls of Mass General or Boston City Hospital. It was then that Nick had volunteered the address of his old acquaintance, Micky Carpenter, DDS. A burly man in scrubs working out of a basement in Dorchester, who had greeted them at the door upstairs, bleary-eyed and not at all thrilled to be awoken at such an early hour.

"Thought you were still inside," was all he'd said, before he let Nick and Hailey into the first floor of his office. It was little more than a reception desk and a single dental chair as scuffed and weathered as the one in the basement that Nick now occupied.

"Been out a couple of weeks," Nick had responded.

Micky had hit them with a mild smile. "You work fast." And then: "You got cash?"

Once downstairs, it had taken the stitchman less than ten minutes to assess Nick's injuries, shoot him up with an antibiotic and a mild painkiller, and hook up a bag of saline to his uninjured arm. Nick wasn't going to be as good as new, Micky had told them, but as good as he could get in the storage room of a dental office in Dorchester.

As she watched the man work the last few stitches into the skin of Nick's shoulder, and listened to their banter, it was obvious to Hailey that this wasn't the first time Nick had made use of Micky and his underground "facility"; she'd seen enough movies to know that this sort of place existed—but still it unnerved her: the harshness of the setting, the thick scent of antiseptics, sweat, and blood, the clutter around her, shelves lined with medical supplies, a garbage can full of used bandages, thread, and gauze. Forty-eight hours ago she was an MIT grad student in applied math, with an apartment in Central Square, a roommate, and a full course load. She might have supported herself through card-counting, and she'd only called herself Hailey Gordon as long as she cared to remember—but her life had been comfortable, if not simple.

All that was over, and now she and Nick were being sought after by the police, the FBI—and worse. Getting arrested in a hospital emergency room might have been the safest outcome they could hope for, at the moment. And in truth, multiple times over the past two days Hailey had considered them turning themselves in. But she also knew that being arrested didn't just mean potential jail time—at the very least for being involved with trying to sell stolen art; it would also mean the end to their quest.

Even in that basement storage room, she could still hear the sound of that replica Liberty Bell ringing in the back of her thoughts, the rising waves of that strange tone reverberating through her very bones. She could see the lead musket balls that Nick had held in his hand—for a brief moment, shifting in color, in *chemical structure*, to something *else*. Shiny, smooth, glinting even in the low light.

Gold.

And almost before she could truly believe that it had actually happened, that a bell had been the alchemical device known in historical literature as the philosopher's stone—the moment had disappeared, the power of that sound had waned and dissipated, the musket balls had suddenly shifted back to nothing but cold, dark lead. Revere's last bell—the Liberty Bell, despite what the

27

history books had told generations of readers—had not been the culmination of his scientific journey, his own quest to build the most powerful device in human history. His last bell had been an experiment, a proof of concept, and, in the end, a failure.

But Hailey was certain that failure was not the end of the story; she only had to open her handbag, which was sitting next to her stool on the cement floor of the storage room, to see the golden box she'd found hidden on the USS *Constitution*, to know that Revere's experimentation had not ended with that odd- if not awful-sounding bell. *From she who made the box.* The secret was still out there, somewhere; the philosopher's stone existed, hidden away for centuries, and though Hailey and Nick had reached what appeared to be a dead end in that courtyard of the Massachusetts State House, the trail was not entirely cold.

As Micky finished tying off the stitches and stepped back from the dental chair, Hailey could see in Nick's eyes that he was just as determined as she was to keep chasing. He started to swing his legs over the side of the chair, when Micky put a gloved hand on his chest.

"Hold on, Nick. You lost a fair amount of blood and my stitches are good, but you tear them out before you heal and you aren't getting a refund."

Nick didn't put up much of a struggle, and Hailey could see how pale his cheeks were.

"He's right," she said. "You need to rest. At least for a few hours."

She looked around the room. It was small, sketchy, and a bit worn down, but it didn't look like it got much traffic.

"What about here?"

Micky grinned. "Accommodations like this don't come cheap."

Hailey leaned down and opened her handbag. She could feel Micky's eyes widen as she dug into the pile of yellow casino chips.

No doubt, he knew what they were. His expression had changed to something hungry. But then Hailey glanced toward Nick, whose own expression had changed. A warning, which Micky seemed to understand, because he raised his hands, palms out, and backed up a step. Then he did some calculating.

"A thousand for the medical care, another five hundred for the room. But you're both gone by sundown tonight. And no wrestling matches. I have to keep the place relatively sterile."

Hailey rolled her eyes, as she counted out the chips. "Does he look like he's in any condition to wrestle? Anyway, it's just going to be Nick. I have somewhere I need to be."

Nick started up again from the chair. "It's my area of expertise," he grunted. Then he paused, the exertion obviously affecting him.

Hailey shook her head, as she handed the chips to Micky. "We don't have any choice. And it's not a bank, it's a museum. I think I'm capable of getting inside a museum."

Micky was watching the exchange, and then he got that hungry look again. "Maybe I can help. I mean, that is, if you're so inclined."

He looked toward Hailey's handbag. When Hailey finally nodded, Micky's grin doubled in size.

"Really is good to see you again, Nick. You're fast becoming my favorite customer. Keep this up, and I'll throw in a couple of crowns—on the house."

CHAPTER FOUR

The trip over to Charlestown had been much quicker and easier than Hailey had anticipated; in exchange for a couple of green casino chips added to the yellows and blacks he'd already acquired, Micky had been happy to shuttle her in his beat-up Buick, which had been parked in the alley behind the dental office. Along the short, twenty-minute drive, the muscular dentist had filled Hailey in a bit more about his relationship with Nick, whom he'd known for more than a decade and had fixed up a half dozen times over the years. Up until today, minor cuts and bruises: broken glass from climbing through windows, a twisted ankle from falling off a warehouse roof a couple years before he got locked up, and once, the removal of a half an inch of barbed wire that had gotten lodged under Nick's palm during a getaway that hadn't gone as smoothly as he had planned. Micky claimed to have a soft spot for Nick— compared to some of the animals from the neighborhood that he'd worked on, Nick was nearly a saint. A saint with sticky fingers, sure, but—according to Micky—he didn't have a violent bone in his body. "A lover, not a fighter," Micky had expounded, fishing with a wink. When Hailey didn't respond, he kept on talking— and didn't quiet down until they were only a few blocks from the Navy Yard, and he saw all the flashing red and blue lights.

Hailey had expected a police presence, so near the scene of the previous night's action, but she hadn't counted on such a huge operation. As their Buick drifted closer, she counted a dozen police cars and at least three Coast Guard vehicles, acting as support for a pair of boats still making circles beyond the docks jutting out from the edge of the Yard. She couldn't tell if there were divers in the water, but she could guess that they'd spent the better part of the night searching the murky harbor for the dark-haired woman's body—or what was left of it—and for the artifact she'd held in her hands when she'd gone over the side of the *Constitution*. Assuredly, the FBI agent had told the police officers and the Coast Guard about the bronze eagle, which meant they'd spend as many resources as necessary to retrieve whatever bits of it might have survived getting hit, head-on, by cannon fire.

"A beauty, ain't it?" Micky said, as they turned onto a side street just a block away from the police operation. It took Hailey a moment to realize he wasn't talking about all the flashing lights, but the tall triple masts rising up above the buildings to their right, casting moonlit shadows toward the roiling harbor. "Went aboard with my nephew last summer. You know they still take the thing out into the ocean a few times a year? Have a crew, and everything. Even the damn cannons still work."

Hailey's cheeks flushed, but she simply pointed toward the curb. "This is close enough."

She wasn't focused on the ship but on a low, rectangular three-story building that squatted a few dozen yards away, one of the original shipyard buildings that had been restored in the 1970s. She'd done a little research on Micky's laptop computer in his dental office before they'd left Nick, sleeping off his painkillers, in the basement; she knew the building had once housed a pump system before it had been refitted for the constant flux of tourists that had been flocking to Pier 2 since the *Constitution* had been opened to the public many decades before.

Once Micky had put the Buick in park, Hailey steeled herself and reached for the door handle.

"Ten minutes, tops. Keep the engine running."

Her own voice sounded strange in her head; it was like her cadence had changed to fit the circumstances. This really was more Nick's wheelhouse; as a card counter and a sometime conwoman, she used math to beat the system, her brain to take money from faceless organizations like casinos, and her cunning and craftsmanship to trick institutions like MIT. She didn't break into places and steal things. Even though at this moment, all she was trying to steal was information, but she knew she was crossing a line.

It didn't help that she was dressed for the part. The uniform that Micky had provided, after a fair amount of negotiation, was a little loose on the legs and felt rough against her shoulders and back. And the shirt and dark jacket were surprisingly heavy, which probably had more to do with the shiny buttons and badge affixed to the front.

"If we'd had more time," Micky had said, looking her over, "we could have driven up to my storage unit in Wilmington and made you a statie. The fit is a lot more comfortable and nobody ever questions a statie. But this should work."

Hailey hoped he was right. To her inexperienced eyes, the BPD desk sergeant's uniform Micky had provided seemed authentic. Another cop might wonder why a desk sergeant was out in the field, but no civilian would question a woman wearing blue and a badge. And Hailey had certainly worn her fair share of costumes before. She'd hit casinos in tight skirts and wigs, doctor's coats and scrubs, business suits, and a multitude of athletic gear. She'd even once dressed as a Vegas magician's assistant, all sequins and sparkles.

She'd never tried law enforcement before, because just putting on the uniform was technically a crime. But, she knew, by now she was well past "technical" crimes.

"Ten minutes," she stressed again.

And then she headed for the museum entrance.

———

The irony was not lost on Hailey as the bored security guard with the peach fuzz mustache buzzed her in through the side door of the USS *Constitution* Museum, which took up much of the first quarter of Pier 2. Micky had been right; the guard hadn't questioned the appearance of a cop during the predawn hour. Even if they hadn't been a stone's throw from an active crime scene, nobody looked twice when someone showed a badge and used a stern voice. And no doubt officers had been in and out of the museum all night, checking to see if what had gone down on the deck of the *Constitution* had somehow bled over to the nearby museum.

Still, Hailey was trembling as she made short work of the narrow hallway that led from the heavy loading door, which she made sure closed tightly behind her, to the set of stairs leading up to the entrance desk, where the guard was waiting. From the looks of the young guard—twenty-two at most, with sprouts of hair on his chin that matched the mustache and a mop of reddish hair reaching almost to the collar of his gray uniform—the kid would have let a mailman inside, if he'd hit the buzzer hard enough. As Hailey had reminded Nick, this wasn't a bank, it was a museum, and not one known for containing anything of particular value. Hailey wasn't even sure if that would have made much of a difference: case in point, the famous Gardner Heist that had started all of this had gone down almost in the same fashion. Two guys, dressed as cops, buzzed in through a side door. Most of the world thought they'd come for paintings; Hailey knew better, but that didn't matter now.

The guard barely raised his heavy-lidded eyes as he led her through the entrance and into the warmly lit first floor of the museum; ahead of them stretched a warren of colorful exhibits dedicated to the history and construction of the tall ship parked on the other side of the pier. Even areas of the walls and ceilings were paneled in wood, obviously meant to instill the feeling that she was standing on the deck of the great ship itself.

"You here for something in particular?" the guard asked. "I mean, you guys have gone through the place enough times already, I'm not sure there's anything left to fingerprint."

Hailey stepped past him, scanning the exhibits on either side. She could see the first floor had been designed to showcase the ship in roughly chronological order, from its construction and launch in 1797 to its battles against the Barbary pirates in the First Barbary War, and culminating in the battles it was most known for, which had taken place during the War of 1812 against the British, during which the *Constitution* had sunk five British warships in short order. Most of the exhibits seemed circumstantial: artifacts and paintings behind glass cases, video monitors spinning stories in carpeted vestibules that were tucked behind replicas of various sections of the ship. But there were also more elaborate dioramas, including a full cutout of the hull of the *Constitution*, showing the many levels of the warship, and an entire upper floor where visitors could imagine themselves being served aboard the ship during its heyday; it sported re-creations of its decks, sleeping quarters, captain's cabin, mess hall, and even one of the cannons that bristled along the ship's firing deck.

But Hailey wasn't interested in playing tourist, and she hoped to never see another Revolutionary Era cannon up close again. She continued scanning the first floor until she found what she was looking for. A door, beyond the exhibits highlighting the various battles of the War of 1812, labeled Archives.

She hurried her pace, and the guard rushed to keep up. When he saw where she was heading, he cleared his throat, and his voice went up an octave.

"Ma'am? I mean, sir? Officer? The other officers already walked through the archive room with my supervisor, and it's been locked up tight since—"

"Yes, I know," Hailey said, as she reached past the cuffs on her belt to retrieve her cell phone—a burner that Mickey had helpfully provided for a couple more chips, "but my captain wants me to get a few more photos of the room before we call it a night. I assume you've got a key?"

The guard had caught up to her, breathing hard. They were passing an exhibit of the most well-known of the *Constitution*'s victories, against the HMS *Guerriere*. Hailey glimpsed details of the famous incident—images in the form of paintings and video, some artifacts that might have been real or re-created, and plenty of descriptive text: The two ships had stumbled across each other on August 19, 1812, four hundred miles south of Halifax. The British ship had fired first, raking the side of the larger *Constitution* with cannon shot—one of which had famously bounced off the copper-sided hull of the *Constitution* and gave the American ship its nickname, Old Ironsides. Hailey knew, without reading, that it had been Paul Revere who had covered the ship with that copper, a technical feat that might have been accomplished only by the greatest metalworker and technologist of the time. She also knew that it was during the opening shots of this battle that the original bell, hung in the mast of the *Constitution*, had been shot off by the *Guerriere*. It was one of the many injuries the great ship had endured before it eventually outmaneuvered and sank the faster British ship. These damages sent the *Constitution* directly back to the Navy Yard in Boston for repairs after it burned the listing hulk of the *Guerriere* and sent it to the bottom of the Atlantic Ocean.

Hailey stepped past the *Guerriere* exhibit, then reached the door to the archive room and squared herself toward the guard, who seemed undecided as to what he was supposed to do.

"You could certainly call your supervisor again," Hailey said, her voice tight. "I'm sure he'd appreciate being dragged back over here so I can take a few photos."

The guard bit at his lower lip, then shrugged and reached for his keys.

"I'm sure it's fine," he said, going to work on the lock. "We're just trying to be helpful. Don't usually get this much excitement around here. I mean, a homicide on the USS *Constitution*—"

"You want to be helpful?" Hailey said. She brushed past him the second the door clicked open. "I could sure use a cup of coffee. These overnights are rough."

The kid watched her move into the room and seemed about to say something else, then shrugged again and headed back toward the front of the museum.

Hailey figured she had a few minutes at most, so she moved quickly. She found a light switch on the wall to her right, and it took a few seconds for the fluorescent tubes lining the high ceiling to flicker to life. Ahead of her, the archive room was rectangular and institutional, lined on both sides with large filing cabinets labeled mostly by year. It looked almost exactly as it had in the photos she'd found online in Micky's office, when she'd done a quick but deep dive into the museum's collection. She'd always been good at combing the internet for hard-to-find information, which in the past she'd used to help keep her false identity moving smoothly along. Sometimes she'd needed to forge documents, or construct backgrounds, or case casino security operations, and that meant she'd had to become extremely computer literate.

She'd known that a museum dedicated to the tall ship, which itself was an historical monument, would be filled with records detailing every moment of the *Constitution*'s journey from its birth, in the Boston Shipyard 230 years ago, to modern times; there was a wealth of information here, but her focus could be narrowed down to a matter of days that to most historians might have seemed inconsequential and thus overlooked. People wrote books and made movies about epic, famous battles such as the one between the USS *Constitution* and the *Guerriere*, but nobody shopped scripts about the days after the battle, which the battered ship spent in drydock, being repaired.

Hailey had found something hidden on the USS *Constitution*—what she had thought would be Paul Revere's final bell, but had actually been the bronze clapper from a bell that was arguably as famous as the Revolutionary hero himself. Hailey believed Revere had put the clapper aboard the famous ship for a reason, perhaps to transport it somewhere, on the safest vessel in existence at the time. She didn't know where Revere had intended to send the clapper, or for what purpose, but she did know approximately *when*.

It took Hailey a few minutes to find the filing cabinet labeled with the proper dates—the last weeks of August 1812, when the *Constitution* entered the dockyards for repairs after the famous battle, and the same time period when Revere was working his way toward his final bell—and another moment to pull the heavy cabinet door open and retrieve the armful of documents she found inside. The documents were mostly in folders held closed with metal clasps, though there were many loose pages as well, sealed in protective plastic covers. Since she didn't have time to find a proper space to work, Hailey dropped to her knees in the center of the room and began spreading the documents out on the shiny linoleum floor.

She wasn't sure what she was looking for; she had already done a basic search online at Micky's office, researching visits between Paul Revere and the USS *Constitution*, which dated back to July 1797, when James McHenry, the secretary of war at the time, had first requested that the ship "be coppered on the Stocks before she is Launched into the Water." Revere, already in his sixties at the time, and the leading metalworker of the era, provided the copper, as well as the 242-pound bell that was later shot off the boat during the battle with the *Guerriere*. In 1803, Revere again refitted the ship with his copper—the original sheathing had decayed—but beyond that, there was no mention of any more connections between Revere and the ship. If indeed he had returned to the ship with the clapper, it had gone unnoticed by history as far as Hailey could tell—which seemed unlikely, considering how famous Revere had become, especially in the Boston area. Although it was possible he'd delivered the clapper on one of his earlier visits, it didn't seem likely to Hailey, since he'd continued his obsessive manufacturing of bells for an entire decade after 1803. If her theory was correct, that he had been attempting to perfect his philosopher's stone through those bells, then the clapper was the integral part of his final creation, which he would have been forging around the time period of the War of 1812.

As she went to work on the folders and files on the floor in front of her, she did not expect to find any obvious mention of Revere visiting the ship during that period; if such a thing had happened, it would certainly have made its way into history books, and might very well have been part of the exhibit in the museum. But that didn't mean there couldn't be some connection between Revere and the ship—some evidence that hadn't made its way online, because on its own it seemed meaningless to the uninitiated.

She worked as quickly as she could, keeping her ears tuned for the return of the security guard with her coffee. Most of the pages and folders in front of her were filled with dry accountings of the various repairs the ship had gone through when it had reached dock, from replacing areas of the main deck and masts, to refitting the sails and completing metal work on the dented exterior of the hull. Sifting from file to file, she eventually located a page documenting the Revere bell that had been destroyed by cannon shot. It was a handwritten note, on the top of a stack of similar personal letters and documents, written by some sort of mechanical engineer using language of the time that was difficult for Hailey to decipher, other than the words she could easily recognize—*bell, housing, cannon round-shot.*

But she wasn't here to read about the bell that had been destroyed—the thread she was following had to do with something that was brought onto the ship, not taken away. Still, she was intrigued by the personal nature of the handwritten letter, which was addressed to a friend of the engineer's—and she began to sift through the rest of the pile, which were all similar correspondences written by the crew working on the ship at the dockyard.

She was near the bottom of the pile when she found something that seemed interesting enough to read twice. It was a much shorter correspondence than the rest, barely two paragraphs, written in the scrawl of a young boat hand named Joseph Wright, who was apparently writing home to his parents from the ship, still docked at the harbor. Hailey had only read the first sentence of the boy's letter, struggling her way through his cacophonous handwriting and the nearly foreign phrasings and spelling of the time period when her curiosity perked. After telling his parents how excited he was to have survived the battles at sea, and how he would soon be getting leave to come home, the boy had mentioned, almost offhandedly, that the return to the shipyard had taken longer than expected because of an unplanned stop—off the coast of Rhode Island.

Hailey didn't believe she'd noticed anything in the exhibit on the other side of the archive room door saying anything about the ship stopping near Rhode Island after the battle with the *Guerriere*. Nor had she read anything online about the detour, though she had no reason to doubt what appeared, at least to her untrained eyes, to be an authentic document. When she read the next few lines of text, her heart ran a little faster.

According to Joseph Wright, the ship had been met briefly by a woman, someone important enough that the captain himself had invited her on board. But the meeting was brief, and within an hour the ship had been back on its way to Boston.

The rest of the letter made only one more mention of the woman: In signing off to his mother, Joseph apologized for how long it had been since he'd been home—but for that, the boy had joked, his mother could blame the woman, who hadn't only held up a lowly boat hand, but had briefly disturbed the journey of "the most powerful ship in the Republic."

Hailey stared at the letter for a long moment before placing it back in the pile with the rest. It wasn't a smoking gun—no mention of Revere, or the clapper, or anything being carried aboard the ship. It might have been nothing, a bit of gossip that had no connection to Revere's final bell. It could be meaningless, unrelated to what she'd found hidden on the USS *Constitution*; no doubt, a ship returning from battle so far from Boston might have numerous reasons to stop along the journey, and may well have made many such stops—events so innocuous and unimportant, they didn't even make it to the museum exhibits dedicated to the ship, and probably got bare mention in the history books.

But still—something about the letter triggered Hailey's instincts. She'd learned a long time ago not to ignore her instincts.

She rose and hastily carried the documents back to the filing cabinet. She already had her phone out, ready to pretend to take pictures, as she heard the footsteps of the security guard returning through the exhibits beyond the open archive room door—but her mind still whirled through what she'd just read. She paused by the open filing cabinet, quickly took a picture of the letter from the boat hand, and shut the cabinet door.

There was no way to know whether what she had just found had a connection to Paul Revere and his final bell or was an insignificant bit of color from a young man's letter home to his mother. But still, it felt like a thread worth following.

In the first paragraph of the letter, the boy had included the woman's name—a name Hailey didn't recognize, but that didn't mean anything. Hailey wasn't an expert on eighteenth-century American history. She was a mathematical prodigy, a card counter who was exceptionally good at solving puzzles.

She didn't wait for the security guard to make it to the archive room; instead, she headed quickly through the door and brushed right past the earnest kid, nearly knocking the proffered coffee cup right out of his hand.

Hailey didn't know much about Revolutionary Era history, but she certainly knew someone who *did*.

CHAPTER FIVE

The resounding *click click click* of Adrian Jenson's Italian cycling shoes skittering against aging, polished limestone echoed through the cavernous basement level of Harvard's Widener Library. As the professor navigated his way through the labyrinthine stacks—monolith-like rolling shelves that rose ten feet in the air on either side, loaded with books of varying sizes, colors, and levels of dust and grime—he barely kept pace with the lanky undergrad who led him along, a kid barely out of high school that Adrian believed was named Greg, or Craig, or maybe even Doug—*but who could really keep track?* Since his escort had greeted Adrian on the steps of the gargantuan library so many stories above, the damn kid hadn't stopped chattering on about the early hour, the crisp weather outside, and the difficulties of fulfilling Adrian's request. Adrian had dutifully done his best to tune out most of the boy's garble. In Adrian's opinion, the only breed more nauseating than a Harvard professor was a Harvard undergraduate, but the oddness of the hour had negated the possibility of any of Adrian's colleagues at the university—only a few miles distant from his own Tufts campus—showing up in person to assist in his inquiry. Which, all in all, was probably for the best, since Adrian wasn't about to explain the reasons for his sudden request. *Nor was he certain he could.*

The truth was, he didn't really know why he was traipsing through the tomblike library at six thirty in the morning. And he couldn't have even begun to describe his mental state, after the events of the night before. He had showered and dressed, donned his usual Lycra bicycling pants and shirt for the ride over from Tufts, partially hidden beneath a tweed jacket supporting his leather saddlebag. But his normally brilliantly coiffed halo of curly blond hair was disheveled, and no doubt his eyes had the wild cadence of someone who had barely slept in the previous forty-eight hours. There were bruises on his backside and left hip, where he had hit the Beacon Hill cobblestones when the eighteenth-century pistol he had fired had knocked him to the ground, and various scratches and bruises on his hands and arms from scrambling away from the mess of the gas lamp he'd made. Surprising, how powerful the dueling musket had been. The sound of the blast still reverberated through Adrian's thoughts.

And on top of that, he was nursing a hangover of epic proportions. He couldn't blame the undergrad—Brad, maybe?—for his pounding headache, any more than he could fault the young man for his complaints about the difficulty of the task Adrian had laid out for him. It must have seemed a strangely frantic call, passed along to the poor boy by a middling associate professor in the eighteenth-century European Classics department, the only Harvard faculty member Adrian had been able to reach at such an early hour.

If Adrian had been able to find what he was looking for on his own campus, the loquacious undergrad would still have been happily asleep in his dorm. But as first-rate a university as Tufts was— certainly, at the moment it sported the top Paul Revere expert in the country, if not the world—its library system paled in comparison to its overachieving neighbor two stops down the Red Line.

In truth, there were few places in academia that could rival Widener Library, in terms of its size or the wealth of its collection. Donated to the university, circa 1915, by the grieving mother of a book-obsessed graduate who had unfortunately perished on the *Titanic* along with his wealthy robber-baron father, the giant stone library housed a compendium of knowledge that was almost *mythological* in scope. Three and a half million volumes of books, contained along nearly sixty miles of shelves, surging ten levels deep into the very earth. It was not uncommon for students to find themselves lost in the mazelike lower levels. One particularly grating ritual involved pairs of students purposefully losing themselves among the many carrels and compartments that graced the stacks, for purposes part carnal, part ceremonial.

Over the years, Adrian had spent more than a few late nights ignoring the whispered tittering and barely covered moans of these adventurous undergrads, as he'd delved into manuscripts from the various private collections owned by the library. For two years back in his early years at Tufts, he'd even had his own cubicle on Basement Level Seven, tucked between two of the rolling stacks dedicated to Paul Revere's early years, when he was known only as an engraver, silversmith, and sometime dentist, and not the man who'd ridden a borrowed horse through the countryside, decidedly *not* at midnight, not on his own, and not, successfully, warning *anyone* about *anything*.

During those research jaunts to the hallowed Harvard library, Adrian had always done his best to avoid needing the help of the library's "staff"—usually undergrads on work-study programs who'd decided late nights in a poorly ventilated, two-hundred-year-old literary tomb beat slopping baked beans at one of the many dining halls scattered across the campus. This morning, however, Adrian had had little choice.

What he was searching for, at this moment, was far off the generous path of his expertise.

"Took me the better part of an hour to find these," the undergrad said, juggling what appeared to be a heavy sheaf of documents held together in a leather binder, as he led Adrian through a pair of rolling stacks toward one of the carrels in the far corner of the basement level. "As far as I can tell, nobody has requested anything from this collection in years."

Adrian responded with a sound that was somewhere between a sigh and a grunt. He had to suffer the young man's presence, but he didn't have to socialize with the boy. *Theseus had been forced to fight a Minotaur in his labyrinth, but he didn't have to converse with the creature, only chop off its head.*

When they finally reached the carrel, which was about as secluded as Adrian could hope for, the boy set the folder on the center of a low, wooden desk, next to an aging, Tiffany-style lamp. The chair attached to the desk looked about as comfortable as a Minotaur's horns, but Adrian didn't expect to be here long. The kid stood for a moment, as if he was expecting something—and Adrian gave him a look.

"Unless you intend to turn the pages for me, I can take it from here."

The kid paused, glancing at the folder, then back at Adrian. "It's just—these are originals—I'm supposed to stay with them."

"By all means," Adrian said, pushing past the boy. "Stay with them—"

And then he pointed back toward the far end of the basement level. "From over *there*."

Adrian hit the last syllable with the tone he reserved for his own students when they had the audacity to suggest he keep office hours, or mentor them on their theses, or help them with the various papers he'd assigned—papers they'd never had any hope of completing. *Undergrads.* Adrian had always believed the worst aspect of academia was all the damn students.

The kid looked away nervously, then shrugged and hurried back through the stacks. Left alone, Adrian lowered himself into the chair and opened the leather binder.

Two hours later, Adrian's shoulders ached as he leaned over the low wooden desk. The leather binder lay open in front of him, the yellowed documents spread out beneath the meager cone of light cast by the faux Tiffany lamp. As the undergrad had exclaimed, most of the pages were indeed originals, though a few were obvious copies. The collection, as stated on a tag hanging from the binder, had been donated to the rare books section of Widener by something called the McCaroll Foundation, collectors of eighteenth-century historical documents.

Though Adrian was an expert on the time period—specifically the Revolutionary Era, and even more specifically the life and activities of Paul Revere—he had only a passing knowledge of these particular documents: letters, actually, written between two characters from the time period. One famous, exceedingly so—in fact, perhaps the most famous name of the era—and one almost entirely unknown. Neither were closely associated with Paul Revere.

Or at least, that was what Adrian had believed and would have staked his impressive reputation on—until somewhere between twenty and twelve hours ago.

The reason he'd been unable to sleep, had tossed and turned even though he'd drunk enough eighteenth-century brandy to silence a garrison of Minutemen—was a brief memory of something he'd read years ago, back when he himself was still in graduate school. Something that had come from this very collection, reprinted in various history books but never really making its way into mainstream public consciousness.

Adrian leafed back through the papers on the desk in front of him, to a yellowed page near the very top. A handwritten letter. Written to a woman named Catherine Ray, on the sixteenth of October, 1755.

He'd read the letter from start to finish four times now, but he went through it again, slowly, line by line. Of course, he was adept at deciphering the flowery language of the time—in some ways, he was more comfortable perusing eighteenth-century documents than he was sifting through the detriment that passed as literature in his own time. But even so, this particular letter was a bit flowery for his tastes. Surprising, because it had been written by one of the most educated men of the times—perhaps, the smartest man of his era:

Dear Katy
Philadelphia Oct 16. 1755
 Your Favour of the 28th of June came to hand but the 28th of September, just 3 Months after it was written. I had, two weeks before, wrote you a long Chat, and sent it to the Care of your Brother Ward. I hear you are now in Boston, gay and lovely as usual. Let me give you some fatherly Advice. Kill no more Pigeons than you can eat. Be a good Girl, and don't' forget your Catechise. Go constantly to Meeting—or Church—till you get a good Husband; then stay at home, and nurse the Children, and live like a Christian. Spend your spare Hours, in sober Whisk, Prayers, or learning to cypher. You must practice Addition to your Husband's Estate, by Industry and Frugality;

Subtraction of fall unnecessary Expences; Multiplication (I would gladly have taught you that myself, but you thought it was time enough, and wou'dn't learn) he will soon make you a Mistress of it. As to Division, I say with Brother Paul, Let there be no Divisions among ye. But as your good Sister Hubbard (my Love to her) is well acquainted with The Rule of Two, I hope you will become as expert in the Rule Of Three; that when I have again the Pleasure of seeing you, I may find you like my Grape Vine, surrounded with Clusters, plump, juicy, blushing, pretty little rogues, like their Mama. Adieu. The Bell rings, and I must go among the Grave ones, and talk Politicks. Your affectionate Friend

B Franklin

P.S. The Plums came safe, and were so sweet from the Cause you mention'd, that I could scarce taste the sugar.
Miss Catherine Ray

Even the undergrad—Greg? Brad? Chad?—would have immediately recognized the name of the letter writer. Benjamin Franklin, perhaps the most famous of the Founding Fathers, certainly the most famous American of the eighteenth century. Ask ten strangers on the street of any city—let alone Boston—and you'd assuredly see instant recognition. *Ben Franklin?* "Invented" electricity. Signed the Declaration of Independence. Wore spectacles. Maybe less would know that he'd started the first major printing press, that he'd invented numerous other world-changing devices—such as the lightning rod, the Franklin stove, swim fins, and bifocals.

Fewer still—perhaps those who had suffered through a multipart documentary, or plunged into one of the various biographies that had been published over the years—would have known about the man's more cosmopolitan endeavors. How he had spent much, if not most, of his time abroad, in London and Paris. How he'd actually been a latecomer to the Revolutionary effort, had in fact opposed many of the early adventures of the other Founding Fathers. Specifically, Franklin had been a vocal opponent of the Boston Tea Party and, as Adrian had taught in many of his lectures, had openly considered Paul Revere little more than a thug and a terrorist. Indeed, where Franklin was of high breeding and education, famous, and one of the wealthiest early Americans, Revere was a man who worked with his hands and had no problem getting dirty. Franklin was high class, although he did have his moments.

In that respect, he was a legendary rogue, and his affairs were almost too numerous to document. There was Deborah Read, to whom he'd been common-law married when he'd first arrived in Philadelphia after his childhood in Boston. Margaret Stevenson, his landlady in London who also became his lover. Polly Stevenson, the aforementioned landlady's eighteen-year-old daughter. And Madame Brillon, one of his many Parisian fancies. *Early to bed and early to rise, indeed.*

But the letter in front of Adrian, though flowery and full of veiled flirtations, mixed in with a full heaping of what Franklin called "fatherly advice," had not been written to one of Franklin's more well-known sexual dalliances but to a much younger, "platonic" paramour, as she'd been described in various biographies of the man. From what Adrian remembered of the woman, which wasn't much at all—Catherine Ray, Caty, or Katy—was somewhat of an enigma in history, who had met with Franklin only five times over his life. They were usually in the company of Franklin's sister, who was somewhat of the woman's mentor. Catherine Ray spent most of her early life in the quiet confines of her birthplace, the tiny sanctuary of Block Island off the coast of Rhode Island.

Even so, Franklin had corresponded with the woman for much of his life, writing similar letters to her all the way until the final weeks before his death at the age of eighty-four.

Although Adrian hadn't remembered much about Catherine Ray, he had indeed remembered this particular letter that Franklin had written her. It was this letter, and specifically a single line at its closing, that had kept him awake until just a few hours ago, when he'd hurriedly showered, dressed, and headed for Widener.

He leaned close to the page, mouthing the words as he read them out loud:

"The Bell rings, and I must go among the Grave ones, and talk Politicks.

Your affectionate Friend, B Franklin."

As closings went, it wasn't terrible; it was loaded with importance, Franklin showing off his high status to a young woman who obviously was impressed by him. But more important, to Adrian, the words signifying that importance—"The Bell rings, and I must go among the Grave ones, and talk Politicks"—all capitalized. And it was that first emboldened word that was now piercing Adrian's thoughts like a red hot fireplace poker. Because he knew, as he had learned all the way back in graduate school and still remembered, this phrase, in this flirtatious little letter from Ben Franklin, arguably the most famous man in the world at the time, to a nobody of a mistress, was the very first mention of the Liberty Bell in recorded history.

And this mention didn't make any historical sense.

The reason Adrian had needed to see the original manuscript for himself, not a copy like he'd read in graduate school or could easily find on the web, was to see for himself the capitalization, the important way it had been presented—the *anachronism*.

Because at the time that Franklin wrote this letter, in October 1755, the Liberty Bell was not a thing of importance, not an object of notice, not even, in fact, known as the Liberty Bell. Though the modern conception of the Bell was that it was a symbol of the American nation, in the eighteenth century it was simply a bell—and one with such a peculiar and awful tone that it was nearly melted down for scrap on multiple occasions. Later stories claiming it was rung at the signing of the Declaration of Independence or at the start of the Revolutionary War were clearly false; the Bell, as it became later known, did not become special or famous until much later in history, during the abolitionist movement of the late 1830s, when an article in the *Hartford Courant* branded it as a symbol of freedom and gave it the name "Liberty." Prior to the article in the *Courant*, it was merely the State House Bell, when it was mentioned at all.

At the time of Franklin's letter to Catherine Ray, the Bell was simply "a bell." Commissioned by the Colonial Legislature of Pennsylvania to hang in their State House, cast twice, by English bellmakers and the American industrialists Pass and Stowe because neither party could get the sound quite right, it was hung unceremoniously at the top of the Philadelphia State House tower, where it eventually fell into disuse before being resurrected by the abolitionist movement.

Over the past two days, Adrian had been forced to entertain a completely different view of the object in question. The idea that Paul Revere might have been involved in casting the thing as his final bell—that it had something to do with some insane conspiracy involving Revolutionary Era alchemists—it was almost too maddening to think about. But even if any of it was true, why would Benjamin Franklin have had reason to consider it as anything beyond an unimportant bell? And why would he have felt the need to mention the bell—the Bell—in a letter to his platonic mistress?

Sitting there at the desk, staring down at the letter, at the odd closing at the bottom of the page, Adrian pursed his lips tightly together. This bothered him more than he could put into words. History was supposed to make *sense*. Real historians like himself didn't need to suffer the indignations of fantasy and fiction, because history was *fact*. Adrian had prided himself on living a life surrounded by fact.

But beginning two days ago, fantasy had been encroaching on his world, his life, and this letter, this "Bell," seemed to be rising up at him right out of that murk of fantasy.

He glanced behind himself. The undergrad wasn't within view. He'd likely grown bored of policing a folder full of scrawled letters and returned to his desk on the first floor. Adrian went back to the document, then made a sudden, impetuous decision.

He reached into his saddle bag, which was on the floor by his feet, and retrieved an empty manila envelope. Then he carefully took Franklin's letter to Catherine Ray from atop the pile on the desk, slid it into the envelope, and placed the envelope back in his saddle bag.

His heart pounding, he put the rest of the documents back in the leather binder, then rose from the desk and headed back through the stacks.

———

Adrian was breathing hard, the sweat trickling in warm rivulets from beneath his polycarbonate bicycle helmet, as he peddled the last few yards to the curb in front of East Hall, 6 The Green, in the center of the Tufts campus. It had been a familiar ride from Harvard Square to Davis, but he'd nearly been sideswiped twice—by an Uber driver in a boxy Kia, shouting obscenities in a language Adrian couldn't identify, and then by the Number One bus, as it careened down Mass Ave. In both cases, Adrian knew he was to blame; normally, he was an expert cyclist, moving like a snake through the traffic that beleaguered Cambridge like a biblical plague. But this morning, he was not himself. He had not been himself for days, firing muskets in the streets of Beacon Hill, accompanying fugitives to multiple landmarks across the city, stealing documents from the basement of Widener Library.

His face reddened even deeper at the thought of the letter in his saddle bag. He didn't know what it was worth, but the financial value of the document didn't matter. It was a piece of history; more than that, if it was discovered in Adrian's possession, he could be arrested and would certainly lose his tenure at Tufts. He would be banished from academia.

But he hadn't been able to help himself. He needed time with the document to understand what it meant.

He leaned his bike against a post in front of the building and quickly secured the forward tire with his industrial-strength carbon steel lock. Then he undid his helmet and started toward the building's steps.

He'd made it halfway there when he noticed the two figures on the patio by the door. The man was leaning against a railing, wearing what appeared to be a brand-new denim jacket and matching pants. He looked worse for wear, but then again he'd always looked that way to Adrian, like someone who had crawled out from under a bar table in South Boston. But the woman, she seemed almost alight, her athletic body full of energy beneath slacks and a white buttoned shirt.

Hailey Gordon stepped forward when Adrian paused halfway up the steps, and he fought the urge to turn and run.

"It isn't over?" he finally asked, knowing the answer from the look on the young woman's face.

"I think it's just starting," Hailey said. "We rang the bell, and it worked—for a brief moment—but in the end it failed."

Adrian digested what she'd said. *It worked—for a brief moment.*

"Lead—to gold?" he mumbled, not believing.

She nodded. "As I said, briefly. But it was only temporary. In the end, the bell wasn't the philosopher's stone."

Adrian shook his head. This was all too much. Fantasy. He didn't want to believe her, and so he wouldn't.

"Well, I can't help you," he said, curtly. "This may not be over for you, but it's over for me."

Hailey was right in front of him, blocking his way. "Actually, I think you're the only one who *can* help us."

She held up her phone. Despite himself, Adrian looked at the screen.

It was a picture of a letter. Different from the one he had in his saddle bag, but of similar age. He'd made it halfway through the first paragraph, when his stomach dropped. Because he saw the name.

Catherine Ray.

CHAPTER SIX

Monet had his lilies.

Van Gogh had his stars.

Curt Anderson allowed himself a grin, as he stepped back from his latest work of art—careful to keep both feet on the fresh hotel towel that covered the shiny porcelain tiles near the center of the obscenely oval marble bathroom. The oversized bathtub in front of him was of a similar geometric shape, and equally marble, though of a slightly pearlier color; the water that filled it, nearly to the brim, was decidedly less pearl and more crimson—and growing darker and thicker by the second.

Curt deftly removed his rubber gloves as he continued to survey his work; it really was a masterpiece, clinically precise but also poignant. The way the man's thick elbows crooked over the rounded edges of the tub, while his wrists remained submerged, crossed against his chest. His head was still mostly above the water, and if Curt was lucky, the corpse would remain artfully afloat over the few hours it would take for the hotel cleaning crew to make the discovery and call the authorities. It was strangely important to Curt that the man's face be visible, even from across the bathroom, when the first homicide detectives arrived on the scene. It wasn't just that the picture Curt had created would lead them to the most likely conclusion that the man in the tub with the sad countenance—Curt had worked hard to position the lips and eyes in just such a way as to exude depths of despair—had slit his own wrists, but because Curt was especially proud of the image he'd created.

With a final kiss to the air, which smelled vaguely of peppermint, from the bubble bath Curt had added at the last minute to the thickening tub water, but also the faintly iron scent of seeping blood, he turned and stepped from the towel to the carpeted hallway that led out of the bathroom and into the living room of the vast casino suite.

The living room was even more garish than the bathroom: elliptical, rather than oval, with mostly leather furniture, an oversized TV covering one wall, and windows, so many windows, running all the way around the outer curve of the space. High up, of course, and even from across the living room, Curt could see the skyline of the city around him blinking like a neon scar above the serpentine boardwalk.

Curt hated Atlantic City, but at least, to him, it held a sheen of honesty, unlike Vegas, its cousin out west. In Vegas you had the same commercialism, the same sense of desperation, the same throb of a city designed around sin and greed. But Atlantic City wore its poverty right out in the open—the grime of New Jersey barely hidden beneath a light dusting of neon-infused makeup. Vegas lived on hope; Atlantic City, fear. In Vegas, there was always the thought that around the next corner, something magical might be waiting. In Atlantic City, you avoided corners, because that was where the neon ended and reality reared its dark and ugly head.

The casino twelve floors below where Curt was standing was a perfect example. From the Boardwalk, it was a magical sight; surrounded by fountains, statues of chariots pulled by horses, the façade of a coliseum rising up into the sky. It wasn't until you got closer, stepping past the shiny slot machines and crowded blackjack tables, and noticed peeling paint on the walls and scuffed and aging carpeting warping up from the addled floorboards, that you realized you were as far from Ancient Rome as you could be. The spot had once been a run-down Howard Johnson's, and at its core, was still a cheap hotel dressed up to attract tourists from New York, New Jersey, and Philadelphia, usually on the last few twists of a downward spiral.

Case in point: Jerome Finney, the man slowly seeping into the bathtub a few yards behind Curt. Once Curt had gotten the list of employees of the construction site who had potential access to the underground lab—a list provided enthusiastically by the extremely helpful foreman, after a fashion—it hadn't been difficult to pinpoint Curt's latest mark. Although the list had been surprisingly long—digging crews, electricians, machine operators, as well as the staff of the Heritage Foundation, who were less likely to walk off a worksite with stolen artifacts, but one had to be thorough—it had only been a matter of cross-checking financial information to figure out the most likely candidate.

Curt hadn't performed the grunt work himself; the Family had a division for that sort of thing, young men and women in windowless rooms in cities all over the world, working computers and phones, connecting with credit card companies, banks, even crypto exchanges. The Family's tentacles were a marvel to behold, and it hadn't taken them long to uncover the half dozen markers excavator operator Jerome Finney had accrued at various casinos and gambling halls throughout the tristate area.

And it had been equally easy for the Family's support staff to flag the sudden infusion of cash into Finney's checking account: six thousand dollars, deposited one day ago. It wasn't surprising when the man had called in sick after such a payday, and arranged a junket to Caesars, which held his biggest marker. Rather than pay off the debt, he'd done what everyone who came to Atlantic City eventually did; he headed straight to the tables to make a deep hole deeper.

Unfortunately for Mr. Finney, losing another six grand at a

blackjack table had only been the beginning of his string of bad luck. Being a little less careful than he should have been with a drink he'd left unattended in the high roller's lounge gave Curt the opportunity he didn't even really need—and after that, Finney was more than happy to let a helpful stranger guide him to the elevators and back to his suite on the twelfth floor.

It hadn't taken long, once they were alone in the suite, for Curt to get what he needed from the man. After that, it was only a matter of what the first law enforcement officers on the scene would find—a Jackson Pollack, like what Curt had left for them in the underground cavern at the worksite—or something more akin to Picasso, full of emotion, color, pathos, as he'd created in the bathroom. Sometimes, you made a statement, even when it might make more sense to be delicate. Certainly, the scene in the underground laboratory would draw attention, but sometimes that couldn't be avoided. Curt had been in a rush, and missing bodies would have caused nearly as much of a disturbance as three men tied to chairs. And to be fair, Curt had been working off some fairly reasonable frustration. Not emotion, exactly, but some disturbing feelings of inadequacy that had needed to be righted as quickly as possible.

The truth was, Curt didn't often suffer anything that could be mistaken for emotion; that had been one of his many gifts, bequeathed over his difficult childhood. Not the fault of his mother—who had died in childbirth—or even his father, a wealthy American banker living in London, who'd had no interest in or use for the child who he believed had killed his wife. Curt hadn't been molded by his parents, but by the older children in the boarding school in Switzerland where he'd been sent, at the age of eight. At the time, a thin, slight, quiet boy, with no family or friends to speak of, a bit of clay to be twisted, prodded, and punched into shape by those older, tougher, vaguely sadistic boys.

Curt would have been the first to admit that his response to the situation far exceeded what was necessary. Where other children might have internalized the misery and abuse, gone on to live fairly normal lives, their scars hidden away, Curt had instead given the world his very first work of art. It had taken three months to plan, and only minutes to accomplish: an "accident" in the school's woodshop, involving a malfunctioning circular saw, that had put two of the older boys in the hospital. Though there wasn't enough evidence to clearly implicate Curt, he ended up in military school back in the UK, which in turn landed him in the British Army, then Special Forces, and then a disciplinary discharge for being a bit "aggressive" while serving in the field during the disturbance in the former Yugoslavia.

Not everyone understood Curt's art. But after his discharge from the Special Forces, the Family had recognized his usefulness and had been more than willing to indulge him. For more than a decade, he had overseen other operatives, stepping in only when his brand of aggressiveness seemed warranted.

At the moment, he was more deeply involved than he had been in years; the operative he'd taken over for had been talented but, in the end, sloppy. She had overreached and paid the price. And Curt, too, had underestimated their quarry—the dull throb that still pained the lower half of his left leg, giving him a slight limp, was a potentially permanent souvenir of his own carelessness, and perhaps the impetus for the display he'd left in the underground lab.

But he was far from deterred; if anything, he was more engaged than ever. The new thread the Family had given him to follow was beyond intriguing. As he crossed the garish living room in two quick steps, his mind shifted back to that pier in Boston, when Mr. Arthur, his liaison to the Family, had shown him the photo of the engraving for the first time.

Curt paused at the edge of the living room, thinking of that photo, which was still in the breast pocket of his jacket. Ben Franklin and Paul Revere, huddled together in a laboratory not unlike the underground cavern where he had left the bodies in the chairs, looking over the elements of an experiment—historical or mythological—that had changed the very course of history.

Then he looked down at the open suitcase that sat on the thick shag carpet next to one of the many leather couches that filled the ellipse of a living room. Right in the center of the suitcase, on top of unpacked clothes—an object, half wrapped in a towel. The item taken from the underground lab that the pawnshop owner hadn't bought from Finney, perhaps because he couldn't calculate what it might be worth—or whether it was worth anything at all.

And to be sure, the item was strange. Curt wasn't sure why Finney had lifted it from the lab, along with the engraving, possibly because it was small enough to fit in a backpack, or under the folds of a jacket. Or perhaps because it was oddly appealing in shape—a round, metallic looking ball, about the size of a grapefruit, hanging in the center of a curved frame by a gossamer of wire.

Curt bent to his knees, the effort causing shards of pain in his damaged left leg, which he deftly ignored. He unwrapped the towel a bit more, then ran a hand over the metallic ball, feeling its smooth surface. Then he shrugged to himself, took his phone out of his jacket, and snapped a quick photo, which he texted over a secure server; the response from Mr. Arthur came immediately:

Await further communication.

Curt actually shivered, reading the words. Mr. Arthur was a different sort of artist, who worked even deeper behind the scenes than Curt ever had. Even after a decade, Curt knew very little about the man, beyond that he spoke for an organization that was bigger and more powerful than Curt could begin to decipher. Another tentacle, to be sure, but one that moved with the power of the beast behind it. Always polite, always sophisticated—but Curt knew Mr. Arthur could have him replaced as easily as he'd replaced the operative before him. And even so, Curt knew that Mr. Arthur was also an operative; Curt had only met the power behind Mr. Arthur once, when he'd first been brought into the Family—and the only thought he'd had at the time was that she had not been what he had expected. But since then, for a decade, his only communication with the Family had been through Mr. Arthur.

A full minute passed, as he waited in the hotel suite—then his phone finally blinked again. To his surprise, the text he received wasn't a message, but an image. Staring down at the screen, it took him a moment to realize what he was looking at appeared to be an image of a painting. Oil on canvas, he thought, and then he used his fingers to enlarge the image.

And then he paused. He glanced down at the device in the unrolled towel—and then back at the enlarged painting.

A chill moved through him—not an emotion, he wasn't even sure he would recognize an emotion if he'd had one—but an instinct.

More texts rapidly appeared on his phone. Information, rumination, and, in the end—a destination. Curt wasn't certain what it all meant—but he knew what part he had to play, where his particular set of skills were needed.

Lilies.

Stars.

He cocked an ear back toward the bathroom, from where he could barely hear the soft trickle of water, dribbling over the edge of the tub. Then he bent down again, carefully wrapped the object back into the towel, tucked it under his arm, and headed for the door.

CHAPTER SEVEN

Nick Patterson was fighting every instinct he'd developed over the previous two decades of his life as he followed Hailey into the swirl of tourists moving toward the revolving glass doors of a modern, oddly shaped building that seemed to gently list down the banks of the Charles River. To his left, looming above the revolving doors, was one of the more anachronistic sights in a city rife with seeming time warps: a thirty-foot-high tyrannosaurus rex, with outstretched claws and open jaws—while just a few yards away, a WWII-era duck boat waited patiently at the curb, painted bright pink and garlanded with flowers and lights, filled with noisy kids sporting necklaces bristling with duck-shaped whistles.

"This place," Nick said, as he moved close enough to Hailey so she could hear him over the whistles, "is about as far from lying low as you can get."

She didn't answer, just kept shuffling behind the crowd toward the glass doors. No doubt, she was feeling it, too; Nick could see the little hairs raising on the back of her neck, beneath the baseball cap she'd borrowed from one of the offices neighboring Adrian Jenson's. Nick had on a matching hat—Red Sox, of course, because around here everything was Red Sox—but he wasn't fooling himself into thinking a hat would make much of a difference.

They were probably the two most wanted people in the city,

and every nerve in his body was telling him they should be going to ground, or finding a way out of town. Instead, they'd headed to one of the biggest tourist attractions in Boston.

He slid into the revolving door a step behind Hailey and got spun out on the other side into an overly air-conditioned, open atrium. To his left was an information desk, and directly ahead, the turnstiles that led deeper into the building. But his attention was drawn to an exhibit to his right, mostly ignored by the tourists heading for the turnstiles. An alcove, really, shielded by glass, tucked into a corner next to a row of lockers available for rent. Nick didn't have to move closer to know what was behind the glass. He could remember it clearly: the brightly colored circular Aztec calendar on the floor, and above it the enormous brass ball with a tapered point, suspended from a long, thick wire that rose thirty feet to the ceiling, sweeping back and forth in wide, graceful arcs.

Nick remembered the exhibit well, because the only time he'd been in this building before, that exhibit was as far as he got.

"I used to love this place," Hailey said, as they followed the crowd toward the turnstiles. "I'd spend whole days here when I first arrived in Boston. For a twelve-year-old obsessed with science, this was basically heaven on Earth."

Nick's memories of the place were not as pleasant. As a kid growing up where he did, with the sort of father he had, the Boston Museum of Science was as foreign a place as MIT. His dad would never have made the trip across town, or spent whatever it cost for a ticket to pass those turnstiles—and by the time Nick had his own money, in his early teens, he was more interested in stealing car radios and smoking cigarettes in the parking lot of the nearest 7-Eleven. The only time he'd actually stepped beneath that welcoming T. rex as a kid had been on a fifth-grade class trip, before he'd dropped out of school altogether a year and a half later. And on that visit, he'd only made it about this far; while the teacher was leading most of the class through the turnstiles, he and two buddies had stopped at the pendulum, watching it swing back and forth behind the glass. It was one of his classmates—a kid named Jessie Leary—who'd first noticed the service door to the left of the glass. Locked, of course, but that hadn't been much trouble for Nick, already a budding juvenile delinquent. A minute later, he and his friend had been taking turns hanging from the two-hundred-pound brass ball.

Nick had spent the rest of the class trip sitting out front by the curb with a BMOS security staffer, and the next two days serving out a school suspension—not his first, and certainly not his last.

"Foucault's Pendulum," Hailey commented, misinterpreting Nick's gaze toward the glass walled exhibit. "Named after a French physicist, and his 1851 experiment to prove the theory of the Earth's rotation. The pendulum swings back and forth, while the Earth revolves beneath it; every hour, it knocks over another pin on the calendar below, tracking those revolutions. So simple, and so ingenious."

Her face lit up as she spoke, and Nick had to stifle a smile. Incredible, how smart she was, and how much joy she got out of all the things she'd learned—almost all of it self-taught. Her family history was even more tragic than his own—an orphan, raised in the foster system until she'd gone off on her own before she was even a teenager. That she'd been able to gain entry to MIT, had even excelled as a grad student, was made no less impressive by the fact that her high school transcripts were fake, and much of what she'd told the university was fiction.

As they passed through the turnstile and Hailey showed the museum employee their tickets, purchased online, via her burner phone, Nick tried to imagine what it had been like for Hailey, wandering through this museum by herself at the age of twelve. Alone, figuring out how to live, survive, thrive—and yet eager to feed her mind in a place like this. A natural chameleon, she'd probably been able to blend in with the tourists, families, and class trips filing through the various exhibits. Perhaps she'd scavenged food in the cafeteria, or hidden away after the museum closed down for the night, finding shelter during the difficult Boston winters. Nick had always seen his own childhood as fairly desperate: His mother had died when he was young, his dad was usually too drunk to care what he was up to, and he'd always been far enough below the poverty line to give him the proper incentives to push him toward a life of crime—but compared to Hailey, he'd had it easy. And yet, instead of robbing banks, she'd been working to get advanced degrees.

On the other side of the turnstile, the museum opened into a brief inner atrium, brightly lit by vast windows overlooking the Charles River. In the distance, Nick could see another duck boat, similar to the one on the curb outside, but this one chugged along across the curved band of choppy water. Stairs led down to a lower floor of the museum, and hallways led off in opposite directions; Hailey had already turned toward the right and was leading Nick into the main section of the building—another wide-open space, with a hallway that ran like a balcony around the open center of the building. Beyond a glass railing to Nick's left, he could see down to the lower floors; hanging in the air, suspended from the ceiling two floors above, a giant globe, speckled with oceans, land masses, swirling cloud systems. On either side of the floor, dozens of exhibits, all colorful, brightly lit, done up in molded plastic. To the right, an Arctic Adventure, decked out with fake snow drifts and hanging icicles. Beyond that, something to do with robots, tons of working gears and moving metal arms. Everything was interactive, and crowds of mostly children worked through the various halls, bouncing off of everything, a chaotic swarm of sound, motion, energy.

Nick felt immediately overwhelmed, his nervous system spiking, but Hailey was moving past the exhibits at a near jog. She led him by something called "Wicked Smart," which showcased inventions from the Boston area—and then they were racing by a glass railing. Nick could see the top of an enormous dinosaur exhibit, and rising up from the floor below—the skeleton of a T. rex, similar to the one outside but now turned inside out. Below, he could barely make out display cases filled with more bones, fossils, dinosaur footprints—and then they reached a glass door leading into a narrow, darkened hall.

The hall was crowded, but Hailey pushed through, Nick stifling his nerves as he followed. He couldn't tell if anyone around him looked like law enforcement—but at least the place was too dark for anyone to get a good look at his or Hailey's faces.

A few steps in, and Nick realized they were on the upper floor of an exhibit. Hailey continued to push through the crowd until they reached another railing, and Nick looked down—nearly twenty feet below, toward a massive raised stage. In the middle of the stage was a man in a bright orange museum jacket, already halfway into some sort of presentation. But the man wasn't the main focus of the crowd; behind him, rising up past the second-floor balcony where Nick and Hailey stood, were two giant rounded pillars, each at least thirty feet high. The pillars ended in huge spherical metal balls, strangely lit from behind by an orange light. As the man talked, Nick could hear a strange sizzling sound that seemed to come from the pillars; the air around Nick felt suddenly charged, and the hair on his arms and neck began to tingle.

Without warning there was an ear-shattering crack, and a huge bolt of electricity fired between the giant metal balls. A second later, more bolts exploded outward from the curved surfaces and careened off at wild angles above the stage.

As the bolts crackled above, the man on the stage spoke to the audience, and after a sentence or two Nick was able to follow the talk—a brief history of electricity, from its discovery by the ancient Greeks, who had noticed that when certain materials were rubbed against amber—silk, for instance—sparks could be created. Almost simultaneously, he said, the Chinese observed the peculiar hunting style of the electric eels native to their lowland rivers. Then he described how, by the 1700s, mechanical advances allowed scientists to harness this "electric magic," as it was known, using what was essentially considered a parlor trick to entertain royalty.

"There he is," Hailey whispered, interrupting Nick's concentration on the man onstage. She pointed toward a figure at the front of the audience on the first floor.

Adrian Jenson was unmistakable in his tweed jacket and cycling pants. His hair was less disheveled than it had been when Nick and Hailey had confronted him on the steps to his office, but he still had that saddle bag over his shoulder and, no doubt beneath the jacket, the same neoprene that covered his legs.

Nick felt an involuntary urge to grimace; he didn't care for the professor, and it wasn't just the way the foppish academic looked down on him. Most "respectable" people had a similar opinion of Nick, even before he'd become an ex-con. Adrian, to his credit, was dismissive of everyone; he was an equal opportunity snob. But the professor had a way of making Nick feel like a perpetual third wheel; despite his loftiness, the history wonk had some sort of reluctant connection to Hailey, which in part was the reason he was still helping them forward—though it was clear he intended to stay at arm's length from the two fugitives as long as he could.

To that end, Adrian had suggested they travel separately to the museum. He had gone by Uber, it being too far for a bicycle; while they had decided to risk the T, switching from the Red to the Green Line, all the while scanning for police, FBI, and worse. So far, they'd gotten lucky, but they were surrounded by people. Even in a dark tourist attraction, sooner or later their luck was going to run out.

Adrian didn't seem to be concerned by the crowd. His attention was entirely on the giant metal balls on the huge pillars, which had settled down to a soft flicker, as another figure moved next to the man in the orange museum jacket. This time a woman, around Adrian's age, with auburn hair pulled back in a tight ponytail. She was wheeling behind her what appeared to be a large metal cage, at least six feet tall, with a bar running perpendicular through its center. On top of the cage was another metal bar, rising straight up, like a cylindrical steeple.

"Give a warm welcome to Visiting Professor Angela Barrett," the man in the orange jacket continued, "on loan to us from King's College in London, by way of Boston University, where she's just completing a six-month sabbatical."

The woman smiled at the crowd, then spoke in a thick English accent.

"Ladies and gentlemen, the year is 1752. And a former printer, practiced statesman, and future revolutionary had recently moved from right here, in Boston, to the political center of the new continent—Philadelphia. This soon to be famous Founding Father, a man who would one day grace your hundred-dollar bill, was about to change history."

As she spoke, another museum employee joined her on the stage. On the man's wrist stood a live dove, its head cocking back and forth as it surveyed the darkened room.

"We're all familiar with Benjamin Franklin and his famous experiment with a kite," Barrett continued. "As the story goes, on a stormy afternoon in June of 1752, Franklin made a kite out of a handkerchief, suspended by a pair of strings made of hemp and silk. He and his son strolled into a field, attached a metal wire to the top of the kite, and sent it aloft toward the heavens. Franklin held the kite by the silk string but allowed the hemp to travel down from the wire all the way to a large metal key, which he'd tied to the bottom."

The audience seemed engaged by her words, but every eye was on the bird. As Barrett spoke, the museum employee placed the bird inside the large metal cage. The bird immediately flew to the bar bisecting the cage's center, then stood quietly, cleaning its feathers with its beak. The employee shut the cage door, then exited the stage.

"From the key," Barrett continued, "another wire ran into a glass jar backed on both sides by conductive metal. This container—a Leyden jar—was essentially a crude battery. As the storm billowed above, Franklin and his son slowly steered the kite high, high, high into the sky."

She looked up, and as she did, Nick heard the loud sizzling sound again as the huge columns began to power up.

"At the time, there were many names for it. Early man considered it a manifestation from their gods—bolts hurled by Zeus, or by Thor, or by Indra. During the Middle Ages it was given its name—'lightning.' Franklin, who had given up his printing press to dedicate his life to the study of the electrical phenomenon, sometimes referred to it as 'liquid fire' or even 'hellfire.' But by any name, what Franklin proved that night, with his kite and his key, was that the phenomenon often lighting up the night skies over London, Paris, Philadelphia, and Boston was essentially the

same phenomenon thrilling royals in courts all over the world—
'electric magic.' Or, as we call it today, 'static electricity.'"

And suddenly, the crack rang out again, and huge bolts of
lightning fired from the two giant metal balls. The bolts crackled
directly down to the cage and hit the cylindrical rod rising from
the top, then sizzled along the barred sides to the floor. The bird,
sitting in the middle of the cage, continued cleaning its feathers,
completely unharmed and unfazed.

"Franklin collected that electric magic into his Leyden jar by
way of the key hanging from his kite. We have done something
similar. The bolts generated by our Van de Graaff generator are
attracted to the highly conductive lightning rod, then are harmlessly transported along the outside of the cage to the ground."

The crowd was watching the bolts raining down from the generator, while Nick focused on Adrian; the professor had his arms
crossed against his chest, and his face was a mask of pure disdain.

"Some of you might have heard the term 'Faraday cage,'" Barrett continued. "It was named after British scientist Michael Faraday, who in 1836 demonstrated that electricity could travel across
the surface of a conductive material without affecting its interior.
But in actuality, it wasn't Faraday who invented the protective
cage. It was Ben Franklin, more than eighty years earlier, who discovered the effect, using a cork ball suspended in a metal cylinder."

As she spoke, she noticed Adrian in the front row for the first
time; she didn't pause, but Nick thought he noticed a slight upturn
to her smile. Not amicable, so much, as something approximating
pity. There was obviously no love lost between the two professors.

"Despite the common perception, Benjamin Franklin did not
'invent' electricity. He *tamed* it. He showed the world that bolts
of lightning, believed throughout history to be the manifestation
of gods, was the same liquid fire created by cloth against amber,

stored in Leyden jars, springing around Faraday cages, seeping out of electric eels. Because of Franklin, today our entire world runs on liquid fire. And without it, we truly would be left—in darkness."

The room went black, as the lights were suddenly doused. There was a brief pause, then applause from the audience. Nick felt Hailey pushing him backward, toward the glass doors.

"Dramatic," he said.

Hailey nodded, but he could tell she was as swept up as the crowd of tourists around them.

Then again, the way Adrian had been staring daggers at the British woman onstage—maybe the Van de Graaff generator and the unsinged dove were just the opening act.

By the time they had found the two professors in the back corner of the sprawling museum cafeteria, at a round table pressed up against a vast picture window overlooking the undulating waves of the Charles, Nick could see that things were not going well.

Adrian, his hair flopping over his ears, was gesturing wildly with both hands as Nick and Hailey approached. The woman was leaning back in her chair, her visage still emanating an almost palpable sense of pity.

"What's wrong with a little drama?" she said, laughing in response to whatever Adrian had just thrown her way. "It's mostly children, Adrian. Children love stories. And special effects."

"Children also love clowns. If they want special effects, let them go see a magic act. You've already got the bird, maybe next time try a rabbit and a hat. It's *unbecoming*. Worse yet, it's fantasy. It's not facts, and it's not history."

Hailey lowered herself into the open chair next to Adrian. Nick hung back, choosing a seat at a table two feet over, close enough so that he could still hear the conversation but far enough away that he had a good view across the rest of the cafeteria. At least Adrian had been smart enough to choose a spot far from the main crowd, with a view of the cash registers, which acted as a natural choke to the steady stream of tourists moving in from the rest of the museum.

Nick hated being out in public like this, and even more, he hated the idea of bringing someone else into their orbit. Adrian had been vague about Angela Barrett—what his connection to her was, or how much of an ally she might be. He noted only that she had the necessary expertise that he lacked; an amazing admission, Nick had thought at the time, considering how full of himself Adrian could be. Even more amazing, now that he'd seen the two of them together, Adrian obviously had more distaste for the woman than he had for Nick, which seemed almost impossible. She didn't seem overly thrilled to see Adrian, either—and if she had known that Nick and Hailey were wanted fugitives, she no doubt would have probably run for the nearest security guard.

"It's mostly history," Barrett countered, barely noticing Hailey or Nick. "The main beats, at least."

"Angela," Adrian said. "A key dangling from a kite."

Barrett laughed.

Nick glanced at both of them. "There wasn't a key?" he couldn't help asking.

Adrian's eyes glassed over for a brief moment. "Almost assuredly Benjamin Franklin never flew a kite into a lightning storm and turned himself into a fried revolutionary for the benefit of his autobiography."

There was a pause, then Barrett sighed. "Adrian is correct, of course. He's usually correct."

"Usually?" Adrian spat, but the woman continued.

"The experiment was most likely a myth, as were many of the stories we know today of Franklin. He did, however, conceptualize the experiment, first in a letter in 1750 to his friend in London, Peter Collinson. In that letter, Franklin proposed the idea of a 'lightning rod' to capture 'electrical fire' from the sky. The Collinson letter then circulated to Paris, where French physicist Thomas Dalibard actually carried out an experiment with the rod, to some success. It wasn't until June of 1752, however, that Franklin contemplated using a kite and a key, in an interview he gave to the *Pennsylvania Gazette*. It's unknown whether he and his son actually performed the experiment; a German physicist, George Willhelm Reichman, killed himself a year later attempting something similar, and it's broadly assumed that had Franklin actually charged a key in the manner he'd described, he would have suffered a similar fate."

Adrian sat silently through her monologue, and Nick could see a glum respect enter his demeanor. As much as it obviously pained the man to admit, Barrett was indeed an expert on Franklin. Whatever Adrian and Barrett's past might be, he had felt the need to reach out to her—and the fact that she had been willing to meet, at such late notice, meant the respect they had for each other—academically at least—went both ways.

"What about the Faraday cage?" Hailey asked. "Was that actually Benjamin Franklin?"

Barrett nodded, her eyes still on Adrian. "Franklin indeed invented the Faraday cage eighty years before Faraday. Franklin was a genius—perhaps the greatest scientific mind of his era. His inventions were numerous. The lightning rod and the Faraday cage were two of his more important creations. But he also invented an indoor heating device—the Franklin stove. And bifocals. Even swim fins. The list goes on and on—there was good reason that he became the most famous of the revolutionary heroes."

"Franklin was far from a revolutionary," Adrian huffed.

Barrett raised an eyebrow, but Adrian continued before she could break in.

"Up until the war, Franklin could nearly have been described as a loyalist. He was enamored with everything European. He embraced the British way of life. He was a man of class and breeding. He dressed in the English style. And he did not think highly of the rabble in Boston."

"A bit of an exaggeration," Barrett started.

"Not in the least. After the Boston Tea Party, Franklin referred to Revere and his 'Mechanics' as little more than terrorists. He considered Hancock and Adams as minor barbarians. He much preferred his colleagues in London and Paris."

"But once war was declared, he became one of the fiercest defenders of liberty—"

"As was all the rage in the parlors of Paris; Franklin was certainly more comfortable in a royal court than on a colonial battlefield."

Nick coughed, and the two professors looked at him. He could feel the cafeteria getting more crowded, filling up with families, teenagers, groups of children carrying plastic trays to tables on either side. They didn't have time for a debate on Franklin's loyalties.

Adrian gave him a glare, but then seemed to understand—and reached down into his saddle bag, withdrawing the document he'd taken from the Harvard library.

"It's not Franklin's Revolutionary War heroics—or lack thereof—that interests us. It's something a bit more—unsettled."

He slid the document in front of Barrett, who needed to only read a few lines before looking up.

"Catherine Ray?" she asked simply.

Adrian nodded toward Hailey, who retrieved her phone—and showed the screen to Barrett, revealing the second letter from the boat hand of the *Constitution*.

"According to this," Hailey said, "the same Catherine Ray—Franklin's platonic paramour—interacted with the captain of the USS *Constitution*, perhaps delivering something to the ship on its way to port after its famous battle with the *Guerriere*."

Barrett's eyebrows rose. Before she could respond, Nick added the kicker, because it didn't seem like anyone else would.

"We think there might be some sort of connection between Benjamin Franklin and Paul Revere—and we think it somehow has to do with this Catherine Ray."

Barrett seemed to really notice Nick for the first time. Hailey could pass for one of Adrian's graduate students, but Nick, in his jeans and new jeans jacket—courtesy of his stitchman entrepreneur—looked like a guy who knew less about Revere the revolutionary than he did about Revere the rough-and-tumble township south of Boston.

She turned back toward Adrian.

"Caty Ray—in this letter, Franklin spells it with a *K*, but in all other correspondence, its 'Caty' with a *C*—has always been a bit of an enigma. Very little has been written about her or her relationship with Franklin. Although she's usually considered one of his conquests, it was clear that there was no intimacy there—more a father-daughter sort of connection. And yet, it was a very deep connection, conducted mostly via letters, from 1754 all the way to 1790, the last letter being sent just days before Franklin's death."

Nick's longest relationship, outside of his family, hadn't lasted four months, let alone four decades. That someone as famous and powerful as Ben Franklin would keep up a platonic relationship with a much younger woman, mostly via letters, for so long, was difficult to comprehend.

"What we do know about the two of them," Barrett continued, "is based almost entirely on Franklin's letters, and on a handful of documents preserved in archives mostly in and around Block Island, a small bit of sand and marsh nine miles off the coast of Rhode Island, where Catherine grew up. She and Franklin met in Boston at the home of Franklin's sister, Jane, who was Catherine's sister's mother-in-law. Even though Jane was much older than Caty, they had become very close, and when Benjamin visited Boston, he and Caty struck up a friendship."

Barrett lifted Adrian's document off the table and peered at it through the protective clear plastic. Although she must have known that this letter—clearly an original artifact—should not have been outside of a library archive or museum, and certainly not in a crowded cafeteria, her expression showed more curiosity than concern.

"Their first meeting went well enough that Franklin invited the young woman on a trip to Newport—a multiday journey, by carriage, that would surely have appeared unseemly at the time. But throughout their correspondence, it was clear that nothing untoward happened between them, either on that trip or after. Not for Franklin's lack of trying; as you can see from this letter, his writings contained an almost constant undertone of flirtation."

She paused, one of her long fingers running over the lines of lavish text beneath the clear plastic.

"This letter—their first—is fairly unique. Much more poetic than the rest, the language taken to flowery extremes. And see how he addresses her as "Katy"—so informal Franklin was always extremely precise in his writing—perhaps the purposeful misspelling was some sort of inside joke between the two of them.

No doubt, the letter as a whole is laced with meaning we can only guess about."

Then she looked up, most of her attention on Adrian.

"But a connection to Paul Revere? That would be going a bit further than subtext. I don't have to tell you that Revere and Franklin did not have much in common. Though they were both born in Boston, they were from different classes and separated by almost thirty years."

"But they would have certainly known each other," Hailey said. "And didn't Revere travel to Philadelphia, after the Boston Tea Party?"

"The Suffolk Resolves," Adrian said. "September of 1774, Revere rode to bring notice to the First Continental Congress, calling for a boycott of all British goods. But Franklin would not have been in Philadelphia at the time. He didn't return from his first long trip to London until 1775."

Barrett had paused, still focused on the letter to Catherine Ray.

"Oswald Eve," she said, suddenly.

Adrian looked at her.

"Oswald Eve?" Nick asked, feeling himself getting impatient. The crowd felt very close, now, as the tables around them continued to fill with visitors. "Some sort of eighteenth-century holiday?"

"Not a holiday," Adrian said. "A person. The owner of the only gunpowder mill in the Americas, a key figure in the American Revolution."

Barrett nodded. "November of 1775, a year before the war broke out, the Continental Congress began to get worried. Outgunned and outmanned, the colonial army was at a huge disadvantage—made immensely worse by a severe shortage in gunpowder, the lifeblood of eighteenth-century armaments. Oswald Eve, a difficult man by any measure, refused to share his technological expertise with the young republic, choosing instead to keep a stranglehold on the gunpowder supply. So the Congress sent a special messenger to visit Eve's gunpowder factory outside of Philadelphia, armed with a letter of introduction and whatever power the fledgling government could muster."

"That messenger——" Hailey started.

"Revere," Adrian said.

"Midnight Ride aside," Barrett said, "he was basically the premier postal worker of the time. You needed a message delivered, you sent Revere."

"You sent Revere," Adrian countered, "because like Eve, he was a master technologist, who was already the leading metallurgist of his time. But Eve was a special sort of brute; he treated Revere poorly on his visit, refused to share any secrets with him."

"Correct," Barrett said. "Revere was prepared to return home to Boston when a second letter of introduction arrived at Eve's factory. This one, lesser known to history, wasn't written by the sitting Congress. It had been sent by a close friend of Eve's named William Greene, a powerful politician, businessman—and future governor of the state of Rhode Island."

She paused, looking up from the letter.

"Who also happened to be the second cousin of Catherine Ray. And who, eventually, married her, despite her continued literary flirtation with Benjamin Franklin."

Nick was trying to digest what she was saying, while keeping his eyes on the crowded cafeteria. Adrian seemed slightly stunned by the connection to Catherine Ray, but he managed to gather himself enough to continue.

"Eventually, Oswald did give Revere a tour of his gunpowder factory. Even though Eve refused to share any of his technological secrets, Revere saw enough to begin planning his own gunpowder endeavor, and when he returned to Massachusetts, he did indeed launch his own mill, which was a huge supplier to the Continental Army. Without Revere's gunpowder, it isn't certain that the rebels could have fought the British to a standstill, let alone win the war."

"And Ben Franklin?" Hailey asked. "Would he have been involved, in some way, with this effort?"

Barrett shrugged. "Franklin was certainly a contemporary of Eve's, and a social acquaintance. They were both important scientists of the era, both living in Philadelphia, and both wealthy members of the city's upper class. If Revere had gained access to Eve's good graces via an introduction connected to Catherine Ray, it's not a huge jump to conclude that Benjamin Franklin, her confidant and in some ways older mentor, had somehow been involved. Perhaps, even, he'd choreographed the encounter—giving Revere the edge he'd needed to bring home to Massachusetts the secrets that led to his own successful gunpowder factory."

"For the war effort?" Hailey asked.

Adrian shook his head. Barrett shrugged again, ignoring him.

"Franklin hadn't given up the notion that diplomacy could avert war, but he was a pragmatist. He might have realized the need for more gunpowder, or he might have had some alternate reasons for assisting Revere. The association with Catherine Ray is intriguing; if Franklin was indeed working behind the scenes through her, it would have allowed him to move the scales without outing himself to his London counterparts. Catherine Ray was a perfect cover: a young ingénue, a pretty girl from the wilds of Rhode Island— nobody would suspect that she was more than a potential conquest for the famous Franklin."

Nick was doing his best to follow along, but his attention had inadvertently shifted to a table about twenty feet to the left, near the center of the cafeteria. A young man had settled into one of the chairs facing their way, maybe thirty years old, athletic build, short blond hair bordering on a crew cut. The man seemed overdressed for the museum—dark slacks, collared shirt, dress shoes with rubber treads. Nick didn't see any children near the man, and though he had a cafeteria tray in front of him, he hadn't touched the food on the tray.

"You say Revere came back from Philadelphia and built his own gunpowder factory," Hailey said, obviously piecing things together. "If it really had been Franklin pulling the strings behind Revere's exploratory mission to Philadelphia, perhaps the connection didn't end when Revere returned to Boston."

Barrett was focused on her now.

"Not Boston but Canton. Revere built his own gunpowder factory—along with a copper mill—in Canton, along the Neponset River. It's a Paul Revere Heritage site now. Open to the public. They're in the process of building a museum."

Adrian was rubbing his eyes. "There's not much there," he said. "An old barn, a restaurant, a nice park. Nothing left of the original gunpowder works or the copper mill. I've toured the site a dozen times. I've even written a paper comparing the original footprint of Revere's mill to its current state."

"The original footprint?" Hailey said. "Like, a map?"

"Map, geological survey, materials, etc. I can pull it up for you, but it's not going to help; as Dr. Barrett said, there's nothing much there anymore. They've only just broken ground on the museum, and their Revere collection is paltry. Some silverware, a cannon—"

But Hailey didn't seem deterred. In fact, she seemed the opposite—determined.

"Adrian, you said yourself, this letter that Franklin wrote to Catherine Ray was the first mention of the Liberty Bell in history.

And this same Catherine Ray visited the USS *Constitution* on its way to port, right around the time Revere had something related to that bell placed on board. And now Catherine Ray, again, is connected to Revere's visit to Oswald Eve, after which he returned to Canton and built a factory—"

"A *gunpowder* factory," Adrian said. "To supply the war effort."

"Maybe," Hailey said, simply.

Barrett was staring at both of them, and seemed about to say something, but Nick suddenly felt his heart speeding up beneath his bruised ribs. He was still watching the man with the near crew cut at the table halfway across the cafeteria—and though the man wasn't looking their way, he'd pulled his cell phone out of his shirt pocket and had pressed it against his ear.

"I think we have to move," Nick hissed.

But Adrian ignored him, as he continued his argument with Hailey. "Even if Franklin did help Revere get access to Eve's technology, there's no reason to believe that Revere and Franklin continued any sort of association; Franklin and Revere were from different worlds, separated by more than thirty years, political opposites—"

Nick felt his frustration growing. He kept his eyes on the man across the cafeteria, who still had that phone pressed against his ear. As he listened to whoever was on the other end of the line, his head swiveled—right toward Nick and Hailey.

"Hailey," Nick coughed, but it was too late.

Nick saw recognition flash across the man's face. And then the man was up from the table and moving right toward them.

CHAPTER EIGHT

For a brief second, everything around Nick seemed to freeze, like images painted across a pane of glass. Then his instincts took over, and a strange calm swept over his nervous system. He immediately knew the man was a plainclothes cop, probably an off-duty detective, maybe BPD. He'd definitely made Nick and Hailey; he'd probably have no idea about the other two—Adrian and Barrett—which meant they weren't in danger. But Nick and Hailey needed to *move*.

Nick grabbed Hailey's arm. She looked up and saw the man for the first time. Then they were both on their feet.

"I'll draw him back the way we came," Nick whispered. "You head for the parking garage."

Nick took a step back from his table, and the man, still a dozen yards away, paused—trying to decide if he was going after Nick or continuing toward Hailey. Nick needed the man focused—so he hooked a foot around the leg of the chair behind him and gave it a good yank.

The metal chair hit the floor with a loud clatter, silencing the cafeteria; then Nick was darting backward through the crowd, and the man—working on instinct as well—made the split-second decision to come after him.

Out of the corner of Nick's eye, he saw Hailey suddenly scoop the document from the table, jam it into Adrian's saddle bag—which she then slung over her shoulder before sprinting in the opposite direction. Adrian shouted after her, but Nick knew she'd done the right thing. The stolen Franklin letter was better off in the possession of a fugitive than a history professor.

Then Nick's thoughts were entirely on his own predicament, because the man with the crew cut was right behind him and coming fast.

Nick skirted the closest table, then jammed himself between a pair of teenagers carrying trays piled high with food: hamburgers, fries, at least two fountain drinks. Nick let his hip connect lightly with one of the teens, not hard enough to knock the kid down but solid enough to jostle the kid's tray—which went over in a chaotic blast.

The kid cursed but Nick was past him. The plainclothes cop had to spin off to the left to avoid the cascade of food, giving Nick just enough time to make it to the cashier's line, which he sprinted through—and a moment later he was back in the main area of the museum, heading in the direction he and Hailey had come from.

The museum was more crowded now, as it was a few minutes before noon. The crowd gave Nick just enough cover to slide his way through the museum gift shop—loaded with displays of overpriced stuffed dinosaurs, shelves of crystalline rocks and astronaut ice cream, bins brimming with electronic toys and boxed crafts. As he went, entirely out of instinct, Nick scanned the shelves for anything that he might use as a weapon, or at least a distraction. Then he was back out of the store and heading toward the museum exit—when he saw the lights. Cop cars, at least two already screeching toward the curb; another blocking traffic.

Christ. Nick made another snap decision and cut in the opposite direction, back toward the turnstiles leading toward the interior of the museum. The security guard manning the turnstile held up a hand as he saw Nick moving toward him, but Nick wasn't about to slow down.

He barreled past the guy and through the turnstile, which spun behind him at full pace. Then he was moving right, sprinting toward the escalators. Nick pushed past a family of three, then climbed up the moving steps, trying his best not to knock anyone over as he ascended.

He burst out the top of the escalator onto the upper floor and dove to his right, past a giant fake sequoia cut open to reveal two centuries of rings. Then he was beyond the great tree and into some sort of traveling exhibit having to do with grasslands, speckled with tanks holding various plants, animals, and interactive mechanical irrigation devices, most crowded with kids pushing buttons, pulling levers, generally touching anything they could touch. As Nick moved through the grasslands, he cast a glance behind himself. He saw the cop just five yards behind, shouting into his phone as he ran. The man had a hand on his hip, where he might have had a sidearm—but Nick knew there was no way he'd pull out a gun in a museum crowded with kids.

Nick continued forward. Directly to the left was another exhibit, some sort of physics display full of pulleys and swings and spinning devices. He considered trying to lose himself among the machines—but then noticed another exhibit directly ahead. A door, beneath a large picture of some sort of enormous insect.

Nick didn't think; he dove straight ahead, pushed through the door—and found himself in a long hallway lined with glass cases on either side. Glancing through the glass as he ran, he saw bugs— all shapes and sizes, from sticklike creatures crawling up and down cactus-like plants, to flying insects with oversized wings pirouetting across neon-lit backdrops.

He cut deeper into the exhibit, which grew more crowded the farther he went. The hallway forked left, into another hallway—and then, Nick realized, a slightly more open area with walls made entirely of what appeared to be thick glass. The area was full of people, all of whom were facing the walls—and as Nick looked past them, he could see why. Behind the glass—the continuous motion of what appeared to be thousands, if not tens of thousands—of beetle-like insects. Rust-colored, each at least three inches long, moving like a kinetic storm across the inside of the massive, wrap-around tank.

"Nick Peterson!" Nick heard a shout from behind him, and he whirled, backing into the crowd, which quickly moved out of the way.

The plainclothed cop was now only a few feet in front of him, holding a badge in the air between them like it was some sort of flaming torch. The man's other hand was still on his hip, and Nick could see the grip of a police issue .38, in a leather holster that was already snapped open.

"This is a misunderstanding," Nick tried, still backing up. The crowd had moved to both sides, and Nick could suddenly feel cold glass against his back. He glanced up—trying not to notice the squirming motion behind the glass—and saw a sign above his head, describing what was inside the tank: Madagascar Hissing Cockroaches—*Gromphadorhina portentosa*—native to the Island nation of Madagascar, three to four inches in length, wingless, excellent climbers . . .

"We can work that out back at the station," the man said, stepping forward. "There are a dozen officers right behind me. So let's not make this any harder than it needs to be."

Nick felt an inadvertent smile touch his lips. This cop knew his name, but obviously nothing else about him; with Nick, things always tended to go harder than they needed to. He tried to move back—but the glass was solid behind him. His left hand opened against the cold, smooth surface; he could feel the skittering of the enormous insects on the other side, could hear the hissing rising through the glass. But it was his other hand that caught his focus; sliding into his pocket, his fingers closed around the item he'd snagged from one of the museum gift shop shelves. Rough, heavy, about the size of a baseball.

"Nice and easy," the cop said, his hand moving from the hilt of his gun toward a pair of handcuffs peeking out of his front pocket.

"Nice and easy," Nick repeated.

And then he yanked his right hand out of his pocket. The cop's eyes went wide; maybe he saw the shiny crystalline rock in Nick's clenched fist, or maybe he just saw the way Nick's arm arced back toward the glass, his muscles tightening against the inevitable—

The rock hit the glass with a loud crack; one more swing, in quick succession. Faults spiderwebbed outward from the point of impact, and then the glass shattered inward. The cockroaches poured out around Nick, bouncing off his shoulders and legs and skittering around the back of his neck, then fountained across the floor in a maelstrom of moving legs, flickering flightless wings, and hissing, so much hissing.

Which was followed by screaming, as the crowd rushed in every direction, trying to get away from the tide of insects. Nick threw himself forward, right past the stunned undercover cop—and then he was in the crowd, being buffeted down the hallway back toward the exit of the exhibit.

A moment later he was back on the top floor of the museum, sprinting as fast as he could past the crowd. He could hear the cop shouting behind him but he didn't look back; instead he increased his speed, heading right for the escalators leading down.

And then he saw the uniforms—at least four, maybe six—pushing their way up the crowded moving steps. Nick didn't think—he skidded to his left, racing past the entrance to the escalators, searching for another way down. Directly ahead—maybe fifty, sixty feet—he could see a door marked Stairs—but he knew it was too far, they'd be on him before he'd gotten down three steps. Instead, he glanced to his left—the glass railing was chest high, and beyond it, the drop had to be at least thirty feet to the floor below. But peeking up toward the bottom of the railing, he saw bones; huge, crisscrossing bones, connected to each other by long metal bars, beckoning toward him like some sort of evolutionary gift from above.

The T. rex skeleton. Stupid, Nick hissed to himself, crazy. But he knew that stupid and crazy was his only option. He ran straight for the railing, caught the top with his good arm, and then was hurtling over the top.

He hit the T. rex right above the wide-open jaws, as his arms grasped at the huge bones crisscrossing the skeleton's head. The entire display pitched downward beneath his weight, shaking like it had been caught in an earthquake. But the metal bars held, and the T. rex groaned and spasmed but did not collapse. Nick clambered downward, bone by bone, from the creature's enormous head to its elongated neck, then down the sprawling rib cage. Below, he could see tourists pointing and backing away, and above he could hear shouts from the police officers—but a moment later he was at the bottom of the skeleton's chest, maybe ten feet above the carpeted floor. He let himself drop, and landed in a painful crouch. In front of him were two kids, maybe twelve years old, eyes wide.

Nick handed one of the kids the crystalline rock he'd jammed back in his pocket—and then he sprinted past them. Directly ahead, he saw the entrance to the same stairwell from the floor above. He hit the door with his uninjured shoulder, then took the steps three at a time, bouncing off the cinder block walls. A minute later, he crashed out into the parking garage. Dark, crowded with cars in parallel spots, curved ramps running up and down. Nick whirled back and forth, searching for which way to go—

"Nick!"

Hailey was coming around the corner from wherever she'd been hiding; she still had Adrian's saddle bag over one shoulder and a terrified look on her face. She knew they only had moments before the garage was crawling with cops. On foot, they'd never make it.

Which meant they had to steal a car. Nick scanned the spots closest to them; lots of late-model SUVs, a handful of compacts— something older would be easier to break into, much easier to start. Anything past the late '90s meant a fob or push-button starter, which made hot-wiring out of the question. The bigger problem was going to be getting out of the garage; they didn't have a parking ticket, which meant blowing through the gate in front of a half dozen cop cars—a hell of a lot tougher than it looked in the movies.

But then Hailey was pointing to the right. Nick saw it—a delivery truck pulled up by a loading door. The back of the truck was still open, but whatever was being delivered had already been moved inside by the driver.

Nick felt his adrenaline spike, as he rushed to the driver's side door and climbed up into the seat. As he'd suspected, the key was sitting on the console between the cupholders. Hailey went around the back—shutting the rear doors—before coming around to slide into the passenger seat next to him.

Nick started the truck and then they were snaking down the ramp toward the exit, which consisted of three gated lanes—and a separate gate marked Service, watched over by a windowed booth.

Nick could see the lights from the police cars in the receiving circle beyond the exit, but he kept his pulse steady as he headed for the service gate. He nodded toward Hailey, who lowered herself down below the dash. Nick knew they only had a few seconds before the police locked down the garage—but he didn't dare gun it down the exit ramp. Instead, he remained at a steady pace, heading slowly toward that lowered gate, praying that whoever was in the booth wasn't paying much attention, simply saw the delivery truck and let them through.

Just as he reached the bottom of the ramp, the gate went up. Nick could see someone waving him through from the other side of the booth's window—and then he was past the exit and moving right by the nearest cop car, which was empty, devoid of motion other than the spinning, flashing lights—no doubt, the occupants still racing around the museum.

Then the truck was sliding out of the museum receiving circle and into the steady stream of lunchtime city traffic, the cop cars, duck boats, and giant T. rex fading away, inch by inch, in Nick's rearview mirror.

CHAPTER NINE

Sometimes, it was the simplest forms of art that ended up being the most powerful.

Zack Lindwell absentmindedly ran a finger along the edge of his shiny brass FBI shield, which hung from a lanyard slung around the collar of his dark blue official windbreaker, as he watched the two men cross the circular atrium ahead of him. Zack was keenly aware of the tension in the vast, glass-walled room—more of a rotunda than a traditional exhibition hall—which housed only a singular artifact, two thousand pounds, bronze, darkened by age, and yet utterly familiar because it was remarkably similar to the replica Zack had been standing next to just six hours earlier.

The men didn't say anything as they reached the curved hollow base of the beast. The senior of the two men dropped to both knees and peered beneath the lip, while the other used gloved hands to push the massive artifact a few inches forward on its frame, to give his colleague a better look. Zack tried to keep his focus on the two men and not the crowd, held back by numerous uniformed park rangers, that was growing on the other side of the glass walls on every side.

It was a little after noon. By now this rotunda, and the museum dedicated to that single, ultrafamous artifact behind Zack, should have been packed with tourists. Bathed in the shadows of

Independence Hall, Liberty Center—which housed the Liberty Bell, and told the story of its provenance and import through a chronologically curated series of documents, paintings, recreations and video montages—was inarguably one of Philadelphia's biggest tourist attractions. Normally, every day over twenty thousand people stood where Zack was standing, marveling at the famous, indelibly cracked hunk of bronze—and yet, at the moment that number was down to three, due entirely to that little brass fleck of art hanging from Zack's chest.

The truth was, at the moment Zack's FBI badge had about as much value as the brass it had been molded from. The two men surveying the Bell in front of him were officially under the auspices of the Parks Commission, and he had no real authority over them. Worse yet, as the head of the Art Crimes Division of the FBI in an entirely different city, Zack had almost no jurisdiction in Philadelphia.

He had been lucky enough that his counterpart at the Philadelphia Bureau had been away from his desk when he'd called from his car during the trip south from Boston; it hadn't been difficult to bully the second-level supervisor into granting ten minutes alone with the Bell and the assistance of a pair of experts from the museum's artifact staff. When the man's supervisor returned from whatever lunch he'd been attending, Zack would have to have some fancy dialogue prepared to explain what he was doing in Philadelphia, and how it connected to the Gardner theft. Crossing state lines during an investigation as broad and important as the biggest art theft in history wasn't unusual, but tying the most famous historical object in the country to those missing paintings would have been challenging enough—if Zack had any solid evidence to go on. Instead, what he had were snippets of conversation he'd overheard while lying paralyzed on the deck of the *Constitution*, and an object that made about as little historical sense as a half billion dollars' worth of art vanishing in the '90s, never to surface again.

"Everything seems in order," the man on his knees said, as he peered beneath the lip of the bell. He sounded mildly disappointed, which wasn't surprising. When Zack had first explained his interest in the Bell to the two museum employees, they'd both been skeptical of the idea that the clapper Zack had taken from the replica bell in Boston was anything more than a well-crafted hoax. It was only when Zack had shown them the preliminary report put together by his forensic team—who had just begun the radiological dating process of the bronze, and the chemical analysis of its construction—that the two men had perked up. The man on his knees, Dr. Samuel Hodge, a recently retired history professor from the University of Pennsylvania, had quickly followed through on Zack's request to shut down the exhibit for a quick examination.

"Nothing's been disturbed," Hodge said, slowly climbing out from under the lip of the bell and rising to his feet. He was portly, with a belly that flopped a few inches over his belt, but there was a springiness to his movements that seemed incongruous to the clearly evident wrinkles covering most of his pear-shaped face. He struck Zack as the sort of retiree he'd often encountered in museums—people who'd left academia because of age or overwork, only to find themselves temperamentally unsuited to sit on the sidelines. They were eventually drawn back to the objects of their previous curiosities, even if that meant donning a museum uniform and spending their days playing tour guide.

"The original clapper is exactly where it's supposed to be," Hodge continued. "I'm not sure what you found in Boston, but I'd stake my reputation on the fact that what we've got here is the same hunk of junk that Pass and Stowe delivered in March of 1753."

Hodge and his younger colleague—a taller, thinner version of the retired professor who referred to himself as Dr. Clagsdale—shared a grin with each other at what must have been an inside joke. Zack wasn't an expert, but he'd gleaned enough from his cursory research on the bell to understand Hodge's jab. The Bell standing in the glass atrium in front of them was actually the third and final attempt at fulfilling the Pennsylvania Assembly's mandate for a new bell to hang in the nearby State House. The original bell had been cast in England at the Whitechapel Bell Foundry but had immediately cracked upon its first ringing. Local metal workers John Pass and John Stowe agreed to recast the bronze beast, but they, too, ended up delivering a bell that fell vastly short of expectations. When rung, it produced a sound so dreadful that it was immediately suggested the thing be melted down and sold for scrap. Instead, Pass and Stowe took the bell back to their foundry and tried again. The third and final bell wasn't much of an improvement on the second; its sound was described as both brittle and nauseating, and there were even reports of people becoming physically ill by its ringing. Instead of scrapping the object, however, a new bell was forged for daily use, while the Pass and Stowe bell was brought out for "special occasions"—such as the coronation of King George II. Eventually, this awful-sounding "hunk of junk" became known as the Liberty Bell, which attracted tens of thousands of tourists a day.

"Could there have been multiple clappers?" Zack asked, as Hodge brushed wrinkles out of the knees of his uniform. "If Pass and Stowe were trying to fix the quality of the tone made by the bell, might they have tried out different ringing mechanisms?"

Hodge glanced at his colleague, who seemed to be losing interest by the second. The man was glancing at the crowd outside the glass walls, clearly ready for Zack to be on his way.

"Anything's possible," Hodge said. "But there's nothing in the historical record about a second clapper. Quite frankly, it's doubtful Pass and Stowe had the technical ability to improve on the design they had inherited from Whitechapel. Pass had never made bells of his own, and Stowe was barely out of his own apprenticeship at a brass foundry. A 1975 metallurgical analysis of the bell revealed the two men had gotten their alloys wrong; they'd used cheap pewter instead of pure tin, and their mix of copper was entirely off. The assembly would have been much better served going with a foundry that knew its bells. But you know how it is—people love to buy local."

Hodge grinned at his friend again, who was already heading back toward the main entrance to the museum, no doubt to begin the process of reopening the building to the public. Zack didn't have any reason to stop the man; there didn't seem to be anything here to connect the clapper he had back in his lab in Boston to the Liberty Bell. And even if Pass and Stowe had tinkered with different evolutions of the Bell, trying to get it to sound better, Zack had no idea how that connected to Hailey and Nick, the missing Gardner paintings, or Napoleon's eagle, which had ended up in the Boston Harbor. The only vague connection he could think of was that the eagle had also been cast in bronze—around 1814—which would have put it within sixty years of the casting of the bell.

But Pass and Stowe were not expert bronze workers, though, and they were unlikely to have had anything to do with the eagle. According to Hodge, they'd been tasked with the Liberty Bell only because they were local. Similar to how everything from the time period in Boston that involved copper, or metallurgy in general, had been crafted by Paul Revere.

"Did they consider reaching out to someone like Paul Revere for help?" Zack asked, as Hodge followed his colleague toward the doors, and Zack went with him. "He was one of the leading experts in bells of the time, wasn't he?"

Hodge shrugged. "Revere loved his bells. And maybe if his found-ries had been closer to Philadelphia they might have gone to him. But there's nothing that I know of connecting Revere with the Liberty Bell; if there was, you can bet we'd have a wing dedicated to him in the museum. Boston was a long trip at the time, and though Revere was skilled in the use of copper, he was considered somewhat of a lowlife in these parts; the Assembly wouldn't have reached out to someone of his status, no matter his expertise. Pass and Stowe would have much more likely consulted a figure such as Benjamin Franklin about the awful sound quality of their work."

Zack looked up, surprised. "Franklin worked on bells?"

"Not that I know of," Hodge responded. "But he was keenly interested in the science of sound."

"I thought his thing was electricity."

"His thing was *everything*. The man had his hand in so many inventions of the era, he makes DaVinci seem lazy. Electricity was his main focus later in life, but in his earlier years he spent a lot of time studying how sound worked. He'd actually developed a way of measuring sound frequencies using glasses—work which led to the invention of his famous *armonica*."

Zack had heard of the instrument before, also known as the "glass harmonica." Franklin had gotten the idea for the invention while watching a friend making music at a party by running his wet fingers around the rims of half-filled wine glasses. Franklin had believed he could improve on the endeavor by turning the glasses on their sides; his armonica was made up of thirty-seven glass bowls mounted along an iron rod. Using a foot pedal, Frank-lin could spin the bowls, and by running his wet fingers over their glass rims, produce music.

"An amazing instrument," Hodge continued. "Franklin invented the device in 1761; within a year, it was all the rage across Europe. The armonica was even outpacing pianos in concert halls—a phenomenon that seemed poised to change the course of classical music for generations."

Zack raised his eyebrows. He'd thought Franklin's instrument had been little more than a curiosity of the time; though he'd seen one or two in museums over the years, he'd certainly never watched anyone play the device.

"You don't hear much armonica these days," he commented.

"Because a few months after armonica fever began sweeping through the parlors of London and Paris, a strange thing started to happen. Reports began to spread of people getting sick during armonica performances. Audiences, musicians—people began to experience intense nausea, dizziness, a few even more advanced neurological problems. Then a rumor surfaced that an eight-year-old boy died during a concert."

"Died?" Zack repeated.

Hodge shrugged. "There have been many theories—lead poisoning resulting from the paints used on the glasses, coincidence, hysteria—whatever the reason, the PR got to be too much to ignore, and the armonica disappeared from parlors and concert halls alike."

Zack shook his head; he assumed that many of the stories that had led to the demise of the armonica were exaggerations, if not outright fiction. But still, the idea that some people might have gotten even mildly ill from listening to a musical instrument seemed insane to him. Then again, hadn't Hodge just told him that the bell in the glass-walled atrium behind him had sounded so awful that people had been struck sick?

His thoughts were interrupted by a vibration coming from his jacket pocket.

Retrieving his phone, he saw that the call was coming from the Philadelphia field office. As he followed Hodge to the Bell museum entrance, he pressed the phone to his ear and heard the overexcited voice of the FBI agent he'd spoken to earlier in the day. Zack had asked the man to notify him if any reports came in concerning crimes involving anything historical in nature—not that he'd been expecting a Gardner painting to appear the morning of his visit to the city. But from the sound of the agent's voice, it appeared his shot in the dark had at least nicked a target.

"Stolen art?" Zack asked, as the agent breathlessly gave him an address.

"Artifacts," the man replied. "But not a simple robbery."

Zack felt something cold in his chest. "Homicide?"

"Plural. And, well—it's not pretty."

It never was.

Twenty minutes later Zack was breathing through a handkerchief as he followed a gloved and suited CSI technician through one of the oddest, most chaotic homicide theaters he'd witnessed—and that was saying a lot. No matter how many corpses he'd seen in his twenty years as an FBI agent, it was always difficult not to be affected by the sight and smell of death, especially in close quarters with bad ventilation. But this crime scene was uniquely disturbing.

Even as he'd made his way down the ladder to the underground archeological site, he'd felt increasingly uncomfortable. It didn't help that a dozen or so CSI technicians in their white smocks and masks and gloves were already picking over everything with the technology of their trade—DNA vacuums, fingerprint panels, electromagnetic detectors. Intermixed with the sherlocks were a group of officials from the Heritage Society of Philadelphia, led by a man with a ringlet of white hair and frantic eyes who kept nearly slapping the CSIs to keep them from touching anything. His authority wasn't helped by the fact that the skin above his gauze mask was decidedly greenish, or that every once in a while Zack could hear the man gag.

Zack couldn't blame him. As he moved through the theater and into the deepest chamber of the site, the acrid smell became almost overpowering. Even the CSI techs were giving the three chairs on the far side of the chamber a wide berth.

Moving closer, Zack fought the urge to look away. The body on the right was perhaps the worst; the young man on the left had gone much faster, it appeared. But the one in the center—mouth gaping open in a wide scream, face stricken and already marbling—Zack shook his head, let his gaze switch from the chairs to the strange device beside them. Old, made mostly of wood, with a foot pedal and a strange glass bulb at the top.

"It's called an electrostatic machine," the man from the Heritage Society explained, coming up behind Zack, his voice muffled by his mask. "The foot pedal causes the globe to spin; the charge is developed by the metal threads in the cloth rubbing against amber, which then runs through the Leyden jars, then into those leads and then—"

"I get the idea," Zack interrupted. "Mr. Caufield?"

The man nodded and held out a gloved hand, which Zack shook. Beneath the latex the man's fingers were trembling, and there was a strange gulping to his breathing. Certainly, being this close to such violent deaths was a shock to the poor scholar; but there was also a strange brightness in his eyes that made him look much younger than he obviously was. In a way, he seemed as fascinated by what had happened here as the CSI techs.

"It's quite an incredible device," he continued between breaths.

"The simple pedal action can accumulate an impressive static charge—over one hundred thousand volts, which can easily be stored in the parallel jars."

"Enough to cook a man from the inside," Zack commented. That quieted Caufield, and Zack tempered his thoughts, switching tracks. "You've seen one of these before?"

"In a museum. Not out—ah—in the wild. No one has, not for at least two hundred years. It's quite valuable. Handmade, perhaps by Mr. Franklin himself."

Zack raised his eyebrows. He'd read the series of texts on the drive over. He knew that a construction crew had uncovered the site a few weeks earlier, and that the Heritage Society considered it a major discovery and were in the process of tying the site to Benjamin Franklin, who apparently had operated numerous scientific facilities in the Philadelphia area. None like this, however—underground, undocumented, sealed off from the world for centuries. Even without the dead bodies, the find would have eventually ended up splashed across the front pages of newspapers and covers of magazines.

"I imagine there are a lot of valuable items down here." Zack looked at the shelves that ran along the walls on either side. "I know you've been cataloguing everything since the place was discovered. Do you know if anything has gone missing in the past twenty-four hours?"

Caufield waved a gloved hand at one of his colleagues, who was hanging back behind the CSI techs. The man—of a similar age as Caufield, with thick glasses above his mask—shuffled forward, studiously keeping his gaze averted from the chairs and the bodies. He had a folder under one arm, which he produced. Caufield flipped it open in front of Zack. The folder's pages were filled with what looked to be Polaroid photos, pinned to handwritten descriptions. Zack recognized many of the objects, from the mundane—test tubes, beakers, specimen scales—to more complicated, archaic devices, such as the electrostatic machine, the Leyden jars, various types of microscopes, and even a small smelting furnace for more complicated metal work.

Caufield flipped pages until about halfway through the folder, then pointed toward a photo taped near the center. Zack looked closer and saw that the Polaroid showed what appeared to be an engraving—two men in a workshop, both familiar. As were the two objects between the men.

"A kite," Zack said, stunned. "And a key." He looked at Caufield. "I didn't know that Ben Franklin was associated with Paul Revere."

"Other than the fact that both were involved in the Revolution, they weren't. Certainly Revere had nothing to do with Franklin's work on electricity, or his proposed experiment with the kite and the key. Which is why this engraving is so interesting, and valuable."

Zack looked more carefully at the images of the two men. Franklin, wearing his familiar bifocals, hair wavy and full. Revere in a tricornered hat, a minuteman uniform. No doubt, an odd carving. Franklin would have been a much, much older man, and yet in the image the two looked to be fairly young men. Curious.

"Is this the only item you've found to be missing?"

Caufield shook his head. He didn't need to flip more pages— the next missing item was on the same page, two photos down.

"This was on the same shelf as the engraving. Both items—gone."

Unlike the engraving, the second missing item was much harder for Zack to recognize. The Polaroid showed some sort of device, perhaps mechanical: a curved frame rising out of two small jars that appeared filled with some sort of gray liquid, and between the curves of the frame a brass-looking ball was suspended in the air by a gossamer-thin thread.

Zack stared at the Polaroid for a full beat. The device was

strange, and he had no idea what its function might be, but it wasn't entirely unfamiliar. He realized he had seen it before.

"These were on the same shelf?"

The man nodded, then guided Zack toward the far wall of the chamber. He pointed to one of the shelves, and Zack could see the space left by the missing items, between a row of beakers and a box that was filled with balled-up wires and what looked to be a collection of different sized chunks of amber. Next to the amber, Zack noticed a leather case, partially open. He could see a pair of square-framed eyeglasses sitting in the case, the thick lenses caked with dust.

"Are those—"

"—bifocals," Caufield said, nodding. "We haven't yet checked the prescription. But what a find, if indeed they are—"

He stopped himself, too excited to finish the thought. Then he shrugged.

"Our initial estimation is that this laboratory was operating somewhere between the late 1770s and the early 1780s. Mr. Franklin would have been in his seventies at the time—by then he was nearly blind without his glasses. He would have been wearing them all the time."

"So these would be what—a backup pair?"

Caufield shrugged again. His attention had drifted back toward the other side of the room, where the CSI techs had moved back to the bodies in the chairs. Soon, they would bring out the black plastic bags, and begin the task of moving the bodies to the morgue. There, the ME would spend the rest of the day determining the gruesome details of what, exactly, a two-and-a-half-century-old machine could do to the internal organs of a construction site foreman and two unlucky security guards.

While Caufield's skin shifted back through different levels of green, Zack's own attention moved back to the folder, which was now tucked back beneath Caufield's crooked right arm. Zack didn't need to see the Polaroid again; now he clearly remembered where he'd seen the odd device before. Not in a laboratory, or even a museum.

"You think whoever did this—" Caufield paused, choking back a heave "—also took the missing items?"

Zack shook his head. "Whoever did this was looking for something that wasn't here."

Zack didn't know what the device was, or why it was important. But he did know someone had been willing to kill for it. A machine that had been sitting on a shelf in a lab—Ben Franklin's lab?—that had been sealed away from the world for more than two and a half centuries.

He couldn't know for certain, but the chances were that what had happened here was connected to the violence that had occurred over the past two days back in Boston. The missing Gardner paintings had led him to the deck of the USS *Constitution*, then to the Liberty Bell. Now he had just seen evidence that linked a vicious triple murder to an engraving depicting Ben Franklin and Paul Revere.

Somehow, history was being rewritten in front of him. Something that was supposed to be as stable and fixed as painter's oil on a canvas. But Zack knew that as permanent as art often seemed to be, the meaning embedded in a painting could shift and turn, and was, in the end, as variable and chaotic as the brushstrokes that had gone into creating it.

A specific subset of those brushstrokes began dancing behind Zack's eyes. He headed quickly back through the chamber, toward the ladder leading up to the city above.

CHAPTER TEN

It was a sight so pure and natural that for the briefest of moments, maybe the time between the rise and fall of a single heartbeat or the flicker of a butterfly's wings, Hailey was completely lost in the view.

The heron had appeared out of nowhere, white and curved and glorious, swooping down from a cloudless midafternoon sky toward the glassy, meandering twists of the Neponset River. At the last second before it plummeted beak first through the glassy water, the heron pulled up. Its outstretched wings skimmed the surface of the river, sending up a spray that nearly reached the grassy bank just a dozen yards from where Hailey and Nick strolled hand in hand, like the dozen other couples wandering through the manicured park. Then the heron was back in the air, rising toward the clouds, its beak empty and its wings flapping against the stiff New England breeze. Whatever it had seen through the water had eluded it; whatever had sent it spiraling down in that determined plummet, so solid and real, had simply—vanished.

Hailey knew exactly how the heron must have felt. She and Nick had been strolling the grounds of the Paul Revere Heritage Site in Canton—a pretty, upscale suburb twenty miles south of Boston—for more than forty minutes now, and so far they had found nothing more solid than the spray of water off of the giant, white bird's outstretched wings.

In fact, there was precious little at the location that even hinted at its connections to the Revolutionary Era—the age of Revere, Franklin, the mysterious Catherine Ray. When she and Nick had first pulled up to the park, Hailey had thought they'd gotten the address wrong.

Besides the nine-acre glade, bisected by walking paths lined with benches and picnic tables, the Heritage site consisted of a grand total of two buildings: a yellow barn, obviously still under restoration, surrounded by a half dozen construction vehicles, and a large, brick, rectangular building with a cantilevered roof and oversized picture windows. The building consisted of a museum and a restaurant; the barn, according to a pamphlet Hailey had been given by one of the construction workers, would one day house a second museum. That collection would detail the history of the site from its origins as a copper and gunpowder mill owned by the Revere family, through its years as one of the largest rubber plants in the Northeast, to its current status as a family-focused bit of protected parkland that had doubled residential housing values in the surrounding neighborhoods.

As they'd left the delivery van next to a bulldozer at the edge of the lot by the park entrance, Hailey had suggested that they act like a couple as they looked around the grounds. After what had happened at the Museum of Science, she'd wanted to play things as low-key as possible; Nick's eyes were still wild from the chase through the dinosaur exhibit, and she was afraid that on his own, he looked about as natural as a man who'd recently left prison and had just climbed down a T. rex skeleton to escape the Boston police could look.

In front of the brick building, they'd run into a group of school-age children on a class trip; while hanging back behind their tour guide, they'd learned that the building had been reconstructed to match the original copper factory, which had stood in roughly the same spot. According to the guide, this site was where Revere and his family had perfected his methods of rolling copper—and where he had pressed many of the sheets that had ended up plating the USS *Constitution* and the dome at the top of the Massachusetts State House.

Eventually, Revere had moved from copper to bronze—crafting the many bells that had dominated the later part of his career as a metallurgist. Along with bells, he'd cast an army's worth of cannons, which had been used in multiple wars, all the way through to the Civil War between the states.

By the late nineteenth century, the Revere family's hold on the property had dissipated, and a new concern had moved in, exchanging the copper and bronze factories for a massive rubber mill, which had been the focus of the area's industry for decades. The mill had consisted of about a dozen buildings—but eventually, as the rubber industry dwindled, the buildings had gone into disrepair. Years later, a residential corporation had bought up the land, parceled out most of it for high-end condominiums, and donated the nine-acre section in the center back to the city of Canton.

The brick building that housed the museum had been constructed along plans Revere himself had left behind; the second floor was filled with Revere cannons, models of the USS *Constitution*, and of course shelves and display cases filled with Revere silverware. The restaurant on the first floor served locally sourced seafood with a New England flair.

Before separating themselves from the class trip, Hailey had noticed that the tour guide had made almost no mention of the gunpowder factory; it had been little more than an addendum to the guide's monologue about Revere's accomplishments. As far as Hailey could tell, no part of the original gunpowder factory still existed. Once they had moved a few yards down one of the walking paths toward the river, Hailey had used her phone to retrieve the maps Adrian had given her from his paper on the factory and had done her best to overlay the original plans with a map of the heritage site she'd pulled off the internet.

"There doesn't seem to be anything left of it," Nick said under his breath, as they passed a couple pushing a stroller. "I'm not sure what you're expecting to find."

Hailey didn't answer. Instead, her eyes focused on her phone, she led him closer to the embankment running down to the water. According to what Adrian had sent her, the original footprint of the factory ran past where the water began; she surmised that before the dams that were holding back the Neponset had been built, much more of this area had been usable land.

"Let's go over what we know," Hailey said. "Revere went to Philadelphia at the behest of the Continental Congress. An introductory letter got him in with Oswald Eve, who basically blew him off. Then a second letter got him deeper inside Oswald's operation, deeper enough that he could come back here to build his own factory."

They were close to the embankment now. Hailey noticed a group of trees right where the grass sloped down to the water. The trees were odd, with reddish leaves, not the sort of trees that speckled the rest of the park.

"If Catherine Ray arranged the meeting, it's possible that Oswald wasn't the only one Revere met that day in Philadelphia. Oswald wasn't interested in helping Revere build a gunpowder factory— but perhaps the entire meeting was a ruse of sorts. Revere had been sent to find out the secrets of gunpowder, but he'd really been after something else entirely."

She paused in the pathway, still focused on the trees with the reddish leaves. Then she reached into Adrian's saddle bag, which she'd taken from the table in the museum and was still slung over her shoulder. She retrieved the translucent folder containing the letter that Adrian had lifted from the library at Harvard.

Nick watched her for a moment as she scanned the letter again. Then his eyes were back toward the water.

"The bird is back. I think it's some sort of egret—"

"Heron," Hailey corrected. Then she beckoned him next to her. "Look at this."

She pointed toward the last line in the letter. A postscript, added at the very end, after Franklin had signed off. A strange, almost poetic postscript.

PS. The plums came safe, and were so sweet from the cause you mention'd that I could scarce taste the sugar.

Nick read the words. Then he shrugged. "The old man liked her plums."

Hailey laughed, but there was a slight buzzing in her chest. Like when she was working on a particularly difficult puzzle, and pieces started to look oddly familiar.

'I don't know much about Ben Franklin," she said. "But I do know that he loved his wordplay. And he was an expert and early adopter of the art of cryptography."

"Codes," Nick said. They had both gotten pretty familiar with the art themselves over the past couple of days. "He wrote in codes, even to his mistress?"

"If that's indeed what she was."

"What do you mean?"

"Benjamin Franklin was a fixture in European society right up until the Revolutionary War. Paul Revere was basically a terrorist.

You heard the professors; when Revere went to see Oswald Eve the first time, he was basically kicked out of the man's factory. People like Oswald Eve, and Benjamin Franklin—high society—couldn't be seen consorting with a man like Paul Revere."

Nick nodded. Certainly, he knew what it was like to be ostracized because of where he'd come from.

"If someone like Benjamin Franklin wanted to work with a man like Paul Revere," Hailey continued, "what better way than to mask it through an intermediary?"

Nick thought for a moment. "You're saying it was better optics to seem like he was consorting with a mistress."

"Franklin had dozens of mistresses. But only one Catherine Ray. Who he kept up a platonic, literary relationship with all the way to the end of his life."

Suddenly, Hailey headed toward the trees with the red leaves. Nick followed. Hailey could see the heron out of the corner of her eyes, diving back toward the river. Before the bird hit the water, Hailey reached the closest of the trees. Her attention shifted entirely to the leaves and the small, roundish fruit she found growing between them. Too high for her to reach, but she could see—

"Add botanist to the list of your skill sets," Nick commented, impressed.

"I spent my childhood reading, while you were busy breaking into cars."

She got a half smile from Nick out of that; but her focus was now past the trees, where the grass dropped off quickly down toward the river. The water was louder here; though the river was gentle, she could sense the power of the current, and she instantly understood why Revere had chosen the area for his factories. Before electricity, water had powered the world for centuries, if not millennia. Before Franklin, and his kite and his key, the only currents that mattered ran between earthen banks, not through copper wires.

And yet, as she moved beyond the trees, she realized that the ground beneath her feet was no longer all grass and earth. She used the toe of her shoe to scuff the grass and mud aside—and saw what appeared to be brick, cut into imperfect squares, beginning a few feet past the trees and running all the way down into the water.

She felt Nick's presence next to her. He dropped to one knee and touched the brick with a finger.

"That's—odd. And old. Really old."

Hailey didn't respond right away. She glanced behind them; she could no longer see the two buildings or any of the construction equipment, and none of the tourists, couples, or families were nearby. As far as she could tell, they were alone.

"I need to see where this leads," she said finally. She kicked off her shoes and started toward the edge of the water.

"You're serious?" Nick asked, but it was a pretty stupid question. By now, he knew her better than that.

The water was cold against her feet, and the bricks sloped downward almost immediately, so that she was up to her knees within two small steps. To her surprise, the current that had seemed so gentle from up on the grass was much stronger now; it pulled at her legs as she took a few more steps, deeper and deeper. The bricks felt rough against the bottoms of her feet—rougher than she would have guessed. Another few steps, and the water was up to her waist. Nick was watching her nervously from the bank, his eyes questioning when she suddenly stopped. The bricks had flattened out beneath her feet in some sort of artificial plateau that ran at least a rectangular yard around where she was standing.

She was deep enough now that she couldn't see her feet, but something about the roughness of the bricks against her toes intrigued her. It wasn't uniform, and there appeared to be some sort of pattern to the sensation.

She needed a closer look. Fully aware of how insane it probably looked to Nick, she held her breath and dropped down into the water, then pushed herself through the cold current until she was only a few inches from the bricks.

She ran her fingers along the surface, feeling the roughness as it ran between the edges of the individual squares. As she'd guessed, the roughness did seem to be in a rough pattern, and as she ran her fingers along it, she realized it was a rough ellipse around three feet wide at its center, then tapering off on both sides. Like some sort of hatch, or window. Before rising from the water, she used her fingernails to dig into a section of the roughness, and dislodged a two-inch chunk of whatever material was between the bricks.

She burst back up through the surface of the river, breathing hard as she shook the water from her hair. Then she clambered back up to where Nick was standing, completely drenched but not caring, but instead, focused on the bit of material in her open palm.

Some sort of black and shiny rock, granulated and rough, with slivers of a silvery material running through it. Hailey touched a bit of the rock to her tongue, then looked up at Nick.

"Potassium nitrate, a bit of charcoal, and a hint of sulfur."

Nick raised his eyebrows.

"It's basically solidified gunpowder. Mostly saltpeter, so very low yield."

"Meaning what?"

"Meaning it will burn, but it probably won't blow up."

Nick was still staring at her.

"This isn't naturally occurring," Hailey said. "Not the bricks, and not this gunpowder. It's shaped like—well, a trapdoor. Sealed up, maybe before the river ran over this part of the park."

Sealed up—but with a mechanism that would unseal it. She thought for a moment. "We need something that can generate flame underwater."

Nick glanced toward the water, mulling over what she was obviously contemplating. Then he looked back toward the museum and the barn.

"Give me ten minutes," he said.

And then he was heading back up the path.

It was more like fifteen. Nick was breathing hard when he finally hurried back between the plum trees, a small, gun-shaped black device in his hands. Hailey recognized the acetylene torch immediately; she'd used similar devices plenty of times in her lab, during numerous engineering courses. No doubt Nick had swiped it from one of the construction vehicles by the barn. Hailey wasn't certain the torch would stay lit underwater for very long, but she guessed it would probably spark—and hopefully, that would be enough.

She held the torch up in front of her, then turned back toward the water. "Old tech, meeting even older tech."

And then she was walking back down the brick path.

This time, she barely noticed the cold, and a moment later she was again nearly waist deep. She took a deep breath then submerged herself, holding the torch out ahead of her. She had her finger against the trigger as she placed the barrel of the gun-like device right against the rough stone between the bricks. Then she pressed the trigger as hard as she could.

It happened suddenly—a bright yellow flash in the water, followed by a deep blue sparkle that spiraled outward along the cracks between the bricks. There was almost no sound, but Hailey could feel the pressure and the heat against her cheeks even through the current. She floated backward, her face caught in the growing blue glow, as the sparks traced the curves of the ellipse in the bricks. As it reached the two most vertical points, there was a sudden crack—and then the entire center of the ellipse caved inward. Water gushed down, filling what was apparently an air pocket beneath the bricks. Hailey felt herself being pulled forward, and rather than fight back, she pushed downward, diving through the opening. She felt a brief sense of fear—she knew, intellectually, this was probably stupid—but her curiosity was overwhelming. She needed to know where this led.

Two kicks of her feet and she was through the elliptical opening. Three more feet down and there were more bricks, a solid floor, but she turned her attention to her right. The water was rushing down a tunnel, more brick on all sides, and was filling it quickly from bottom to top. But ahead, she could see that the tunnel sloped upward, above the water level. Obviously, some sort of cavern ran beneath the riverbank where she and Nick had just been standing, directly under the set of plum trees. Still holding her breath, she swam as fast as she could along the tunnel, letting the water push her along—and then her head broke through the surface, and she gasped for air.

A few more feet and she was able to climb out of the water. The cavern stretched out a good ten feet ahead of her; the floor was more brick, the walls curved upward, the ceiling appeared to be made of packed earth. The air was thick and musty, and the scent of sulfur was strong. She wondered how much more of the solidified compound ran behind the walls. It was dark—almost pitch-black. As she moved another foot out of the water, she could make out shapes ahead of her, but even squinting she couldn't pick out what they were.

And then she heard a splashing behind her, and a cone of light flashed around her. She saw Nick coming out of the water, his burner cell phone held above his head, the flashlight mode on.

"I'll be damned," he said. "Micky wasn't full of shit. These things really are water resistant."

Hailey turned back toward the chamber. "Good thing," she said. "We don't want to use anything like the torch in here."

"I figured. Is that sulfur?"

"This might have been some sort of gunpowder storage room."

But then her eyes adjusted to the low light from the cell phone, and she began to recognize the shapes. Along the curved back wall ahead of her—bells. All sorts of sizes, from one that appeared to be just a foot tall, all the way to one that had to be close in size to the Liberty Bell. A dozen of them, all flashing bronze as Nick turned the phone back and forth.

"Revere bells," he whispered. "Christ."

She wondered if he was calculating how much they might be worth. She considered reminding him how much the things weighed—no way they were getting them out the way they'd come in.

"What the hell is that?"

Nick was pointing past the last bell. Hailey took a step forward, her damp foot almost sliding against the brick floor. Beyond the curve of bronze, against the wall—a strange console of sorts, about the size of a small piano. But instead of piano keys, she saw what appeared to be round glass bowls nested together along a metal rod. Beneath the console, she saw what appeared to be foot pedals.

She crossed to the device, awed by the simple beauty of the thing: the polished curves of the bowls, the way they interlocked with a gear-like mechanism leading down to the pedals. Without thinking, she placed one of her bare feet on the closest pedal and gave it a pump.

The bowls began to spin. She placed a finger, still wet from the water, against the edge of one of the bowls.

A strange, soft, dramatic noise filled the chamber, somewhere between a hum and a note. As she pressed her finger harder against the bowl the tone grew deeper, almost palpable. She felt wonder, but also a vague sense of unease. Such a strange noise, like nothing she'd ever heard before.

"What is that?" Nick asked.

"It's called an armonica. I've seen pictures—never seen one in real life. Benjamin Franklin invented it."

She lifted her finger off of the bowl, and the silence returned, heavier than before. She heard Nick's footsteps behind her—he'd crossed past the smallest bell and was at a row of shelves that had been pushed against the wall. One of the shelves was lined with leather pouches. He lifted one—maybe hoping for coins, or gold—but the pouch looked malleable against his fingers.

"Powder," he said.

Gunpowder, she assumed. She was more interested in the other shelves in front of him, and she quickly moved away from the armonica and joined him past the bells. Beneath the shelf of pouches, one shelf was entirely taken up by bound notebooks and loose papers—yellowed, old, but in surprisingly good condition. No doubt being sealed up in an underwater cavern helped preserve the pages—but even so, she was thrilled to still be able to make out the writing on the pages. Calculations, running line after line—mathematics, but not any sort of math she was familiar with. The few symbols she did recognize had to do with frequency, wave theory, cycles—the mathematics of sound.

"I think this is a lab," she said, flipping through the pages. She then turned to one of the bound books and worked open the tie.

"Dedicated to working with sound. Revere's bells—Franklin's armonica—"

And then she paused. She'd gotten the bound book open, and this time, she recognized many of the symbols inside. Not because she was an applied math major at MIT—but because she'd spent the past few days digging deep into the pseudoscience of alchemy.

The book was filled with alchemical symbols. Elements and compounds, planetary metals, processes—many that she recognized, such as the symbols for Air, Earth, Fire, and Water, the images depicting Sulfur, Lead, Iron, and Gold—and the broader concepts—pentagrams, the sun in various forms, and then a symbol she knew pertained to the philosopher's stone—the ultimate alchemical device that was supposed to transform base metals into higher forms, such as lead into gold. The symbol— a circle surrounding a triangle surrounding a square surrounding another circle—was splashed across numerous pages in the bound volume—but Hailey couldn't begin to interpret what the book was, other than a catalogue of these symbols.

Still, the very fact that she'd found these symbols here, in the location of Revere's gunpowder factory, along with the bells and the Franklin armonica—seemed pretty good evidence that Revere and Franklin had been working together. On the mechanics of sound—as Revere developed his many bells in search of his philosopher's stone—and perhaps the armonica fit into that experimentation. But if Franklin was involved, perhaps that science had continued in a different direction.

Her thoughts were interrupted by Nick again, who had stepped past the end of the shelf and was peering at something directly against the wall of the chamber.

"This looks promising."

Affixed to the wall was a cloth painting, hanging in an ornate wooden frame. The painting was simple, probably oil against canvas, and was in the still life style Hailey had seen in museums—in wings dedicated to art from the seventeenth and eighteenth centuries, she seemed to remember. As in many of the still lifes she'd seen in museums, this painting depicted a bowl of fruit—but only one type of fruit, reddish purple and spherical, piled high in a shiny glass bowl.

Nick didn't need to wait for her response. He reached forward and lifted the painting off the wall.

Behind where the canvas had hung, there was what appeared to be a heavy iron safe embedded directly into the brick. In the center of the safe sat a cylindrical combination lock made up of dials, four across, with letters instead of numbers.

"It's a codex," Hailey said.

"Only four," Nick said. "Shouldn't be that hard, should it?"

Hailey glanced at him. "Right. Only 14,950 possibilities."

"Ah."

Nick was looking around the sides of the safe, perhaps contemplating another way in. Dragging the thing out of the wall would be quite a feat, and Hailey didn't relish the idea of trying to move something iron in a room that stank of sulfur. One spark, and who knew what would happen?

But thinking it through, she had the sudden idea that maybe things didn't need to seem so complicated. The chamber was hidden—but not from everyone. The letter from Franklin to Catherine Ray had been their invitation; which meant that if indeed Revere and Franklin had built this place, they had wanted it to be eventually found, or why embed clues in the letter at all?

She moved next to Nick and ran her fingers over the cylindrical codex in the center of the safe. Four letters. An invitation—not

116

a deterrent. *Could it be that simple?* She reached forward and began spinning the dials. Putting the letters one after another.

C. A. T. She was about to put the last dial in place, when Nick touched her arm.

"Hold on," he said. "The professor—Barrett—she said something about this letter being different than all the others. The way Franklin spelled her name—"

"A *K*," Hailey said. "That's right. In this letter he spelled her name with a *K*. It couldn't have been a mistake. Franklin was very precise with language. It would have been on purpose."

She quickly moved back to the first dial and changed the *C* to a *K*. Then she went to the last dial and twisted it until the *Y* was right in front.

There was a loud click, followed by a metallic clang. Hailey felt an odd breeze against her face and smelled something almost smoky, but her attention shifted immediately as the front of the safe swung outward.

The space inside was about the size of a locker, and Nick reached inside. At first, Hailey thought that whatever he was retrieving had been bundled up in what appeared to be a thick gray blanket, but as Nick unfolded the material, she realized that all that the safe contained *was* the blanket. It was folded over itself four times, so tightly that the creases were sharp and defined. Fully unfurled, the blanket was rectangular and long enough to reach the floor, a half an inch thick, gray knit, vaguely institutional looking. Along the top edge, beneath Nick's fingers, Hailey could see a sewn-in series of numbers and three letters: *9241777WSP*

"Strange thing to keep in a safe," Nick murmured.

Hailey took the blanket from him and gave it a closer look. She didn't see any other marks or writing on the blanket, other than the numbers and letters along the edge. But she did notice an odd scent, vaguely metallic and just the tiniest bit sweet—almost sugary, coming off the material. She was about to mention the scent to Nick when a much stronger smell wafted toward her, seeming to come from the wall behind the safe.

"Is that—smoke?" Nick said.

It was hard to see in the dim light from Nick's phone, but the air seemed to swirl along the wall—and then Hailey saw a flicker of blue between the bricks, running outward from where the safe door hung open, toward the ceiling.

Hailey's eyes widened, as her mind made sense of what she was seeing.

"We need to get out of here," she said suddenly.

She tucked the blanket under her arm, then stepped back from the safe. The blue flickering was more pronounced now, snaking away from the safe in multiple little rivulets. She didn't know if the gunpowder within the walls had been sparked accidentally when they'd opened the safe—or if it had been designed to ignite when the safe was opened. Either way, it appeared that this safe was meant to only be opened once—the blanket, whatever its significance, came at a price.

"I think you're right," Nick said, his eyes widening, but Hailey was already moving.

She took the bricks in three steps, then leapt forward toward the water. She didn't notice the cold as she submerged herself, then kicked forward back into the tunnel, fighting with all her strength against the current. She felt Nick's strong arms behind her, his body in the water as well, pushing her forward, and then suddenly there was a roar. A wave of pressure slammed into them both, and Hailey tumbled forward much faster than she'd ever been able to swim, as the water rushed against her in a vicious swell. She felt herself lifted upward—then suddenly she burst through the surface of the river. Looking wildly back toward the direction they'd come, she could see billowing blue flames beneath the water—and then Nick burst forth next to her, gasping for air. As she watched, the flames sucked back inward toward the tunnel, and then there was a rumble. Up on the river's bank, an area of grass surrounding the plum trees suddenly collapsed downward, like a balloon that had just deflated. Then—silence.

Hailey breathed hard as she made her way back to the shore. The bells, the armonica, the chamber—all of it submerged and buried, leaving nothing but an indentation in the grass as evidence that it had ever existed. Another moment, and Hailey and Nick would have been buried as well. Two fugitives swallowed up beneath a Paul Revere heritage site, as lost as the history they were attempting to recover.

She reached the river's bank and crawled up onto the grass, then splayed out on her back, the blanket on her chest. Nick pulled himself onto the grass next to her, his breathing rapid and more than a little pained. For the moment, they were still alone, though no doubt other people in the park had heard the muffled explosion. They needed to keep moving—but for the moment, Hailey wanted nothing more than to remain physically still, while her thoughts continued to race forward.

She wasn't sure what they had found—but she was certain it was proof of Paul Revere and Benjamin Franklin's connection, by way of Franklin's "mistress," Catherine Ray. And whatever it was, it revolved around Revere's quest to attain the secret of alchemy—to create his philosopher's stone. Revere's bells, Franklin's armonica—experiments toward a goal—were pieces in a puzzle that Hailey was determined to put together, no matter the risk.

CHAPTER ELEVEN

A familiar calm moved through Zack's limbs as he strolled through the marble and stone hallway bisecting the first floor of the Philadelphia Museum of Art, a massive complex rising up above the Ben Franklin Parkway near the center of the city. Sixty thousand square feet contained vaulted exhibit spaces, arched auditoriums, and magnificent Frank Gehry–designed public spaces that made the location one of the premiere museums in the Western hemisphere.

To Zack, these sheer stone walls and arched ceilings, this over-air-conditioned air that smelled faintly of antiseptic cleansers and aging canvas, felt like home. Though he'd only been to this particular museum a half dozen times over his career, he had spent much of his life in places like this, taking refuge in halls deliberately designed to feel impersonal, hallowed temples to the miraculous, historic art, objects, and artifacts housed within.

Zack's childhood had never been storybook. His father, a beat cop in New Haven, Connecticut, had done his best after the cancer had taken his mother when Zack was little older than twelve, but navigating one of the roughest cities in the Northeast as a single dad hadn't left much room for levity. Zack hadn't made it easy on the man; he'd run with a tough crowd as a teenager—including a pair of cousins who had mastered the art of petty theft before they'd graduated from middle school—and he had been kicked out of multiple high schools and even arrested for possession of a firearm at age sixteen. Meanwhile, his dad had gone to work each morning fully expecting it might be the day he'd need to draw his service revolver; and Zack had watched him go, then spent most mornings ditching school to watch his cousins lift car radios and knock over ATM machines.

A lenient judge and a short stint in juvenile hall set Zack's mind straight. Not wanting to end up in prison like his cousins inevitably would, he'd begun visiting the local art museums on the nearby Ivy League campus, the stone buildings that cast shadows over the alleys where his dad spent his afternoons. At first, it had been the architecture that had drawn Zack, the lofty ceilings and the sense of impenetrable, immortal history emanating from the turrets and towers of buildings that seemed more like churches than museums. But then, over a period of months, Zack had begun falling in love with the art itself. Paintings from eras he'd barely learned about in school, alive with color, stories told through the brilliant brush strokes of artists long dead and buried.

His father was injured on the job during the summer before Zack's senior year in high school. Fortunately, his pension had paid for six months of a private school education, which had given Zack the chance to study the artists whose art had saved him from the streets. In that short time leading up to his graduation, Zack had attained an encyclopedic knowledge of the different periods and styles that had woven through the centuries. Not only could he name an artist or a work from the slightest bit of canvas, he could tell if a painting was a copy, or if a print was a first edition or a third, or if a sculpture was a fake.

By the time he'd gained entry into that same Ivy League school whose museums had turned his life around, he'd decided on a career path. He'd paired an art history major with a degree in criminal science, a path that had led directly to his joining the FBI upon matriculation, and he'd worked his way up the ranks of the Art Crimes Division.

Turning a corner and passing through a pair of double glass doors, Zack entered the American Wing of the museum; immediately, his heart started to move faster, and the familiar excitement of being deep into another investigation made him thankful for the few good choices he'd made in his early life that had somehow trumped all the bad ones.

He'd been through this wing before, on one of his trips to the museum. He hadn't been to the Philadelphia art mecca on business—though the museum had been the center of a handful of major thefts over the years. One, in the 1970s, had involved two paintings by Marcel Duchamp that had been stolen from the customs area of Kennedy Airport while in transit from the museum to a traveling exhibition. Three men had been arrested trying to sell the Duchamps for fifty thousand dollars apiece. A second major theft had involved a stolen Rodin sculpture, which was eventually found in the basement of a downtown residential apartment building, hidden under a sewer line.

Neither were high-profile like the Gardner theft, but the art community here had been tangentially related to that heist as well. In 2003, rumors had arisen that a number of the Gardner paintings had been offered for sale by criminals associated with the Philly mob. The sale had never taken place, and the paintings had never surfaced—but numerous theories had flitted about the FBI's halls suggesting the paintings could be stashed somewhere in the city.

Zack had not been part of the teams that had gone through basements and warehouses surrounding Philadelphia over the course of the next decade, but he had seen drafts of the publicity letter that

THE MISTRESS AND THE KEY

had been read at a press conference in 2013, asking the public in the Philadelphia area to keep an eye out for the famous works of art.

Zack slowed his pace as the American Wing opened in front of him. A clean, white space with walls covered in paintings on both sides, mostly focused on works of oil from the eighteenth and nineteenth centuries. Passing an alcove dedicated to Native American works to his left—including a large wooden totem pole depicting Sacagawea, the Shoshone woman who had helped Lewis and Clark in their expedition to Louisiana—he headed for a series of paintings along the far wall of the exhibit dedicated to the Revolutionary Era. Even from yards away, the lush, dramatic colors jumped out at him, as he took in battle scenes, naval escapades, the odd landscape. Most of the paintings were large, such as one showing William Penn's signing of his treaty with the Native Americans of the region, dating to 1772.

The back half of the series was dedicated to paintings by the single artist who perhaps defined the time period—certainly, the most renowned portraiter of the eighteenth century, a man who had spent his childhood in Philadelphia before emigrating to London a decade before the Revolution began.

Though Zack was generally familiar with the works of Benjamin West, he was far from an expert; he knew that West's most famous painting—which was hanging in the center of the wall dedicated to his art—was *The Death of General Wolfe*—an enormous, lavish piece set during the French and Indian War, and one of the most reproduced paintings of the period. He also knew that West had founded the Royal Academy in London under the patronage of King George III, who referred to him as the "American Raphael." He knew West had been born in Pennsylvania, had supposedly taught himself art but was functionally illiterate, that he'd painted mostly portraits in the 1750s, but after moving to England had become quite famous for historical scenes; and although he was American, he'd never spoken out against the English crown and was quite possibly a loyalist.

Zack continued browsing the man's work in the back of the American Wing. It was obvious that West favored large canvasses, bright colors, intricate backgrounds, and details—but Zack didn't linger in front of any of the enormous frames depicting battles, treaties, or religious architecture—instead, he moved quickly toward a much smaller painting, near the very end of the West-centric wall.

Compared to *The Death of General Wolfe*, this particular painting was just a sliver of canvas—barely thirteen inches tall, ten inches across. The date on the small plaque next to the frame put its provenance at 1816, which would have only been a few years before West's death, at the age of eighty-one. But even though the painting was small, it was as detailed and lavish as West's larger works—impressive, considering the man would have been in his late seventies, close to death at a time when the average lifespan was many decades shorter.

Unlike many of West's larger works, this book-sized painting was a portrait; the man in the center of the slate was both recognizable and oddly unfamiliar.

Sweeping white hair, rotund form, bald head—the visage of Benjamin Franklin was clear to anyone who'd ever opened an American history book or glanced at a hundred-dollar bill. And yet, it was an odd rendition of the most famous Founding Father. In the painting, Franklin was dressed in a billowing red cape, one of his hands uplifted toward the heavens. Directly above, a tremendous storm exploded across the night sky, and floating off to the left was the infamous kite from Franklin's experiment. The equally infamous key hung from the kite, separated from Franklin's

outstretched fist by little daggers of electricity. And to Franklin's right and left, naked cherubs seeming to help him with his work, one of whom was inexplicably dressed as a Native American.

But it wasn't the oddly dressed cherub, the kite, or the electricity that caught Zack's attention as he leaned close to the small painting; he was immediately focused on something in the left-hand corner of the painting. Zack moved so close he could see himself reflected in the glass of the painting's tiny frame.

In the left corner of the painting, tended to by a pair of the semi-naked cherubs, there was depicted some sort of strange mechanical device, consisting of a golden sphere suspended from a wooden frame. The sphere seemed to be floating at first, but when Zack moved even closer to the frame, he could see that it was actually hanging from some sort of gossamer thread. And from the sphere he could see what appeared to be a bolt of lightning streaming down toward a glass jar placed below.

Staring at the device in the painting, Zack felt the hair on the back of his neck begin to rise. He had seen this device just twenty minutes ago, in the photo the expert from the Heritage Society had shown him. It was the very same device that had gone missing from the homicide site where three men had been shocked to death by a 250-year-old electrostatic machine, quite possibly designed and built by the man in this West painting.

Zack exhaled, still staring at the device. He knew that Benjamin West had been a close friend of Franklin's; they had lived close to each other in London, had frequented the same restaurants and clubs, and had both been favorites of King George III. It was no surprise that West had chosen to do a portrait of Franklin—after all, Franklin was the most famous man of the era, as big an international celebrity as had ever existed. More than that, in many parts of Europe he was considered an almost holy icon—his invention of the lightning rod had saved countless lives, especially in the crowded cities of London and Paris, where many buildings were made of wood; previous to Franklin's harnessing of electricity, lightning was a true and arbitrary threat.

But even so, why did West wait until 1816, twenty-six years after Benjamin Franklin's death, when West himself was so near the grave, to paint such a portrait? And why this small portrait—simply titled *Benjamin Franklin Drawing Electricity from the Sky*—which seemed so out of West's style, mixing religious and historical elements and nearly deifying his subject in stark contrast to the more realist works that lined the hallway to Zack's right. In this portrait, Franklin seemed a saint—even a superhero—caped and surrounded by naked cherubs. His kite and key weren't being struck by lightning—quite the contrary, Franklin was literally "drawing electricity" from the storm, as if he had gained power over the elements, over lightning itself. Why had West portrayed his close friend as someone so much larger than life?

As Zack concentrated on the painting, another thought struck him. The experiment depicted in the painting had supposedly taken place in 1752, when Franklin would have been a relatively young man in his forties. But the depiction in West's painting was of an old man—white flowing hair, wrinkled face—and yet, again, there was something wrong about that face.

Zack paused, remembering something Caufield, the man from the Heritage Society, had told him earlier that day. Staring at Franklin's face in the painting—a tingle moved through him. He reached into his pocket, and dug out his phone. Then he began dialing.

———

Twenty minutes later Zack was still in front of the portrait of Benjamin Franklin; he'd receded a few feet back toward a bench that had been placed beneath two larger works depicting more scenes from the French and Indian War. But he was still standing, one eye on Franklin while the other surveyed the hallway around him. The American Wing was still sparsely occupied; there had been an ebb and flow of art gazers during the time Zack had spent waiting, but nobody had strolled past West's larger works. A few tourists had shuffled through the Native American alcove behind him, some stopping to take pictures with the Sacagawea totem pole—but as far as Zack could tell, nobody was interested in Franklin, despite his cape, his cherubs, or the FBI agent standing a few feet away.

Zack was left alone with his thoughts, right up until the moment he saw Caufield hurrying toward him down the hallway, followed closely by a young man in a dark suit that screamed *federal agent*. Zack recognized the young FBI agent he'd met earlier in the Philadelphia Field office—Angus Rappaport, he remembered, basically a kid right out of Quantico, long limbed and jittery with the excitement of a newly minted agent, something that would undoubtedly fade as the years went by. For his part, Caufield didn't look happy to see Zack, or to be in the art museum at all; his ring of white hair now framed a look of sheer dismay, and his wrinkled hands clenched a small plastic bag so tightly Zack thought the man's fingers might puncture the material. But through the plastic, Zack could clearly see the oblong leather case, which was still partially open—revealing the pair of antique bifocals, exactly as Zack had seen them on the shelf in the underground lab.

"This is highly irregular," Caufield hissed, as he reached Zack. "We weren't planning to remove these from the site until we had performed our radiographic exam; it's quite possible these are a unique specimen—certainly, incredibly valuable and of historic note. They should be in a sanitized exam room, or a museum—"

"They are in a museum," Zack said. "And I only need them for a moment. Then you can have them right back."

The man paused, suddenly catching sight of the portrait in front of them both. His mouth opened, then shut, as he took in the visage of Benjamin Franklin. Then he looked at Zack again, confused.

"This is highly irregular," he repeated.

Zack nodded, then held out a hand. "May I?"

Flustered, Caufield glanced at the younger FBI agent, who was removing a pair of cloth gloves from his jacket. If the younger man had any idea what was going on, he certainly didn't show it. His face was all eagerness and excitement as he gave Zack the gloves.

Zack pulled them on as Caufield reluctantly opened the plastic bag and gingerly retrieved the leather case, holding it out so that the spectacles were in front of Zack. Zack carefully lifted them out of the case. They were incredibly light, with frames that felt like wire. The lenses were thicker than he'd expected—and when he looked closely, rather than a single line across the glass that he would have expected from bifocals, there seemed to be many little lines, and the glass itself seemed to bulge in certain places.

"Are these supposed to look like that?" he asked.

Caufield coughed. "They're extremely old. We don't know what sort of temperature variations or changes in humidity might have occurred in that lab over the past two and a half centuries. The atmosphere in the underground chamber—"

"Seemed pretty stable to me," Zack countered.

"There were three dead men tied to chairs."

"I mean apart from that."

Caufield coughed again. Zack noticed that he was no longer looking at the spectacles; he was focused on the small portrait. He seemed to have noticed what Zack had noticed—because his eyes were a little wider than before.

"You said it yourself," Zack said. "In his later years, Benjamin Franklin was almost never seen without his glasses. West was one of his closest friends—why would he paint Franklin without his most recognizable feature?"

The FBI agent was looking along with them.

"Maybe because superheroes don't wear glasses?" he tried, his voice higher than Zack had remembered.

"There weren't such things as superheroes in the eighteenth century," Caufield said. "The concept wasn't invented for another two hundred years."

Zack couldn't wait any longer; without a word, he raised the spectacles and placed them over his eyes. Caufield gasped—but

Zack barely noticed, because as he stared at the painting through the glasses—suddenly his entire world began to spin.

The image in the painting hadn't changed; Benjamin Franklin was still in the center of the slate, wearing that cape, his arm raised, electricity dribbling from the stormy sky—but now, there was something else, something *more*.

"My god," Zack whispered.

Above Franklin's head, embedded deep into the billowing storm clouds, a line of lavish text had appeared. Big, swooping letters, dark blue against the smoldering sky.

"FREEDOM IS A LIGHT FOR WHICH MANY MEN HAVE DIED IN DARKNESS."

Zack read the words out loud, as Caufield and the FBI agent stared at him. The words seemed familiar, but Zack couldn't quite place where he had heard them before. He took the spectacles off, blinked hard. He could see that Caufield was still staring at him, so he handed the older man the glasses. Caufield paused for a moment, but then curiosity got the better of him, and he put them on. He looked at the painting—and gasped so hard he nearly choked.

"How is this possible?"

He quickly took off the glasses and handed them back to Zack.

"It's actually not as rare as you might think. It's an artistic technique based on a process called anamorphosis. A method used by artists to distort or hide images from unknown spectators for almost as long as there has been art."

"An optical illusion?" the other FBI agent asked, eyeing the glasses in Zack's hand with obvious envy. But this time Zack wasn't going to share; he knew everything this man saw would be reported back to his supervisor at the Philly field office, and for now Zack wanted at least a little breathing room to figure out what was happening around him.

"The technique of anamorphosis goes all the way back to cavemen times, actually. Stone age paintings found in the cave in Lascaux use anamorphosis—horses and bison painted on one of the cave walls seem distorted almost to the point of obscurity—but when viewed from a different floor, they appear perfectly rendered. A painting by a German artist named Hans Holbein in 1533 has what appear to be white and gray slashes across the bottom—but when viewed from one particular angle, the slashes form a perfect skull. Da Vinci was also a practitioner of the technique, but it really came into its own in the seventeenth century—usually for political reasons. After the execution of King Charles I, many paintings included secret portraits of the dead king, which could only be seen with the use of mirrors, or polished cylinders devised specifically for the task."

The young agent shook his head, still looking at the spectacles. "Crazy."

"Not so crazy when you think about the fact that often throughout history, painting the wrong sort of portrait could get you killed. There were many good reasons to keep certain images hidden, and the only real limitation to the technique is the skill of the artist."

As Zack spoke, his mind whirled back to his last moments with Hailey and Nick on the *Constitution*—to the snippets of conversation he had heard when he was nearly dying, to the vision of that bronze eagle from the Gardner theft, lost to the dark waves of the harbor. Secrets hidden in artistic objects—secrets that could get people killed, that *had* gotten people killed. And here, in front of him, in a two-hundred-plus-year-old painting by Benjamin West, a clue came through a message visible only with glasses that might have once been owned by Benjamin Franklin.

Zack took another breath, then put the spectacles back on and faced the painting again. He read the words over, trying to remember where he'd heard them before. Then he realized—something else was off in the painting, there was some sort of shape around the words. He took a step back, almost running into the bench behind him. And then the shape took form.

The shape was a tombstone. The top of its arch surrounded the words, which he read out loud again.

"FREEDOM IS A LIGHT FOR WHICH MANY MEN HAVE DIED IN DARKNESS."

His jaw trembled, because he remembered where he had read those words before.

And suddenly, he knew exactly where he needed to go next.

CHAPTER TWELVE

Ten yards away, bathed in the shadow of the Sacagawea totem pole, beneath a painting of a pair of Native Americans crossing a river in a handmade canoe, Curt Anderson sat quietly on a carved wooden bench, between an elderly man reading a museum brochure and a young woman nursing an infant in her lap. The infant was cooing as it fed, while Curt smiled warmly. Inside, he felt nothing.

Though his eyes were similarly vacant, his entire attention was across the hall from the alcove, on the FBI agent who was still momentarily in front of the painting, though he'd just removed the antique spectacles for the second time. Curt was less interested in the older man next to Zack, or the younger FBI agent; his entire being was attuned only to Zack Lindwell, and the tiny beads of sweat that had suddenly risen above the skin on the back of the agent's neck.

Curt knew, deep down in his center, that Zack had just seen something in the painting that was not visible to Curt or to anyone else in the museum hall. Although he hadn't been able to hear what the three men had been talking about from his perch in the Native American alcove, he had immediately recognized the antique glasses—he was certain he had seen them in the underground lab. He could not have known that they would somehow be important to his mission—and in fact it was quite by accident that he was seeing them again now.

He had arrived at the gallery thirty minutes before Zack and had spent the interim time before the agent had arrived gazing at the same Benjamin West portrait of Franklin, to no avail. He had been led to the spot most likely in the same manner as Zack—by the device, which was now in a shipping container on the way to the Family, for closer inspection.

It hadn't taken the Family long to match the device with the image in the West painting, once their experts had received the photo Curt had sent them from the hotel room in Atlantic City. No doubt they'd had more than one team on the task, which made Zack's own investigative work that much more impressive. Curt had actually been surprised when he'd seen the agent coming down the hall, and he had slunk away to the alcove just in time. Not that the FBI agent would have recognized him; they had never truly crossed paths before. Curt was certain that no photograph of him or file on his background had ever found its way into Zack's hands—or, for that matter, across the desk of any federal agent in any country in the world.

Whatever files had once existed about Curt, from the time he'd traded boarding school for military service, or during his years as a highly trained special ops soldier in various wars before the Family had taken him under their wing, had been meticulously scrubbed. He was quite sure no photos of him existed in any databanks; in fact, Curt Anderson wasn't even his real name, nor the third or fourth iteration of his identity. He'd changed his spots so many times over the years, he wasn't even sure what type of animal he used to be.

He truly was a man with no past. And his present was entirely focused on Zack and the painting—and whatever was in that painting that Curt, across the hall, could not possibly see.

Whatever it was, it had clearly galvanized the FBI agent, who was suddenly heading away down the hall. Curt let him go, because to do anything different would only be a waste of time. Zack Lindwell had proved to be a valuable asset, despite himself. The museum, the streets outside, the city of Philadelphia—these were all places filled with cameras that the Family could easily access. Curt could remain moments behind the FBI agent no matter where he went. He already knew which rental car Zack Lindwell was using, what hotel he was staying at, even what the man had eaten for breakfast before he'd arrived in Philadelphia. It would be no problem following the agent wherever he went next.

Only when Zack and his entourage of two had reached the entrance to the American Wing did Curt finally rise from the bench, smiling again at the woman with the baby, and cross to the Benjamin West painting for a last, glancing look. Franklin, the cherubs, the device. All so wonderfully and needlessly dramatic. But he knew the real drama wasn't in the sweeping brushstrokes, the vibrant colors, or the historical moment depicted within. The real drama was whatever was hidden beneath, a secret Curt was certain he would soon understand.

He waited another beat, then turned and followed the FBI agent from the room.

CHAPTER THIRTEEN

Adrian had always assumed that his high intelligence would end up being his downfall. Even as a child, his teachers at the elite prep school in northern Connecticut, where he'd convinced his parents, both professors of sociology at Hartford, to let him attend, had been telling him he was too smart for his own good; but he'd come to realize it wasn't his intelligence, per se, that was the problem. It was intelligence married to *inquisitiveness*; as St. Augustine had surmised, the path to hell was paved in foolish curiosity, a trait Adrian had attempted to stifle throughout his adult life. That he was failing now, so thoroughly, meant he deserved whatever misery was inevitably heading his way.

At the moment, the view in front of him was less inferno, fire, brimstone, and more glass, steel, and abject banality. At least the interior of the building he'd just entered appeared clean and polished; usually, train stations were grimy, caked in exhaust and the scent of too many humans stuffed together in too small a space. But thankfully, Route 128 Station, named charmingly after the nearby highway that connected many of Boston's more placid suburbs to the city itself, looked more like a crashed space station than the usual Amtrak depot.

Adrian quickly bypassed the ticketing area, which was staffed by a pair of women in blue uniforms chatting noisily about the latest celebrity gossip; one of the women clutched a magazine displaying a photo of a couple who were either in love, falling out of love, or somewhere in between. Adrian could not have identified either person in the photo, nor could he understand why anyone would care about the love lives of total strangers; but for once, he couldn't bring himself to judge the Amtrak employees.

He had traveled across town—a distance that was even too far for his bicycle—for the historian's equivalent of such voyeuristic gawking. That the celebrities he was chasing had been dead 250 years didn't matter; Adrian had come to this train station to engage and indulge in fantasy—a sin even more virulent than curiosity.

Traipsing through the train station, he thought back to his latest indignity—the scene at the Museum of Science. When the plain-clothes officer had chased after Nick, he'd nearly knocked Adrian right out of his seat, upending trays of food from the surrounding tables. Adrian had still been picking French fries out of his hair when the uniformed officers had arrived.

Thankfully, the police hadn't seen enough to connect the two fugitives to Adrian; he'd simply told the officers that Hailey and Nick had interrupted his lunch with a colleague to ask for a ride out of town, and when refused, had stolen his saddle bag on their way out of the lunch room. To Adrian's surprise, Barrett had backed up his story—and it wasn't until the officers had left them that she'd winked, and exclaimed:

"You've finally surprised me, Adrian! You're not the boring fuss I'd assumed. Perhaps you're not a total lost cause."

The fact that she didn't seem concerned at all that she'd spent the morning with Boston's most wanted made him think even less of her moral state—though clearly, he had long since lost the right to judge anyone, least of all a woman who, he grudgingly had to admit, knew as much about eighteenth-century history as he himself. She had shared a lunch with Hailey and Nick; Adrian was risking his entire career—maybe even his life—by continuing to associate with them.

On cue, he caught sight of the bedraggled pair in the far corner of the vast waiting area of the station. It was an open space with incredibly high ceilings that cantilevered up to a bank of fluorescent lights. Rows of metal chairs were spread out around the room, perhaps a hundred or more—but less than a dozen people milled about, and none seemed to notice the two fugitives, despite how disheveled they seemed.

As Adrian got closer, he saw that both Nick and Hailey looked actually *damp*; Nick's denim was sticking to his muscled chest, and Hailey's hair was back in a ponytail, her cheeks glistening with moisture. Although they had mentioned the river in the brief phone call on their way out of Canton, Adrian had not thought through the details of what they had gone through to procure the artifact that had brought him to the train station; because once Hailey had sent him a photo of the item, it had consumed his attention—primarily because he knew exactly what it was and, more important, what it meant.

It wasn't until Adrian was a few feet from the pair, when he caught site of the blanket draped casually over Hailey's knees. His lips turned down and he hurried to her, lowering his voice.

"Are you insane? That's not some throw your grandmother gave you. It's a piece of American history."

Hailey gestured to the chair next to her, as Nick moved to one directly across, so they could converse without anyone nearby listening in. Adrian lowered himself angrily, then reached out and carefully took the blanket off her knees and held it close to his face. He, too, could smell the strange, almost noxious sugary scent that Hailey had described on the call, but he was more interested in the writing stenciled into the upper edge of the soft material. His heart pounded as he read the numbers and letters.

9241777WSP

"Adrian?" Hailey asked. But Adrian didn't respond.

His mind was whirling. The moment Hailey had sent him the picture of the blanket, and this notation, he had known what it meant. But seeing it in person, feeling the gray material in his hands—it hit him solidly in the chest. Here was proof of a connection between Benjamin Franklin and Paul Revere that was not documented in any history book. This blanket, found in a safe in the remains of Revere's gunpowder factory, hidden behind a combination lock that opened to the name of Franklin's supposed mistress, was a guidepost to Adrian. This blanket, and that notation at its edge, were the reason he had told Hailey and Nick to meet him here, in this train station. He knew that after he told them what it meant, they would be traveling far from Boston, and a stolen delivery truck was too easy a target for law enforcement, which would surely be searching for them.

Hailey was watching him carefully as he handled the blanket, and finally couldn't contain herself.

"Why are we here? What is this—"

"—blanket," Adrian finished for her.

"Of course it's a blanket," Nick said. "Looks almost institutional, except for how old it must be. Something military? Why was it in a safe?"

Adrian shook his head. "Not military. But yes, institutional."

"Prison," Nick stated. "It's for a prison."

Instead of continuing, Adrian reached inside his jacket and removed the pair of items he had gathered—with much effort—after his phone conversation with Hailey. He handed the first, a small package with brown wrapping covered in foreign lettering, to Hailey but kept the second, a glass vial filled with clear liquid. Acquiring the package had been the more difficult task; Adrian had rushed to three different exotic markets before he'd found it on the back shelf of an East Asian grocery deep in Boston's Chinatown. The liquid in the vial, on the other hand, had only involved a brief visit to one of Tufts' chemistry labs and a bit of bullying of an undergraduate lab assistant.

Hailey was looking the bag over, feeling the weight of the powdery contents inside, but Nick was still focused on the blanket, his eyes moving to the letters and numbers at the edge.

"Nine two four one seven seven seven—" he started, but Adrian didn't want to wait for the gears in the man's head to finally click together.

"September fourth, 1777," Adrian said shortly. "A fairly significant date in Revolutionary history."

"And the letters? WSP?"

"An abbreviation, if I'm right. But I think we'll know for sure in a moment. You have the torch?"

Nick brought the device out from the pocket of his jacket. The acetylene torch was about the size of a handgun, with a small canister attached for the fuel. It looked dryer than the man's clothes—thankfully they had taken care with it, because it was going to be necessary if Adrian had correctly analyzed what Hailey had told him about the blanket. Now that he was holding it himself, smelling that faint metallic, sugary scent, he was almost certain that he had.

"I've got it, but I don't understand," Nick said. "You're so excited by this blanket, you want us to light it on fire?"

Adrian rolled his eyes, but Hailey had already pieced it together before Adrian needed to explain.

"Invisible ink," she said. "Some sort of solution that bonds with the cotton in the blanket. You need heat to catalyze whatever chemicals you've brought to reveal what's hidden in the cotton."

Adrian nodded. "Benjamin Franklin was not the spymaster that Paul Revere was, but he did indeed enjoy and employ subterfuge; famously, he used a method of hiding messages in materials made of cotton—clothing, blankets, and the like—that had been taught to him by a French military contact, Pierre Joseph Hyacinthe, the Chevalier de Monts. I was able to dredge up a letter written to Franklin by the chevalier in the historical records, which detailed the concoction, which was made from dissolving aluminum and lead bath salts in water."

"The metallic, sweet scent," Hailey said.

"Correct. Apparently, according to the chevalier's letter, whatever message has been hidden by the method is revealed by heating the cloth in *eau de garance*; which, after much digging, I've determined to be powdered madder—an East Indian root used to make hair dye—and sulfuric acid."

Nick eyed the vial, but Hailey was already opening the package of madder. She took the vial from Adrian, carefully undid the top—pulling her head back against the noxious scent that now filled their corner of the train station—and dumped the powder from the package into the clear liquid.

She refastened the top of the vial and gave it a good shake. Obviously, she had worked with chemicals before, which didn't surprise Adrian. The girl was, after all, both a fugitive and an MIT graduate student.

She nodded to Adrian, who unfolded the blanket and lay it across the empty chair next to her. Nick stood, shielding the trio from view from the rest of the mostly empty waiting area. Then Hailey uncapped the vial and carefully began pouring the contents over the blanket. As the liquid soaked the cotton material, Nick leaned forward and held the acetylene torch underneath the blanket, careful to keep the blue flame low and far enough away from the threads so that nothing ignited.

There was a dull hissing, and the noxious smell from the sulfuric acid grew stronger. As Adrian watched, he began to see etching appear in the cotton material of the blanket; what first appeared to be scratches, beginning right below the notation in the upper edge of the blanket, formed into row after row of numbers. Seemingly random, but spaced regularly, separated in places by what looked to be Greek letters. Hailey continued spilling the *eau de garance* farther down the blanket; after a few dozen rows of numbers, the scratches changed form—and slowly, through the hissing, shapes became visible. It took a moment, but Adrian realized they were now looking at a crudely drawn map, broken into squares, intersected by what looked to be paths. There were shapes along the outer edges that appeared to be buildings, the biggest of which was in the shape of a horseshoe. From the horseshoe a dotted line ran through the other squares and wound along the paths to a spot halfway across the blanket.

"What the hell is this?" Nick whispered.

Adrian didn't respond. He was looking at the horseshoe-shaped building, a feeling of excitement rising inside of him. He believed he knew what he was looking at, which meant he had been right about the notation at the top of the blanket, and what it meant.

"September fourth, 1777," he said. "The date fits. That's what it would have looked like then."

"What?" Nick asked.

But Hailey, finally capping the vial as the liquid still seeped toward the farthest corners of the blanket, was focused on the rows of numbers above the map.

"That spacing—this is a code."

Adrian nodded. He had seen it, too—and he could take it a step farther than Hailey, for the same reason he had correctly guessed at the use of Chevalier's invisible ink.

He withdrew his phone from his pocket and did a quick document search over the servers connected to his office on campus. It took him less than a minute to locate the text he was looking for— an obscure political book by a French-born Dutch writer and diplomat of Franklin's era, a man named Charles William Frederick Dumas. The book, *Bouquet's Expedition*, was a fairly obscure treatise on a 1764 military expedition against the Ohio Indians. Translated into English, the book had sold well in the colonies before the war, but its import became evident much later, based on a short, single-page introduction the author had added in an English edition that had been printed shortly before the war had broken out between Great Britain and the Americas.

Adrian turned his phone so that Hailey could see the page of writing. She started to read, then stopped—although the paragraphs seemed to contain a fairly innocuous bit of tripe about Dumas's methods of writing, the wording was odd, and sometimes repetitive. Hailey didn't need to read far to understand, given her abilities in the field of cryptography.

"It's a cipher," she said.

"A fairly famous one," Adrian responded. "Charles Dumas, living in the Netherlands, was a favorite agent of the nascent republic, and, as an admirer of Benjamin Franklin, taught him the use of what later became known as 'Dumas's Cipher.' A fairly simple substitution cipher at that, which instantly became Franklin's favorite method of hiding messages in plain sight. This intro, consisting of 628 letters, corresponds to 628 numeric options; many of the letters are repeated, so there are multiple numbers associated with the more common letters. But as long as you had access to his treatise on the war with the Ohio Indians, it was just a matter of simple substitution."

Hailey reached into her bag and pulled out a notepad and a pen. Her face had that look Adrian recognized—where he was inquisitive despite his best efforts, she threw herself entirely into her enquiring nature. She lived for things like this, and within minutes she was deep into the process of decoding the numbers still solidifying in rows in the cotton of the blanket, as the solution ate deeper into the fabric. Quickly, her notepad filled with letters broken into words; the Greek letters a rough guide to where phrases ended and began.

Adrian read the words as she added them; she'd made it through only a few rows before he began to shift in his seat. Not only had he been correct that this blanket was real evidence that Franklin and Revere were working together, but the words hidden in the cotton revealed an even deeper connection:

My dear friend and colleague, Mssr Revere. Though our efforts in parallel—to crack the code and find the key—have yet to yield solid fruit, we have indeed gone from root to limb to leaf. From the bell to the bowls, so close and yet so far. But the direction is certain, and I believe my newest endeavor will lead us to our fiery conclusion. We are so close—but the device that will power our republic is now in danger...

Poetic, and yet it seemed clear to Adrian; Franklin and Revere were working together, trying to crack the code of alchemy, to find the key—the infamous philosopher's stone—that had the power to transform materials. Not simply lead to gold, though that was the most illustrative and familiar goal of the alchemical sciences—but the idea was, once you had the power to transform materials at their basic levels, you could engineer just about anything.

"From the bell to the bowls," Hailey said. "Revere's bells, and Franklin's armonica. They were experiments that brought them close, but in the end, they were failures. Franklin's newest endeavor—his work in electricity? This device he speaks of, being in danger—"

Adrian didn't respond. Instead he gestured toward the row of numbers on the blanket that Hailey hadn't yet translated. She went to work, and when she finished, she, Adrian, and Nick read the words together. Nick was still holding the torch, but the blue flame was so low it was barely a flicker.

"The British are coming," he read. Then he looked at Adrian, who shook his head.

"Not those British. September fourth, 1777—nearly a year into the war, and things were not going well for the American colonies. The British were working their way up the East Coast. After the Americans had faced disaster in the Battle of Newport—Revere himself had taken part in the failed skirmish—the British moved all the way to the outskirts of Philadelphia. Two days later they would take the city."

"Philadelphia," Hailey said. "That's where Benjamin Franklin was—presumably he sent this to Revere, two days before the British took over."

She looked back at the blanket. Beyond the last row of numbers—"The British are coming"—was the map, with the dotted line leading to a spot near the center.

"The device," she said, "in danger. This message, this map—Franklin was asking for Revere's help in securing whatever it was he was working on, before the British took over."

She looked at Adrian. "You knew that we would be going to Philadelphia," she said. "You recognized the notation on this blanket. Do you also recognize this map?"

Adrian looked at the horseshoe-shaped building in the drawing, then at the intersecting paths. He nodded.

"The device," Nick said, toward Hailey. "You think it could be—" And then he stopped, midsentence.

Adrian saw that Nick's attention was now focused on the bottom corner of the blanket, below the edge of the map. The torch in his hand had reached that area of the material, and an image was slowly taking shape. Nick pressed the trigger on the torch, letting the blue flame rise a few inches toward the material. The image grew more detailed, more distinct.

Adrian's eyes widened. The shape of the thing was odd, but clearly familiar. Adrian felt the immediate urge to turn away—not just *turn* away, but *run* away. But he knew now that he couldn't. He felt Nick lean forward over his shoulder, staring at the image on the blanket.

Then Nick said what they all were thinking.

"It's a key."

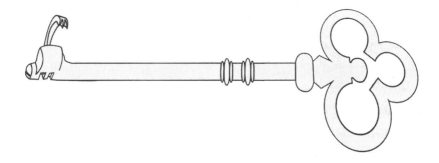

CHAPTER FOURTEEN

The sky had gone a deep, gunmetal gray as the sun dipped below the horizon; flickers of moonlight peeked through the thick clouds, offering glimpses of soft white between the manicured trees that lined the intersecting, cobbled paths. Barely eight p.m. on a Tuesday, and yet the park was already wrapped in an otherworldly feeling. Just a few hours earlier, these paths were alive with tourists, families, kids walking bikes, and carts pushing everything from hot dogs to Middle Eastern fare. But now Zack was essentially alone, as he traipsed through the eight-acre, cubic glade of grass, trees, and paths that squatted in the center of the city of Philadelphia, embraced by office buildings, high-end residences, and historic sites. Around one corner, Independence Hall and the glass enclosure where Zack had spent his morning with the Liberty Bell; nearby, the Ben Franklin Parkway and the grand art museum where he had spent the late afternoon.

Six hours earlier, when Zack had finally digested what had appeared beneath the brushstrokes of the Benjamin West painting of Franklin—*Drawing Electricity from the Sky*—he'd quite literally run down the famous front steps of the museum, Caufield in tow, intending to head straight to this park and these paths. West had hidden a message in the painting—his strange homage to Franklin—and had put the key to unlocking the message

147

directly in the homage itself. Purposeful, perhaps directed subterfuge; the fact that West, a close friend of Franklin, had included both the strange device from Franklin's lab and the hidden message in the same work of art didn't seem like a coincidence. West—and, by extension, Franklin—were speaking to Zack across centuries, and he was doing his best to listen.

The message—and image—hidden in the painting had sparked his memories, and he had an idea where he needed to go—but after leaving the museum, he'd switched tracks. Though he knew where the message was leading, there was something about it that hadn't made sense. Instead of heading directly to the park, he'd explained to Caufield the bare bones of what he needed to find information about—and together, they'd headed directly to the older man's office at the Philadelphia Historical Heritage Society.

After four hours in an archive room, reading through files, Zack had found what he'd needed. Although Caufield had been with him as he'd dug through the information, he'd set out on the next phase of his investigation on his own. No doubt, if Zack had asked, Caufield would have been right next to him in the park, rushing along the winding path through the sparse trees, excitement rising as he went. Perhaps, even, he would not have balked at the heavy metal tool Zack carried under his right arm, which the FBI agent had borrowed from the garage depo at the local FBI headquarters on his way to the park. Having seen the words and image in the painting, Caufield would have known exactly what Zack had intended to do with the tool, and despite his cautious nature, his own professional curiosity might have pushed him to contemplate the same course of action.

Zack took a deep breath, feeling the weight of the tool as he turned a final corner and moved between a handful of trees. Even in the darkness, he could make out the glade of stone ahead, at the

end of a long stretch of pathway. On either side of the trail leading up to the stone he could see tall metal flagpoles, bearing flags
high above that fluttered in the wind. He couldn't see the colors
or designs on the flags, but he knew they were the emblems of the
original thirteen states of the new republic that had gone to war
with the British, as well as the first American flag. As he moved
past, he noticed that the second pole on his right was leaning
inward toward the path, and the stones at its base had been damaged; perhaps a recent storm, parade, or protest had knocked the
pole loose, and it hadn't yet been repaired. He doubted it would
remain that way for long; he knew that Washington Square was
one of the central gems of the city, surrounded by some of the
most expensive real estate in the area.

He also knew that it hadn't always been that way. From his
research, he'd learned that the ground he was moving over had
once been a graveyard—not just a graveyard, but many graveyards,
graveyards upon graveyards. When he blinked, he could almost see
the corpses piled so deep beneath the path he was moving down,
they might well have been viewed as the foundation of this central
area of city itself.

Washington Square had been a part of Philadelphia since the
city was founded in 1682, and despite its central prominence in
the fledgling metropolis, it had spent its first century as a potter's
field—a burial ground for the city's unwanted—the poor, criminals, suicides, and victims of plague and murder. It was no wonder
that during the Revolutionary War, the Square became a burial
ground for soldiers killed in the various nearby engagements—
both American and British. This was followed by even more bodies
thrown into the mix after the yellow fever epidemic of the 1790s.
The bodies only stopped being buried in the area by the turn of the
nineteenth century because, as was commented at the time, "there

were so many burials in Potter's Field that no more could be made without disturbing the remains of those previously interred."

Zack could only imagine what the place had looked like two hundred years ago, before the burial grounds were eventually filled in with dirt, then grass and trees; so many bodies, mostly unnamed and unmarked. But tonight, he had come to Washington Square for one particular grave—and one particular body, though it was, indeed, unnamed.

He reached the edge of the stone glade and paused. There were benches to his right and left; directly ahead, the glade ended in a raised area, also made of stone; in the center was a carved-out circle, embraced by a low iron chain; in the middle of the circle, a metal cage, containing a burning, eternal flame, flickering bright orange in the darkness. Behind the flame, a huge stone sarcophagus stood in front of an enormous granite wall. On a high pedestal above the sarcophagus stood a tall bronze statue. The statue was immediately recognizable: George Washington, a replica of the most famous statue commissioned by Washington himself, by French artist Jean-Antoine Houdon. Zack had read that it was Benjamin Franklin who had convinced Houdon to come to America to cast the mold for Washington's visage, and the finished statue was considered the most accurate likeness of the Revolutionary War general and first president ever carved; it even included the oddly indented shape of Washington's chin and jaw, a result of his famously trauma-plagued teeth. It was reported that by the end of his life, Washington had only a single tooth left in his mouth and was reliant on the rudimentary dentistry of the time to eat and speak.

But Zack was not interested in Washington's dental issues, or the statue in front of the granite wall, or even, for the moment, the stone sarcophagus. His attention had already shifted from the general to the words that had been carved directly into the granite. Huge letters, directly above Washington's head:

FREEDOM IS A LIGHT FOR WHICH MANY MEN HAVE DIED IN DARKNESS

Zack felt his head swimming as he read the quote, exactly as he'd seen it in the painting by Benjamin West. A hidden message, in a portrait that had been painted in 1816.

His thoughts still swimming, he let his eyes drive to the paragraph of text embedded in the wall beneath the quote.

THE INDEPENDENCE AND LIBERTY YOU POSSESS ARE THE WORK OF JOINT COUNCILS AND JOINT EFFORTS OF COMMON DANGERS SUFFERINGS AND SUCCESS—

Washington's Farewell Address, 1796.

If it had been that paragraph that he had seen in the painting, he would not have had to spend the afternoon with Caufield going through archived letters and documents. Lifted from George Washington's farewell address, there was nothing anachronistic about these words appearing in a painting from 1816. But the previous quote—"Freedom Is a Light for Which Many Men Have Died in Darkness"—had not been uttered by Washington. It had, in fact, been crafted by a copywriter at an advertising agency, for the express purpose of appearing on this monument—in 1953.

On the way out of the museum, Zack had suddenly remembered this fact—just as he'd remembered visiting this monument on one of his handful of trips to Philadelphia. Though the Tomb of the Unknown Revolutionary War Soldier was lesser known than the similar monument in DC—the Tomb of the Unknown Soldier—or most of the tourist destinations on the Freedom Trail back in Boston, it had stayed with him, perhaps because of the simplicity of its message. This tomb—the skeletal remains that were presumably hidden within that sarcophagus—didn't have a name, because it was meant to represent any soldier who had perished during the Revolution. Especially with a war lodged so deeply in the past, in the mythology of the founding of America—it was easy to forget the violent cost, the misery and death behind the myth.

Up until today, Zack had believed that simple monument had been the result of a revitalization effort by a group of local businessmen and politicians, hoping to raise property prices in the area around Washington Square; but combing through the archives, he had learned that in fact the idea to honor the fallen soldiers of the Revolution went back much further. In the summer of 1789, a committee had been gathered of Philadelphia's most prominent citizens; the goal was to find a way to honor Washington, not only with a park bearing his name, but with a monument built in his name. Unfortunately, the committee had stumbled in its efforts to raise the money needed for such a project, and even the naming of the park had been tabled for what amounted to another two decades. It wasn't until 1816 that the former graveyard was renamed after the first president.

But during that meeting in 1789, plans for a memorial were indeed struck, if not brought to fruition. And according to multiple letters Zack had found in the archives, the leading voice among the famous Philadelphians at the meeting was none other than Benjamin Franklin—who had returned to his home in the year before his death, presumably to be surrounded by family as his health took a turn for the worse. Although the details were scarce,

Franklin himself had been behind the push to build a monument honoring both Washington and those who had fallen in the war for America's freedom. A yellowed, hand-sketched map Zack had found in one of the many letters had even included details on the monument—where and how it should be crafted, down to the size and shape of the sarcophagus.

After both Franklin's and Washington's deaths in the following decade, the idea for the monument had fizzled—until the early 1950s, when a new committee was finally formed, this time of real estate barons and political opportunists. Hoping to draw more visitors to the area, this more modern cabal stumbled onto the original plans of a monument dedicated to Washington and those who had served in the war he'd overseen, and they found their way to the same spot Benjamin Franklin had suggested. They'd also borrowed his idea of interring the bones of a soldier in a raised stone coffin—and had dutifully begun digging in the Square for an appropriate corpse to fill the role.

As the story went, it took nine tries—nine holes in the newly updated park—to find a body of the appropriate age, gender, and injuries. In fact, the skeletal remains they ended up using were found in a plot that had apparently been used for a soldier who had distinguished himself in the battle over Philadelphia, before the Americans were overrun. The only problem was, upon digging up the remains, the committee's experts couldn't be certain whether the corpse had belonged to an American soldier or a Brit; and the wounds to the man's skull could have been caused by anything blunt—a musket ball, or even a hoe.

In the end, they decided it didn't matter what uniform the man had worn; a casualty of war was worth honoring, no matter whose orders he'd followed. They'd acquiesced to Franklin's designs and, as a last act, had apparently even incorporated his final thoughts on the monument directly in the granite wall. Although the conception was that a copywriter had written the phrase about Freedom, Light, and Darkness, Zack had found the same phrase in Franklin's last letter about the monument, which he'd written to the committee that had been meeting that summer of 1779.

FREEDOM IS A LIGHT FOR WHICH MANY MEN HAVE DIED IN DARKNESS. Zack mouthed the words, as he took another step toward the granite wall. And then his focus shifted to the stone sarcophagus at its base. He looked down at the heavy metal tool under his arm, then slowly brought it forward. *Was he really going to go through with this?*

Did he have a choice? Franklin's own words, hidden in Benjamin West's painting, had brought him here, to this spot that Franklin had chosen. To this spot, to this coffin, that contained—well, Zack had no idea. But whatever it was, it was something, or someone, Franklin had meant to be buried there. And through West, something, or someone, Franklin had apparently meant for someone to one day find it.

Zack took a deep breath and started forward.

He had made it less than two steps when suddenly an arm whipped around his neck from behind, and something pressed hard against his mouth and nose. For a brief second he smelled something sickly and sweet—and then his legs went weak.

And everything turned black.

CHAPTER FIFTEEN

itting, Hailey thought to herself, as she watched the moon's reflection glint off the thick glass windows of the four-story limestone building at the corner of Sixth and Walnut, on the edge of Washington Square. The rectangular panes of glass were barred in iron—either an homage to the building that had once stood in this spot 230 years before, or in response to the realities of life at the center of a city that was constantly in transition, a melting pot with one foot lodged firmly in its patriotic history, another stepping forward toward a chaotic, urban sprawl.

Hailey had only been to Philadelphia once before, when she was a little more than sixteen. She'd gone on a whim; even at that young age, she'd understood that self-education was going to be the key to shifting from survival mode, a state she'd been living under since she'd escaped her desperate childhood at the age of twelve, to thriving as a young adult, among peers from some of the best private and public schools in the country. She'd already come up with a plan to fake her way into MIT, her university of choice, due to its focus on math and science, but she'd known that a con as intricate as becoming a student at one of the top schools in the world was going to need to be based in substance. Beyond forged secondary school documents, she needed to play the part—which meant she needed experiences to build on. There was only so much you could learn from books.

That trip, she'd taken a Greyhound bus from the terminal at North Station, not the six-hour train from Route 128. And when she'd arrived, she hadn't had a plan. She'd merely walked the city, breezing by the historic buildings and more modern corporate behemoths. She hadn't stopped, even, to see Independence Hall or the Liberty Bell. She'd thought of them as things from the past, as lifeless as the bronze and stone from which they were carved.

Looks, deceiving.

She shifted her attention back to the building that took up most of the corner in front of her. Writing carved into the stone above the thick double doors a few feet away told her it was an insurance building of some sort; the pillars holding up the nearby entrance seemed imposing for a place full of actuaries and accountants. But perhaps the pillars, she now knew, were a nod to a past that was much more alive than she'd previously assumed.

"Before they burned it down to make way for this monstrosity," Adrian commented from a few feet behind, "there was also a fence and a gate, high and iron, much more frightening and imposing than these pillars. Behind that, the building was an immense horseshoe, built around a yard that was about an acre in area. Everyone in the city knew this place by its appearance, but more so, by its reputation. Now, however, most Philadelphians walk right by, never imagining the misery that had once called this corner home. Unless, of course, they notice the sign."

Hailey didn't need to look in the direction Adrian had indicated; she'd seen the sign on the walk over, rising up from a jag in the sidewalk. Dark metal, with gilded yellow lettering:

Walnut Street Prison

One of the nation's first urban penal institutions, it confined felons, prisoners of war, Tories and debtors from 1775 to 1838 . . .

When Hailey had first seen the sign, realization had hit her; this was why Adrian had told them to meet at the train station in Boston. He had known their destination, even before she had decoded the words on the blanket or revealed the map and the strange image of the key. It had been the notation on the edge of the blanket—the date, September 4, 1777, followed by the letters "WSP"—that had allowed him to make what he would probably call an educated guess.

"The Walnut Street Prison isn't just one of Philadelphia's more brutal secrets," he continued. "It's a direct connection to Benjamin Franklin."

Hailey glanced at Nick, as Adrian continued in one of his monologues—explaining the history in the way only he could, equal parts edifying and patronizing. Apparently, Franklin's association with the WSP had begun at a cocktail party at his home, just blocks from this spot, when Franklin had gathered a group of Philadelphia notables to form something he'd called the "Philadelphia Society for Alleviating the Miseries of Public Prisons." Franklin and his pals had embarked on a radical plan to change not just the Walnut Street Prison but the nature of imprisonment around the world.

"Franklin believed that criminality was a moral failing, a moral disease, that could be cured by solitary repentance. The Pennsylvania System, as it was later called, led to the establishment of solitary confinement—the idea was, you isolate every prisoner, separate them from society and each other, and give them a chance to mend their own minds."

Nick's face turned cold as Adrian spoke, and Hailey could only guess at what he was thinking. Nick knew, intimately, what living inside a place like WSP could be like.

"Before Franklin's mucking about," Adrian said, "this was one of the worst places on earth. Common cells where hundreds of prisoners were thrown together, often naked. There were reports of extreme abuse, violence, pestilence."

Hailey shivered as a breeze touched her neck, and she glanced away from the building, toward the park across the street. Washington Square seemed so peaceful and quiet, lined with trees and bisected by empty paths. She could see a fountain in the distance, spouting water high into the air. It was hard to match the view with what Adrian was describing.

"Franklin and his friends alleviated many of the physical problems—providing clothing and blankets, such as the one in your bag—but they exchanged the physical misery for what turned out to be pure mental torture. Prisoners were brought into the prison hooded and chained, then sent to windowless cells to spend twenty-four hours a day, alone. Many poor souls were driven mad, many more ended up committing suicide. Everyone who went in, came back different—but it wasn't the panacea Franklin had hoped for. It did, however, put this spot on the map—the WSP turned into a touchstone that eventually became internationally known."

He turned away from the building and pointed into Washington Square. "I'm not exactly sure where the map leads, but I don't think we'll be going very far."

With that, he headed across the street. Hailey looked at Nick again, who only shrugged. With a last glance at the former Walnut Street Prison, he turned and followed Adrian—with Hailey one step behind.

———

Adrian kept mostly to the path, his oddly circular gait reminding Hailey of a cyclist still turning pedals, even far from his mount. Within moments, the former prison and the street and iron gates surrounding the Square were no longer visible; they were deep into the park, winding between the trees.

Adrian continued to talk as they walked, telling Hailey more than she wanted to know about the ground beneath their feet. How originally it had been a cemetery—that in fact every step probably put them over dozens, if not hundreds, of dead bodies, some going back as many as three hundred years. As Adrian talked, Hailey could see Nick was more interested in the scenery around— he was casting glances left and right, making sure they were still alone. Hailey knew that it was all part of his nature—that even before he'd been to prison, he'd grown up in streets that were often dangerous; he'd learned from an early age to be cautious and careful, always ready to fight or run.

"A graveyard," Adrian was continuing, as he led them down the path. Hailey had taken the blanket out of her backpack a handful of times since they'd entered the park, but Adrian seemed to have the dotted line they were following memorized by now, "mostly colonists, American soldiers, and Native Americans—but that all changed in September of 1777. George Washington had been soundly defeated at the battle of Brandywine. The British general, William Howe, charged toward Philadelphia, then the home of the Continental Congress, the leadership of the Revolution. He thought he could end the war by taking the Congress, but by the time he marched into the city, the Congress had moved to York."

"Must have been a sight to witness," Hailey said, as they passed between a pair of trees that looked like spruce, then around a low hedge. Behind the hedge, she noticed a small area of the park had been roped off, and behind the ropes she could see boxes of what

looked like period clothing, as well as crates containing props—
fake-looking sabers, more authentic-looking muskets, plenty of
three-cornered hats. She assumed that someone was planning a
reenactment, or a parade; thankfully she didn't see anyone nearby,
this late in the evening. "People fighting the British in the streets—"

"Quite the opposite. Before the Brits arrived, most of the rebels
had run north and west. The citizens who remained were largely
loyalists. But the British were not pleasant guests; they set up shop
in the richest homes and treated the colonists quite brutally. As
for the Walnut Street Prison, it became home to captured revolutionary soldiers, who died by the dozens every night. They were
dragged out and added to the bodies already filling these grounds."

Hailey glanced down at the path, then shivered. Adrian
continued.

"Thankfully, the British occupation was short-lived. The Patri-
ots were in Valley Forge, consolidating. Then the French entered
the war. Lafayette brought his fleet, and the British quickly abandoned Philadelphia. They simply fled in the middle of the night."

His pace had suddenly slowed. Around them, the park was now
intensely dark—it had to be close to midnight. Ahead of Adrian,
Hailey began to see shapes—it took her a moment to realize she
was looking at flagpoles, rising up on either side of the path. Ahead
of the flags, she saw what appeared to be an area of stone—and in
the center, something flickering orange.

"But going back—September fourth, 1777," Adrian said, quieter now as he slowed his pace even more. "The British were days
away from occupying the city. Benjamin Franklin asked Revere's
help in securing something of great importance. Whatever it was,
assumedly it was hidden here—then hidden again, by way of invisible ink and a map."

His words drifted off. They were close enough now that Hailey could see that the orange flicker was from a flame, at the center of a circle of stone, embraced by a low metal chain. Behind the flame, shadows danced up a high statue of George Washington in front of a massive granite wall. But in front of the statue—a large, stone sarcophagus.

Hailey's eyes widened. Adrian was staring, too—and he started when Nick reached out and touched the professor's arm. Hailey looked where Nick was pointing, toward a bench off to the right.

There was a figure slumped on the bench. Not sitting, exactly, but leaning strangely, legs out in front, head back against the stone.

A homeless man, Hailey assumed; they'd seen many on the way to the Square, most in the cool shadows of trees—but then she squinted, saw the figure's face—and realized she *knew* him.

"The FBI agent," she whispered, her chest tightening. She had seen him splayed out before, on the deck of the USS *Constitution*. This time, he looked different. Not stiff, or stiffening. But slumped. His chest seemed to be rising and falling.

Hailey started toward him. Nick reached out for her, but she was determined, so instead he followed. Adrian, she noticed, receded in the opposite direction; he looked spooked by the jarring presence of the federal agent on the bench. Alarm bells were going off in Hailey's mind as well, but she had no choice—she'd saved this man once before, and she couldn't leave him lying there.

She reached the bench, dropped to one knee, and put a finger against the man's throat. She felt a pulse and exhaled, relieved.

"Is he . . . ?" Nick asked, but before Hailey could speak, a voice answered for her, as a figure moved out from the other side of the sarcophagus, not ten feet away.

"Dead? Not yet. I hadn't decided what to do with Mr. Lindwell. Eliminating FBI agents can get so complicated. They're not usually the sort you can just, say, toss off a building and be done with."

Hailey's stomach shrunk as she looked toward the voice, still on her knees by the prone FBI agent. She recognized the thin, angular man immediately. He was dressed impeccably in a pale blue linen suit. His torso was narrow, his knifelike jaw jutted out beneath a sickeningly calm smile, and his arms and legs were knotted with muscle beneath the suit's thin material. His hands were empty for the moment, no weapons visible. But she'd seen the man move before and she knew how quick and strong he was. The fact that he was outnumbered wasn't going to make any difference.

The man took a step forward, revealing an object behind him. Propped up against the edge of the sarcophagus was a large metal contraption—something she'd seen before, in an MIT engineering lab. *A hydraulic jack, used to lift heavy objects.*

"I can't tell you how pleased I am that you've found your way here," the man continued, taking another smooth step toward them. Hailey tossed a quick glance past Nick at the word "both"— realizing that Adrian had vanished backward into the park. Not surprising, considering how skittish the man had gotten at the sight of an Amtrak employee, let alone a man like this, coming out from the shadows of a tomb.

"Saves me the trouble of hunting you down," the man said. "But I am impressed by your tenacity; you've been one step ahead of my employer for so long, I'm somewhat surprised that I got here first."

He was close now, less than six feet away, separated from them only by a curve of the low chain that surrounded the eternal flame. Beyond the light from the fire, the darkness had seemed to thicken around their corner of the park as the moon moved between the clouds. The only sound was the rustling of the trees.

And then the man sighed. "My employer would probably prefer that I keep you both alive long enough to find out how you got here. What threads you followed to this tomb. But I've seen how resourceful you can be."

Hailey felt Nick tense next to her. She wanted to search around the bench for something to defend herself with, but she couldn't take her eyes off the man, that cool, emotionless look on his thin face. Inches away, she felt more than heard the FBI agent stir on the bench—but then his breathing went rhythmic again. He would be of no help. His limbs were as lifeless as a rag doll, and his slacks were rustling like leaves in the breeze. And then she saw, in the corner of her vision, a slight bulge down the FBI agent's left leg, inches above the ankle. Beneath the material, a shape that could, just maybe, be—

"Perhaps we split the difference," the thin man said.

And suddenly he lunged toward Nick. As he moved, the man's left hand made a flicking motion and a long blade appeared from the sleeve of his jacket—a cruel-looking combat knife of some sort, gleaming in what was left of the moonlight. The knife cut through the air ahead of him as he halved the distance in the blink of an eye.

But Hailey was moving, too, and she had much less space to cover. Her right hand went up the FBI agent's leg and her fingers found the leather holster; a second later she had the small handgun free, and she rolled back against the bench, lifting the barrel toward the diving man.

The man saw her at the last moment and twisted to the right, his knife missing Nick by inches. Hailey pulled the trigger, and there was a deafening explosion, followed by a flash of bright light. The man's body jerked to the side, a splash of blood spraying from above his left elbow. The knife spun out of his hand, but the man stayed on his feet, twisting almost three hundred degrees as he continued toward Nick.

Nick leapt at him, and the two collided. Nick tried to grab the man in a wrestling move. But the man was way too fast; even with his damaged left arm, he pulled free of Nick's grip. His knee went up and caught Nick in the stomach, and then his right arm came down, elbow first, against the back of Nick's head. Nick dropped to the concrete, then rolled to the side, right underneath the metal chain surrounding the flickering flame.

Now the man whirled toward Hailey, who was aiming the handgun for a second shot—but before she could pull the trigger she saw a flash of metal coming toward her. Another hunting knife, from the man's other sleeve. The blade slashed across the back of Hailey's hand where she gripped the gun, which clattered to the stone beneath her feet.

A searing pain tore across the skin of her hand, warm liquid splattering against her wrist and forearm. She staggered back, grabbing at the wound. It wasn't deep, but it was long, a twisting, ugly red tongue running from her knuckles almost to her wrist.

The man was now standing in some sort of combat crouch between her and Nick, who was still on his back on the stones, just a foot away from the flame. The man's injured left arm hung uselessly at his side. But in his right hand was the second knife that he'd just used on Hailey, as long and terrifying looking as the first. He glanced at Hailey, then turned toward Nick, on the ground. Then back again to Hailey.

"I think maybe I misjudged the greater threat. I doubt I'm the first to do that."

He cocked his head toward Hailey's wound, which she gripped with her free fingers.

"Don't worry about the hand," he said. "We'll get some ice on that as soon as I'm finished with your friend."

He turned back toward Nick, then stepped gingerly over the

metal links into the circle of stone. Another step, and he'd be right on top of Nick, that knife flashing toward Nick's throat. Hailey forgot about her hand and started forward, knowing it was suicide, but also knowing she had no choice—

When out of the corner of her eye she saw a shape moving through the darkness. A figure dashing out from between the trees of the park like an apparition, culled right from the pages of a history book.

Eyes wild, teeth gnashing, glowing halo of hair bouncing high with each wild lunge of his spandex-covered legs.

CHAPTER SIXTEEN

Nick was on his back, the stone slabs cold and hard against his denim shirt, as he watched the angular man and his outstretched blade streaking toward him through the air—when suddenly there was a flash of motion from behind the man. For a brief second Nick's mind couldn't decide if what he was seeing was real, or a hallucination brought on by inevitable, impending death. But then he saw the hair, and the shape in front of him took form.

The professor, Adrian, diving out of the park at full speed, holding a musket, tipped with a terrifyingly long—if most likely plastic—bayonet, aimed directly at the back of the linen-suited killer. For whatever reason, Adrian hadn't been content with the faux Revolutionary Era weapon; he'd also donned a blue minuteman jacket, which he'd no doubt found in one of the prop crates they'd passed in the park. It fit snugly over his shoulders and was so short on his arms that it looked like something he'd borrowed from an eighth grader's closet. But the brass buttons running down the front flashed in tune with the bayonet, which surged directly toward the center of the angled killer's back.

But the man was too fast, trained too well. At the last moment, he felt the wind of Adrian's attack and whirled. The plastic bayonet skimmed his chest as he turned, and the blade caught the material of his shirt. It was surprisingly sharp enough to tear away a ribbon of cloth directly above the man's diaphragm. The man's knife spun free, but his hand shot out like a lurching snake and he grabbed the musket by the barrel, yanking Adrian forward at full speed. Adrian's feet left the ground as he lost his balance and skittered forward across the circle of stone, narrowly avoiding the flame at the center. He hit the ground and rolled, then came to a stop hard against the raised sarcophagus. He sat there, dazed, staring back toward Nick.

In front of Nick, the killer looked at the musket in his hands, then brought the barrel down against his knee, cracking the bayonet off. He then tossed the broken musket to the ground at Nick's feet and held the bayonet up to get a better look at the blade. Plastic, but thick and almost two feet long, tapered into a point as sharp as a shark's tooth.

"This might actually do," the man said. He glanced toward Adrian, sitting stunned against the tomb, and then back at Nick. "You've got interesting friends."

The sudden look in the man's narrow eyes was the most terrifying thing Nick had ever seen. Not primitive anger; this was pure determination. This man was going to kill him and feel nothing at all.

Nick crawled backward against the stone. His flight reflex was kicking in; he wanted to get up and run, but he knew he'd never make it. He could feel the flame warm against his back. He was only inches from the fire now, so close he could smell the butane coming up from beneath its base. He looked wildly around himself, but the only thing close enough to reach was the broken musket, faux wood attached to the long metal barrel.

And then, as he wriggled back another inch, he felt something in the back pocket of his pants.

He paused as the realization hit him. Then he reached forward, ignoring the pain coming from various body parts—his shoulder, head, stomach—and grabbed the broken musket.

"What are you planning to do with that?" the angular man asked, amused.

Nick slid back another foot so that he was right alongside the flame at the center of the stone circle, so close the heat was almost searing the bare flesh where he held the musket. He looked directly at the man holding the bayonet. "I'm going to shoot you with it."

The man's eyes widened. Then he smiled. "That's the spirit," he said.

And then he lunged forward, the bayonet ahead of him.

But Nick was moving, too. His left hand went behind his back and into his pocket. He grabbed the leather pouch he'd lifted from the cavern in Revere's gunpowder factory, then jammed it into the hollow barrel of the musket. He whirled to the side, and as the man arched toward him, Nick shoved the musket—barrel first—into the center of the eternal flame.

The gunpowder in the pouch erupted in a massive flash of light, followed a second later by a sound so loud it seemed to crack the very air. The musket tore out of Nick's hand and fired directly upward, stock first—hitting the man in the direct center of his chest. There was a horrible cracking sound as the man's ribs shattered, then the man was lifted off the ground and flung backward. His body twisted in the air, then tumbled back against the stones, finally skidding to a lifeless stop at the edge of the park. His body appeared caved-in at the center—the musket rising right out of his chest, barrel up.

Hailey raced to Nick's side, and both of them stared at the body. Adrian made a noise—something between a grunt and a moan—and then rose from next to the sarcophagus. The professor's face was pale, his minuteman jacket torn at the elbows. Most of the brass buttons had fallen off. Nick could see one of the buttons melting next to the eternal flame, which was still spitting blue sparks from the bag of gunpowder.

"That's not the proper way to load a musket," Adrian finally said, his voice wavering.

Nick almost laughed, but then shards of pain moved through his stomach where the man had hit him with his knee. Hailey helped Nick up. When he saw her hand, and the wound stretched across the skin, he no longer thought about his own pain. Adrian tore a strip of material from what was left of one of his sleeves, and Nick wrapped it tightly around Hailey's hand.

Adrian took a step toward the body with the musket sticking out of its chest, then seemed to think better of it. Nick didn't need to tell the professor what they all knew: The man was dead. Nick had no illusion that he would be the last to come after them. After all, he hadn't been the first. Whoever he worked for seemed to have vast resources and was chasing the same treasure they were seeking. For the moment, they had a head start.

But their head start would be brief.

The two explosions—the FBI agent's gun and the gunpowder—would draw law enforcement. Nick couldn't hear sirens yet, but he knew in minutes the place would be crawling with cops. Even in Philadelphia, two explosions weren't something that people ignored.

Hailey had obviously come to the same conclusion, because she was already reaching for the hydraulic jack on the ground next to the sarcophagus.

CHAPTER SEVENTEEN

Adrian's heart was pounding like he was pedaling his way up Beacon Hill in tenth gear, as he watched Hailey lift the hydraulic jack and head toward the sarcophagus. Nick was rising from the ground to join her, but for the moment Adrian felt frozen in place. His mouth was dry, his eyes wild, and he could feel rivulets of perspiration trickling down his back.

He still didn't know what had possessed him—and *possessed* was certainly the right word. He could still feel the tight material of what was left of the minuteman jacket against his shoulders.

He had charged that man, actually charged at him, bayonet raised. That it wasn't a real bayonet made little difference. For a brief moment, Adrian had styled himself a soldier; he wasn't sure what would have happened if the man hadn't turned in time— would he have actually attempted to plunge that plastic bayonet into the man's back?

Thankfully, Adrian had been about as adept at war as Revere; the only reason he was still alive, he presumed, was Nick's quick thinking with the gunpowder and the musket, turning its barrel into a projectile. Nick wasn't a genius, but he was cunning; between his survival instincts and Hailey's intelligence, Adrian had to admit they were quite an impressive pair.

"This is pretty simple," Hailey was saying, as she set the jack in position by the sarcophagus. "Plant the base against the ground, put this lever beneath the lid. It's basic physics."

To Adrian, there was nothing basic about what she was obviously planning to do. When he'd first seen the map appear on the blanket, he'd known they would be crisscrossing Washington Square. He'd recognized the Walnut Street Prison immediately and had made a rough guess as to which part of the Square Revere and Franklin were leading them toward. But his thoughts hadn't settled onto the Tomb of the Unknown Revolutionary War Soldier until they'd approached the flags leading to the stone glade.

As he watched Hailey preparing the jack, he thought back to the letter from Franklin to Catherine Ray, and to the single line from that letter that had started them on this journey.

"The Bell rings, and I must go among the Grave ones..." he whispered, and both Hailey and Nick turned to look at him.

He knew that Franklin had, in no small part, been responsible for this monument to the Revolutionary casualties; the brilliant, powerful Founding Father might even, somehow, have steered the placement of this tomb to this particular spot. But was it really possible that he'd endeavored to have something—or someone—interred in that coffin, centuries later? That he and Revere had conspired to hide something—intentionally, or after the fact—in a way that would protect it indefinitely?

With the British closing in on the city, and Franklin about to run to Europe, not knowing if or when he'd ever return—perhaps he had seen it as the only safe option. Whatever was hidden was obviously important—both Franklin and Revere had described it as so powerful it would change the balance of world power. Perhaps they thought it so powerful, so valuable, they'd rather inter it, perhaps beyond both of their deaths, rather than have it fall into the wrong hands.

"Ready," Hailey said, as she secured the jack beneath the lid of the sarcophagus. Then she stepped back.

Nick reached for the lever. Just as he touched the handle, Adrian heard the faint sound of sirens in the distance. Then, the sound of metal against stone echoed through the darkness. Nick strained against the jack, the muscles of his forearm rippling beneath his shirt. There was a loud creak as the lid came up. Nick got under the edge and pushed it as hard as he could. The lid slid off the side of the sarcophagus and crashed down to the stone ground below.

Adrian couldn't help himself and moved next to the pair. He was hit immediately with a gust of moldy, damp air, and nearly choked. He pressed a palm over his mouth, then leaned over the sarcophagus to see what was inside.

The skeleton looked impossibly old, more brown than white, lying on its side. The torso was wrapped in an American flag, but not the modern iteration; Adrian could see the circle of stars representing the thirteen original colonies twisting around the jutting bones of the skeleton's rib cage.

Hailey was leaning even closer than he was, peering up and down and around the bones.

"There's no sign of any key," she said.

Nick reached into the space, feeling the stone floor of the sarcophagus, then underneath the skeleton itself. He shook his head. *Nothing.*

Adrian felt almost relieved. The idea that Franklin and Revere could have hidden something in this place, and that it had remained hidden for centuries—it was almost as absurd as the notion of a philosopher's stone itself. But then—the blanket, the map, the image of the key. *The bells, the armonica.* The evidence seemed clear—Franklin and Revere had been working together. They had left clues. The fact that he and Nick and Hailey had been led to this place—that the FBI agent and the killer had arrived here as well, following unknown clues of their own—there had to be *something*.

Adrian had a sudden thought. He stepped back and reached for Hailey's bag, which had fallen to the ground somewhere before the battle with the killer. He quickly opened the bag and retrieved the blanket.

He could hear the sirens more clearly now, as he carefully unfolded the soft gray material. But the sirens didn't matter—his mind was spinning, contemplating, thinking.

Nick was looking back at him. "What is it?" he asked.

Adrian had the blanket fully unfolded. He pointed at the image near the bottom. "The key," he said.

Now that he was looking at it again, carefully, it looked—odd. At first glance, like an antique house key, but on closer inspection the edges seemed sharper, and the point was strange, curved outward on two sides. Less like it would *fit into* something, and more like it might *pry open* something.

The sirens grew louder, making Adrian think faster. "The key," he repeated. And then it fully dawned on him. "It's not Franklin's key. It's *Revere's*."

"What do you mean?" Nick asked.

"Revere was a metallurgist. A technician. A spy. But he was also something else. And one of the most talented of his time."

Hailey looked at him. He rolled his eyes.

"What are they teaching you in school? The state of American education—"

"Professor."

Adrian moved to the sarcophagus, pushing by Nick.

"Revere was a *dentist*. The premier dentist of his time. Although he didn't, as popular conception has it, work on George Washington, he was the Revolutionary equivalent to a dentist to the stars."

He paused and leaned forward over the open coffin. "And apart from working on the notables of his era, Revere invented the art and science of forensic dentistry."

"Forensic dentistry?" Nick asked.

"The technique of identifying dead men by their teeth. Revere pioneered the practice—in fact, the very first case involved the corpse of Revere's colleague, Joseph Warren, with whom you are familiar—"

"The Bunker Hill Monument," Hailey said.

"Correct. Warren had died at the Battle of Bunker Hill, and his body had unceremoniously been thrown into a pit with dozens of other corpses. It was Revere who searched him out and identified him by his particularly odd bite."

Hailey was suddenly looking at him, hovering over the coffin. "The key—"

"It's not a house key," Adrian said. "It's a Revolutionary Era *dental* key. Used to remove fillings, or implants, from a man's teeth."

She thought with him. "If Revere could use a key like that to take things out of someone's teeth—you think maybe, here, with this corpse, he's done the opposite. Forensic dentistry, but backwards."

Adrian took a deep breath, then reached down into the sarcophagus. He wanted to close his eyes but forced himself to keep them open. His hands found the skeleton's skull, his fingers trembling as they touched the rough material. He could see the dent in the upper part of the bone—where the poor soldier had been hit in the head by something blunt. He had a brief vision of the musket barrel hitting the chest of the killer who had besieged them—then quickly shook the thought away. There was no time to waste.

He found the jaw, grabbed it tightly in his fingers, and gave it a good twist. There was a crack—and the bottom of the jaw came free, rather easily. Adrian jerked back, lifting the lower jaw out of the sarcophagus. He held it up in front of Hailey and Nick.

The teeth that remained were yellow and crooked, dangling at horrible angles. Adrian turned the jaw over, revealing the lower palate—and then he saw it: Carved directly into the bone, a series of numbers.

51.6460 0.8026

And beneath the numbers, a line of text.

Fais Ce Que Tu Voudras

He looked at Hailey. Her cheeks were flushed. Perhaps she had translated the French. Adrian didn't wait for her to say the words out loud.

" 'Do what thou wilt,' " he said.

She looked bewildered, almost as confused as Nick, who was standing next to her.

Adrian could barely hear the sirens over the rushing in his ears. He wasn't confused, or bewildered. Because he knew exactly where the words *led*.

CHAPTER EIGHTEEN

Slithering, gunmetal gray, a pulsing rope of muscle beneath ridged scales, four feet long from tail to teeth, moving through the murky water in sweeping, elliptical arcs. Each twist of its body carried it closer and closer to the glassy surface of the aquarium, sending ripples of water in outward, concentric circles.

"Make it spark, Mommy! Make it spark!"

A few feet from the wall of the eighty-gallon aquarium, Athena Stavros smiled as she watched the two boys press their matching faces against the glass. Although they were physically identical, she didn't need to see the boys' expressions to know it was Castor and not his brother, Constantine, who had spoken the words. Castor had always been the more curious and excitable of the twins; even now, his little body could barely contain itself as he peered through the glass, every inch of his four-foot form shivering in tune with the frantic motion of the creature inside the tank.

Constantine, for his part, stood quietly at the glass, hands crossed behind his back, little fingers interlocked. Six years old and already a thinker, like his grandfather. Castor, on the other hand, had much more of Athena herself in his veins. The need for excitement, action, instantaneous feedback. *Instant gratification.*

Athena took a step forward, her bare feet sinking into the shag rug that covered most of the circular "solarium." Though the tank was eight feet across and nearly five feet high, it seemed small in the vastness of the brightly lit room; behind Athena sat a pair of low leather couches, beige in tune to the equally beige carpet. The walls, too, were beige, rising twelve feet to the cantilevered ceiling. Which, at the moment, was partially opened to the warming rays of the midmorning Mediterranean sun. When the heat of the day progressed, Athena would have the crew close the ceiling, but for now, the warmth felt good on the back of her neck as she joined her two sons at the edge of the tank.

"You want to see him spark? You too, Constantine?"

She was smiling now. The boys always had this effect on her. No matter how difficult the day had been, her boys made the hard things . . . soft. A part of her knew, it was as much chemical as it was spiritual; the endorphins released by familial love were similar to the highs of opioids. But chemical or not, it felt good to be around them. To see them smile and learn and grow.

She moved past the boys to the low counter on the far side of the aquarium. The counter was made of driftwood polished so severely Athena could see herself in its surface. The counter had been purchased by one of her crew in an art gallery in San Torini, on the same trip in which they'd acquired the aquarium, not two days ago. Of course, the tank and the counter had been much easier acquisitions than the aquarium's lone occupant. Athena could still vividly recall the delivery, as she'd personally met the helicopter—one of the three aboard her yacht—at the rear pad on the third deck, two stories above the solarium. The man who had accompanied the delivery was supposedly the best in the business, and still he'd complained incessantly about how difficult the quarry had been to procure.

Reaching the driftwood counter, Athena focused on a small wire cage sitting on its top shelf; she carefully retrieved one of the half dozen white mice scurrying behind the links, holding the writhing little animal by its long, winding tail.

As she lifted it high above the aquarium, the mouse swung around, teeth bared, trying to reach her fingers. Castor, watching, gasped—but Athena laughed.

"It's only instinct, child. The mouse sees me as a threat, and his instincts kick in. It's not personal. And there's no thought involved. The poor animal can't possibly know that I'm not the threat at all. Nor that he was born for such a purpose."

With a look at Castor, then Constantine, whose expression showed none of the fear that crossed his brother's face—she tossed the mouse over the top of the aquarium and into the water.

The mouse hit with a splash, then began paddling its little paws. The two boys had quickly returned to their place right up against the glass. Castor's face was so close his breath was making a cloud against the surface.

Behind the glass, the murky water had gone unnaturally still. There was a pregnant moment, and Athena felt a thrill move through her. She watched the mouse, paddling away against the water—when suddenly, there was a swirl below the creature, and then the ribbon of gray flesh was surging upward.

A second before it reached the mouse, there was a loud crack, and a spark of light flickered through the murky water. The mouse's body spasmed, then it froze, its muscles stiff as wood.

The eel leapt upward, mouth wide, and took the mouse whole. Then with a flick of its tail, it plunged back downward toward the bottom of the aquarium. A moment later, the water was still again.

Castor clapped his hands together. Constantine just stared and then, almost imperceptibly, nodded. Thinking, always thinking, calculating. Just like her.

The electric eel was one of Earth's most fascinating creatures. A trick of evolution, electric eels were not actually eels—they were a type of "knife fish," ray-finned fishes native to Panama and South America. Usually found in deep rivers, where almost no light penetrates, the electric eels had developed an internal organ made up of electrocytes—disc-shaped cells piled together like a battery. The eel's nervous system synchronized the cells by releasing a neurotransmitter connecting the negative and positive charges within each cell, creating the equivalent of a five-hundred-volt battery—more than four times the voltage of an average wall socket. The eels could send an electric shock at will, stunning or killing prey much larger than themselves. As large, even, as a human; there had been many reports of swimmers being shocked into unconsciousness in Panamanian rivers, only to drown moments later.

"Again!" Castor shouted, but Athena shook her head.

"Not until after your studies, boys. Celia is waiting for you in the classroom."

Both boys made noises, but Athena only smiled and ushered them away from the tank. As much as she enjoyed seeing them entertained, she had not gone to the trouble of acquiring the eel for their amusement. It was for her own education—when there was something new to learn about, she had always made it a point to be thorough.

She led the two boys across the solarium to a pair of glass doors that whiffed open at their approach. The boys gave her hugs, one after another, then ran through the doors and down a carpeted hallway. Athena waited a moment until they were out of view, then exited the solarium herself and headed down the hall in the opposite direction.

From the solarium, it was a short walk to the main lounge of Deck Three of the floating paradise Athena had called home for much of her adult life. In the objective portion of her brain, she knew that her upbringing would have seemed exotic and incomprehensible to most; Deck Three of the *Kratos* stretched four hundred feet alone and contained a pair of swimming pools, a movie theater, a salon, and four elevator bays leading to Decks One through Seven. The *Kratos* was the third largest superyacht in existence—at 515 feet, it was only half a foot shorter than Russian oligarch Roman Abramovich's *Eclipse*. But the *Kratos* had been outfitted with accommodations that had cost more than twice those of the *Eclipse*. Where Abramovich had two helipads and a submarine capable of reaching depths below five hundred feet, the *Kratos* had, in addition to its three helipads and two submarines, a runway that could be extended from the stern and could accommodate a P-2 Search and Rescue Jet, which was kept in a specialized hull below one of the seven onboard swimming pools.

Like the *Eclipse*, the *Kratos* was outfitted with security well beyond what would normally be considered necessary for a vessel of its size. An armory stocked with the latest firearms, a battery of antimissile surface-to-air projectiles, state-of-the-art radar and sonar jammers; most of the equipment was defensive, though the *Kratos* did have a few combat secrets that even Athena was only vaguely aware of. Her father had always been both paranoid and obsessed with preparedness.

Athena increased her pace as she moved through the main lounge, passing beneath the two identical chandeliers dripping crystal that hung from the soaring, sixteen-foot-high ceiling. Above the chandeliers, Deck Four—fourteen bedrooms, most unoccupied. Her family was small—just her two children, who always traveled with their school tutor, and her brother—Gabriel—who at twenty-two used the *Kratos* as a stopover between lavish parties. At the moment, he was probably sulking in his room, since gliding up the East Coast of the United States would not be a particularly useful location for him, considering his lifestyle. He was much more at home in the Mediterranean, island hopping between Mykonos and Ibiza, even tolerating the proximity to their ancestral home—her family's private island of Tarantus, where her father now permanently resided.

But Gabriel didn't have any say in the travel course of the *Kratos*; because of Athena's father's condition, she now made those sorts of decisions. In everything but name, she was now—and had been for some time—the de facto head of the Family.

Her eyes dimmed as she moved to the elevator bay at the rear of the main lounge. Although she had been preparing to take over for her father for much of her life—he'd first started showing symptoms of the disease that would eventually take away his cognitive abilities when she was in her early teens—it had still been a shock when, days before her twenty-eighth birthday, he had made the decision to hand her the reins. He had been mostly still competent at the time, and she had resisted; a decade and a half later, she knew he had made the right decision—when it had still been his to make.

The elevator whiffed open. She entered and placed her palm on the security panel halfway up the back wall. The elevator started downward, moving silently through the spine of the ship. The ride was only a few moments—two decks, to the lowest portion of the vessel—but it felt much longer. When the doors whiffed open again, Athena stepped out into another carpeted hallway.

This area of the ship was the only part of the *Kratos* that was not accessible to her boys, the crew, or to Gabriel. Even her younger brother was only vaguely aware of the Family's inner secrets— their true purpose, or quest—or, as Athena liked to think of it, her own personal *birthright*.

Not the wealth the Family had accumulated over many

generations, making it wealthier than many small countries. Not the island she would eventually inherit when her father succumbed to Alzheimer's. Not the *Kratos* itself, which she would happily share with her brother.

Her birthright was something else, something intangible—a secret *knowledge* that had guided her actions for many years now, and in recent days had taken over her entire world.

She moved quickly down the hall, passing works of art on both walls. If an art historian had been walking beside her, he would have gasped at each framed object—a Van Gogh, a Picasso, a Matisse—each more valuable than the last.

She briefly slowed as she reached the last painting, near the end of the hall—brand-new to her collection. No doubt, any art historian would have immediately recognized this work as well: the little ship battered by the crashing waves, the figure of Jesus in the center, tending to the terrified sailors. Rembrandt, of course, but not just any painting by the great Dutch master.

The Storm on the Sea of Galilee wasn't just perhaps his greatest work—it was the central painting in the biggest heist in recorded history, stolen along with ten other paintings from the Gardner Museum in Boston in 1990. Unbeknownst to the outside world, it was a heist that had been paid to order, by her father, Silian Stavros IV. A heist that in fact had had nothing to do with the Rembrandt— or any of the eleven paintings stolen that night. A heist that had only to do with Athena's *birthright*, something that went back much further than the 1990s—generations, centuries, even millennia. All the way back to Alexander the Great, in fact, the Greek king who had conquered most of the world a thousand years before Christ. It was Alexander who had plundered Egypt—but it was one of his generals, Atticus Stavros, who had made the discovery that had set into motion a quest that had lasted generations.

The modern conception of alchemy was actually a bastardization of the original pursuit, which had begun in ancient Egypt along the banks of the Nile and was originally centered around the Egyptian belief in life after death. The art had begun as a crude form of chemistry, with the goal of preserving bodies at the moment of death—in a process now known as mummification. But contrary to the modern conceptions of the purpose of mummification, the goal was not to preserve the lifeless form of a king for future worship; the goal of the chemical process was much more ambitious. The ancient Egyptians believed that the perfected chemical process would one day bring their kings *back to life*, either in this world or the next.

Along with untold material riches plundered from the treasure houses in the great Egyptian cities along the Nile, Atticus Stavros brought the secrets of this fledgling "chemistry" back to his native Greece; *Khemia*, the Greek word for "Egypt," became shorthand for the black art of transformation—merging the Egyptian science behind mummification with the Greek's own views of the elements of nature.

Over the centuries that followed, the Stavros family passed these secrets down from generation to generation—along with the wealth they had conquered and continued to accumulate—and was eventually the basis for an international trading empire that stretched across the known world. When the dark ages hit, the waves of religion sweeping across the Mediterranean pushed the study of alchemy, as it had become known, deep beneath a network of secret societies and coded language. Even so, the Stavros family continued to prosper. They never gave up on the quest to uncover the powerful promise the Egyptians hoped for—mastery over the chemical nature of material life. While the majority of the Stavros empire had to do with the mundane accumulation of wealth and power—Athena's grandfather had moved the family from shipping into oil and arms and had amassed a fortune that could be counted in the tens of billions—there had always been a segment of the Family focused on monitoring the advances—real or exaggerated—within the underground alchemical community.

The infamous, and to the outside world, *mythical*, philosopher's stone—the Holy Grail of alchemy—had not been among the plundered items Atticus Stavros had brought home to Athena's ancestral private island all those millennia ago. But in many ways, he'd acquired something even more powerful—a belief that such a world-changing Holy Grail could and did exist, just out of reach—and it was this belief that had been the engine driving the Stavros family to the heights it had achieved. It was this belief—this birthright—that continued to drive Athena, especially now that the Holy Grail seemed so suddenly within her grasp.

She shivered as she exited the hallway, and entered a smaller, carpeted cabin at the very stern of the lowest level of the *Kratos*. To her right, along the curved wall of the cabin, she passed a circular hatch, which she knew led to the submersible bay. To the left, another hatch led to a chamber known only as the Vault, which contained objects too valuable to even display; eventually, once she'd had her fill of the Rembrandt in the hallway behind her, the *Storm* would find its place on a shelf behind that hatch, perhaps never to be viewed by anyone, again.

Directly ahead of her, in the center of the carpeted cabin, another item of similar fate: standing on a low pedestal, a bronze eagle—horribly damaged, one wing melted over, burn marks running up and down from beak to claws. The finial from the Gardner Museum—the entire purpose of the heist her father had financed, more than thirty years ago.

Paul Revere's eagle, crafted by a French bronzier from a mold the Founding Father had never intended to be cast. Her father had paid for the eagle to be stolen from the Gardner—but had not himself known the true import of the item—the secret mathematical message embedded in its wings. It had taken the girl—Hailey, as she called herself—to uncover what the Family had missed, an alchemical advance that dated back more than two hundred years. *A nobody of a girl, a con artist, a card counter—*

"I have to admit, this was a new one. Clients have sent jets and helicopters—but this was my first submarine."

Athena turned toward the voice. Beyond the hatch leading to the submersible sat a wholly unremarkable woman, perched awkwardly in a chair; behind the woman, one of Mr. Arthur's security personnel—a tall, chiseled blond man Athena knew as Sven, whose muscles were so defined Athena could see them through the material of his gray suit. The chair and the security man were both situated between a pair of stone busts by Michelangelo that her father had purchased at a Sotheby's auction about a year before he'd become bedridden, more than a decade before. The busts, of Brutus and Caesar, had come as a pair, as they had been unearthed together from a ruin outside of Rome, in the late 1970s. Her father had only truly been interested in the Brutus—and not because it was a uniquely charming visage of the legendary traitor to the Roman dictatorship. Over the years, Athena's father had become quite an expert in the life and works of the great Italian artist; the Family had one of the largest private collections of Michelangelo's personal notebooks, many of them never seen by anyone other than the Family's own archeologists. It was one of those notebooks that had led Athena's father to the bust—nothing more than a mention really, pointing to a secret hidden in the "darker pair of two titans of Rome."

Athena's father, like Athena herself, had always been attuned to the details of their shared quest. Upon hearing of the impending sale of two busts that had been unearthed together—the only pair of the "titans of Rome" by Michelangelo that had been displayed together—he had immediately made moves to acquire them. The price didn't matter, nor would he have allowed any rival, or rule of law, to stand in the way. Had he needed to hire thugs to rob Sotheby's instead of simply outbidding a field of private collectors, he would have done so without hesitation.

Michelangelo—like Revere, Benjamin Franklin, and so many other great names in history—had been a student and practitioner of the alchemical arts and had hidden many messages from the discipline within his works. Although there were no indications in the artist's notebooks that he'd had any special knowledge of the philosopher's stone, the possibility of some sort of secret within the unearthed bust of Brutus was too tempting to pass up.

Once he'd acquired the bust, he'd immediately had it sent to one of his labs for a full radiographic workup. And true to the notebooks, there had been a secret inside the titan of Rome. The stone bust had a hollow core in which sat a gemstone—not the mythical philosopher's stone but a pure yellow sapphire, over sixty carats, making it the largest, gem-quality yellow sapphire ever discovered. Although the gem was priceless, Athena's father had left the bust of Brutus intact. The yellow sapphire—the alchemical symbol of Saturn, which represented the metal lead—would remain hidden, as Michelangelo had intended, until the Family had achieved its primary purpose.

"I must say," the woman continued, hands still clasped, as she glanced at the busts on either side of her. "I was quite surprised by the invitation. My understanding was that Mr. Arthur handled all of the Family's business. As much as I'm honored to meet you face-to-face, Ms. Stavros, I am curious as to what I owe this unique pleasure."

Athena shifted her attention from the bust of Brutus to the woman, and looked at her more carefully. She had never met this woman before—but of course her reputation was well known to Athena. And seeing her in person—Athena was not disappointed, but at the very least, confused. The woman was truly *unexceptional*. In fact, she was so average, if she'd been walking past in a café or stood in a crowd outside a theater in any city in the world, Athena would have looked right past her. Five foot six, with a bob cut that would have suited a high school librarian. Her body was rounded, not overweight, but not seemingly fit, either. She was wearing a tan pantsuit that was tight around the middle, and her skin was almost as beige as the carpeting in the ship's solarium.

Remarkable, how unremarkable the woman was. Athena could see that Sven was equally surprised by the appearance of the woman—he must have also known of her reputation, but even so, he couldn't conceal the obvious look of contempt spreading across his chiseled features.

Athena caught the man's eye, and he quickly stiffened. With a nod, she sent him over to the wet bar in the far corner of the cabin, where he quickly retrieved a pair of crystal wineglasses, already half filled with a delicate red from one of the Family's many vineyards.

"The honor is all mine," Athena said, as Sven handed a glass to her, then the woman in the chair. "I've been an admirer of your work for many years now, and I was extremely pleased that Mr. Arthur was able to secure your assistance; we've had a series of, shall we say, setbacks. I believe a woman of your considerable skills can help us get back on track."

The woman nodded slightly, her bob cut barely moving with the motion. Her fingers looked thick against the delicate glass of the wine goblet. It was truly hard to believe that Athena was looking at one of the most dangerous women in the world. An operative who had worked for organizations as disparate as the Russian mob and the Mexican cartels, with a personal kill list that included over forty political assassinations. According to her reputation, she was nearly a force of nature, and yet in person she was, entirely, beige. So beige, in fact, that the nickname that had followed her from childhood—from the days when she first began catching notice as a teenage operative—an orphan, raised, trained, and employed by Catalina separatists in her native Spain was La Nadie—literally, "the Nobody."

It seemed impossible. Athena took a deeper sip from her own glass, then, more out of curiosity than anything else, gave Sven another imperceptible nod.

It all happened in an instant. So fast, it reminded Athena of the electric eel striking down the mouse. Sven reached into his jacket for his gun; in that same moment, the woman in front of him kicked her feet against the floor, sending her chair backward into Sven's groin. As he hunched forward, she sprang up out of the chair, the wineglass still in her hand. She shattered the glass against the side of Sven's head, leaving only the stem, sharp as a shard— which she pinned against his throat, right above the jugular.

Sven let the gun drop to the floor, as La Nadie turned toward Athena. The glass at Sven's throat dug into his skin, just enough to cause a trickle of blood to run down to the collar of the security man's shirt.

"Did I pass the interview? Or would you like me to take this man's throat out as a souvenir? Would be quite a waste. I was hoping he could give me a tour of the ship. I've always found something oddly redundant about swimming pools on boats."

Athena nodded again. The woman lowered the stem, and Sven stumbled back, hand at his neck. La Nadie gave him a wink, then turned back to Athena.

"Now that we're all friends again, let's talk about your setbacks, and see how I can be of service."

Athena grinned, as she sent Sven back to the bar for a fresh glass of wine for her newest associate. She felt certain—the Family had never been closer to its goal, nor she to her birthright. With this woman's help, one day soon Athena would take a hammer to the bust of Brutus—and that day, ironically, the yellow sapphire inside would be a mere trinket compared to the wealth and power her birthright would unleash.

CHAPTER NINETEEN

Ladies and Gentlemen, we've just passed twenty-two thousand feet on our way to a cruising altitude of thirty-six thousand feet. We anticipate a smooth crossing, and I've instructed our flight attendants to dim the cabin lights..."

The captain's monotone, tinged with a heavy British accent, drifted like a lullaby through the canned air of the Boeing 777 wide-body transatlantic jet, as the vessel continued to rise above the low cloud cover. Even though the seat belt sign was still illuminated, Hailey was moving carefully and quietly down one of the two aisles that ran through the "club" cabin—British Airways' most current euphemism for coach, which was itself a euphemism for cattle. As far as Hailey could tell, the rear two-thirds of the plane was only slightly more comfortable than the sort of transportation one might expect between a barn and a slaughterhouse— but the farther she padded up the carpeted aisle toward the front section of the plane, the nicer the accommodations became.

Even so, when she'd jammed into her narrow seat in club for takeoff just twenty minutes before, she had been wide-eyed and filled with adrenaline. She had never been on a plane this big. She'd flown before, but only short hops, flights that had always connected somewhere she didn't need to go and had never wanted to see. Certainly, she'd dreamed about one day traveling the world—seeing cities in Europe or Asia or India—but the day-to-day rigor of surviving had always been like a visor pulled down against her dreams.

And yet now here she was, in a giant steel cylinder rocketing upward over the Atlantic Ocean. It was all so overwhelming, and she almost felt her knees buckle as she exited the club cabin and made short work of whatever British Airways was calling business class.

The plane was nearly full, most of the seats on either side occupied by men in suits, and the odd couple in more comfortable leisure wear. She didn't see many children, but then again, she now knew how much it cost to fly from Boston to London—part of the reason her eyes had been so wide since takeoff—and the few families she'd passed were back in club.

As overwhelmed as Hailey was, she could only imagine that Nick felt even worse. When she'd left her seat, she had passed him two rows up—jammed between an overweight woman with a pocketbook on her lap and a teenager with headphones, bobbing to some metallic sound that reverberated loud enough to be audible from the aisle. She and Nick had avoided sitting together on the off chance that anyone might recognize the two of them together from some news report—but even if they'd been next to one another, she would have left Nick behind in his seat, at least for the moment. When she'd passed, he'd had his eyes closed, leaning back against his headrest. Either asleep, or close to—no doubt he was beyond exhausted, his body battered. It was the first chance either one of them had had to actually rest since this had all started.

For Hailey's part, as tired as she was, she'd found it impossible to stay still. Her mind was whirling—in no small part from the rapid stream of activity that had led them to this place. The machinations involved in getting two fugitives onto an international flight had been substantial, a process that had begun with Nick reaching out again to Sully, his loyal stitchman, who had connected them to a counterpart in Philadelphia. This time, their savior wasn't a general dentist but an endodontist—a man who fixed root canals as a profession, but crafted and sold passable US passports on the side.

Ironic, Hailey had mused, after their discovery at the Tomb of the Unknown Revolutionary War Soldier, that this underground network consisted of dental professionals—but then again, as Adrian had explained on their way to the airport, dentists had always occupied an odd pedestal in American culture. It wasn't until the late 1800s that dentists had to register with any guiding body or professional guild, and it wasn't until the 1920s that there was even a framework guiding dental work, though hardly anyone stuck to anything that could be considered a standard of care. Jewelers, blacksmiths, apothecaries, even priests practiced dentistry as a side hustle through the eighteenth, nineteenth, and much of the twentieth centuries. Traveling vaudeville performers would pull teeth as part of their acts. And in some cases, dentistry could be a truly macabre profession—when Napoleon's army was defeated at Waterloo, teeth were pulled en masse from the corpses littering the battlefield and sold to dentists around Europe to be used as false teeth.

That a network of dentists was also moonlighting for underground criminals hadn't surprised Adrian at all, but he'd sent Hailey and Nick on ahead on their own to meet with the endodontist—a man with hands the size of frying pans who was happy to take the rest of Hailey's casino chips in exchange for a pair of passports under the names Allison Powell and Carl Morgan. Hailey had been nearly paralyzed with fear as she'd gone through airport security with the fake passport, but Nick had kept her calm with a firm hand on her shoulder. The more federal crimes you committed, he'd whispered, the easier it got. That had gotten her to smile at exactly the right moment, and the TSA agent had simply waved them through.

Hailey continued up the aisle until she reached the thick curtain separating business class from first. Pushing through, she was glad to see the first class flight attendants busily preparing their food carts up at the front of the plane. Quickening her pace, she quickly noticed how much nicer the first class cabin was than the rest of the plane; the air seemed to smell better, almost flowery, and most of the window shades were drawn, leaving a soft blue light emanating from the ceiling. Most of the people she passed were already settled in their pods, lying flat in the reclining seats, many with covers pulled up to their chins. But in the fourth row from the front, she caught sight of a cone of orange light—a seat still in sitting position, and an easily recognizable figure hunched forward over his open tray table. Adrian's hair almost seemed to glow, as he focused on the open books spread across the table in front of him.

Approaching the professor, she found it hard to square the image he now presented—the consummate intellectual, poring over texts he'd borrowed from one of the many university libraries in Philadelphia while Nick and Hailey had been busy with the endodontist—with the man who had come out of the mist in Washington Square holding a fake musket tipped with a hard plastic bayonet. No doubt his actions, as insane as they seemed, had saved her and Nick's lives. And it wasn't the first time he'd saved them. She knew his motives weren't entirely altruistic—he was driven, like her, to seek answers, and the mystery unfolding in front of them was simply too enticing for him to pass up. But even so, as difficult and strange as the professor could be, Hailey owed him—well, everything.

He didn't look up until she'd reached his seat and her shadow obscured one of the open books on the table in front of him. He glanced at her, and a grimace crossed his lips.

"They really need to install doors between the cabins. Those curtains are clearly too skimpy to keep the riffraff where they belong."

She knew he was only partially joking, but she pushed into his pod anyway, using her hip to make room for herself in his seat. His grimace turned to a glare, as he grudgingly shifted aside.

"I'm sure this isn't allowed. And I believe the seat belt sign is still illuminated."

"We've done a lot worse over the past two days. If the flight attendant comes for me, I'll be sure to warn her about your skills with a bayonet."

As Adrian blushed, Hailey glanced down at the open book on the table; to her surprise, she saw that much of the page was taken up by an odd drawing, of what looked to be some sort of very large monkey. But as she peered closer, she saw that it wasn't merely a monkey; someone had strung a pair of sharp horns on its head and had painted some sort of design across its face. And it appeared to be holding a pitchfork, as it lurched through what seemed to be a dark cave.

"I like monkeys as much as the next girl, but I'm assuming you aren't flying us to London to visit a zoo."

Adrian sighed—but Hailey immediately recognized his expression. Obviously, she intended to interrupt Adrian's research, so he might as well use the opportunity for one of his customary lectures.

"It isn't a monkey, it's a baboon. And it wasn't traipsing through any sort of zoo. This baboon is actually quite important; the end point to a story that involves some of the most famous men of London. Politicians, writers, philosophers. And even one particular American Founding Father: our friend, Mr. Benjamin Franklin.

Adrian shifted the book so that Hailey could see the second book he had open on his table. Emblazoned across its open pages: a picture of a triangular crest. And in the center, the words Hailey instantly recognized from the corpse in the grave of the unknown Revolutionary War soldier:

Fais ce Que Tu Voudras

"Do what thou wilt," Adrian translated, though Hailey knew just enough French to have already figured them out herself. "You might recognize them from more recent applications, of course. Popularized in a recent song, I believe, and on a television show or two. Perhaps before that, from writings of the occultist Aleister Crowley, who used them as sort of a trademark. But in truth, they come from a much more complicated and historically significant provenance."

He turned the page of the second book, to another picture—this time, a portrait, of a man in Renaissance clothing reading what seemed to be a Bible. Strangely, there appeared to be a naked woman perched next to him, and yet the man had a halo over his head. But the halo was odd—within the gilded ring was a face.

"Francis Dashwood," Adrian explained, pointing to the man in the portrait. "A wealthy and powerful Duke who lived in London in the early eighteenth century. Dashwood, along with his colleague—the Earl of Sandwich—were the founders of an institution—secret, at first, but eventually infamous—generally known as the Hellfire Club."

Hailey raised her eyebrows. "Quite a name for a club."

"With quite a history," Adrian said. "Private *men's* clubs catering to the powerful and wealthy had sprung up all over London at the turn of the eighteenth century. Dashwood's, however, was clearly the most significant—beginning first in a London establishment called the George and Vulture Inn, around 1730, and then moving to Dashwood's own estate, on which he built an actual monastery dedicated to hosting his like-minded associates, in secret, in the decades that followed."

"A monastery? Dashwood's club was religious?"

"Quite the opposite," Adrian said, lowering his voice. At some point while Adrian was speaking, the seat belt light had gone off, and one of the flight attendants had started down the aisle, offering drinks to the first row of passengers.

"For the Hellfire initiates, 'Do what thou wilt' was more than some witty club motto," Adrian continued. "It was their raison d'etre. Dashwood was famously against any form of religion—a true, atheistic hedonist. He founded the Hellfire Club to be a place of debauchery, where his rich and powerful friends could meet—always at night, away from prying eyes—to indulge in the sort of conversation—and activities—that would have been scandalous in the palaces and political halls of the era. What began as a private meeting place for twelve of Dashwood's close friends ballooned to a club with dozens if not hundreds of members. Dashwood's Hellfire Club grew over a period of two decades—and as the years progressed, rumors swirled—of strange rituals, occult activities, sexual orgies—even, at times, human sacrifices."

The flight attendant had made it another row, but Hailey was glued to the seat, her eyes wide.

"Rumors," Adrian repeated, waving a hand. "Most of them likely false. Journalists of every era—but especially the early eighteenth century—had a penchant for dealing in fantasy, and historians are often no better. As it turns out, there are no actual records of what went on at Dashwood's Hellfire Club. There were records—but Paul Whitehead, the final secretary and steward of the club, and once one of Dashwood's closest friends, had them all burned when he was on his deathbed."

"Seems a bit dramatic."

"These were dramatic times. Whitehead went a step further— upon his death, he had his own heart removed, placed in a jar, and given to Dashwood to inter within the shuttered club, as a final bit of closure. As I said, dramatic times."

Hailey whistled, low. Then touched a finger to the portrait of Dashwood. "So all the religious imagery—"

"A humorous ruse. The painting was made by a famous portraitist, William Hogarth, who was also a club member. It's a parody of famous religious images of Francis of Assisi, which were prominent at the time. The Bible in the picture is actually an erotic novel— *Elegantia Latini Sermonis*—and the face in the halo is in fact the Earl of Sandwich, Dashwood's cofounder, and one of the most powerful and famous men of the era. Hogarth might just as well have included any number of the famous faces who filled the Hellfire Club's roster: Robert Vansittart, one of the more powerful judges of the time; Thomas Potter, the son of the Archbishop of Canterbury; and the famous politician and journalist, John Wilkes."

Adrian shifted Hailey's attention to the other book on his table—to the drawing of the baboon.

"It was Wilkes who was responsible for this, shall we say, atrocity. Apparently, a live baboon was kept by the Hellfire Club as a mascot—and was rumored to have been involved in numerous rituals, and possibly some of the debauched escapades that took place. One particularly lively night, Wilkes decided to use the baboon to play a prank on the Earl of Sandwich; Wilkes dressed the baboon as the Devil, then set it loose on the earl—who became so hysterical and frightened, he got down on his knees and began to confess his sins. Once the prank was revealed, the earl became so incensed, it created a rivalry between the men that might have contributed to the club's eventual demise."

Hailey shook her head. It all seemed so fantastical—that this was real history was shocking. When she imagined London in the eighteenth century, she did not picture baboons dressed as demons, or famous, powerful politicians hanging out in a place called the Hellfire Club.

"Boys," she said, simply, which got a bit of a smile from Adrian.

"Indeed. And perhaps the most famous rake mingling with Dashwood, Wilkes, and the Earl happened to be our old friend—Benjamin Franklin."

"Franklin was a member of the Hellfire Club?"

"He was a friend of Dashwood's, and during his years in London he was invited to many of their secret meetings. It's unclear whether he was ever an official member. But he did spend time on Dashwood's estate."

The flight attendant was only one row away now, close enough that Hailey could hear her British accent as she asked the passenger in the pod in front of them what he wanted to drink. But still, Hailey made no move to head back to her seat.

"And in September of 1777, as the British were about to take Philadelphia, Franklin asked Paul Revere to help him hide something—and with Revere's help, presumably, buried a clue in Washington Square—'Fais ce Que Tu Voudras.'

"More than that," Adrian said, speaking faster and even lower now. He went back to the second book, turned a page. Another picture—a hand-drawn map.

"This is Dashwood's estate—West Wycombe, as it was known. Here's the monastery—but the really interesting stuff is actually underground. As Dashwood's club grew in members, he'd had a series of tunnels dug beneath the monastery, deep into this hill here, and moved the club's meetings underground."

He touched his finger to a corner of the map, in the center of what appeared to be one of those underground tunnels. Hailey could see, next to his finger, a row of numbers.

51.6460 0.8026

The same numbers that had been carved into the palate of the skull they'd found in the Tomb of the Unknown Revolutionary War Soldier.

"Coordinates," Hailey said.

Adrian nodded. "Latitude and longitude. Franklin would not have been a stranger to Cartesian coordinates. He created the *Farmer's Almanac* and was an experienced mapper and traveler. Perhaps his association with the Hellfire Club was much deeper than history has yet recorded."

Adrian paused to think a moment. When he spoke again, he sounded almost reluctant.

"Although Dashwood founded the club in London at the George and Vulture decades earlier, the first meeting of the Hellfire Club at Dashwood's estate—West Wycombe—occurred on April thirtieth, 1752, during a holiday known as Walpurgis Night. It's a Christian feast that celebrated an obscure saint, an occasion Dashwood no doubt thought an ironic date on which to launch his relocated gathering. But the night didn't go well; too many of his friends arrived, and the space beneath the monastery wasn't prepared for such a crowd. So according to my research, Dashwood planned a second inaugural meeting, which was held forty-two days later—on June tenth, 1752."

He paused, as if he didn't want to continue.

"Is that date significant?" Hailey prodded.

Adrian coughed, then pushed aside both of the two books that were open on his table. Hailey saw that there was a third, smaller book beneath them—another history book, dedicated to the same time period, the mid-eighteenth century.

Adrian opened the book to a marked page. In the center was a painting.

"That's Benjamin Franklin, isn't it?" Hailey said. "Is he wearing a cape?"

"*Benjamin Franklin Drawing Electricity from the Sky*," Adrian said. "A famous painting by the artist Benjamin West, a close friend of Franklin's who also lived in London—and was a member of the Hellfire Club. But West's association with the club isn't the relevant point here—it's the act itself, portrayed in this portrait."

"The kite and the key," Hailey said.

"The kite and the key," Adrian repeated. "Franklin's famous experiment with the kite and the key, drawing electricity from the sky. That event—mythical or not—supposedly occurred on June tenth, 1752."

Hailey felt her heart pounding. "The same day that the Hellfire Club had its first meeting, in the tunnels beneath Dashwood's estate."

The flight attendant was moving to Adrian's row, and Hailey knew she had to head back to her seat. But before she rose and stepped into the aisle, she looked at the professor. "It can't be a coincidence, can it?"

He didn't answer. His expression was back to a grimace, but this time it had nothing to do with her presence in the first class cabin. History, again, was being rewritten in front of him—fantasy was flirting with reality. And Hailey knew nothing was more painful to the Professor. But Hailey wasn't concerned with Adrian's sensitivities.

As she finally slid out of his seat and started back toward the curtain that separated the first class cabin from the rest of the plane, her mind swirled through everything she had just learned. Much of what was known about the Hellfire Club was rumor—the only records about it had been burned hundreds of years ago, by a man who then donated his actual heart to be interred in the club, forever. Whatever had actually occurred at the Hellfire was lost to history.

But Hailey, Nick, and Adrian had uncovered a message leading them directly toward that very history—etched into the palate of a man who had died during the American Revolution, by Paul Revere and Benjamin Franklin.

Fais ce Que Tu Voudras

A motto of debauchery, of a secret underground club of wealthy, powerful men. But when Hailey closed her eyes, she didn't see politicians, judges, journalists, or even Franklin, the scientist and Founding Father who had given the world the blessing of electricity. All she saw was that hand-drawn baboon—dressed as the Devil—dancing through a dark, foreboding cave.

CHAPTER TWENTY

Eight hours later, Nick's head felt like it was spinning at a hundred RPMs as he trudged up a winding dirt path that serpentined between never-ending lines of perfectly manicured hedges. To Nick's right and left, he could see rolling hills that bled into flat plains; it was too dark to see the grass, but he assumed it would have been lush and green, considering how damp the air felt, and the way the thick mist clung to the meticulous, landscaped curves. Adrian had mumbled something about the bucolic-looking fields when they'd first arrived at their destination—some place called the Chiltern Hills, thirty minutes outside of London—as having the appearance of a grass-covered Rubenesque painting, lounging beneath the British moon. Nick hadn't known what the hell Adrian had meant by that, but he'd known the comment hadn't been intended for him, anyway. To the professor, Nick was an unpleasant third wheel—though, Nick assumed, Adrian wasn't too thrilled with his second wheel, either, no matter how smart Hailey was or how good an audience she seemed for his constant soliloquies.

The professor loved his bicycles, but to Nick, the foppish man seemed to want to go through life on a single, lonely wheel.

For his own part, Nick would have happily let the scholar finish what had already turned into an eight-hour journey on his own.

As deeply as he was invested in their quest, from the minute he'd stepped off the plane at Heathrow, Nick had felt like he'd been caught in the center of a cultural tornado. He'd been buffeted by sights and sounds that he was barely equipped to digest. He could have blamed these feelings on his five-year stint in prison—but the truth was, his entire life's landscape had been a form of steel walls and iron bars. In thirty-two years, he'd never really gone *anywhere*, or seen *anything*.

By the time they'd gotten in the hired carriage at the taxi stand outside of Heathrow—a big, black, bug-shaped car—Nick had fallen into a near silence, just trying to compute the sights and sounds around him. So many people, from so many places; the anachronistic architecture, as they reached London and wound their way through the narrow streets, passing churches, museums, colleges made the oldest sections of Boston look positively new. Even as the day shifted to night, and the lights of the more modern sections of the city blinked like a forest of Christmas trees mangled together after a fierce storm, Nick felt like a kid in the back of the cab. Adrian had already taken charge—guiding the taxi driver on a bizarre shopping spree, hitting a handful of stores that Nick couldn't identify for items the professor didn't bother to explain. A pair of retractable shovels, a length of strong climbing rope, a small, handheld pickax; not the sort of souvenirs you'd find in the tourist shops surrounding Buckingham Palace or the British Museum.

And when Adrian had given the driver their final destination, Nick had watched the man raise his thick, fluffy eyebrows before shrugging and heading for the outskirts of the city. And now here they were, hiking up the English countryside.

Hailey and Adrian were a few feet ahead, talking in low tones; Nick figured they were continuing the conversation they had started on the plane, snippets of which he'd heard as they'd walked nervously through customs. At the time, he'd been more concerned about their fake passports standing up to the gruff customs officers than whatever Hailey and Adrian were discussing, but once they'd breezed through—the passports proving the endodontist's skills at forging documents, if not his acumen at root canals—Nick had done his best to pay more attention.

Apparently, the palate they'd found in the skeleton in the Tomb of the Unknown Revolutionary War Soldier was leading them to something called the Hellfire Club. The thought that Ben Franklin—the kindly looking man on the hundred-dollar bill, renowned for the kite and the key—was a member of something so illicit seemed incredible to Nick. But then again, if Nick had learned anything in prison, it was that it was impossible to judge anyone by their appearance. People were complicated, and historical figures no less so than the people he'd met in the prison yard.

Nick was breathing hard as the path wound through the last of the hedges; up ahead, Adrian and Hailey had slowed, and Nick could see why. A hundred yards in front of them, at the top of a low hill, he could make out a church of some sort, rising up into the darkness. But instead of a cross, at the top of the church Nick saw what looked like a metal sphere, flashing in the moonlight streaming through breaks in the thick clouds.

"St. Lawrence's Church," Adrian said, quietly. "This is the peak of West Wycombe Hill, the center of Dashwood's ancestral estate. You see the orb—it was used by Dashwood and his friends as part of a messaging system; one of Dashwood's associates—and a founding member of the Hellfire Club, Joseph Norris—had a similar sphere atop an obelisk on his estate twenty miles to the south. The men would flash messages to each other, using torches or reflected sunlight."

Adrian started forward again. At first, Nick thought Adrian was leading them toward the entrance to the church—but at the last minute, the professor chose another stone path that wound around the building, and back into more rows of hedges. Another hundred yards, and they broke through again—and Nick found himself facing another old-looking building.

"Another church?" Nick said, catching his breath. The heavy pack on his back dug into his still healing shoulder; Hailey had wanted to help carry the supplies Adrian had picked up in London, or put some of them in her saddle bag, which was over the professor's shoulder—but Nick had felt strong enough to carry the load. Third wheels had to do what they could to feel useful now and then.

The building in front of them certainly did look like a church—arched windows, stone walls, turret-like towers—but this building had the appearance of being much older than St. Lawrence's Church and was mostly in ruins. Parts of the construction had been built right into the hill. The ruins were surrounded by a fence made of high iron bars, and behind the bars, Nick could see what looked to be picnic tables, surrounding colorful umbrellas. Around the tables someone had placed a series of gas lanterns, which lit up the front of the stone ruins like the entrance to some sort of Gothic haunted house.

"Not a church," Adrian said. "A cave. Or more accurately, a system of tunnels attaching a series of caves, carved right into the hill, beneath the ruins of a twelfth-century monastery, known as Medmenham Abbey."

"The Hellfire Club," Hailey said, quietly. "These are the tunnels."

Adrian nodded.

"Built from the remains of a chalk mine, actually. Dashwood originally attempted to helm his club meetings in the abbey above the tunnels; but his club grew quickly and the abbey was too open to the nearby public; local villagers looked on the club with understandable concern."

"Pitchforks and torches?" Nick asked.

"We're in England," Adrian responded. "Harshly worded edicts and noticeable expressions of disgust."

He walked to the fence. There was a chain lock across the entrance, but there didn't seem to be any signs of people nearby.

"During the day, this place can be quite the tourist attraction," Adrian said. "People come for tours of the caves. Sometimes, the current owners even hire it out for events. The tunnels and caves aren't exactly Buckingham Palace, but there are plenty of people who'd spend a handful of pounds to see where a bunch of lords and politicians might have once held satanic orgies."

He glanced back at Nick, then toward the bag on Nick's back. Nick unslung the pack, reached inside, and found the small pickax. He eyed the chain lock, then glanced around them.

"This will make a little noise," he said.

It took two hands and a bit of leverage, but he managed to get the lock open without losing any of his stitches. The three of them waited another moment, making sure nobody had heard the effort; then they were through the fence and moving past the umbrellas and the picnic tables toward the arched entrance to the hill beneath the monastery. Directly above, at the peak of the arch, Nick could see the words, emblazoned above the entrance:

Fais ce Que Tu Voudras

As they reached the opening beneath the words, Nick reached back into his pack and retrieved three flashlights, which Adrian had purchased during his shopping spree. This time, Adrian was happy to let Nick lead; Hailey was close enough to Nick's side that he could feel her breath against his neck.

Nick followed his cone of light into the first tunnel—a rounded passageway leading directly into the hill. The walls on either side appeared to be white brick; on either side, small plaques and framed drawings told the history of the club, from Dashwood's founding to its demise, when Paul Whitehead, the club's steward, had burned all the club's files and records.

At the end of the first tunnel, which was brief enough that Nick could cross it without raising a sweat, there was a wooden door. He was about to reach for the pickax again when Hailey tried the knob—unlocked. Behind the door, another tunnel. Here, the air was suddenly much thicker and damper than outside. This tunnel curved softly to the right and began to descend deeper into the earth. Nick still led, but his pace slowed; the farther they moved from the entrance, the darker it became, and the more reliant they were on the orange cones coming from their flashlights.

Behind Nick, Adrian had one of the books he'd brought on the plane open in his hands, partially lit by his cell phone, which was also out ahead of him; Nick had glanced at the map a few times on their way to Dashwood's estate, but he had never been particularly good at following 250-year-old drawings. He knew that Adrian wasn't just following the thick lines that represented the tunnels themselves; he was also using his phone's GPS to track the coordinates of where they were heading. It was complicated work—the professor nearly stumbled multiple times as he tried to focus on the phone's screen, the map, and Nick and Hailey's progress. The deeper the tunnel descended, the rougher the going went; the walls and floor had become rock, not brick—carved but not entirely smooth. At some points, as the tunnel curved in more of a serpentine pattern, the walls became so narrow that Nick's shoulders almost touched both sides at once.

Another turn, a few more yards in silent shuffling along the stone floor—and Hailey gave Nick's shoulder a squeeze, then pointed to his right.

Carved right into the stone wall, Nick saw huge Roman numerals:

XXII

Beneath the carving, someone had hung a plaque containing the remnants of an eighteenth-century poem that supposedly referred to a secret passage that existed somewhere within the caves and tunnels they were moving through. Hailey read the opening of the poem out loud:

"Take 20 steps and rest a while;
Then take a pick and find the stile
Where once I did my love beguile.
'Twas 22 in Dashwood's time,
Perhaps to hide this cell divine
Where lay my love in peace sublime."

When she finished, Adrian looked up from his book and phone.

"Ah yes, the secret passageway. Apparently, it was supposed to lead to a stairway with twenty-two steps—the Endless Stairs—which lead either up to the monastery, or down—somewhere. More myth, most likely."

He turned back to his map and phone and ushered them ahead. But as they continued down the tunnel, Nick could see that Hailey was mouthing numbers as they went—counting down the first twenty steps from the poem. Before she'd reached the end, the tunnel turned again, and Nick saw that to their left was a barred opening to a small cave. Inside, two mannequins. Nick shined his flashlight on the two figures: One was instantly recognizable.

"Benjamin Franklin," Nick whispered.

Adrian looked up again. The Founding Father was dressed in clothes of the era, hunched over, wearing his signature glasses and holding a lantern.

"Yes, with Dashwood. But there's so much wrong with this I don't know where to begin," Adrian commented. "At the time of his visits to the Hellfire Club, he would have been a much younger man. And those shoes are from twenty years after his death."

Nick noticed that Hailey wasn't paying much attention to the Franklin mannequin; she had gone from counting steps to repeating lines from the poem as she walked.

" 'Where lay my love in peace sublime,' " she said. "I don't think that, in particular, has anything to do with a set of stairs. It's about a woman—'in peace sublime.' I think someone who died here."

Adrian coughed. "The White Lady, perhaps."

"Who?" Nick asked.

"One of the many ghost stories about this place. The White Lady. Her name was Sukie, the story goes, and she served drinks at the George and Vulture. A beautiful barmaid who had rejected all of the local men and instead flirted with a wealthy aristocrat visiting from somewhere far away."

They'd moved past the cave with Benjamin Franklin and were winding down another dark tunnel.

"The local thugs decided to play a trick on Sukie. They forged a letter to her, ostensibly from the aristocrat, asking for her hand in marriage. A meeting was arranged here in the tunnels beneath the monastery; Sukie was to arrive in her white wedding dress. But when she reached the tunnels, instead of the aristocrat, she found all the local lads, and was understandably incensed. As the story goes, rocks were thrown, and one hit Sukie on the head, knocking her to the ground. She died here, and the thugs buried her body."

Hailey's eyes had gone wide.

"Her ghost has supposedly haunted the tunnels ever since," Adrian finished. "An apparition in a white wedding dress, floating around looking for vengeance, or lost love, or both."

Even Nick shivered at that, and the tunnel around him felt even more claustrophobic than before. It didn't help that suddenly he started noticing strange carvings on the walls on either side—most of them round or oval, at different heights, scratched right into the rock. At first, he thought they were just geological formations—but when he shined his flashlight on them, he realized—they were faces.

Hailey saw them too, and slowed her pace. Directly to the left, one of the faces appeared to be representing some sort of wizard—with a pointed hat and a flowing beard. Another, nearby, had a cornered hat. Adrian noticed their attention and came close as well.

"The members of the Hellfire were encouraged to carve self-portraits into the walls. The wizard—that's Dashwood himself. The rest are unknown—anonymous club members, the way they saw themselves."

Some of the pictures seemed macabre, even frightening. Ghostly shapes, impish, some demonic—made even more unsettling by a gurgling sound coming from up ahead. Shining his flashlight forward, Nick saw that there was some sort of stream bisecting the tunnel up ahead. Whether it was natural or man-made, the stream seemed cut directly into the rock, deep enough in some areas to have a series of stalagmites rising up out of the water like gnarled fingers reaching into the darkness.

Adrian wasn't looking ahead toward the stream; he had paused a few feet behind Nick, and was holding up his book, the map lined up with the wall.

"Strange. If I'm reading this right, the coordinates we're after are—through this."

"Twenty-two," Hailey said, finishing her count.

Nick looked at her. She shrugged, then shined her flashlight along the wall, past Adrian and his map. One of the visages caught their attention; it was odd, round, but with a catlike face, half of which was taken up by a wide smile. Above the cat's face was what appeared to be a flower of some sort carved into the wall.

"Twenty-two steps," Hailey repeated. "But that's not a woman." She paused, thinking. "The name of the woman in white. Sukie. That's not a common English name, is it?"

"Certainly not of the time," Adrian said. "But it can be a derivative of the name Susan."

"What sort of derivative?" Nick asked. "It sounds Japanese."

"Not Japanese," Adrian said. "It actually comes from ancient Hebrew. Soo-ki. It means 'lily.' A flower associated with fertility, and the Virgin Mary."

Hailey nodded, shining her light on the flower carved into the wall.

"The Virgin Mary would certainly have fit in with the symbolism of the Hellfire Club. A wholesome image turned into something darker—a ghost haunting these tunnels."

She was thinking as she spoke, and then her flashlight focused on the cat face beneath the carved image of the flower. "What does this look like to you?"

Nick was a second faster than Adrian. "A cat."

"But what sort of cat?"

Nick didn't have an answer to this one.

Adrian looked at Hailey, then finally coughed. "Cheshire."

Nick had heard the name before. From the storybook *Alice in Wonderland*. He hadn't read it, but he knew about the cat in the book, the one with the huge smile. A cat that could turn invisible— leaving only that grin, floating in the air.

"When did Lewis Carroll write *Alice in Wonderland?*" Hailey asked.

"*Alice's Adventures in Wonderland,*" Adrian corrected. "Eighteen sixty-five, I believe."

Hailey wrinkled her brow, but Adrian's eyes shifted.

"But the image of the Cheshire Cat goes back much further than Lewis Carroll," he said, quietly. "The theory is, Carroll got the idea of the cat with the crazy grin from a carving on the wall of St. Wilfrid's Church, in a town called Grappenhall, which was close to Carroll's birthplace in Cheshire. Alternatively, a twelfth-century 'Smiling Cat' in St. Nicholas Parish Church, in Surrey, was another possible inspiration—"

"Both these cats," Nick commented. "In churches? Why?"

"A smiling cat is a very old symbol of vulgarity and vice, going back well beyond the early eighteenth century. Its use in churches could have something to do with the notion of sin; which would explain its use here, though for opposite reasons."

Hailey moved closer to the smiling cat on the wall. "But there's more to the Cheshire Cat than vulgarity," she said. "In *Alice's*— excuse me, *Alice's Adventures—in Wonderland*, the Cheshire Cat has the ability to become invisible. More accurately, the cat fades out until all you see is his teeth. Although it might just seem like a literary device, the phenomenon is actually the basis of a pretty complex scientific process."

Now Adrian looked as confused as Nick felt. Hailey reached past the professor to the pack on Nick's back, and rummaged inside. A moment later she was back next to Nick, holding one of the items Adrian had bought for their expedition. No doubt, since they were tunneling, Adrian had grabbed anything he thought might be useful underground. Nick saw that in Hailey's hand was a length of rope ending in a heavy weight—a plumb line, used to gauge depth or measure the verticalness of a sheer wall.

She glanced at Nick. Her eyes were strange, her face excited.

"Lean forward. Focus on the cat's face. Specifically, the smile. Don't blink if you can help it."

Nick knew better than to argue, and did what she asked. Hailey held the plumb line between his face and the wall and began to swing the metal weight in front of his eyes. He did his best to keep staring at the cat's smile, as the weight went back and forth, back and forth.

"Hailey," Adrian said, from behind Nick. "I'm not sure what—"

"Just wait," Hailey said. "This is my lane."

The weight kept swinging. Nick's eyes started to water, and he fought the urge to blink. He was about to agree with the professor—when he noticed something strange. The cat's face was beginning to—disappear. "What the hell?"

Hailey's voice was tinged with excitement. "It's called binocular rivalry. A visual stimulus presented to one eye is suppressed by a competing visual stimulus presented to the other eye. The suppression occurs because the visual cortex in the brain can only process one image at a time, so it must choose one or the other."

As she spoke, the cat continued to vanish, little by little. Most of the outline of its head was already gone, the eyes were going next. The smile was still there, etched into the rock.

"Your eyes are trying to fixate on the stationary object—the cat carved into the wall—but your brain is trying to make sense of the moving weight. Every time it makes the choice to try and comprehend the weight—"

"—the cat vanishes," Nick whispered.

For a brief second, all that was left was the smile—and then that, too, disappeared. And yet, there was something still there, in the stone. An imprint that he had not been able to see before the cat's features had vanished. An indentation—that didn't look natural at all. Nick realized, suddenly, what he could now see.

He turned toward the professor. "Your bag," he said.

The professor didn't move fast enough, so Nick crossed to him and yanked the saddle bag open. Reaching inside, he quickly found what he was looking for—a delicate item wrapped in cloth.

He moved back to the wall, and used his fingers to find the indentation that was now no longer visible, hidden beneath the image of the cat. Then he carefully unwrapped the cloth—revealing the upper palate and front teeth they'd taken with them from the skeleton in the Tomb of the Unknown Revolutionary War Soldier.

It had been Adrian's idea to bring the item from Washington Square with them—believing eventually that it should end up in a museum, to be studied by scholars for years to come. They'd all felt a sense of fear bringing the palate and teeth through customs—but if any agents had seen it on the X-ray machine, they hadn't made any fuss, probably assuming it was a set of false teeth. Now, Nick was only glad that Adrian had been thinking ahead—even though the professor could not have realized how prescient he'd actually been.

Nick turned the palate over so the teeth were facing forward—and pressed them into the indentation in the wall.

"What are you doing," hissed Adrian. "That's an artifact—"

But Nick wasn't listening. The teeth fit exactly into the indentations, as he had guessed from what he'd seen.

There was a loud metallic noise—and suddenly, a section of the wall directly in front of him jerked back a few inches. He put his hands on either side of the Cheshire Cat—and gave the wall a hard push, using all of his weight.

The section of wall moved back, as if on rollers. There was a gasp of cold air that hit his cheeks—and then the section of wall *dropped*. A second passed in silence, and then there was a loud splash from somewhere below.

Nick leaned forward a few inches—the opening was pitch-black. He pointed his flashlight downward and saw water—the stream up ahead obviously ran down through the rock—but the water seemed to be splashing around something, an object sitting in a shallow area, blocking the flow. It appeared to be some sort of chest, maybe wooden. Warped by time and the stream, but it appeared intact.

Adrian and Hailey moved next to him to look.

"Christ" was all Adrian could say.

Hailey was opening Nick's bag again, returning the plumb line in exchange for a heavier and longer length of rope.

Nick was breathing hard as Adrian and Hailey helped pull him the last few feet back over the ledge and into the tunnel; he hadn't actually needed the rope for the way down, which turned out to be a six- or seven-foot drop to the shallow stream. The water swirled at his bare feet like frozen claws. It had been much colder than he'd expected, but it hadn't taken him long to get to the chest or haul it back up the wall to the opening in the tunnel.

The chest wasn't heavy, and as Nick set it down on the floor between Adrian and Hailey he worried that it might come apart at the seams. It was obviously extremely old, and mostly unmarked. The only carving he noticed in the wood was directly on top; it appeared to be the image of a heart.

"Something to do with the woman in white?" Nick pointed.

"Or maybe to do with Mr. Whitehead, the club secretary," Adrian responded, "whose heart had been placed in an urn inside the tunnels. In 1829, an Australian soldier on leave visited these tunnels, and reportedly stole the organ, leaving only the urn behind. Whitehead's ghost supposedly travels these tunnels along with the woman in white, searching for his missing heart."

Nick shivered, telling himself it was mostly because of the cold water he'd just stepped through to retrieve the chest. He watched as Hailey attacked the warped clasps beneath the heart. A second later the clasps came undone, and she carefully pulled open the top of the chest.

She seemed confused by what she saw inside. Nick moved closer as she retrieved the contents—a small sheaf of yellowed, parchment-like paper, tied together by red string. Nick could see the top page, which appeared to be covered in—

"Are those musical notes?"

Adrian pushed past him to take a closer look. Hailey undid the bit of string, and gently shuffled through the pages. More notes, handwritten and complex, running through row after row of musical bars.

"It's a composition," Adrian murmured. "A folio."

Hailey got to the last page—which appeared to have been torn in half. The notes on the page ended abruptly at the tear, halfway into a musical bar.

"It's unfinished," she said. "Or missing its ending. Was this written for piano?"

Adrian reached out and took the sheaf from her, turning back to the first page. There was writing at the top of the page, swirling letters in what might have been pen ink.

"It says here it's an adagio—'*Harmonica.de.glass.*'" He looked up.

"Franklin's invention," Hailey said. "The armonica."

Nick felt a rush. He thought back to the instrument he'd seen in the underground cavern beneath the remains of the gunpowder factory—the strange instrument with the glass bowls, whose music had reportedly made listeners ill. Hailey had hypothesized that Franklin had been experimenting with Revere on using sound as a means to alchemical power—that the philosopher's stone could have something to do with a perfect tone. Revere had attempted to create that tone with a bell, to limited success. Franklin, too, had experimented with sound, creating the armonica, before shifting his scientific focus to electricity. Could this unfinished Adagio have something to do with their alchemical experiments?

Then Nick noticed that Adrian had gone still, his face pale. The professor was staring at that first page of the folio. He didn't seem to be breathing.

"Are you OK?" Nick asked.

Adrian lifted the first page so gingerly, his fingers barely seemed to be touching the parchment. He turned it so Nick and Hailey could see. Hailey shined her flashlight directly at the page, where Adrian was suddenly pointing.

Above the first bar of music, in small, handwritten letters—a sequence of numbers, and then a date—March 1778. Next to the date, a name.

"That can't be real," Hailey whispered.

Nick read the swirling letters with some difficulty. Then he blinked, and read them again:

Wolfgang Amadeus Mozart

CHAPTER TWENTY-ONE

Adrian shifted uncomfortably against the stiff leather of a garish, Louis XIV chair situated in the corner of a bookshelf-lined office on the third floor of the History Wing of King's College, London. He barely attempted to stifle the look of pure disdain fluttering across his face. The office—twice the size of Adrian's own—was filled with antique furniture, thick carpeting, and display cases loaded with artifacts. The walls beyond the bookshelves were covered with framed eighteenth-century paintings—many of them reproductions, but a few that seemed authentic. The picture window behind the mahogany desk across from him looked out over the college's main court—a sliver of manicured grass stretching between a pair of four-hundred-year-old, castle-like buildings, already centers of the world's academic universe when Tufts, where Adrian worked, was little more than a grazing hill for some early American settler's pestilence-ridden herd of cows.

And yet, Adrian's disdain wasn't entirely due to jealousy. King's College was one of the most esteemed universities in the world, and the collection of artifacts and art filling the office was impressive. But the setting and décor were disjointed, almost chaotic. Adrian guessed that was what came from specializing in the history of a man whose life had been long and complex, and whose personality seemed to waffle by the decade, from conservative and buttoned-up to famously vulgar and profane.

The chair Adrian was sitting in was from a collection derived from Benjamin Franklin's years in Paris, where he had served as ambassador for the newly formed American republic. In a glass case directly to Adrian's left, he could see a chronological companion to the chair—a long metal pole, darkened by years and use, tapered to a point. A plaque above the case explained that the metal was a genuine Franklin lightning rod of Franklin's French era; it had once been attached to the steeple of a church only a few blocks from the Bastille. Next to the rod, another section of the case was dedicated to the many trinkets and souvenirs that had been sold in Parisian shops during Franklin's stay—everything from medallions and necklaces bearing Franklin's likeness to snuff holders, canteens, and playing cards. Because of the lightning rod, which had saved thousands of lives across the French capital, Franklin had attained a celebrity status well beyond his political position.

Next to the case, Adrian recognized another invention of Franklin's era—the first design of a flushing toilet—with Franklin's face imprinted on the lid. Above that, the wall was hung with a variety of circular saws, many with hand cranks attached, the smallest the size of a cell phone—though Franklin hadn't invented the saws, he'd improved on the design. And on the other side of the immense desk, Adrian could see a genuine Franklin stool—a chair that could transform into a set of stairs—and behind that, a pair of Franklin swim fins beneath a shelf containing a half dozen bifocals.

Item after item after item, a disjointed menagerie that made Adrian wince. But he knew that much of his discomfort had more to do with the fact that he was sitting in Angela Barrett's office than with the office itself. It wasn't simply that he disliked Barrett;

it was the indignity of having to come to her, of all people, for the information they needed.

Hailey and Nick sat next to him on a velvety love seat, where they'd settled after milling around the display cases just long enough to make Adrian uncomfortable. They might have thought nothing of two colleagues like Adrian and Angela visiting each other for information on their related fields; but Adrian prided himself on being an island. He had never needed another professor's help before, and it was doubly painful reaching out to Barrett, of all people.

Unfortunately, she was the only one he could think of with the necessary expertise to understand what they had found in the Hellfire caves.

He glanced over at Hailey. Though her backpack was still over her shoulder, and his own saddle bag was on the floor between them, she had the folio of yellowed parchment pages on her lap in front of her. Though they had since covered the aging artifact in a plastic binder they had picked up in a stationery store, Adrian could still see the rounded notes and horizontal bars of the handwritten first page of music through the clear cover. Blinking, he could also see the torn last page—how the score ended abruptly, an unfinished manuscript, one that clearly should have been sitting in a museum and not at the bottom of a stream behind a secret passageway in an eighteenth-century labyrinth of former chalk tunnels.

Surprisingly, Hailey's own focus did not appear to be on the artifact on her lap. Instead, her eyes had drifted to the far wall, settling on one of a half dozen framed paintings hanging on the far side of the picture window. All of the paintings were from the Revolutionary Era, most large canvasses having to do with famous moments from the war itself, but Hailey's focus was on the smallest of the bunch. Not an original—a print in a solid silver frame, about the size of a hardcover book. Immediately recognizable because Adrian and Hailey had recently peered at the very same image, on the flight from Philadelphia.

Benjamin Franklin Drawing Electricity from the Sky—the portrait by Benjamin West. Up there, on Barrett's wall, in all its strange glory; the flowing cape, the cherubs, the odd devices and allusions, and of course, the key and the kite. *The experiment that probably never happened, and yet still, somehow, changed the world.*

Adrian's thoughts were interrupted as Angela Barrett finally swept into the office, closing the door behind her. A small smile crossed her lips as she moved past Hailey and Nick and around to the other side of her desk, where she lowered herself into a chair similar to Adrian's own. Then she leaned back, crossing her arms against her chest.

"This is a delightful surprise," she said, settling her eyes on Adrian.

He did his best not to squirm against the leather beneath him. He reminded himself that the last time Barrett had seen the three of them, Hailey and Nick had been running through the Museum of Science being chased by undercover police officers. Adrian should have been thankful Barrett had agreed to meet them at all, considering the circumstances.

"I appreciate your willingness—" he started, but she waved a hand.

"As long as we're not planning some sort of a jailbreak, I'm happy to lend my expertise. Your text indicated you've found something interesting?"

Adrian searched her tone for a hint of anything patronizing. The last time he'd been in this office, more than a decade before, things had gotten fairly ugly. At the time, he hadn't come to Barrett for her "expertise"—he'd come for an apology.

The incident still gnawed at him, and probably always would, as it was one of the formative embarrassments of the early part of his career. Four years into his postdoctorate work, he'd been invited to speak at a conference on the King's College campus, in a theater packed with forty of the top eighteenth-century European history scholars in the world. Adrian's presentation had gone well, of course—an amplification on a paper he'd written about Revere's failed campaign in Newport, which had already earned him numerous accolades in the scholarly press—but just as he'd finished speaking, he'd noticed a raised hand in the front row of the auditorium.

Barrett had begun her line of questioning innocently enough. "Isn't it possible that your focus on Revere's failures as a commander obscure his contributions as a strategist?" From there, it had only gotten worse, as Barrett had politely and deftly torn apart much of Adrian's thesis. Worst of all, she hadn't been entirely wrong; his mumbled responses were wholly insufficient, and by the end of his allotted time, he'd sweated through his tweed jacket, having taken a solid hit to his psyche if not his career. If he'd already been considered quite the peacock among his colleagues in Boston and London, Barrett had clearly just plucked out a handful of his plumes.

After his speech, he'd come directly to this office, demanding an apology. Barrett had called him absurd: *Adrian,* she'd told him, *you need to lighten up about these sorts of things. Disagreement is perfectly acceptable among equals.* He'd sputtered something back at her that he no longer even remembered, and hadn't spoken to her again until the meeting at the museum.

And now here he was, back in her damn office, seeking her help. The indignity of the situation was overwhelming, leaving Adrian with a momentary lack of words. Luckily, Hailey was there to fill in the silence, as she pushed the plastic-covered folio across Barrett's desk.

"This is going to be a bit hard to believe," Hailey started, and then dove into a brief description of how they'd found the folio in the Hellfire caves, and why they believed the musical manuscript had been hidden in the chest by none other than Benjamin Franklin.

Adrian knew how insane it all sounded and watched Barrett's face for signs of incredulity. But all he saw were furrowed brows and a spark of amazement in her dark, doe-shaped eyes. She had already seen the name on the first page of the folio, and was carefully fingering through the musical bars, page to page, obviously awed by what was in front of her. As Hailey continued, explaining that she'd already searched the pages for any sort of hidden codes or secret messages and had come up empty, she noted their theory that this folio had some connection to a project Franklin had been working on with Paul Revere—one which Hailey left purposefully vague in her retelling.

As Hailey finished speaking, Barrett remained focused on the pages, so quiet and still that for a moment it seemed like she wasn't even breathing. She'd gotten to the last, unfinished page, where the rest of the manuscript had apparently been torn away—then returned to the first, and was rereading the title and, of course, the swirling signature. Finally, she looked up from the folio, first at Hailey and Nick, and then toward Adrian.

For a moment, she seemed unwilling to speak. Perhaps she was waiting for Adrian to tell her that this was all some elaborate prank—some way of getting back at her, perhaps, for the slight he'd obviously never gotten over. But when Adrian simply met her eyes, then nodded slightly, Barrett seemed to understand—this was real. And the academic wheels behind her gaze began to turn.

"Taking this at face value," she said, quietly, "it's a spectacular artifact. But putting aside for the moment the many questions I have about what has led you to this—beyond the fact that I'm holding what appears to be a previously unseen manuscript by the greatest composer in history, I'm immediately struck by the date—March 1778."

"My understanding," Adrian interrupted, "was that Mozart did come to London, and was heralded by the court of George III, where Benjamin Franklin spent much of his time—"

"Correct," Barrett said. "But that was much, much earlier; Mozart visited the court of George III in 1764, and at the time he was a boy—just eight years old, a prodigy, on his first European tour. He played a series of concerts for the rich and powerful, and even wrote a piece for the Queen. He might well have crossed paths with Franklin, but at that age Mozart was little more than a curiosity, a child touched by God. It was his only formal trip to England; after a year of touring Europe, he returned to Salzburg and spent the next decade building his reputation as a great composer, but he struggled financially throughout his career. In 1777, he finally resigned his position in Salzburg and traveled to Europe again—reaching Paris in March of 1778."

Suddenly, Barrett was up from her desk and approaching a short filing cabinet situated between two of her glass display cases. She rifled through a drawer, then returned with a bound sheaf of pages, some sort of academic work in progress. She dropped back into her seat and began rifling through the sheaf.

"As you know, beginning in 1776 and continuing through the end of the Revolutionary War, Benjamin Franklin lived abroad, sent by the fledgling Congress to enlist allies and to try to negotiate for peace. Although England was Franklin's first love, his lengthiest period of exile was spent not in London but in Paris. He arrived in 1777 as a true celebrity—one of the most famous men of his era, a Founding Father, but also a savior of the French people."

Perhaps noticing Nick's blank look, she nodded toward the lightning rod in the glass case behind her.

"It can't be emphasized enough how important the discovery of the lightning rod was. Especially to the French; their entire capital was essentially constructed of wood. Lightning had been a bane of French existence for centuries. Franklin's rod turned 'hellfire' into something controllable. He was heralded as a hero."

She continued flipping pages.

"Mozart, on the other hand, had not arrived in Paris as anything close to a VIP. Although his talent was known worldwide, the market for composers—no matter how touched by God—was miniscule. Apart from a gig writing for the Paris ballet, he was professionally shunned, and had a reportedly miserable stay in the City of Love. His mother became ill and passed away. He himself grew extremely sick—and began to deteriorate, both physically and mentally. He remained for barely a year, then left, never to return."

She abruptly stopped flipping pages, settling on a chapter near the center of the academic work—and pointed to a typewritten title.

Franklin, Mozart, and the Great Supper

Adrian raised his eyebrows, and Barrett blushed.

"Not my best turn of phrase—but to be fair, it was only a year after my doctoral thesis, and I was still finding my footing. This is a paper I wrote about Franklin's early months in Paris—and this chapter was almost a throwaway bit of gossip—about an evening that had taken place during Mozart's stay in the city, in which Franklin and Mozart had indeed crossed paths."

She glanced down at the paper, but it was obvious she didn't need to read the words to remember what she had written, years ago.

"As I said, Mozart's visit to Paris did not go as planned; although the composer had become close to the Paris Opera's ballet master— Jean-Georges Noverre—and had been commissioned to work on a handful of pieces, the work quickly dried up, and Mozart ran low on funds. As his mother grew ill, Mozart found himself searching for a patron to support the rest of his stay. He befriended a French architect by the name of Louis Portione, who invited the young composer to stay in a room above one of the city's many Masonic lodges, where he remained until his mother's death in July of that year."

Hailey was glancing at Adrian, who ignored her—but Barrett seemed to notice, glancing up from her paper.

"Yes. It's fairly well known that Benjamin Franklin was a Freemason. Although he regarded the group and its rituals with some level of amusement, he did attend meetings and was a member of various lodges around Europe. In Paris, the lodge he was most familiar with happened to be the Maison de Pierre—'the House of Stone'—where Mozart had been staying. This chapter in my paper was about an evening Franklin had spent at the De Pierre, dining with Mozart and a handful of architects, engineers, and scientists."

Adrian saw that Hailey had moved forward in the loveseat.

"This 'House of Stone'—is it still there?"

Barrett smiled. "It's Paris. *Everything* is still there."

"So if Mozart and Franklin had been involved, and somehow this folio was the result of some sort of collaboration—"

"I wouldn't book my trip to Paris just yet," Barrett interrupted. "Yes, Mozart and Franklin did meet, at least on this one occasion, but perhaps more intimately during the composer's stay in the French capital. And yes, Mozart was known to have composed a few pieces for Franklin's famous glass instrument—the armonica was, after all, more popular than the piano for a short span of time. Further, if I'm understanding even a bit about what you've been chasing—Franklin and Mozart might have shared a deeper interest in, shall we say, the pseudo-sciences. I'm sure you're familiar with Mozart's *The Magic Flute*."

Adrian cleared his throat, having been silent long enough.

"Tripe, compared to his other works. Written in haste for a lowbrow audience. Filled with fantasy—"

"—and imagery and symbolism from the occult," Barrett finished for him. "*The Magic Flute* is also rife with Masonic tokens, as well as nods to alchemy. The number three—which is heavily related to both Freemasonry and alchemy as the most stable number, representing order—is the basis of the entire work. Three children, three slaves, three ladies, even the music itself was composed in E-flat major, with three flats. And the flute—a magical instrument—might even be symbolic of the ancient idea of a philosopher's stone..."

Barrett paused, noticing the looks on her guests' faces.

"An object which I feel you are familiar with. So it's not entirely out of the realm of possibility that Franklin inspired a Mozart composition, which he wrote while he was out of work in Paris. A work that appears to be missing its ending, but that doesn't mean we need to travel across the Channel to search for the rest of this folio."

She closed her own paper and turned back to Mozart's.

"Original manuscripts of the great composer can be found all over London. The British Museum has a sizable collection, of course. And many of his early works are kept in a special chamber at Buckingham Palace."

Nick coughed. "Breaking into Buckingham Palace might be beyond my skill set," he commented.

Barrett stared at him. Adrian felt his cheeks warm, but Barrett only seemed momentarily slowed.

"Thankfully we don't have to break into anywhere. Since March 1778 means Paris, I know exactly where we need to begin our search, and it isn't Buckingham. The largest collection of Mozart's Parisian works is much nearer."

"Here at King's College?" Adrian asked, hopeful.

Barrett shook her head. "No." She glanced toward Nick. "But if I'm still as charming as I was in my university years, I think you'll be able to leave your lockpicking tools at your hotel."

CHAPTER TWENTY-TWO

Thirty minutes later, Hailey climbed up the crowded stone steps of the Regent Park Tube station and stepped out onto the quaintly named, equally crowded Marylebone Road, shielding her eyes from the midmorning sun. The trip had been less than four miles from King's College, but they'd had to change subways twice and been forced to stand most of the way, packed into a mosh pit of businessmen, tourists, and early-lunchers.

The sunlight felt good against Hailey's face, and when her eyes finally adjusted, she saw the two professors ahead of her, moving quickly down the tree-lined sidewalk toward an impressive building made mostly of redbrick and white stone. The building sported multiple chimneys sticking up from its sixth floor, above a curved parapet lined with ornate carvings and many rounded windows. Hailey wasn't an expert, but she guessed that as close geographically as their new destination was to King's College, it was similarly adjacent in time; another two-hundred-year-old campus, established with the help of a royal decree.

Barrett reached the entrance to the building first and paused in front of a large wooden double door that had been propped partially open. There were college students moving in and out, many carrying musical instruments. Though Hailey never had a chance to study any instrument, growing up on her own, she'd heard of the Royal Academy of Music. Home to many an iconic composer and famous musician—in modern times, giving birth to such talents as Elton John and Annie Lennox. Barrett had filled them in on the school's history during the short Tube ride from King's College. Founded by French harpist Nicolas Bochsa and John Fane, the Earl of Westmorland, the Royal Academy of Music had been established under the auspices of King George IV, the same royal who had been responsible for King's College. Catering mostly to classical performers with the immense talent required to gain entrance, the Royal Academy shared classes with King's College. Barrett's relationship to the musical institution went even further back, to her own teen years.

Before she'd discovered history and a love for Benjamin Franklin, she'd explained, she'd been a bit of a piano prodigy herself, playing concert halls all over London while still a teenager. She'd dreamed of becoming a professional and had followed that dream through these same double wooden doors.

"I spent one glorious year on this campus entertaining the fantasy of being the next Martha Argerich," she'd told them, as the subway car had rumbled through the London underground. "But my skills at the keys peaked around the same time that I discovered how much I enjoyed poring through books about the American Revolution. Thankfully, I turned out to be just as skilled at reconstructing the lives of American Revolutionaries as I'd ever been at tickling the ivories."

"I'm sure that's not true," Adrian had responded, but Barrett had let the shot go unanswered.

As they entered the building's lobby through the partially open doorway, Hailey could see the flush of color enter Barrett's cheeks—no doubt, she still had many fond memories of the place, and perhaps missed her former passion more than she'd admitted.

The interior of the building was less staid and historic than its exterior; the floor was paneled in black and white, like a chessboard, and a metal-railed spiral staircase dominated the center of the room, rising up to the higher floors like a twisted, corrugated spine. There was a reception desk directly ahead, staffed by an elderly woman with a bouffant of white hair. Barrett hadn't reached the desk when a thick English accent echoed through the room from two twists up the spiral stairs.

"Angela. How wonderful to see you."

The man sweeping down the steps looked decidedly less than regal; corduroy pants and tan riding boots, and a white shirt that was especially tight around a very plump midsection. The man's face was birdlike, with a chin that extended a little too far over his throat, and a forehead that went so far back toward his tufts of blonde hair, it nearly seemed to come to a point. He might have been handsome once, or at least cherubic, but now looked to Hailey more like a wobbly bowling pin.

"Gregory," Barrett responded with a smile. "Appreciate you meeting me at such short notice. It's been too long."

She seemed to be throwing niceties like confetti, but Gregory appeared to enjoy every smile and word. After a quick exchange of introductions, the man gestured for them to follow him back up the stairs.

"You know I love a good mystery," he said, winking smarmily over his shoulder as he went. "If it's anything music related, I'm sure you've come to the right place."

———

Gregory's second-floor office was much smaller than Hailey would have expected, considering the sign on the door said, "Dean." At the same time, it was obvious Gregory had done his best to make the space just ostentatious enough to be off-putting. There were various awards and plaques lining the low bookshelf that ran along one wall, along with pictures of Gregory himself—much younger, and not as handsome as Hailey had imagined—seated at grand pianos in various halls where he'd toured as an up-and-coming pianist.

Beyond the bookshelf, Hailey saw that the rest of the small space was taken up by instruments of various shapes and sizes. She counted a half dozen violins, and a trio of brass instruments hanging from a rack by the door. By far, the instrument hardest to ignore was a large standing harp in the far corner, made of polished wood, with strings almost as tall as Hailey herself.

As she looked at the harp, Gregory lowered himself into his chair behind the desk, fingers making a bridge beneath his extended chin.

"Quite an instrument, don't you think? It was donated by the Bochsa family a century ago, but I've had it meticulously maintained. Each string has been restrung countless times; steel and catgut, exceedingly high-tensile strength. I'd be happy to play it for you, if you'd like."

He'd switched his attention to Barrett, who smiled back. "As much as I'd love that," she said sweetly, "we're here on pressing business."

He raised his eyebrows, as Barrett came around the desk to stand next to him, closer than she needed to, while Hailey, Nick, and Adrian remained standing in the center of the office. Barrett leaned forward and placed the folio in front of Gregory, opening it to the first page.

The man seemed immediately distracted by Barrett's closeness—but as he followed her long fingers to the page open in front of him, his expression suddenly changed. His eyes widened as he read the title and signature.

"This—is an original?"

Barrett nodded.

Gregory swallowed, then quickly reached into the top drawer of his desk and withdrew a pair of silk gloves and a magnifying glass. It was as if the rest of them had vanished from the room. He slipped the gloves over his fingers, then began examining the folio closer— page by page, in silence—until he reached the torn final page. Only then did he look up, eyeing Barrett, and then the rest of them.

"Quite a fascinating document. Where did you—"

"Not important for the moment," Barrett said, still leaning close to him. "My associates and I are more interested in the folio itself. Have you ever seen anything like this before?"

Gregory turned back to his magnifying glass, running it over the barred notes, then back to the first page, and that signature.

"As you know we have an extensive collection of Mozart's work, with a focus on his Paris period. As for his compositions for the glass harmonica—there are only two that I know of—1791, K.617 and K.356. The 617 was a quintet—armonica, oboe, viola, cello, and flute. A fine piece. I believe I was in Vienna when I heard it for the first time—"

"Gregory," Barrett prodded. "Back to our folio. You can see that it's missing its ending. Your extensive collection—does it include anything that might be connected to this work?"

Gregory shrugged.

"There are a number of partial and unfinished manuscripts in our archives . . ."

He left the sentence hanging, and Hailey felt there was suddenly some sort of negotiation going on in the room. Barrett leaned even closer to the dean.

"I'm sure when we're done with our own research into this folio, it would make a wonderful addition—"

That was all it took. Gregory grinned and reached into another drawer in his desk, retrieving a skeleton key, hanging from a long necklace like string.

"Let's see what we can find," he said, putting the key around his neck and springing up from his chair. Barrett barely got out of the way in time, as he led them all toward the door.

———

Ten minutes later, they had descended four floors below Gregory's office, by way of an aging elevator with a caged door and a pair of stairwells that somehow seemed even older than the building surrounding them. They'd crossed through a subbasement that had been turned into a makeshift museum, filled with exhibits and display cases containing mostly stringed instruments. Violins, violas, cellos, and many other musical devices Hailey had never seen before and couldn't name.

Once they'd passed through the museum, they'd entered another warren of hallways and cubicles, which ended in a short corridor lined on one side with a rectangular wooden bin. The bin was filled with what appeared to be violin strings, wrapped together in bundles that reminded Hailey of floral bouquets, without the petals.

"A project some of the students are working on," Gregory mentioned, as he led them by the bin. "Various strings from all over the world, donated by various universities and violin factories. The students are practicing and testing stringing techniques in a workshop on the third floor and using some fairly sophisticated sound meters to measure tone and frequency."

Hailey had learned more about tone and frequency over the past few days than she would have admitted to the dean. Instead she watched as Gregory came to a sudden stop in front of a closed, heavy-looking door halfway down the corridor. The door wasn't made of wood like the rest of the doors they'd seen in the building; it was lined in some sort of metal and appeared to be sealed on all sides. Gregory smiled at them, then reached for the skeleton key hanging around his neck.

The key flashed as he stuck it into the lock on the door. There was a loud metallic click, and then the door was open. Hailey felt the huff of cool dry air as she followed the rest of the group inside. She had been in enough biosafety labs to recognize reverse air compression—she guessed that the room was temperature controlled as well. No doubt, this was a place where valuable papers were kept.

As Gregory, Barrett, and Adrian spread out into the room, Hailey hung back with Nick and took it all in. The room was mostly stark, almost like a vault; the walls were lined in the same metal as the door, and the ceiling was crisscrossed by fluorescent tubes. There were low tables taking up much of the center of the room, with folding chairs set up around them. The back wall was lined with metal cabinets the shape and height of high school lockers. There were notations on each cabinet—but it wasn't any sort of filing system Hailey recognized.

Gregory seemed to know exactly where he was going. He headed straight for one of the cabinets, and when he got there, Hailey noticed for the first time that there was a combination lock halfway up the cabinet door. Gregory hunched over to work the lock, turning the wheel at the center six times in opposite directions. As he worked the lock, he spoke over his shoulder.

"So tell me, Angela, whatever happened to that cellist you were dating when we last spoke—Harold? Hoover?—I don't see a ring, but nowadays, you know, that doesn't mean—"

"We went our separate ways years ago. People like us, Gregory—it's enough to be married to our work."

Gregory got the cabinet open, then reached inside and rummaged through a long shelf filled with plastic-covered documents. He was mumbling to himself as he fingered through the covers, and Hailey had the distinct impression he was searching for some sort of flirtatious response to Barrett's statement—but lost his train of thought when he found what he was looking for—a large file near the back of the shelf.

He used both hands to retrieve the file, then turned and headed for one of the tables in the center of the room. The file hit the surface with a thud. It was at least fifty pages thick, and before Gregory opened it, he once again donned his silk gloves, which he'd brought with him in one of his corduroy pockets.

"These are all Mozart?" Hailey asked, shocked at the thickness of the file.

Gregory glanced at her, with a look on his face that seemed to imply he was noticing her presence for the first time. Then his eyes drifted to Nick and Adrian.

"Part of a collection that was donated by the Carver family, of East London, when their daughter attended the Royal Academy back in the late '90s," he said, as he began sifting through the open file, page by page. "Quite a talented musician—although for a collection like this, we would have welcomed her even if she could only hit the low notes on a plastic kazoo. Although we are all aware that Mozart was one of the most prolific composers—even with such a short life, his known works encompass over six hundred pieces—and that doesn't include partial works, rough drafts, fragments—"

He suddenly paused, his gloved fingers touching a page near the center of the large open file.

"Fragments," he repeated, tapping the page. "This sheaf contains our uncategorized, unfiled pieces—what we call fragments—many of which we can't identify, others we simply haven't been able to date or connect with larger, finished works. But this . . .'"

He carefully unhooked the page from the file and held it up. Clearly, Hailey could see that there was a tear down the middle—and that the page was filled with musical bars, beginning right at the tear.

Barrett quickly retrieved their folio from Adrian's saddle bag and opened it up to the last, torn page. She put it close to the one Gregory was holding—and it was instantly clear they had a match.

"I see," Gregory said. "Without the other half it had just seemed like notes from an unfinished draft. Maybe for piano, or some sort of opera in progress."

He took the page from Barrett, set them both down on the table, and pushed them close together. The pages connected almost perfectly, musical bars drifting from one side to the other and linking up. Barrett leaned closer, reading the bars with her eyes.

Hailey watched her and realized she was reading the music, letting it play in her head. Barrett had been a concert pianist; obviously, her skills allowed her to *hear* the bars, as if they were being played.

"The first part of the manuscript—when I read the music in my office, it sounded fine, if a little trivial for Mozart. A play on his more famous works. But this—this is different. These notes, connected, sound—strange. Like nothing I've ever played or heard before. Certainly not from Mozart."

Gregory moved next to her and stared down at the now connected page as well. He nodded. "It's ugly, even. Disjointed."

Hailey moved so she could see the notes as well. They meant nothing to her on their own, but she knew they contained instructions—like a code of sorts, or a recipe—but not for any language she understood. She knew that in the past, spies had hidden messages in music; famously, during World War II, pianists were employed to hide messages in simple compositions that could be "read" by other pianists and translated into sentences. But this seemed—different.

She didn't know a lot about Mozart, but what she did know was that as a composer, he was known as a storyteller. He told stories through notes, through melody, through harmony.

She blinked, looked at the notes again, then blinked again. She couldn't hear what Barrett heard, but she could see the rise and fall of the bars, the strange way the notes seemed to climb upward and downward, sometimes tightly together, sometimes apart. And she realized—she was seeing *something*.

She looked up at Nick, who was regarding her quietly. Then she cleared her throat.

"Can we borrow this?" she asked.

Gregory looked at her like she'd thrown something at his head. "Absolutely not," he sputtered. Then he glanced at Barrett. "You know that's impossible, Angela. There's a protocol—"

"What about a photo?" Hailey tried, reaching into her pocket for her phone.

Gregory quickly took the page in his gloved hand and put it back in the sheaf, shutting the folder.

"Out of the question. There's paperwork that needs to be filled out. As I said, there's a protocol for something like this—"

"Gregory," Angela tried, but the dean was shaking his head.

"If I could, I would. You know that, Angela. But like you said, our marriage is to our work—no matter where our hearts may be."

He turned on his heels, headed back to the cabinet, and placed the file back on the shelf. Before any of them could protest, the cabinet door clinked shut, and Gregory gave the combination lock a spin.

"But not to worry; I'll make the necessary calls and we can

begin that paperwork. Shouldn't take more than a few days. In the interim"—he looked at Barrett, as he stepped away from the cabinet and started to lead them toward the door—"perhaps you and I could schedule a lunch, to go over this, and old times?"

Hailey started forward, about to push the issue—but then she felt Nick's hand on her shoulder. His eyes told her to just follow along.

A few minutes later they were back out on the sidewalk in front of the building, as Gregory headed up the spiral staircase toward his office. Adrian and Barrett were both looking at Hailey, waiting for her to explain what she had seen in the completed folio—but she was still looking at Nick, who had a strangely confident expression on his face. With a nod of his head, he asked her to follow— and started around the side of the building. She glanced at Adrian and Barrett, then shrugged—and the three of them took off after Nick, wondering where the hell he was taking them.

CHAPTER TWENTY-THREE

Gregory Cromwell, dean of the Royal Academy of Music, crossed his corduroy covered legs beneath his desk as he leaned back against his cherrywood chair, surveyed his narrow office, and thought happily about how wonderful his morning had gone so far. Imagine—Angela Barrett back in his life after so many years. Coming here, to his school, his domain, asking—nay, *begging*—for his help. Angela Barrett, who had rebuffed him countless times during their university years, but she of the amazing fingers—only passable against ivory piano keys, but electrifying the few times he'd felt them on his arm, or against his hand, even if only for a fleeting shake, or a passing bit of contact. Back then, their relationship had never advanced beyond friendship—but, he wondered, was this morning's visit the beginning of something new?

Certainly, even without the promise of a potential rekindling—or kindling—of something amorous, the morning's visit filled him with excitement. Imagine—not just Angela Barrett returning to his life, but in her hands—an original Mozart folio, even partially damaged, that had never been seen before? It almost made the presence of her strange coterie of friends palatable—even the obnoxious young woman who had asked to borrow a 250-year-old manuscript. Then, of course, there was the strange American with the hair, and the thug in denim—but the folio, that was certainly something. If Gregory played his cards right, not only could he end up with Angela Barrett, but perhaps a new manuscript for the Royal Academy's collection.

He was still grinning to himself at the thought, when the phone on his desk began braying at him; he half expected to hear Barrett's wonderful voice again as he answered on the second ring, ready to schedule that lunch he'd suggested. But instead, it was only the front desk receptionist. It took Gregory a moment to decipher the old woman's Liverpudlian accent—even though she'd been with the school since he himself was a student, she hadn't yet mastered "proper" pronunciation—but eventually he got the gist. Apparently there was a young journalist in the lobby who claimed she had an appointment to interview him for an article on the upcoming Royal Academy performance season. Gregory didn't remember making any such appointment, but then again, it was certainly possible it had gotten lost—in translation—between reception and his schedule. How the Beatles had ever risen to stardom chewing up the King's English was an absolute mystery.

"Poor lass says she really canna reschedule, as she's on a deadline," the receptionist cawed on the other end of the line. "And that they want your profile to be front an' center."

Gregory sighed dramatically. But inside, he was intrigued. Front and center sounded good, even in Liverpool. His morning was only getting better. Barrett's request, which he'd intended, after a fashion—and a lunch or two—to pass along to the archives department, would have to wait.

"Send her along."

He went to work straightening his collar and slicking down his hair, as he passed the moments before there was a quiet knock on the door to his office.

"It's open."

The woman who came through was much as Gregory might have expected. Average height, dressed somewhat frumpy in a gray dress with square shoulders, with her hair in a ponytail and a pair of glasses that seemed thick enough to double as telescopic lenses. Not exactly heavy, but not skinny, either. Certainly, she was no Angela Barrett.

"Thank you so much for seeing me, Dean Cromwell. I promise not to take much of your time."

Gregory detected the hint of a Spanish accent—perhaps Catalonian, maybe Barcelona.

The woman shut the door behind her, then stepped farther into the office. "You know how the magazines can get with their deadlines."

She paused, looking around the room. Taking in the awards, and the instruments.

"Happy to help," he started.

But she continued talking, her words coming fast. "I saw you in the lobby earlier, but you seemed busy—escorting some friends on a tour, I assumed?"

She glanced at him, then continued looking around—her eyes settling on the magnificent harp in the corner of his office. He watched her, a bit confused—she didn't sound like any journalist who had ever interviewed him before. Her tone was almost too—convivial. Like she was talking to an old friend. He tried to steer the conversation along.

"Shall we get started—"

"The woman—she was British, a colleague, I assume?—but the other three seemed quite out of place."

Suddenly she had turned away from the harp and was looking right at him. And somehow, her eyes no longer seemed quite as average or innocent or wide, and her cheeks, though full, had gone a cold, porcelain color that made them seem tighter.

He swallowed. "Which magazine did you say you were from?"

"I didn't. The three others, they were American, correct? The man with the hair—I didn't catch his name. But the other two—Hailey and Nick?"

Gregory stared at her. She smiled, but there was nothing convivial in the curve of her lips.

"What were they looking for, Dean Cromwell?"

He coughed. "Who are you?" he sputtered. He was still in his chair but considered standing, or reaching for his phone. But then he shook his head. This woman—she wasn't something to worry about. She was just—nosy. "I think it would be best if we rescheduled."

The woman sighed and slowly crossed to the harp. Her hand was out, and then she was touching one of the long, glistening strings.

"Excuse me, that's a museum piece."

"Then it should be in a museum, shouldn't it? Let's try again, Dean Cromwell. What were the Americans looking for?"

He realized her accent had gotten heavier. He had an ear for accents—and hers was definitely Catalonian, Barcelona—but not from the upper castes, the rich areas of Sarrià and Pedralbes. This was the tone of someone from the streets. A stark contrast to her average, soft, appearance.

"I'm sorry," he said quietly. "But I think you should leave."

The woman didn't move. Her hand still rested on the harp string, and Gregory shifted uncomfortably in his chair. Now he definitely wanted to reach for his phone, but something was stopping him. This woman—she was asking about Angela's friends, what they wanted at the Royal Academy. Gregory had pretty much ignored their presence—he'd been so focused on Angela—but why was this woman so interested? Obviously, she didn't work for any music magazine. Was she some sort of law enforcement? Were the Americans wanted for something? Was the Mozart folio they'd shown him stolen from somewhere? Had they been casing his own collection?

As he pondered these thoughts, his hand absent-mindedly moved to the rope necklace he still wore—he hadn't yet returned the key to his desk. The metal object had slipped under the collar of his shirt, and he pulled it free. It felt strangely heavy in his fingers, and he glanced down—but instead of the shiny skeleton key, he was suddenly looking at something more rounded—still metal, but not key shaped at all. It was a medallion, made mostly of brass, with an image in the center. With a start, he recognized the image:

Benjamin Franklin.

"What the hell?" he mumbled.

But even as his words tumbled out, he was interrupted by a flash of motion. He looked up from the medallion just in time to see the woman coming around his desk, moving almost impossibly fast. He pushed back in his chair while reaching for his phone, but he was too slow. Before he could touch the receiver, she was behind him, and suddenly he felt something cold and metal and tight against the skin of his neck. He gasped, trying to leap up, but she was strong—way too strong—and she slammed him back down into his chair, then twisted hard, and the metal around his neck grew tighter, tighter, tighter.

His mouth opened but no sound came out. His chest heaved—but no air reached his lungs. He felt the metal around his neck digging into his skin—and suddenly something warm and wet flowed down the front of his chest. He reached up with both hands, grasping at the metal. With a burst of exertion he got one finger between the metal and his throat—but then the woman yanked back, and suddenly blood sprayed down Gregory's wrist, and he watched the tip of his finger tumble down his chest and land on his corduroy-covered lap.

For a brief second, the woman lightened her grip, and the metal at his neck loosened just enough for him to get a single sob of wonderful air. His chest heaved, his eyes were wild. The woman leaned close to his ear.

"I'll ask you one more time. What were they looking for?"

He sputtered and coughed, blood trickling from the corners of his lips. He knew, instantly, that he was going to tell her anything and everything she wanted to know. And a part of him knew, with equal certainty, that it wouldn't make any difference.

Approximately eight minutes later, La Nadie moved gingerly back to the center of the narrow office of the vice dean of the Royal Academy of Music, and surveyed the body that was now slumped forward over the desk near the rear of the room. The poor man looked almost peaceful—if not for the rapidly growing pool of blood extending out around his lifeless head, from the long gash that ran around the skin of his neck. The entire affair had taken a bit longer than La Nadie had expected—but well within the parameters of wet work such as this. *Wet work*, she repeated to herself, as she watched the blood ripple across the wooden surface, then run down the desk's legs toward the carpet. The term had always intrigued her. A Russian euphemism that traced back to criminal syndicates operating in the early nineteenth century, to describe burglaries that had involved the spilling of blood. The Russians—always so poetic, even when it came to murder.

For herself, La Nadie had never had any problem with the blood, probably because she had been initiated into this line of work at such a young age. Abandoned by her birth parents at the age of four in the slums of Can Peguera—an area derogatorily known as the "casas baratas"—or "cheap houses"—region of Barcelona—she had been taken in by the same sort of criminal syndicates that might have coined Russian poetry had they not been so busy mugging tourists and murdering competitors on the street corners of El Raval. By the time she was in her teens, she'd gained quite a reputation among the lowlifes and dangerous people of her neighborhood, not just for her skills as a thief, although she'd been an extremely talented pickpocket. Or her ability to fight, which had surprised everyone around her. It had always been her ability to blend in that had ironically turned heads; she was a shadow in an already dark street corner, beige in an already beige room. Noticed, for being unnoticed. And it was this quality, more than any other, that had attracted the Terra Lliure—the Catalonian nationalist terrorist group that had notoriously carried out hundreds of bombings, murders, and assassinations since its inception in the late 1970s up until its supposed disbanding in the mid-1990s. But as is often the case, the fact that the Terra Lliure had receded from the newspapers by the turn of the millennium didn't mean they had actually disappeared—just that they had chosen the safety of shadows, of beige upon beige. Instead of political violence, the terrorist group had pivoted to professional violence—murder for hire, assassinations for dollars, rubles, Bitcoin, what have you.

The TL had taken a special interest in the little nobody girl from the streets and had continued her training. By the age of sixteen she had grown into one of the most feared hired assassins in the underworld, contracted out all over Europe and the Americas.

Eventually, she had grown tired of the corporate life and had struck out on her own. The TL had understandably taken umbrage at her leaving—arguing that they had invested mightily in her training—but she had successfully made her case for freedom by leaving a half dozen of the organization's upper management in various stages of dismemberment.

Over the past decade, she had plied her trade, becoming increasingly choosier about the missions she was willing to take on. She no longer needed money—she had accounts all over the world containing millions she would never spend—but she truly enjoyed her work when it suited her. She was especially attracted to projects that challenged her.

That was what had drawn her to the Family, and the current mission; with the Family's immense resources, La Nadie would have expected that her own skill set would only have been redundant. That their own coterie of talent—exceptional as their operatives had been—would have been able to handle the complications unfolding in front of them. But even so early into the field, La Nadie had found the situation more complex than she could have imagined.

She took a last look around the office, pleased with her own work. No doubt, the woman at the reception desk would describe to the police the frumpy journalist who had entered Gregory's office—but nobody with her description would come up in any law enforcement databank. And any cameras fitted with facial recognition software that had happened to capture her on her way to the Royal Academy would find nothing of note. Her face was not in any database nor reproduced on any form of ID.

Ironically, it was facial recognition software that had brought her to this place; not via her own sources, but by means of the FBI—the federal agent Zack Lindwell, whom her predecessor had been following and left, thankfully, alive in the Square in Philadelphia. Lindwell had been following Hailey and Nick on his own. An agent in the Art Crimes Division, he appeared to have taken a personal interest in the pair of fugitives, marking them in a private APB that he'd circulated to colleagues around the globe. As far as La Nadie could tell, Lindwell had intercepted the APB when it had discovered the fugitives in London, and explained to his own bosses that his interest was part of a larger investigation—that arresting Hailey and Nick or alerting local police would foil a much more important collar. Whether Lindwell believed the fugitives might lead him to the Gardner paintings or he was following the fugitives for personal reasons made no difference. He had become a convenient, if unknowing, aid to La Nadie's own mission, and she would continue using him as long as he remained so.

Similarly, it appeared that for the moment, Hailey and Nick and the third American—Adrian—were doing her work for her as well. They'd apparently found something that they believed was connected to what the Family was seeking—a folio by Mozart!—and were working on piecing together what it might mean. The poor, still-bleeding dean hadn't known what that might mean—but it didn't matter. It was enough to know that the three of them were moving forward; it made La Nadie's own next steps clear. She needed only to let them continue—until they had either found what they were searching for or hit a dead end. In either case, she would be ready to step in. No doubt she would already be nearby. In the shadows, beige upon beige.

Satisfied with the office and the body slumped over the desk, she turned toward the door. It wasn't until she'd started for the knob that she realized she was still holding the harp string in her right hand, coiled partially around her palm, the glistening metal dripping, wet.

She let her fingers relax, and the string fell to the floor, where it uncoiled, the long metal whipping out like the tail of a snake, painting the carpet with a flicker of bright red blood.

Then she reached for the knob and headed back out toward the revolving stairwell, and the lobby beyond.

CHAPTER TWENTY-FOUR

By the time Hailey had caught up to Nick in an alley that ran along the rear of the building, he had already picked the lock on what looked like a maintenance entrance and was holding the door open for her, waving a hand to rush her along. Adrian and Barrett were two steps behind, but both gave pause before following Hailey inside. Adrian gave Nick a suspicious look, while Barrett just seemed confused; maybe the British professor had assumed they'd gone as far as they could with the folio and would have to wait for her friend at the Royal Academy to turn whatever wheels he was willing to turn. But it appeared Nick had other plans.

"We have to move fast," he said, grabbing Adrian by the sleeve and yanking him through the doorway after Hailey. "Hard-and-fast rule of opportunistic heists—you go quick, or you get caught."

"Opportunistic heists?" Adrian sputtered.

But he didn't resist, and Barrett followed after him. Nick shut the door and started forward, passing Hailey to take the lead down a long hallway that ended at a service elevator. Hailey fought the urge to question Nick as he hit the elevator button, then ushered them all inside when the doors opened. Breaking through a maintenance door on the side of the building was one thing; but as far as she could tell, the lock on the archive room would take work, probably tools—and no doubt there was some sort of alarm system involved if you didn't use the correct key. But Nick seemed so confident—and frankly, it was exciting to see him take the lead.

"Usually heists involve weeks of planning," he continued, as the elevator rumbled downward. "Sometimes months. I planned one bank job for fourteen months, actually. Cased the joint so thoroughly I knew the guards by name, where they went for lunch, what their favorite foods were. I knew their bathroom routines and the music they listened to on their iPhones."

"Didn't you just get out of prison?" Adrian asked.

"Not the point," Nick said. "Usually, planning keeps you safe. But when there's no time to plan—you go in fast, you get out fast."

The elevator doors slid open, and they were back on the museum floor of the building. Nick raced forward, and Hailey rushed to keep up. They passed the various exhibits and instruments, then were in the last hallway, moving fast by the bin full of violin strings. Just before they reached the metal-plated door to the archive room, Nick pulled to a stop, reached into the bin, and removed one of the wiry violin strings. It was particularly thick and strong looking, and he tested its strength with both hands.

"You going to use that to pick the lock?" Hailey asked. "I'm guessing it will set off some sort of alarm."

Nick smiled and shook his head.

"This is a warded deadbolt lock, would be tough to pick with a violin string, no matter how strong it was. Luckily, I've got this."

He reached into his pocket and withdrew Gregory's skeleton key, still hanging from the necklace. Hailey's eyes rounded.

"Opportunity," Nick said. Then he put the key into the lock and gave it a good twist.

The door whiffed open with the burst of cool, dry air, and they were inside, making a beeline for the cabinet at the back of the room. Now Nick had the violin string out. Making it as straight as possible, he slid it into a crevice at the edge of the cabinet door, parallel to the circular combination lock.

"When the dean opened this door, I noticed some wiring along the side panel; my guess is, there's a signal sent to a security booth somewhere each time the cabinet is opened, a sort of fail-safe in case someone gets in here for an unscheduled visit. The violin string should be able to override the signal break and buy us some time."

Hailey nodded, and she saw that Barrett, who was hanging back toward the center of the room, at least looked impressed, if not thrilled to have followed them where they obviously weren't supposed to be. But Adrian had his arms crossed.

"You still have that combination lock to deal with."

Nick glanced at Hailey. "You want to enter the combo, or should I?"

Adrian stared at both of them.

Hailey shrugged. "Either way, but you're closer."

Nick did the spinning: six numbers, which Hailey had memorized, without even meaning to, while Gregory had turned the wheel. Years as a card counter meant memorizing numbers was second nature to her. But Nick had obviously been thinking ahead.

There was the metallic click, and then Nick had the cabinet door open. It took less than a minute for Hailey to find the correct file. Rather than taking the entire sheaf, she quickly worked her way to the second half of the Mozart folio, carefully withdrew it from the cabinet, and headed for one of the tables in the center of the room.

Barrett was watching her, as she placed it on the table, then withdrew their original folio from Adrian's saddle bag. As she flipped to the last page and placed the two torn sides together, Barrett cleared her throat.

"I'm not sure where this gets us," Barrett said. "What is it you're seeing, dear? Some sort of code?"

Hailey ran her eyes over the finished musical bars, again and again.

"Not exactly," she finally said. Then she looked up at Barrett. "This isn't just a performing arts school, right? It's also focused on the technical aspects of music? Sound engineering, that sort of thing?"

"Of course," Barrett said. "There's an entire department focused on engineering, with labs on the third and fourth floors. I hated those floors; I was never wonderful with equations and gadgets. I just wanted to play."

"Even so," Hailey said. "Can you still find your way around those labs?"

Barrett nodded.

Hailey turned to Adrian and Nick. "I'll go with Professor Barrett, and hopefully we can find what I'm looking for. You two— we'll need a place to work."

"What sort of place?" Adrian asked. "A music lab?"

Hailey shook her head. "More like a practice room. Anywhere there's a piano."

"You're going to play this?" Nick asked.

"No," Hailey said, and nodded toward Barrett. "She is."

———

A short elevator ride, three different labs, and a brief search of an equipment closet, with the help of a heavily tattooed, long-haired third-year music theory student who simply assumed, after some leading statements, that Barrett was a professor of classical piano in need of assistance, and Hailey had found what she was looking for. The device was heavier than Hailey had expected, about the size of a small television, but between herself and Barrett, they were able to get it back to the elevator and down to the second floor of the building, where Nick and Adrian had succeeded in their own mission.

They pushed through a pair of doors and then between two heavy curtains into a rectangular room with hexagonal sound-proofing along all four walls, and three rows of cushioned seats leading down to an elevated stage containing a shiny grand piano. Hailey felt her pulse begin to rise. Adrian had already placed the folio in the built-in music stand above the open keys, and Nick was sitting at the bench, pretending to finger the notes, though it was clear he couldn't read music to save his life.

Pushing the device the last few yards to the edge of the stage, Hailey tilted her head toward Nick, who got the message—he moved to help her lift the heavy bit of electronics, while Barrett took his place before the music stand. The British professor's face showed a mixture of emotions—awe that she was really about to play something written by Mozart, by hand, hundreds of years ago and unseen until now, and dismay, because she must have also been thinking that this was all completely insane—and, no doubt, a wild goose chase.

"What do you hope to hear?" Adrian asked, as if reading Barrett's mind.

Hailey found the cord at the back of the device and searched the wall for an outlet. Once she'd plugged it in, the device whirred to life. Most of the front of the boxy machine was taken up by a screen, which was crisscrossed with green lines like some sort of digital graphing paper. Beneath the screen were a series of knobs and levers, sporting bright red digital numbers.

She looked up from the machine and noticed that everyone else in the room was looking at her.

"I've been thinking about this since we found the folio in the

Hellfire Club," she said, wiping dust from the screen on the device. "Benjamin Franklin and Mozart—an odd pairing, to be sure—came into contact in Paris, and they shared an interest in Freemasonry and alchemy."

Barrett's eyes narrowed a bit—no doubt, she'd put enough pieces together to know that this all revolved around alchemy, something she couldn't have considered much more than myth—but she'd come this far with them, and there was no reason for her to turn back now.

"Mozart was known to be 'touched by God'—a musical genius, a prodigy who could create whole symphonies in his head and put them down on paper. And we also know Franklin had been working with Paul Revere in trying to come up with a mathematically perfect musical tone that could affect materials at a base level; it's not a stretch to believe that Franklin might have enlisted Mozart in that effort."

"Revere made bells," Adrian said. "You don't need Mozart to write for bells."

"Revere made bells," Hailey repeated. "But Franklin made the armonica. And we already know that Revere's bells weren't powerful enough—Revere's experiment with the bells showed that indeed the science was possible, but in the end the bells were a failure. If Franklin had given up on Revere's idea, shifted his research into electricity—his key and his kite—then if there is something embedded in whatever Mozart wrote for Franklin's armonica, it will be more complex than a single tone."

They were still all watching her. Hailey knew she was thinking out loud—playing with the puzzle pieces floating through her thoughts. She turned back to the device and hit a lever beneath the screen. A bright yellow line appeared in the center, vibrating slightly with every noise in the room, however slight.

"This device is a calibrated oscilloscope. Effectively, it draws sound."

"What?" Nick asked.

"It takes sound," Hailey said, "and turns it into two-dimensional images by measuring the length and depth of sound waves. Not just notes, or harmony, but the energy behind the waves themselves. It can be tuned to focus on a single source—to edit out background noise and feedback—and essentially turn any form of sound into a two-dimensional picture."

As she was speaking, the yellow line was jumping up and down, rising higher along with her pitch and longer with the depths of each of her syllables.

"Pretty cool," Nick said.

"If you're implying that Mozart might have hidden a visual message in this composition to be read by some machine that wouldn't exist for hundreds of years—" Adrian started, but it was Barrett who interrupted him, not Hailey.

"The device is modern," she said. "But the concept goes back a very long time. The idea that sound can paint pictures goes back to at least the late seventeenth century—the theory originated, in fact, because of a psychiatric condition uncovered by the Oxford philosopher John Locke. He was studying a blind patient who could 'see' the music of a trumpet. To the blind man, certain notes produced corresponding colors and shapes in his mind. Eventually, the condition became known by the name synesthesia. In those cases, the human mind mimics the oscilloscope—often to very detrimental results. A few patients were known to have even gone mad, unable to control their ability to see sound."

"And you think Mozart might have had this ability—this synesthesia?" Adrian seemed displeased with the notion—or perhaps he was just bothered that Barrett had corrected him.

Barrett shrugged. "He was a unique individual, a once-in-a-millennium talent. There's no telling what he was capable of in his short life." Sitting at the piano, she looked up at Hailey. "If you're right, this music doesn't contain a code or secret message. The music *is* the message."

Hailey nodded. Barrett was smart, and quick. And despite how crazy it all sounded, she still seemed willing to play along.

As Hailey watched, Barrett pulled back her sleeves and stretched her hands out over the keys. Hailey noted that the British professor's fingers were incredibly long and graceful, made for the instrument. Barrett nodded toward the device, and Hailey turned a knob, digitally instructing the machine to focus on the central sound in the practice room.

Barrett's fingers touched the keys and began dancing back and forth to the notes, as her eyes scanned through the centuries-old musical bars. And right from the start, the music was strange; like nothing Hailey had ever heard before. Rising up, then jerking sideways, deep, lower half notes then staccato bridges; minor chords twisting together into knots, only to rush forward into open harmonies that rose and fell almost at random. Hailey could feel the music in the pit of her stomach, could almost taste the heavier notes on her tongue, and for a moment it was like her whole body was being pulled in too many directions at once—

"Christ."

She looked over and saw that Adrian had moved directly in front of the oscilloscope's screen, and was bending forward, his eyes wide. Hailey saw—the screen was now full of intersecting yellow lines, arching out at wild angles, coming together and then ripping apart. Barrett was playing faster, now, her fingers frantic against the keys, her brow furrowed and beads of sweat dotting her forehead. She was completely lost in the strange music, playing as if she was in the center of a vast concert hall—but Adrian, Nick, and now Hailey were no longer paying any attention to her because they were all staring at that damn screen. Because the image that was flashing across the glass was no longer chaotic, or random, or wild—it was—

"Christ," Hailey repeated.

The image was instantly recognizable. Hailey watched as Adrian withdrew his cell phone and took a picture of what they were seeing. Nick moved closer to Hailey, leaning close.

"Is this what I think it is?" he whispered.

"It can't be," Adrian responded, also a whisper.

Hailey blinked—but the image was still there, clear as anything she had ever seen, clear and unmistakable—

—and *impossible.*

CHAPTER TWENTY-FIVE

Curved gray walls flashed by on the other side of the pane of glass to Hailey's left, a blur that seemed almost hypersonic, although in the logical portion of her brain she knew it was more like 185 mph, while the low rumble of the train's powerful engines moved through the vinyl seat beneath her. The seat wasn't as comfortable as it had looked in the brochure; but she shared an armrest with Nick, so she didn't really care. He had chosen the aisle, because it allowed him to keep a roving eye on the other passengers. They were near the front of the economy cabin, which stretched twenty rows behind them. Two hours into the journey, he hadn't spotted anyone who didn't look like a tourist—other than Adrian, hair akimbo and eyes wild from what they'd seen on the oscilloscope, seated directly across from Nick on the other side of a small plastic-topped table.

Hailey trembled and took a break from staring at the image captured on Adrian's phone, which was now sitting on the table between the three of them. Around her, the train cabin was modern and surprisingly warm. The interiors had been done up in a dull brown color, the lighting fluorescent but pleasingly soft. The windows were large, running in rectangular strips down either side, and though there was currently nothing to see but tunnel—or, more accurately, Chunnel—the continuous flash of motion lulled her into a strange sense of calm. She had thought that being trapped inside a metal cylinder moving at intense speeds through a series of tubes sunk three hundred feet below the English Channel would have been terrifying. But in truth she was more amazed than afraid by the feat of architectural engineering that had made the Eurostar possible. Above her head to the left, she could see one of the numerous emergency boxes that speckled the train's cabins attached to the wall, sporting a glass fire alarm and a fire ax—but she knew the safety precaution was more for show than anything else; the Chunnel—and Eurostar's state-of-the-art bullet train connecting Folkestone in Kent, England, an hour and a half from London, and Calais, three hours' drive from Paris, but only a short hop by rail—was truly one of engineering's wonders of the world.

As Adrian had put it, on their way to the London Eurostar station, for a thousand years, the Brits and the French had been at each other's throats—and every battle had meant crossing the English Channel—150 miles at its widest points—by whatever means was technologically possible: paddles, sails, steam engines, and eventually turbines. The idea of digging a tunnel between the two countries went back as far as Napoleon; in 1802, the warmongering tyrant had dreamed of an underwater tunnel, sporting immense ventilating chimneys, connecting his armies on either side of the Channel—but his engineers had convinced him that it was beyond their abilities. Eighty years later, the first real attempt at creating an underground crossing was made by a British military officer— Col. Frederick Beaumont, who managed to dig a mile-long tunnel across the Channel before admitting failure.

It took another hundred years for technology to advance to the point where Napoleon's and Beaumont's fantasies could finally become reality. After many starts and stops over the ensuing decades, in June 1988 the governments of France and England, no longer at war, decided to cofinance the endeavor, to the tune of sixteen billion dollars. At the time, it was the most expensive construction project in human history; it took more than six years to complete and employed over fifteen thousand workers—ten of whom died from accidents during the project.

Nearly fifteen minutes into the trip beneath the waters of the Channel, Hailey still felt a palpable sense of awe at what the marriage of a handful of brilliant minds and the sweat of a phalanx of specialized laborers could achieve, driven by a dream that had probably seemed impossible at first. A dream that might have seemed—insane.

She finally let her eyes drift down to Adrian's phone, which was sitting face-up between the three of them on the plastic table-top, the screen lit from within. The photo Adrian had taken in the practice room stared back at her, the glowing yellow lines that had been drawn by the oscilloscope, visually capturing Mozart's musical composition in digital pixels.

Hailey stared for as long as she could, then looked up at Adrian. He was shaking his head, perhaps for the hundredth time since they'd left the Royal Academy of Music. His wild hair and eyes were understandable, as was his expression of disbelief.

Nick, for his part, had obviously come to terms with what they had discovered. He'd been the first to say it out loud, in the back of the taxi to the Eurostar station in London.

"The Eiffel Tower."

Mozart's music had arranged itself into an approximation of the lines and angles of the most famous structure in Europe, perhaps the world. The corrugated iron-beamed tower that was synonymous with the Paris skyline, designed by Gustave Eiffel in the late nineteenth century and debuted at the opening of the 1889 World's Fair. The image captured by the oscilloscope seemed almost a sort of architectural engineering sketch, laying out the supporting structure of the tower, the three main levels, a spine rising up to a sharp peak with what appeared to be an antenna rising out of the top.

Adrian had silenced Nick with a stare in the back of the cab, but Barrett had taken up the cause, arguing with Adrian all the way to the ticket booth in St. Pancras International station. It was clear to her that somehow, Mozart had indeed embedded plans for a structure at least similar in design to the famous Parisian tower in the lost folio; and she had already begun to put together a theory as to how it might have been possible. After they'd bought tickets for the Eurostar—for Adrian, Nick, and Hailey, as Barrett had decided that breaking into the basement archive at the Royal Academy of Music was already a bridge too far, and she had no plans to attach to that indiscretion a Chunnel excursion—Barrett had grabbed a

Paris guidebook off of a gift shop shelf and opened it to a picture of the actual Eiffel Tower.

"There's no question," she'd said. "Though there are copies of the tower all around the world—most famously, Tokyo, Vegas, even China and Romania—this design was first implemented in Paris by Gustave Eiffel. The tallest building in the world for nearly fifty years, until the Chrysler Building in New York surpassed its height in 1930, Eiffel's design was chosen in a fixed engineering competition to inaugurate the Parisian World's Fair."

"Eiffel was born forty years after Benjamin Franklin's death," Adrian had countered. "The Eiffel Tower was built almost a century after both Franklin and Mozart were buried within a year of each other."

Barrett had nodded. But her expression was anything but mollified. "Eiffel couldn't have interacted with either Franklin or Mozart in person, but that didn't mean their paths never crossed."

"The Masonic Lodge," Hailey had said, as they settled into seats outside a station café to wait for their train. "The Maison De Pierre."

Barrett had flashed her eyes at Hailey.

"Exactly. Gustave Eiffel was one of the greatest architects of his era. Beginning in his early twenties, he had begun rising up the ranks of the Freemason organization, and he had spent much time in the De Pierre—which, though lesser known than the Grand Mason Lodge in Paris, was a hotbed of mason activity during the early nineteenth century. There are rumors that Eiffel had even taken his vows to become a third-degree Master Mason in the secret halls beneath the De Pierre, though much of that history is impossible to confirm. Whatever the truth, it's clear that Eiffel could have had access to any secrets Mozart and Franklin might have left hidden, specifically, for someone of Eiffel's skills and status; and where better to leave instructions, such as these, than a lodge dedicated to feats of engineering and architecture? If, as you've been intimating, Benjamin Franklin had used Mozart's genius to hide the plans of something he and Revere had been attempting to build—who better than the greatest architect of the next century to carry those plans forward?"

Adrian had still been reluctant to accept the idea—that Gustave Eiffel's plans for the Eiffel Tower had been originally derived by Benjamin Franklin and hidden in a musical piece by Mozart—as they'd prepared to board the train to Paris. But he'd been willing to agree to share with Barrett any paper that came of whatever they discovered, in exchange for the train tickets—which she'd bought in her own name, in case anyone had followed them to London—and her willingness not to report any of what she'd witnessed to London authorities. Not that any of them had been concerned—Barrett had become a willing ally, as intrigued by the puzzle they were putting together as Hailey herself.

Now deep beneath the English Channel, hurtling toward Paris in a rail-borne rocket, the three of them were all still trying to come to terms with what they had discovered.

"Franklin is in Paris." Hailey was the first to break the silence, trying to simplify it for herself as much as for the others. "He's escaped the British in Philadelphia, and he's confided his plans— whatever new plans he's worked up, after his experiments with Revere had led to a dead end—to Mozart, who's hidden them in a work of music. Then the Revolutionary War ends—why not reveal these plans, before he, Mozart, and Revere are all in the grave? Why hide them for a future engineer and architect to build?"

Adrian seemed reluctant, still, to accept any of this—but he couldn't help himself from answering.

"The same reason we're traveling under false passports, with tickets bought by someone else. The same reason alchemists hid their work behind secret codes and symbols. And even though the Revolutionary War had ended, the late eighteenth century and early nineteenth century was a time of chaos, and extreme flux. The American Revolution led almost directly to the French Revolution; to guillotines and the storming of the Bastille. Flames were engulfing much of the known world."

Nick nodded. He was glancing around the train, still making sure there was nothing out of the ordinary, nothing dangerous around them. Hailey followed his eyes. Across the aisle she saw a family—two kids and a harried mom and dad—huddled around their iPad. Behind them, a French-looking couple holding hands while sharing coffees. Up ahead, at the front of the train car, a young woman leaned against the wall by the lavatory, talking on her cell phone, a to-go container from one of the London station's many cafés cradled in her hands. Hailey turned back toward the table, and the image on Adrian's phone.

"Franklin must have realized that tossing something of immense power into those flames could only end badly; if he'd really succeeded where Paul Revere had failed—if he'd found the secret to the philosopher's stone—he would have kept it hidden away, hoping that sometime in the future, the moment would come when his invention would make the world better, rather than tear it further down."

He'd hidden away the plans for his invention with Mozart's help, in a piece of music, which, in turn, he'd sealed away in the Hellfire Club. Clues had been left behind—perhaps in multiple places—where the right people might be expected to uncover them. Revere's own lab, which had ended up lost to history beneath a river in Canton. And perhaps, the Maison De Pierre, eventually uncovered by Gustav Eiffel, a Master Mason with the technological ability to bring Franklin's invention to life.

Staring at the image on Adrian's phone, Hailey felt her pulse begin to rise. She ran her finger along the screen, following the yellow lines as they rose up the outer edges of the tower, pausing at each of the levels, following the different angles and geometric forms. She paused, as she reached the peak of the tower—where a series of lines from above converged on a single point, slightly below the pointed perch atop the design.

Something about the way the lines came together piqued at her memories; she had seen this before, and it took her only a moment to remember where.

"Revere's bells," she said, thinking out loud. "His alchemical tone—it had worked, but only briefly. The frequency of the sound waves was the right mathematical construct to affect the structure of lead—but not powerful enough to make it permanent. But in Revere's time—in his technological moment—there was no way for him to increase that power, or the output of his bells. But Franklin . . ."

She paused, her words drifting off. Adrian exhaled, finishing for her.

"Franklin endeavored to harness a much more powerful energy than sound."

"Hellfire," Hailey said. She put her finger on the phone's screen, where the lines converged. "Focused together in one place."

"A lightning rod," Nick said. "You're saying the Eiffel Tower was designed to be one big lightning rod."

"But instead of dispersing the electricity into the ground, whatever Franklin had invented somehow focused the energy into here—"

"What's there?" Nick asked.

Adrian shrugged. "Originally, the tower was simply that—a

tower, considered fairly ugly in design. In fact, it was supposed to have been torn down shortly after the World's Fair. But Eiffel had saved the structure by turning it into a "scientific lab" and a radio receiver—where experiments were done in early broadcasting and reception, as well as with wind and weather. There is a science center below the base—and up here, supposedly a small lab. There's also Eiffel's apartment."

"His apartment?" Hailey asked. "For real?"

"The tallest luxury apartment in all of Europe. It was rumored that dignitaries and royals used to sleep over, and Eiffel may have even lived there for a time, though that is in dispute. It's little more than a curiosity now, cordoned off from the tourists."

Hailey tried to imagine it—an apartment a thousand feet above Paris, at the peak of an iron-wrought monolith. But if she was right—if these converging lines on the blueprint Mozart had hidden in a piece of lost music meant what she thought they might— then this perch was more than a place for dignitaries and royals to stare down on the world below. It was, in some way, not a place at all, but a Holy Grail—

Her thoughts were interrupted by a silky voice coming over the train's PA system, announcing that the Eurostar would shortly be exiting the Chunnel and making its way toward Paris.

Hailey took Adrian's phone off the table and placed it in her own purse; she wanted to study it more. Adrian didn't resist—in fact, he looked like he wanted nothing more to do with the image. Hailey knew that eventually he would accept, or at least ignore, his reservations until they'd gotten to the tower and seen for themselves if it was real or not. But he, like the rest of them, had come too far to let preconceptions hold him back.

She touched Nick's arm, signaling for him to let her past into the aisle. "I'm going to splash some water on my face before we reach the station."

Nick started to rise to come with her, but she shook her head— the bathroom was only a few rows away, and she would be quick. She slung her bag over her shoulder and headed down the aisle. Her mind was still whirring—it was hard to believe they were almost in Paris, a city she'd always intended to visit. And even though she had Nick with her, she wasn't going to Paris for romance—but to rewrite history.

She passed the family of four, who didn't even glance at her. The couple, too, ignored her. They were gazing out the window to their left, which was now brightening as the view shifted from the curved walls of the tunnel to the French countryside, a blur of greens and browns beneath an aquamarine sky.

Then Hailey reached the front of the cabin. She sidled past the woman on the phone, who was still picking at her takeout food as she laughed into the receiver, a fork and knife held awkwardly in one hand as she cradled the phone with the other. The woman was chubby and friendly looking, with dark hair pulled back in a conservative little bun. She gave a friendly smile as Hailey went by.

Then Hailey reached the lavatory and pushed her way through the accordion-style door. She secured the lock after she stepped inside. The bathroom was white and surprisingly large for a train, extending a few feet in every direction. The sink was metal and vaguely square, with sloped sides and a faucet like the neck of a giraffe. Hailey leaned over the basin, plugging the bottom and filling the sink slowly with lukewarm water.

She hadn't slept in longer than she could remember, other than a few hours during the flight to London. She'd only changed her clothes once; now she was in slacks and a flowing white shirt, more comfortable than a short skirt—and at least she still had her tennis shoes. The fact that Nick had been able to replenish his denim in London was a small miracle.

She grinned at the thought, and turned off the faucet. Then she carefully lowered her face into the sink, keeping her eyes closed, letting the warmth of the water embrace her skin all the way to her hairline. Finally, she opened her eyes, seeing the metal at the bottom of the basin just inches away, her own reflection swimming in the sheer surface. It was a ritual she had learned as a child, when the world around her seemed so chaotic—the calm and quiet beneath the water reconnected her, made her mind pause and her emotions settle—

And suddenly she saw something through her reflection, a flash of motion behind her.

She jerked her head up, her wet hair flinging back over her shoulders—but before she was totally upright, a frighteningly strong arm wrapped around her neck from behind, yanking her back off her feet. Something sharp and icily cold touched the skin at the side of her neck, right above her carotid artery.

Her eyes went wide as she faced the mirror above the sink. Through the streaks of water from her flinging hair, she could see another face right next to her own.

It was the woman from outside the bathroom, the one who had been eating takeout from a container. But now the woman looked different—not friendly, nor particularly chubby. She wasn't smiling, and though her dark hair was still in a bun, she had discarded the takeout container, and now had only the knife in her right hand. Where the tip of the knife touched Hailey's throat, a tiny trickle of blood ran down her skin.

"I'm going to need the phone, my dear."

The woman's voice had a slight Spanish accent and was

unnervingly pleasant. Hailey realized her bag was still slung over her shoulder, hanging to one side. Terror filled her body—she knew she had no choice, but she also guessed that once she'd handed over the phone, she was as good as dead. This woman was clearly not law enforcement; which meant she worked for the same organization that had already sent two others after them already. This woman, despite her appearance, was no doubt a trained killer.

Hailey trembled, and began moving her hand toward her bag. "Please, you don't have to hurt us. I'll give you what you need."

The woman loosened the knife, letting the point hang a centimeter from Hailey's skin. "Don't beg, it's not becoming. Give me the phone, and then we can discuss what happens next."

Hailey felt the opening of her bag, and slowly moved her hand inside. Her mind was spinning—she only had seconds left. Her fingers touched the cold metal of Adrian's phone—but then the back of her hand felt something else, something both rough and soft at the same time. Realization hit her. Her eyes widened just a tiny bit—but the woman noticed, and the knife touched her skin again.

"Don't do anything foolish," she said, her accent heavier.

But Hailey knew that foolish was her only hope. She drew her hand out of the bag, but instead of her phone, her fingers gripped the folded-up blanket from the safe in Revere's underground lab. There was a vague, sulphury smell as she whipped the blanket forward—and then jammed it into the still full sink.

The second the blanket touched water, an immense hissing filled the room as the dried sulphuric acid from Adrian's *eau de garance* interacted with the H_2O. A plume of acrid smoke shot upward, and Hailey jerked her head back, her mouth and eyes tightly shut.

The plume hit the woman full in the face and she made a screeching sound, then loosened her grip around Hailey's throat.

The knife clattered to the floor. Hailey leapt for the lavatory door, still holding her breath; she knew the air was filled with enough sulfuric gas to incapacitate her assailant for a few minutes at most. She fumbled with the lock—then crashed out into the train cabin, ricocheting off the opposite wall.

People in the closest rows looked up, but Hailey kept moving, careening down the aisle. Nick saw her first, as he rose up out of his seat, followed by Adrian. Nick's eyes widened as he saw her, the rivulet of blood on her neck—and then his gaze moved behind her. Hailey could feel the woman crashing out of the lavatory after her. She glanced back—the woman was rubbing at her eyes, which were bright red and streaming tears. The skin around her lips and eyelids was already swelling up—but her expression didn't show anguish. She looked—intrigued.

Hailey whirled forward again and rushed down the aisle. She took a step past Nick and Adrian, heading right for the emergency panel on the wall of the train. She hit the glass with the heel of her hand.

An alarm blared through the cabin, and shouts and cries reverberated from the passengers on either side. Hailey ignored the noise and reached for the fire ax above the emergency panel. She yanked it free from the wall.

Behind her, she could hear the woman still coming forward. Nick had braced himself for the attack that would surely come, and Adrian was trying to stay out of the way. But Hailey had other plans.

She focused on the closest window. Outside, the green and brown plains had shifted to something more urban; the outskirts of Paris were coming into view. Low, two-story buildings were jammed together beside narrow roads filled with cars. And then, suddenly, darkness—they'd entered a tunnel, the last leg of the trip before the station.

Hailey took a breath, then swung the ax toward the window as hard as she could.

The metal blade hit the center of the glass, and a spiderweb of cracks spread outward from the point of impact. People were screaming now, but Hailey pulled the ax back and swung again, with all her strength.

The pane shattered outward, and Hailey was hit with a blast of warm wind from the interior of the tunnel. There was a terrible screech as the train's emergency brakes clenched tight, and the entire train jerked forward, sending people tumbling from their seats. Nick collided with Adrian, who was clinging to a seatback to keep from cartwheeling down the aisle. Behind Hailey, she heard the woman grunt as she lost balance, still half-blind from the sulphuric gas. Glancing back, Hailey saw she was tangled up in a pair of suitcases that had fallen from the now-open overhead compartment above her head.

Hailey took advantage of the moment and dove forward down the aisle toward the end of the cabin, the ax still in front of her. Nick and Adrian chased after her. Hailey reached the double doors leading out of the train and jammed the ax head between them. Nick added his weight to her own, and together they pried the doors open with a whiff.

There was a three-foot drop to the tunnel floor beside the track. Hailey leapt down, Nick a step after her. Adrian paused in the open doorway, but Hailey grabbed his arm and yanked—and he tumbled out after them. Then the three of them were running alongside the stopped train. The ground was mostly smooth, cement and carved stone, and the curved tunnel wall was only a few feet to Hailey's right. A moment later, they'd reached the front of the train and passed the bullet-shaped control cabin. A pair of wild-eyed engineers stared at them through the windows. Hailey kept going, her legs moving as fast as they could. She could hear Adrian gasping to keep up, Nick pushing the professor along. Behind them, she could hear voices in the tunnel—other people stepping out of the train, maybe the woman along with them—but Hailey didn't look back.

"There," Nick shouted. "Up ahead, on the right."

Hailey saw the door, marked with an emergency light. She still had the ax in her hands, but the door wasn't locked. As she yanked it open, another alarm blared, adding to the cacophony still coming from the stalled train.

The stairwell was cement and metal, winding upward at an intense vertical pitch. Hailey took the steps two at a time, Nick and Adrian huffing behind her. She was no longer thinking, just acting; she could still feel the cold point of that knife against her neck, the warmth of her own blood against her throat.

Three turns in the stairwell, and there was another door. She hit it hard with her shoulder, then was through, and she skidded out onto a tiled floor.

Around her, a brightly lit train station—shops and cafés and ATM machines and information booths, crowds of people surging in every direction—and as she burst through, everything seemed to freeze. All of the people turned to look as the bray of the alarm reverberated against the glass of the storefronts and the shelves lined with everything from croissants to paperback books to electronic equipment. People dove to get out of the way, carving out an empty half circle around them on the tiled floor—

"*Arrêt! Arrêt!*"

And suddenly she saw the gendarmes, coming from every direction, guns out, barrels aimed at Hailey and Nick and Adrian.

Uniformed police mingled with transit security in military gear, handguns next to automatic rifles, all of them pointed directly at them—as the shouting grew louder, more insistent.

"*Arrêt!* Halt!!!"

And Hailey opened her hands, letting the ax fall to the floor with a clatter. Then the closest officers were rushing toward her, guns still drawn, and she saw the flash of handcuffs, and knew, finally, for the first moment since all of this had started—it was finally time to stop running.

CHAPTER TWENTY-SIX

*W*hite upon white upon white.

The sand flashed like ground diamonds beneath Athena's bare feet, as she strolled along the pristine, torturously perfect beach that circled her family's private island. To her right, high, man-made dunes undulated beneath the tropical gusts of wind coming off the Mediterranean, while to her left, the crystal-clear water lapped at the floating dock she had just stepped off, where her leather-lined tender still bounced, tethered by a gold embossed rope to a boathook made of perfectly transparent glass.

In the distance, she could still make out the shape of the *Kratos*, where it was anchored just beyond the shallow reef that surrounded much of the island's southern side. Her father's engineers had spent years negotiating with the Greek government to tear out the annoying coral and build a proper harbor for the 560 foot yacht, so far to no avail. Unfortunately, Athena knew that her father wouldn't likely live long enough to see the grand deck plans he'd had drawn up come to fruition—but she was equally certain that she would one day walk down a crystalline plank to this diamond white beach, rather than endure the short ride on her tender.

That was how it had always worked in her Family—one generation handing off dreams to the next. For generations, the Family's wealth and power—and weblike tendrils—had grown, spiraling outward from this island where Athena now stood—an aptly named, ancient volcanic deposit. And when she closed her eyes, she could almost see those gossamer tendrils connecting her to a network that spanned continents, spanned much of the known world.

Arachne, as the island had been known for more than two thousand years, was the seat of the Family—its heart, its soul—but the Family's power lived in those tendrils. In cities all over the world, the Family's tens of thousands of employees went about their business. Each individual connected to the next, but none ever having any conception of the whole.

London, Berlin, Paris, New York—offices with indistinct names, United Central Bank and Trust; Umbrella Insurance Co.; Republic of Actuarial Sciences—and on and on and on. Offices filled with men and women in suits and ties, sporting laptop computers and leather loafers, drawing salaries and benefits. Maybe some of them knew they were working for a conglomerate with a Greek charter, perhaps a few even understood the charter was owned by a shipping heir worth billions. And a few—a dozen at most—knew of Arachne, the 240-acre island in the Mediterranean, where the scion of the Greek shipping family convalesced—neither asleep nor awake, but still breathing. And they assumed the company he owned was run by a board of faceless, nameless pencil pushers, gray-haired men who met in places like Geneva and Munich to draft company-wide accounting ledgers and emails, parroting earning reports and annual updates, the mind-numbing dialogue of any modern corporate behemoth.

Very few knew anything about Athena.

As a child, she had been beyond reclusive. She had attended the finest boarding schools in Switzerland and France, but had stayed out of the press, had avoided the other socialites and scions of the wealthy, the social entanglements that had felled many before her. In contrast, her brother—Constantine—had made a name for himself in the clubs and brothels all over Europe and Asia. He'd even been arrested twice: once in a sex club in Prague, and then a drug den in Amsterdam. On both occasions he had been sent back to Arachne for treatment, to little avail.

Athena sighed, as she followed the path that led from the beach to the entrance to the main Family compound set a few dozen yards up the dunes. The path was white, of course, as was the building in front of her. Sleek and modern, stretching two football fields in length, and rising four floors into the cloudless blue sky. The windows on the upper floors were bulbous and round, and were complimented by multiple sets of satellite dishes and receivers, bristling upward like the engaged cilia of an insect. Athena knew that from above, Arachne earned its name: not only the eye-like windows and the satellite dishes but the jagged coastlines, the way the coral twisted out from the center of the island like tortured limbs.

No doubt, the Ancient Greeks who had named the island had felt the same. Although they hadn't had access to helicopters and private jets, in ancient times Arachne had sported a pair of peaks from which assuredly the spider-like form of the terra had been clear. Her father's engineers had struggled mightily to level the cliffs, repurposing the ancient stone to build the modern Family compound. Likewise, they had spent years, and millions of dollars, hollowing out the many basement levels beneath the visible buildings—and the mausoleum-like caverns beneath the basements, which housed the remains of Athena's family going back as far as recorded history.

Thousands of years of urns, burial shrouds, sarcophagi—surrounded by statues, paintings, treasures beyond imagination.

Athena had spent many hours touring the caverns—impressed by a past that could fill numerous history books, but she had always returned to the surface intent on the future—which she believed would make all of those history books pale in comparison.

She shivered as she reached the end of the path and the pair of glass doors at the base of the compound, which opened with a whiff before her shadow had time to play across the panes. Inside, the floor was polished marble, and across the front atrium stood a woman in a white nurse's uniform, head bowed, hands crossed at her waist.

"Good morning, Marissa," Athena said, as she met the woman and led them both toward the elevators at the rear of the atrium. "How is he today?"

"He stirred this morning. I think he could sense you were coming."

Athena nodded, tiredly, at the nurse's kindness. It had been a long journey to Arachne from her yacht, which was still off the coast of the Eastern United States, to her private jet, then the flight halfway around the world. Her plane was a refitted 727 Aerobus, which meant it hadn't needed to stop for refueling, but even so, eleven hours in the air was taxing, no matter how luxurious the interior. A steam shower and a king-size bed were simply different at thirty thousand feet.

But over the past five years, Athena hadn't missed even a single one of her weekly visits to her father. Even now, with everything that was happening—so close to the fruition of her lifelong mission—she couldn't have borne to postpone the trip. Because she knew, deep down, that any one of these visits could be the last.

The elevator opened on another polished marble atrium, a vast and circular room dominated by a single piece of furniture—a large bed, bathed in white sheets, surrounded by machines.

Electronic devices and IV tubes and pumping tanks, screens showing vital signs and metallic whirrs and buzzes humming along with the high-powered ventilation system. There were windows on the curved far wall of the room—but the drapes, more white, were drawn. The only real light in the room came from the ceiling, which was paneled in special halogen strips, to mimic natural light without so much as a wisp of the ultraviolet, the harshness of the Mediterranean sun.

Athena approached the bed softly, her mouth going dry, as it usually did when she was here. Though most of her father's body was hidden beneath the white sheets, she could make out the angles and edges of his dagger-like form. He was mostly bone, now; his skin was bleached and cracked, not by sun but by time. His face, visible above the sheets, was like the cliffs the engineers had torn down. Cheekbones jutted against almost invisible skin, a jaw and forehead that were more skeleton than man.

His eyes were open, but Athena knew that didn't mean anything anymore. Her father hadn't seen anything with those open eyes for quite some time.

There was a stool by her father's head, and Athena quickly crossed to it and lowered herself against the cushion. She found his hand beneath the sheets, gently squeezed the fingers, wishing he could squeeze back.

She wanted to believe he could still feel her, hear her, know her. But the logical portion of her brain knew that this was more for her sake than for his. At ninety-seven, her father was mostly gone from the world—a world that he had nearly conquered. Once, he had been a big bull of a man, who would bounce her on his knee on the bridge of the *Kratos*, or in the cockpit of their plane, and explain to her that one day it would all be hers. Not the plane, or the ship—but all of it, the entire world around and below. The ocean, the earth, the sky.

And in quieter moments, alone on Arachne, he would tell her exactly how it would all be hers. Not through the money the Family had accumulated, nor the power they had accrued through their corporate tendrils. But via the secret the Family had been chasing for over two thousand years.

Every book ever written about alchemy, and alchemists, waxed on about the dangers practitioners of the ancient pseudoscience faced, how they were always in hiding, concocting their secret codes, secret symbols, secret languages. But never did any of these books explain exactly *whom* the alchemists were hiding *from*.

Governments, it was inferred. Churches, or kings, or queens. Powerful people who might have seen alchemy as a threat and wanted it for themselves, or to wipe it from the world. But the truth was, none of these structural, temporal powers had any real knowledge of alchemy, or the alchemists who chased its power. Most of them saw it as myth, or fantasy. But still, the alchemists hid—because beyond the governments, churches, kings, and queens, there was, in fact, someone to hide from. An organization more powerful than the temporal structures combined.

For two thousand years, the alchemists had been hiding from the Family. From Athena, from her father, from his father before. From generation after generation, from the men and women interred deep in the caverns many floors beneath where Athena now sat, who had spent their own lives deciphering the codes and the symbols, chasing the discoveries and the advances—and sometimes silencing the threats that threatened to reach the finish line before them.

It was her father, before the coma had taken him, who had uncovered the threads that had led to Athena's current successes. Her father, who, in the early 1990s, had discovered the connection between a strange, bronze eagle that had once sat atop Napoleon's flag and the progress a Revolutionary technologist—and spy—had made toward inventing the Holy Grail of alchemy, the all-powerful philosopher's stone. Had her father's hired criminals done their jobs correctly, the bronze eagle might have been the gateway, while her father had still had his faculties, to that Holy Grail—but instead, it was now left for Athena to finish what her father had begun.

And she was so close now. She wished she could tell her father about what was happening, even now—how the trail had been picked up in London and followed to Paris—how the eagle had only been the first step, how the Revolutionary technologist had passed the baton to another, even more famous Revolutionary. How despite their momentary setbacks—the loss of Curt in Philadelphia, the fugitives barely escaping La Nadie on the train to Paris but ending up in the hands of the French police—Athena had no doubt they were on the trail to success, after so many years of failure . . .

But instead, she could only squeeze her father's hand beneath the sheets and lean forward to kiss his pale forehead. And maybe, just maybe, she saw his eyelids flutter at her touch.

She wished he could somehow understand that finally, soon, everything he had promised her would come true. The sky, the ocean, the world—it would all be hers.

She rose from the stool and headed back the way she had come.

CHAPTER TWENTY-SEVEN

Zack Lindwell stormed angrily down a hallway that was mostly cement, above, around, and below; oversized cinder blocks rose up on both sides to a curved ceiling that made it seem more like he was entering some sort of aging, underground subway station and not the busiest police station in the city of Paris. The fluorescent panels that crisscrossed the ceiling above him flickered a dull orange as he went, casting shadows that intermingled with the steady stream of officers and various lower-level law enforcement personnel that brushed by in both directions, some towing handcuffed prisoners while others pushed dollies loaded with paperwork—the real lifeblood of any police station, even deep into the digital age. Zack knew as many of the faceless, windowless doors he passed were dedicated to the mountains of files, evidentiary documents, and never-ending photocopies of the same as they were to holding cells.

Which possibly explained the terrible mood of the two gendarmes who were presently escorting him down the busy hallway, using their similarly stocky bodies to prod him forward as they went, like tugboats pushing a cargo ship through a narrow channel. No doubt, the incident on the Eurostar that had shut down an entire section of Gare du Nord was going to have the officers drowning in paperwork. And it certainly didn't help that the three captured suspects involved in the fracas were American, or that two of the captives were wanted for questioning by the police department in Boston for a series of crimes that included multiple homicides.

Although the French police had so far kept the situation out of the press, there was no doubt that very soon this was going to be a departmental and international hot potato that no harried gendarme would want to deal with, and certainly not before lunch. But Zack's own mood had nothing to do with the complexity of the situation or any notion of paperwork. It had entirely to do with the phone call he had received not twenty minutes earlier, from his own superiors—a call he had expected to be difficult, but one that had arrived with a ferocity that even the present circumstances couldn't explain.

Zack's past forty hours had been nothing short of insane. After waking up in the park in Philadelphia to the arrival of local Philly PD, he'd found himself in the center of an utterly bizarre crime scene: First, there was the open sarcophagus of the Unknown Revolutionary War Soldier—the corpse inside *mutilated*, part of its jaw missing! And then, even worse, a second corpse—this one impaled with a faux Revolutionary musket, an actual goddam bayonet by its side.

Zack hadn't recognized the dead man, but after finding a bottle of ether in the man's coat pocket along with a soaked rag, he'd been able to reconstruct enough to know that once again he'd had his life saved—and after being informed of multiple images that had been lifted from cameras all around Washington Square, he'd known he once again had Hailey and Nick to thank.

Facial recognition software—which he'd accessed using his FBI authority and the cover of a special investigation—at Logan Airport and Heathrow had alerted him to the fact that whatever

Hailey and Nick had found in the tomb in Philadelphia had led them to England; of course, Zack should have immediately called in his discovery to his superiors and the BPD—but had, instead, opted to keep it a private matter. As a department head on an active investigation, he had a fair amount of leeway when it came to running operations. And he believed he could have made a pretty good case that the search for the Gardner paintings—and the potential resolution of one of the greatest unsolved art heists in history—granted him a little more ammunition than a regular operation. But now, with the incident on the train, he had known there would be hell to pay with his superiors.

Even so, the phone call he'd just gotten, as he'd made his way to the station after his Parisian contacts had responded to his private APB on Hailey and Nick, had been harsher and more pointed than anything he could have expected. He'd predicted a reaming—but not an instant *recall*. His superior had made it absolutely clear; Zack was to cease all private and public operations and return to Washington immediately for a Level One briefing. The designation itself was odd—Level One meant a briefing between him and his direct superior, one on one, no cameras, no filed reports. It was a designation reserved for the highest-level security situations, usually involving terrorism. Zack had never heard of the designation being used for a briefing involving an art heist.

Even with the chaos Hailey and Nick had caused at the train station, Zack couldn't shake the feeling that there was something going on behind the frantic and determined way his superior had recalled him to Washington. Which was why he had momentarily defied orders, and was now moving through the spine of the oldest police station in Paris, flanked by gendarmes.

The truth was, his FBI badge didn't hold any real power here—but professional courtesy went a long way, and in Paris, at least, the FBI still had enough mystique to open a few doors. Zack could tell from the way his escorts were moving, despite their grumpy demeanors—shoulders up, chests out—that they believed they were doing something important. At the very least, escorting an FBI agent to interrogate prisoners sure beat filling out paperwork in a windowless file room.

Two more long hallways, and Zack and his escorts reached a locked door with another uniformed officer standing outside. The shorter of Zack's escorts spoke to the man in hurried French, who also seemed to light up at the mention of "FBI" and quickly went to work on the lock.

The questioning room was small, more cinder blocks on every side, and the ceiling lights had been turned up to an almost blinding yellow. There was a long steel desk in the center of the room, and sitting on one side were the three of them: Hailey in the middle, Nick, and Adrian, the Tufts professor Zack had first seen on footage from the airport, and had identified with facial rec. All three looked like they'd been through the wringer. Clothes wrinkled, scrapes and dirt on their skin. Hailey had a bandage under her jaw, and the top of her white shirt was stained with what appeared to be fairly fresh blood. Zack could see that all three were still in cuffs, though their hands were in their laps. Nick looked the most comfortable of the three—he'd been in handcuffs many times before, and the look on his face told Zack that he'd been in many rooms just like this. But Hailey and Adrian looked terrified; both were squirming in their seats, and Adrian seemed like he was about to pass out.

As Zack moved into the room, all three looked his way—and Hailey's eyes seemed to light up with recognition first. Despite himself, Zack felt a sudden sense of connection—he knew he owed her for his life, twice now—but he did his best to push it away. He knew that as much as he wanted to trust her, at this point she was still a suspect, and she was involved in something that had led to numerous dead bodies.

He shifted his eyes from Hailey to the three gendarmes, who had all crowded into the room behind him. He searched his memory for a bit of passable French:

"Ce c'est bon, j'ai besoin de dix minutes seul."

The three gendarmes looked at each other, then the shorter one shook his head. Asking for ten minutes alone with the three Americans seemed like more than a courtesy to the officers, but Zack wasn't ready to give up.

"The bureau would be very appreciative," he said, in a mix of English and French. "And any information I gather would of course be shared between us. As you might imagine, the FBI is always looking for European partners with a shared sense of commitment to justice in situations such as this."

Zack was laying it on thick, but he noticed that the gendarmes' chests rose a bit with his words, and the shorter of the three only paused a few seconds, before nodding. A moment later, Zack was alone with the three handcuffed Americans.

He pulled up a steel chair on the other side of the desk from them, and then crossed his arms against his chest.

"Most fugitives try to lay low when they're being investigated for multiple homicides and half a billion dollars in missing art. But it seems you three went with a different approach."

Hailey was the first to speak, leaning close over the desk, her voice trembling. "You have to get us out of here."

Zack lifted an eyebrow, but Hailey kept going, her words rushing together.

"There are people trying to kill us, and I don't think we're safe, even here."

Nick was eyeing him, his face still cold, but the professor was nodding vigorously, his eyes watery enough to make Zack think the man was about to burst into tears.

"I'm aware," Zack responded. Twice, he'd nearly died at the hands of the same people who were obviously chasing Hailey and her friends. Clearly professionals, which these three were not. "And these people—they were involved, somehow, in the Gardner heist?"

Hailey nodded.

"But it's not about the paintings. It was never about the paintings."

"The eagle—" Zack started.

"Not about the eagle, either—not anymore."

Hailey looked like she was about to continue, perhaps tell him everything—when Nick nudged her with his elbow, then pointed up toward the ceiling. Zack followed Hailey's eyes. He had to squint against the bright lights—but next to the fluorescent panel, he could clearly see the fish lens of a closed-circuit camera.

Of course, the French would be recording everything. Zack's new buddies in the gendarme weren't fools. Whatever Zack learned, they would learn—and use to prop up their own investigation, and maybe their own careers.

He immediately thought back to the phone call from his supervisor. The vitriolic tone his boss had used during the recall, and the demand for a Level One briefing back in Washington. No doubt, his boss had reasons to be upset—but that didn't explain his vigor, or the Level One briefing. The man had seemed almost—terrified.

Zack had to wonder—was there something else going on back in Washington? Was it possible that his boss, a departmental supervisor in the FBI, had been compromised? No doubt Zack was just being paranoid. If he was smart, he'd get up from his chair, wish the three of them the best of luck, and leave them to their fates. Head back to Washington for his briefing. And move on with his life. No, he wouldn't be the agent to crack the Gardner heist—but he'd have his career, and he had his life.

And sure, Hailey could have done the same; left him to die on the deck of the USS *Constitution*, or perhaps run the minute she'd seen him unconscious at the Tomb of the Unknown Revolutionary War Soldier.

Finally, he lowered his eyes from the ceiling, and looked right at Hailey.

He desperately wanted to know what was going on. Who Hailey thought was chasing her, how it connected to the Gardner theft, and where she, Nick, and Adrian were heading—why they were in Paris, what they had found in London. But he couldn't ask her, not now, not here. And he also knew he couldn't stay in Paris; he'd been recalled, and though he'd made a detour, the FBI wouldn't let him linger much longer.

He leaned forward over the desk and lowered his voice almost to a whisper. "Twice you saved my life. Today, I'm going to do my best to save yours. But I need a promise from you."

He looked from Hailey to Nick. The professor's eyes were too wild to connect with, so he left Adrian to himself.

"Wherever this leads," Zack said, "you end up in my custody. If you're innocent, I'll make sure you're protected. But you need to end up in my hands."

Hailey nodded. It took longer for Nick, but he nodded, too. Then he offered up a half smile.

"How's this gonna work, FBI man? A Parisian jailbreak?"

Zack pushed back from his chair and rose to his feet. "Nothing so dramatic."

He pulled his cell phone out of his pocket and began to dial.

It wasn't going to be simple—the FBI didn't have jurisdiction in Paris, but the US embassy did. And he had friends at the embassy who might not yet know that he had been recalled.

When they figured out what he'd done, he was going to get in enormous trouble. He might even lose his badge.

But he hadn't joined the FBI for a badge.

While he still had one, he wasn't going to use his badge to break these three fugitives out of jail. He was going to use his badge to walk them out the front door.

CHAPTER TWENTY-EIGHT

La Nadie ran her short, cheaply manicured fingernails between the drops of condensation rolling down the sides of her limoncello, as she lounged back against a bright blue, modern-looking chair at an outdoor table at Amore Mio, an elegant Italian bistro on Rue Louis Blanc in the Sixth Arrondissement. She had been seated at the bistro all morning, but the brusque and skinny waiter manning the seven outdoor tables of the restaurant hadn't seemed to care; in fact, after she'd gone through two appetizers and now her second limoncello, the young man had dutifully ignored her, leaving her to give the morning passersby her full attention.

Of course, she wasn't on Rue Louis Blanc to watch the tourists and young Parisians stroll the wide sidewalk in front of her; she was there because of the building a dozen yards to her right; a stone and turreted castle of a building, with a half dozen police cars parked at parallel angles out front.

It was as if the restaurant and the table—situated at such an angle that she had full view of the grand front entrance to the Central Police Station, the largest and most trafficked department in all of Paris, if not France—had been designed to make her morning more efficient. That the bistro also happened to make the best pasta in Paris was a bonus—as was the young man seated at the table directly to her left. Young, French, with high cheekbones and a triangle of scruff around his jaw that no doubt had to be tactfully cared for, like an English lawn. The young man had gone through four cigarettes and one coffee in the past thirty minutes, during which he'd cast a total of six glances in her direction. At the last, she'd tossed back a smile that told him not only was she surprised and flattered by the attention, but after one more limoncello, she'd be inviting him to sit across from her, and perhaps, after, squire her about town.

No doubt, he had pegged her for an American tourist. The shopping bag at her feet, emblazoned with the insignia of the nearest Hermes outpost, was his first hint; and then there were her clothes: jeans that rode up too high around her waist and a farmer's blouse that might as well have screamed Neiman Marcus. On top of that, her hair; she'd traded her bun for a high pile of strands that was almost a bouffant. All in all, she had put on the appearance of a nice Midwestern American girl, on her first trip to the City of Love, ready to be swept off her feet by a Frenchman with just the right amount of scruff.

In truth, the young man's chances with her had less to do with the Italian alcohol in front of her and more to do with what was happening at the police station. As much as she was enjoying the Frenchman's attention, her real focus was on the scene that was occurring at that very moment, on the police station's stone front steps.

She had spotted the FBI agent first, the minute he'd come out through the doors. He hadn't strolled out quietly; he'd been shouting something in French at the two gendarmes directly behind him—putting on quite a show that seemed way out of character, from what she knew of the FBI agent. Though she was too far away to hear what he was saying, she was a good enough lip reader to make some sense of the conversation.

The agent was telling the gendarmes that he was acting under the full authority of the US embassy; that he'd been tasked with bringing terrorists to justice. That he was only following his own orders, and that they could contact the embassy to discuss the situation. The words themselves were illuminating, but when the three fugitives came staggering out of the station, still in cuffs between another pair of gendarmes, La Nadie was able to guess at the rest of the story.

The FBI agent appeared to be using his authority to take the three suspects into his own custody, claiming they were part of a bigger terrorism investigation that had been approved by the US embassy. As much as the French wanted to hold the three suspects, they weren't prepared to get embroiled in what would most likely become a political mess. The FBI agent was talking fast and moving fast—and before La Nadie could even take another sip of her drink, the agent had separated them from the gendarmes and whisked them into a waiting black car with diplomatic plates.

It was an impressive display, especially since La Nadie was quite certain it was all an act. She knew that the FBI agent had been recalled, effective immediately, and had no jurisdiction in Paris—or anywhere, for that matter. Not only because she'd listened in on the phone conversation between the agent and his superior in Washington, but because she herself—via the family's impressive network of resources placed in the highest offices in DC, had been behind the decision to recall the FBI agent. As helpful as he had been to this point, she no longer felt she needed him, and she did not want there to be any more complications to her mission.

Her brow furrowed the tiniest amount, and she was careful to keep her emotions in check, knowing that the young Frenchman at the next table was casting his seventh glance in her direction. He looked about ready to make his move, and she needed to cover up any disgust at herself, and what had happened on the train, that might make its way onto her cheeks.

It had been her own fault. She had rushed things, had attempted to get hold of the phone before she'd needed to, when she could simply have waited until the trio had arrived in Paris and headed to their next destination. She had seen an opportunity—Hailey heading to the bathroom alone—and had acted impetuously.

In truth, she had been curious. She knew that this girl, this trio, had bested two of the most skilled operatives in her line of work, and she had wanted to see the young woman in action for herself.

Well, she had certainly *seen*; it had taken thirty minutes in her hotel suite, bathing her eyes and lips in baking soda and aloe, before she'd recovered enough from Hailey's trick with the sulphuric acid–laced blanket to apply makeup and make herself presentable again. She had to admit, as upset as she was with herself, she was impressed by Hailey—and maybe just a little bit in love.

She let herself smile at the thought, which was perfect timing, because now the young Frenchman had risen from his table and approached her own.

"I am Mattan," he said, introducing himself in heavily accented English. "Would you mind if I joined you?"

La Nadie let her smile widen even more.

"Barbara," she said, in a heavy Midwestern accent, because today, she needed to be Barbara. Indianapolis, Cincinnati? She would fill in the blanks along the way. "And that would be wonderful. It's my first time in Paris and I could definitely use a guide. So many amazing places to see!"

Mattan slid deftly into the chair opposite her, then reached into his pocket for a new cigarette. "Where shall we begin?"

It didn't matter to La Nadie where they began. Before she'd attempted to take the phone from Hailey on the train, she'd seen enough of its screen from her perch by the lavatory—she didn't care where they began.

But she knew exactly where, eventually, they would need to end up.

CHAPTER TWENTY-NINE

There were worse places to plan a heist, Nick thought to himself, as he settled into a high-backed leather chair at a low oak table. The velvet-lined reading room, in a four-hundred-year-old building squatting on the banks of the Seine, was lined with books, on shelves that had to be twenty feet tall. The ceiling above the shelves was curved toward the center, which sported a chandelier that looked as old as the building itself; teardrop-shaped crystal dripped from arms of brass and gold.

There were a dozen similar oak tables crowding the room, but almost all were empty, save for the table closest to the velvet-draped windows overlooking the river. Four college-age kids with slicked hair and skinny jeans had a bunch of maps splayed out in front of them, researching something, no doubt for a course at the nearby university. But other than the college kids, Nick, Hailey, and Adrian were alone, and certainly the only Americans in the building. Apparently, libraries weren't high on any tourist's agenda, even a library as impressive and ancient as the Bibliothèque Mazarine.

From the front entrance of the building—with its high pillars and rounded doors—to its lavish interior, the Mazarine looked more like a well-preserved Roman palace than a public library; but Adrian had explained that not only was it the oldest building dedicated to books in Paris, it was quite possibly one of the oldest libraries in the world, containing more than forty-four thousand volumes and a rare books collection that rivaled any others. There was even an original Gutenberg Bible in its collection, one of the few remaining in existence.

In light of what Adrian had told them on the ride over, Nick had been concerned about the uniformed security guards at the front entrance. However, the armed men hadn't looked up as the three of them had entered, not even to ask for a library card. The place seemed open to anyone, which was yet another bit of good fortune in a morning filled with them.

Nick could hardly believe that the FBI agent had remained true to his word: getting them out of the police station, out of hand-cuffs, and then letting them go in an alley in Paris—without ever having a chance to get them alone and drill them on what they knew. Even in the ride to the alley, the agent had remained in character, assuming the car was bugged like the police interrogation room. The fact that they were all free now and continuing their quest, rather than locked up in a cell or on their way back to Boston to face criminal charges, was utterly shocking. Things didn't usually go Nick's way, and he intended to make the best of it.

He turned his attention away from the shelves of books and the lavish décor to the table in front of him; Adrian had opened a half dozen tomes from the library's collection onto the tabletop, most of them showing different versions of the same image—architectural drawings of the most famous monument in the world.

Everything Nick knew about the Eiffel Tower he'd learned from movies and television. In the photos he'd seen, it had always looked unfinished to him—like the skeleton of a building rather than a completed monument. He knew that it was made mostly of iron, that it had been designed by Gustav Eiffel, that it was lit up by lots

of tiny lights that blinked on New Year's Eve—but other than that, to him it was something you saw on postcards, not in real life.

Adrian was directly across the table from him, bent over one of the open books. Since they'd arrived in the library, the professor had poured himself into the task—probably trying to push thoughts of what had happened on the train, or the feeling of being in handcuffs, as far away as he could.

"Eiffel wasn't originally known for towers or monuments," he said, as Hailey surveyed one of the images—an original architectural blueprint that had been unearthed in letters from the great architect just a few years earlier. "He was more famous for bridges and train stations, and it was his bridges that gave him the idea for this specific design. The tower can actually be viewed as a bridge that has been cut in half, then put together again vertically. The open nature of the beams are to combat the wind, which was a real concern. At its height—over a thousand feet—the winds are often hurricane force."

Adrian had already gone over the basics. Eiffel had come up with the design with the help of two engineers, and won the contract to build the monument to inaugurate the Paris 1889 World's Fair, which was held to celebrate the one hundredth anniversary of the French Revolution. It stood 324 meters tall and was the tallest man-made structure in the world when it was completed. It was made of iron, which was a novel material at the time, and was assembled using a groundbreaking new method called puddling, which involved melting iron and shaping it into the desired form.

The tower was not built to be a permanent structure. Most Parisians of the time were opposed to such a massive and modern-looking tower standing in the center of the city. To help secure the tower's fate, Eiffel proposed that the tower would also double as a scientific research center—that the huge metal structure could act as a radio beacon, and that its height would allow for a unique opportunity for the burgeoning science of aerodynamics.

Notably, when the tower was built in 1889, Eiffel included a total of five elevators in his design, originally powered by steam engines and operated using a system of counterweights and pulleys. Three of them, located in the east, west, and north pillars, were used to transport visitors from the ground level to the first and second levels, traveling at a speed of six meters per second. The fourth elevator was in the south pillar and was used to travel from the second level to the top of the tower. This elevator was known as the "panoramic elevator," as it had glass walls for panoramic views of the city during ascent and descent. The final elevator was located in the west pillar of the tower and was used to transport maintenance workers and equipment to the top of the tower; it was not open to the general public. Although the lifts had undergone many renovations over the years, the basic principles of how they operated had remained the same.

Sifting through the different blueprints, Nick noticed that none of them contained any information on the "apartment" that Eiffel had built at the top of his tower.

"One of the well-known secrets of the monument," Adrian had said with a shrug. He'd pointed to a spot on one of the blueprints, near the viewing platform on the highest level of the tower. "It's approximately here, if I remember correctly. It has a glass door and window you can look through, and it's been kept in mostly the same shape as it was originally."

Now, Hailey pushed Adrian's phone next to the blueprint, its screen open to the image from the Royal Academy of Music. "The lines converge below where you're pointing."

Adrian shrugged. "Maybe my memory is off. Or maybe this is all a shot in the dark."

"You say Eiffel had to present the tower as a scientific research center to save it from being temporary."

"Correct. The land had only been leased for twenty years; Eiffel was looking for reasons to let him keep it standing. Tourism wasn't initially a big draw—people thought the tower was ugly and a blight on the city's skyline. So Eiffel cycled through a number of last-ditch efforts to save his namesake."

Adrian shuffled through the many blueprints. "He added a meteorological lab, one of the most sophisticated of its time. He also ran experiments dropping plumb lines from the top, for physics calculations. And he even added a wind tunnel, to test models for flight. The basement contained a military bunker. But the most influential of his efforts—"

He pointed to drawings of antennae sticking out the top of the tower.

"Radio. In the 1860s it was a new science, exploding out of labs all over America and Europe. Eiffel realized his iron tower was a perfect radio conductor. He ran wires to the top and conducted experiments, communicating with stations as far away as New York City."

Nick was only half listening to their conversation; he had focused his attention on Adrian's phone, at the spot where the lines converged. This was where they needed to go—not the radio antennae at the top of the tower or the military bunker in the basement. They needed to find a way to the highest level of the Eiffel Tower, a monument visited by millions of tourists a year, tens of thousands a day. Obviously, they couldn't go during the hours the tower was open—which meant they had to find a way in at night. Through security—he could only imagine security would be tight, involving armed guards, most likely military.

His eyes shifted to one of the open books on the table. It was an image of the finished tower, and the first thing he noticed were the beams of light coming from near the top of the tower—huge spotlights sweeping the city below.

Adrian noticed his attention.

"From the beginning, light shows were a big part of the tower's appeal. Originally, Eiffel used gas lanterns to power these huge spotlights. But later innovations improved the situation dramatically. Eiffel was close friends with Thomas Edison, and with Edison's help, he installed lights throughout the tower, which ran on a steam generator in the base."

Hailey turned a page in the book Nick was looking at, to a more modern picture of the tower. In this picture, the tower didn't just sport spotlights at the top—it was covered in lights, thousands upon thousands, like stars. Different photos showed the lights blinking, sometimes in unison, sometimes at random. Sparkling like snowflakes in bright sunlight.

"For the turn of the millennium," Hailey said. "They added these bulbs all over the exterior—twenty thousand bulbs—which are turned on every evening and remain lit until one a.m."

"Must be quite a job," Nick commented, "keeping all those bulbs working."

"What are you getting at?" Adrian asked.

Nick touched his jaw. He had cased hundreds of buildings over his life. Had learned the routines of countless security guards, bank tellers, and office workers. But sometimes, it wasn't the routines of the people who worked in a building that made the difference. It was the routines of the *building* itself.

"We need to get here," he said, pointing to the picture of the tower. "But we can't take the elevator or the stairs, we can't go during business hours, and we can't fight our way through security. We need to get here—from the outside."

Adrian stared at him. "You're not suggesting we climb the damn thing."

Nick grinned, but shook his head. "You ever have a Christmas tree, Professor? Imagine a tree with twenty thousand bulbs. What happens with bulbs? They burn out. They short. That many bulbs—it probably happens daily. There has to be a process, a protocol, for repairing those bulbs. When they go out someone gets a call, comes out, and fixes them."

He was already thinking ahead, going through the next steps, figuring out what they'd need and where they might get it. They were in a foreign country, a place as strange to him as the surface of the moon. But this was *his* wheelhouse. This, he knew like the streets of South Boston.

The people who got the call when a bulb blew or something needed to get fixed—these were people Nick understood. It would be difficult, but it was a way in. Because in Nick's line of work, there was *always* a way in.

CHAPTER THIRTY

Hailey fought the urge to grab Nick's hand, even though it was only inches from her own where she gripped the steel pole that ran up the center of the bright yellow double-decker elevator. She'd never been good with heights, and she couldn't imagine a place more terrifying for someone with even mild acrophobia than a double-decker elevator sliding up the interior of one of the four insect-like struts of the Eiffel Tower.

The view through the windows of the chamber they were in was barely obscured by the corrugated metal slats that made up the outer frame of the tower's leg; to Hailey, it seemed similar to the view she would expect from an airplane taking off over the city. Bright, twinkling lights of buildings, the technicolored blur of cars on the avenues and rotaries, the serpentine swirl of the Seine twisting beneath multiple arched bridges. More unnerving still, the cabin was tipped to the side, forty-five degrees from center, as it made its way through the open shaft; Hailey knew that the original design had been modeled off of the funiculars that carried passengers over mountains in Switzerland, working by means of hydraulics and pulleys dating back almost 150 years. Though the workings had been updated and repaired many times over the century and a half since Eiffel's era, Hailey knew that much of the original materials were still in place, functioning as they had so long ago.

But she couldn't show her fear, because for the moment she was not herself. She had traded her slacks and shirt for a bright orange uniform emblazoned with a name tag—Eliose Grand—and the chiron of a well-known French utility company. She had a thick coil of rope fitted with metal-climbing crampons attached to her hip and wore a helmet with a lamp on her head. And her outfit matched Nick's, though he looked much more the part of an electrical repair engineer than she ever could.

Even more important, they were not alone in the elevator. One of the many tower security guards was standing just a few feet away at the controls, with a gun on his hip and a walkie-talkie on his belt that could instantly connect him to the dozen armed police officers at the tower's base.

She had no choice but to keep her fear inside. Looking at Nick, the way he was presenting himself as a bored municipal worker at the beginning of a long night shift, made things easier for her. As good as she was at playing roles—she had had a lot of practice— this was Nick's world.

He had been exactly right. A bit of pointed research in the library had informed them that there was, indeed, a specific protocol for changing the bulbs on the exterior of the Eiffel Tower. Once a night, a photography station on a nearby building would take dozens of photos of the monument, which a team of visual engineers would go through, searching for dimmed or extinguished bulbs. If it was determined that the outages involved equipment failure, rather than electrical shorts, a team would get the call—and maintenance engineers would be on-site within hours.

It was all the information Nick had needed to plan out their ascent. Infiltrating a utility company's headquarters had been child's play; Hailey and Adrian had waited outside on the street while Nick had gone in through the front door, just a few hours ago. He'd returned shortly after with the uniforms and equipment, along with IDs.

Once they'd reached the tower, it had been simple to convince security that they'd gotten the call about a series of lights that had gone out near the peak of the monument. Hailey's French might have been only passable, but Adrian had added a German accent to his own, playing the part of a stuffy and rude German-born engineer well enough to keep the security guards from wanting to press him too hard about anything specific. Once the security guards had checked their IDs and let them through, Adrian had remained behind at the base with his own walkie-talkie in case real police showed up.

Now they were riding up the side of what was once the tallest building in the world. Silent, because Nick didn't speak any French, and English wouldn't make sense to the security guard traveling with them. Hailey had to be content with furtive glances at Nick.

The elevator began to slow as it reached the second level of the tower. At roughly four hundred feet and close to eleven p.m., the city sparkled below like a Christmas tree on its side, but the second-level platform they were approaching, surprisingly, wasn't empty. Hailey could see a few tourists still mingling about, mostly couples. Although the tower was closed for the evening, she knew the latest seating at the famous Jules Verne restaurant that took up much of the second level stretched past nine p.m.; this also explained the handful of impeccably dressed wait staff she saw milling between the couples. Although she couldn't see past the restaurant entrance from the moving elevator, she had seen pictures in some of the books in the library: an elegantly decorated dining room with white tablecloths, crystal chandeliers, and over-sized windows offering panoramic views of the city. Hailey only wished she and Nick could be as carefree as the couples she could see gathering near the elevator platform as the double-decker cabin approached.

Her gaze focused on the closest of the couples: a young French-man with scruff on his angled chin embracing a woman who looked American, a Hermes bag on the ground at her feet. Hailey couldn't see the woman's face, but she could imagine the flush in her cheeks, the sparkle in her eyes, and Hailey felt her own lips form an inadvertent smile. One day, maybe she and Nick would revisit this place as tourists, not as faux maintenance workers try-ing to stay a step ahead of a shadowy organization out to kill them.

The elevator slowed. Nick touched her shoulder and guided her to the doors on the other side of the chamber, opposite the restaurant. The exit doors opened first, as the last tourists and staff waited for the elevator to discharge Nick and Hailey. Then they boarded, and the elevator begin its descent.

Hailey moved with Nick behind the security guard, who led them quickly across the platform and up a short set of metal stairs. They were in the center of the tower now. Directly ahead was another, smaller elevator, this one marked Off Limits. Looking upward, Hailey could see this elevator ran vertically, straight up the spine of the monument. The shaft, surrounded by those open iron bars, disappeared into the darkness above.

The guard hit a button and the elevator opened, revealing a chamber just barely big enough for Nick and Hailey and their equipment. The guard gestured them inside; he would stay behind, leaving them to their work. Hailey tried not to show her fear as she followed Nick into the chamber. Then the doors shut behind them, and they were alone.

The sound of Hailey's own heart pumping mingled with the metallic grumble of the gears that pulled the ten-by-ten elevator higher and higher into the sky. Now there was no way to avoid the view, since the elevator's walls were mostly glass. Outside, the city was receding farther by the second, the lights blending into a strobe-like blur. The only thing between Hailey and a dizzying plunge was the glass, and a sea of iron struts that looked like something that had been soldered together in a high school metalworking class.

Nick reached out and squeezed Hailey's hand. She focused on him, and he smiled beneath his bright yellow, utility company hard hat.

"And you say I never take you anywhere," he said.

The best she could muster was a fake laugh. The elevator shook as the gears continued to churn. She couldn't see the cables above the low ceiling of the cabin, but she could imagine them: huge steel ropes quivering like muscles against the elevator's weight.

Then the grinding grew louder, and she realized they were reaching the third level of the tower—their final destination. She knew from the books that the third level contained a warren-like observation deck, near the center of which perched Eiffel's apartment. The thought that Eiffel, and invited guests, would stay up here for nights on end seemed insane to her. An image flashed in her head from a visit she'd once made to the financial district in downtown Boston: a pair of pigeons roosting on a window ledge, twenty stories above the winding, narrow streets.

"A million rivets," Nick interrupted her thoughts, and she followed his eyes to one of the iron bars flashing by as they continued upward. "That's what Adrian said. They used over a million rivets in the construction. You know, they don't use rivets anymore—not because they aren't strong, but because they are too dangerous to work with. You have to superheat the metal, then sink them into drilled holes in the bars. As they cool, they contract, pulling the metal tightly together. It's almost impossible to get a better seal than rivets. Even though this monument was built to be temporary, the construction process meant it could last forever."

Something about his comment pricked at her. "When the tower first went up, even though Eiffel had grand plans, he couldn't have known if his lobbying would work—he had to assume there was a chance the tower would get torn down after the World's Fair. Why would he put Franklin's invention—something so important Franklin had died without revealing it to the world—in something that might be temporary?"

"Maybe it was another experiment—like Revere's bells—another test?"

"This is a lot of effort for an experiment," Hailey said, looking at the tower around them. "If he was working off of the plans Franklin had designed, hidden in Mozart's composition—wouldn't he have tried to find a more permanent situation in the first place than a monument that was set to be torn down from the start?"

Nick didn't have an answer. The elevator jerked as it settled to a stop in a bay on the third level. There was another churning of gears, and then the elevator doors clicked open, revealing a set of metal stairs leading to a narrow, corrugated metal walkway.

Hailey moved first, Nick next to her. Her plan was to stay as much toward the interior of the platform as she could; though they were carrying climbing gear, she had no intention of going beyond the high railing that ran like a ring around the platform. If she'd read the image on Adrian's phone correctly, whatever they were looking for would be in the center of the tower anyway, beneath the spot where Adrian believed Eiffel's apartment rested.

As she moved, she could feel the wind pressing against her; thankfully, it was a calm evening, cloudless enough that the panoply of stars above the city was nearly as dazzling as the blur of lights below.

To the right of the stairs that led away from the elevator, the platform opened into the viewing area—primarily enclosed, with large, double-paned rectangular windows set directly into the wall. Between the windows were various photos and plaques showing the tower in different states of construction, along with comparative images of other towers and monuments around the world. No doubt, the Eiffel Tower was the most impressive feat of architecture of its time period—twice as tall as its nearest competitor, the Washington Monument. An achievement ahead of its era—made even more impressive by the fact that if Hailey was right, its technical origins went another half century into history, and its theoretical origins even further, perhaps millennia.

She continued around the viewing platform and found another set of stairs leading up to an upper level, with an open-air deck surrounded by a curved chain-link fence. Telescopes and fixed binoculars sprouted around the edges of the deck, aimed through holes in the fence. Above, she saw catwalks extending around the circumference of the platform, and then in the center a ladder leading upward toward the pinnacle of the tower. She couldn't see far up the ladder, but guessed somewhere up there was the housing for the various radio and meteorological antennae that Eiffel had added to his design.

"Over here," Nick said, beckoning. To his right, another set of steps led to a set of doors. There were windows above the knobs, and Nick was peering through.

Hailey moved next to him. Through the glass, she could see the infamous "secret apartment." As Adrian had described, it had been decorated to look just as it had in the late 1880s. The floor was covered in an oriental carpet, and the furniture was low and wooden. There was a console radio in one corner, and cubby holes and alcoves along the back wall filled with nineteenth-century scientific equipment. But the décor was overshadowed by two figures seated in chairs in the center of the carpet, clearly visible through the glass. Mannequins—two older-looking men, dressed nicely for their era. Hailey immediately recognized Gustav Eiffel from the books, but Nick surprised her by naming the other mannequin first.

"Thomas Edison."

Then she also noticed the plaque behind the mannequins, on a table next to an old phonograph, one of Edison's many inventions.

"According to the plaque—and Adrian's books—they were the best of friends," Nick said. "Looks like he visited the tower a bunch of times, even slept in this apartment."

Hailey felt a rush that wasn't due to the light wind coming through the chain-link fencing behind her. Edison, the inventor who had perfected the light bulb and had essentially taken the baton from Benjamin Franklin, experimenting with both sound and electricity. It wasn't surprising that these two famous men of their shared era knew each other—but the idea that they were close friends, that they might have conducted experiments here, together—pushed her thoughts in compelling directions.

Nick tried the door—of course it was locked. But he didn't seem concerned. He reached into his supply bag and retrieved a screwdriver, along with what looked like a metal file.

It took him less than a minute to get the knob turning. He returned his tools to the bag and pushed his way inside.

Shutting the door behind her, Hailey felt her heart rate normalize. They were still nearly a thousand feet above the city, but she was indoors, behind walls. Luckily, she was not also claustro-phobic; the apartment was cramped, despite the various alcoves and cubbies. She didn't recognize much of the scientific equipment around her, but she didn't waste any time investigating—most, she assumed, would be props, carefully placed as background to the two mannequins in the chairs.

Instead, she wound around Eiffel and Edison, and drew Adrian's phone out of her own bag. She opened the screen and studied the spot on the image where the yellow lines converged.

"If I've read this right," she said, "whatever we're looking for will be right below us."

From outside, it had been impossible to see if there was any-thing directly beneath the apartment; but dropping to her knees, she could feel that beneath the oriental rug, the floor felt solid metal, in contrast to the corrugated iron outside on the viewing platform.

Nick knelt down next to her and drew a box cutter out of his bag. Hailey felt a tinge of guilt as he went to work on the carpet, but she didn't see that they had any choice. She hoped it wasn't as expensive as it looked.

It took Nick a moment to get through the thick material, and then together they peeled it back to reveal a solid plate of metal floor beneath. Nick flicked his helmet lamp on, illuminating the smooth surface. He was feeling along the metal with his palm as he shifted the light back and forth—and then he paused.

"A handle?" Hailey asked, hoping.

He shook his head, then lifted his hand—and shined the light directly where his palm had been. Hailey saw, with a start, that there was something carved directly into the metal.

A face. Carved so lightly it would have been easy to miss. But now that she was staring directly at it, caught in the beam from the headlamp, it was unmistakable. Not just a face, but one that was instantly recognizable, because she'd seen it before.

"A Cheshire Cat," she whispered.

Round slits for eyes and that smile, carved into the metal floor. Had it really been here since the tower had gone up 140 years before? Was it Eiffel's nod to the Hellfire Club, to Franklin and Revere? Clearly a message, which meant they were in the right place.

Hailey felt along the floor for another carving, but it was smooth and cold. Nick had shifted a few feet to the side, right under where they'd peeled the carpet back. He aimed his light at where his fingers touched the metal, and then cocked his head.

"See these?" He was touching dark spots in the smooth panel. "These aren't rivets. These are screws."

"I thought the entire tower had been fastened together with rivets."

"These must have been added after the initial work was done."

He reached into his bag and this time removed a battery-powered screwdriver. There was a loud metallic whir as he removed the first screw. It was almost six inches long, dark with age. Then he attacked the next few screws. When he was done, he released the trigger on the screwdriver—but Hailey noticed there was still a loud metallic whir, somewhere in the background. At first, she thought it was some odd echo—then realized it was the elevator being recalled.

She looked down at the walkie-talkie on her equipment belt. The light indicated it was on, but Adrian hadn't alerted them that someone was heading up. Perhaps the security guard was coming back to check on them and had called the elevator back down to get him from the second level.

"We have to work fast," Hailey said. Nick nodded, reached past her, and felt around for more screws. He found a second set just beneath the carpet, and pulled back more material to reach them with the screwdriver.

When the last screw came out, Nick felt farther under the carpet—then grinned. "I've got an edge."

His muscles strained—and then a section of the panel came up with a cough of metal against metal. Nick put the section to one side, and they both looked down. The space beneath was pitch-black, and deep enough that Hailey couldn't guess how far it went down. Nick shined his headlamp past her—and finally she saw the bottom, maybe four feet below. More of a compartment than a room, with solid walls on all sides. To Hailey's surprise, it looked—empty.

"There's nothing here," Nick said.

Hailey's stomach tightened. Nick was right. No device, mechanical or otherwise. She shook her head, despondent. Had they come all this way for nothing? It seemed impossible. The image from Mozart's manuscript, the Cheshire Cat. She leaned her head forward, down into the opening. To her surprise, the air felt thicker down there, and smelled bitter, almost ionized. She squinted her eyes in the dim light from Nick's lamp and noticed that areas of the walls and floor were darkened with burn marks, and that the metal was even melted in some places.

Her eyes widened. Iron was one of the most stable metals in existence. It had a melting point of 2,800 degrees Fahrenheit. But something in this space had generated that level of intense heat, leaving scars behind.

She reached beneath the lip of the opening. To her surprise, she felt strands of thinner, more malleable metal sticking out.

"Copper wiring," she said. "Something *was* here. But it's not anymore."

Her fingers closed on one of the wires; it was frayed at one end. She quickly drew her hand back. It was a clear night, no clouds in the sky—but even so, she could imagine what a lightning strike would be like at the top of the tower. If these wires ran through the peak—

She paused, thinking. *Screws, instead of rivets.* Whatever had been in this compartment had been added after the tower was completed, then removed. Nick had been right. This had been the setting of another experiment, but the tower itself, the design that had come from Franklin, via Mozart—could it have all been part of this experiment? Something like this, on such a scale . . .

Her thoughts paused, as her gaze settled on a corner of the compartment beneath her. There was a shape in the corner—something small and boxy, perhaps another chest like in the Hellfire tunnels.

"Help me down," she said. "I think I see something."

"We don't have much time," Nick responded.

Hailey looked back over her shoulder. She could clearly hear the grinding noise of the elevator returning now, the thick cables pulling the cabin up the spine of the tower toward them.

"I'll be quick," she said, slinging her legs over the edge of the opening.

Nick grabbed her under her arms and helped lower her down. She dropped the last foot to the floor and landed with a metallic thud. Then she crouched, and reached into the corner.

The object wasn't a chest but a case, metallic and small, about the size of an encyclopedia. The case was lighter than it looked, and she quickly passed it up to Nick, who then reached back for her arms. A moment later she was next to him in the apartment. The case was next to Edison's feet. Looking carefully, Hailey saw clasps along the edge.

When she opened the case, the first thing she saw was a sheet of drafting paper. Handwritten notations and numbers ran along one side, measurements and calculations. But in the center of the paper was an image both recognizable and strange. At first glance, it looked much like the image from Mozart's music, which was now emblazoned on Adrian's phone's screen. But not exactly the same—overlaid over the skeletal structure of the tower was something else, curves and lines coming together—another structure superimposed over the skeleton.

Hailey's mouth opened, then closed. She looked at Nick, who was also staring at the drafting paper. Because he, too, recognized the image—not just the tower, but the other structure superimposed over the tower. Because it, too, was familiar—as familiar as the Eiffel Tower itself.

"What is this?" Nick asked.

Hailey's mind whirled. The two images, one superimposed over the other. Calculations and measurements along the side.

"I think it's—an *adjustment*," she whispered.

"There's something else," Nick said. He reached into the case and shifted the drafting paper to the side. There was a second sheet of paper beneath it, thicker, almost the heft of canvas. It was small, about the size of a paperback book. It appeared to be upside down—there were dark colors seeping through the canvas, and Nick took the canvas and turned it over.

"My god," he whispered. Hailey stared at the canvas, not believing what she was seeing. And then her eyes moved back to the drafting paper—and realization hit her.

"You see it?" she asked. "You do see it, right?"

Before Nick could answer, there was a noise, and Hailey looked up toward the door to the apartment. She heard footsteps—and then voices. A woman and a man, speaking in French, laughing as they spoke. The footsteps grew louder, and she saw shapes through the glass in the door. Two people, stumbling as they walked.

"We have to move," Nick hissed.

The couple was coming closer.

"They sound drunk," Hailey said. "If we stay quiet—"

The voices stopped. Hailey squinted through the glass in the doors, and saw that the couple was right in front of the apartment now, locked in what looked like an embrace. Heads close together. They were kissing. There were moans. And then—gasping.

Choking.

Hailey's eyes went wide, as suddenly the door to the apartment swung inward. Silhouetted in the door, a young Frenchman with scruff on his jaw, handsome and thin, standing next to a woman with a bouffant hairdo, too much blush on her cheeks, and a wide smile on her lips. Despite the hair, she was immediately familiar— but even so, Hailey's attention was on the man, because something about him was *wrong*. His head was leaning to the side and his eyes were wide open, but his skin was the color of snow.

Then Hailey saw the Hermès scarf around his neck, twisted so tight it was barely the width of her wrist.

The woman let go of the scarf and the young Frenchman's body crumpled to the floor. She met Hailey's eyes. "I know. What a waste."

Hailey couldn't tell if the woman was referring to the young corpse sprawled out against the oriental carpet, or the scarf.

The woman's eyes shifted from Hailey's face to the two pages in the open metal case. For the briefest moment, the woman's eyes went wide.

"Is that—?" She paused, trying to comprehend what she was seeing.

Nick took advantage of what might be the only chance they would have. He grabbed the metal case and flung it toward the woman's head. She jerked to the left at the last moment, her feet tangling with the legs of Gustav Eiffel's chair—sending both the dummy and herself crashing toward the floor.

Hailey grabbed the two pages from the floor in front of her and leapt for the door. The woman reached for her, but Hailey barely made it past, and hurtled out onto the viewing platform. Her equipment pack bounced against her back as she sprang toward the elevator, which was sitting in its bay, doors still open.

She could hear feet moving behind her; the woman had ignored Nick, as Hailey had hoped, and was coming after her, determined to get the pages in Hailey's hands. But the woman was fast—and Hailey knew the elevator would just be a dead end. She spun to her right, skidding around the edge of the platform—and saw a door marked Avertissement: Exteriore in bright red. Her heart fluttered, but she realized it was her only choice.

She hit the door with her shoulder and careened through.

The wind hit her like an open palm, nearly pushing her back through the door. Beneath her feet was a ledge about two feet long, ending in a low railing. Beyond that—air, sky, nothing. Her eyes went wild as she felt an intense burst of vertigo, and she nearly toppled forward over the railing. Then she screamed at herself to regain control, and quickly shuffled to her right, pressing her back against the iron bars behind her.

Ten steps, and she reached the exterior of the chain-link fence that ran around the main section of the observation deck. She was on the outside of the links now, her back against the fencing. Sliding along as fast she could go.

Then she looked back—and saw the woman stepping out through the door she had just come through, out onto the ledge.

Hailey gasped, hurrying her pace, one foot next to the other. There was no sign of Nick, but she knew he would be somewhere nearby. Unless the woman had gone for him in the interim—from what she'd already seen, she knew this woman was capable of extreme and instant violence.

"There's nowhere to go," the woman shouted after her, voice carried above the wind. "Well, that's not entirely true."

Hailey glanced down, at the lights of the city so far below.

"Is this when you offer me some sort of deal?" Hailey shouted back, still moving forward along the fence. "What we've found, for my life?"

"We're well beyond negotiations, my dear."

Hailey took another step—missing the ledge with her right foot, and for a second she lost balance. She slipped forward, catching herself with a clawlike grip on the fence at the last moment. Her body swung out over nothingness. Then she twisted herself back toward the fence and found that the ledge had given way to a flat rectangular surface, just to the right of the observation deck.

Directly in front of her were a pair of heavy steel cables running up through the teeth of a set of huge gears. She looked around— and realized she was standing on top of the maintenance elevator that led down the spine of the tower. Another low railing separated her from the catwalks leading back to the observation deck. And directly ahead, a covered spiral staircase that led up to the radio antennae at the peak of the tower.

She started for the staircase, knowing full well it would be another dead end—but she'd only made it two steps when she heard a thud behind her.

The woman had leapt the last few feet and had landed just two yards away on top of the elevator. The elevator bounced at her weight, then steadied. Hailey clenched the pages she'd grabbed from the case in her hand, staring wildly. The staircase was still a good five feet away. She'd never make it.

Hailey braced herself, as the woman started forward. She would have to fight. She reached into her backpack with her free hand, searching for anything to use as a weapon. Her hand closed on a box cutter, the same design Nick had used on the oriental carpet. She drew it in front of her, using her finger to open the blade, which was about the size of her thumb.

The woman laughed. "That could leave a nasty little scratch."

She shifted her weight, about to lunge when a flash of motion came from Hailey's left. She saw denim—then Nick barreled into the woman at full force.

But the woman was fast—she twisted right, letting Nick's weight carry him around her, and brought her knee up in some sort of practiced move. The knee connected with Nick's stomach. He grunted and curled to the floor. The elevator bobbed again, the cables groaning. The woman lifted her foot and drove her heel into Nick's side. There was a sick crack—one of Nick's ribs—and Nick rolled away in a near-fetal position.

Hailey started toward him, but the woman blocked her path, standing right next to the pair of cables, and drew something from her back pocket. A metal steak knife from the restaurant on the second level, serrated and glinting silver in the light of the moon.

She glanced down at Nick, who was right at her feet, still curled in a ball.

"Such a romantic gesture. *La magie de la tour Eiffel.* But sadly, also pointless. At least—you'll always have Paris."

Suddenly the woman lunged forward—and came to a dead stop. Her face changed, confused, and she looked down. Hailey followed her gaze.

Her right leg was next to the cable, and there was a thin stretch of what looked like wire tight around her ankle, pinning her to the thick metal. It took Hailey a beat to realize—it wasn't actually a wire, but a violin string.

Nick scrambled back off the edge of the top of the elevator, out of his fetal position. He had his walkie-talkie out and spoke quickly into the receiver.

"Adrian. Call the elevator. Now!"

There was brief French dialogue crackling through the speaker—and then a loud mechanical groan as the cables came to life. Hailey stepped back off the elevator onto the edge of the catwalk leading back to the viewing platform.

"I hear the view's just as good on the way down," she said.

The giant gears began to spin, and the elevator plunged downward, the woman holding the cable with both hands as the wind pulled at her. A moment later, she was gone, descending down the elevator shaft.

Hailey glanced down—in a moment she could no longer see anything but empty darkness. Then she rushed over to Nick, who was already pushing himself to his feet. His face was red, and he was grimacing with each breath, but he seemed well enough to stand.

"I've had worse," he grunted. He, too, looked over the edge of the elevator shaft. "With any luck, she'll be stuck on that thing for a while. I used a sailor's knot. I'm about as good at knots as I am at getting kicked in the ribs."

Hailey planted a kiss on his lips, which surprised them both.

"We need to get moving," she said. "We'll have to take the stairs. Hopefully we can avoid her at the base—but eventually, we'll have to deal with her again."

"She's persistent," Nick agreed.

"Worse than that, she knows exactly where we are going next."

The woman had seen the two pages that Hailey still gripped

in her left hand. Hailey didn't need to look at them again—the images were embedded in her mind. Separate, they didn't mean much—but side by side, they were impossible to ignore.

Like an optical illusion, all blur until you found focus—then as bright and sure as a bolt of lightning from the sky.

CHAPTER THIRTY-ONE

La Nadie braced herself against the smooth roof of the elevator capsule as it lurched to a stop in its base on the second level of the tower, then allowed the momentum to carry her body in a tight roll over the edge. It was a short six-foot drop to the platform, and she landed in a near crouch, ignoring the sharp pain coming from her right ankle. It had taken her half of the ride down the spine of the tower to carve herself free from the violin string with the silverware she'd copped from the Jules Verne restaurant; the string had been surprisingly strong, and Nick had tied it so tight against her flesh that it had been difficult to get the blade levered correctly without cutting too far into her skin. Whatever else she could surmise about the ex con, he was good with knots.

She didn't see any security guards on the platform, but she could hear noise coming from the nearby restaurant, probably cleaning staff finishing their shift.

She briefly considered taking the elevator back up, or heading to the maintenance stairs to confront the two fugitives again. She doubted they'd beaten her to the bottom, since she'd had such a head start—but if they were smart, they'd already alerted security below to come retrieve them. La Nadie didn't want to risk making a fool of herself for the third time.

Instead, she skirted around the elevator and past the restaurant entrance, then headed for the main customer stairs that led down the southern leg of the great tower. The gated entrance was closed, but it took her less than a minute to get through the locks using the same violin string that had been tied around her ankle, which she intended to keep as a slightly bloody souvenir of her own foolishness. Then she was bounding down the steps toward the ground.

To her surprise, she didn't feel despondent at her failure—twice, now—at the hands of the two amateurs. On the contrary, she was elated. Her heart was beating faster than it had in months, and she was actually smiling. She had always liked surprises, and Nick's move with the violin string had certainly taken her by surprise. She had clearly underestimated her quarry, but more than that, she had acted unnecessarily and inefficiently. She had gotten so far by letting them take the lead and solve the puzzles for her.

In truth, the attempted assault hadn't been her idea. The orders had come from Mr. Arthur, who was no doubt becoming impatient, the closer they came to success. La Nadie should have stuck to her intuition; Hailey was indeed a genius, more capable than all the tendrils of the Family combined.

La Nadie reached the bottom step and burst out beneath the base of the tower. To her right, she could see security gathered by the entrance to the maintenance stairs, and perhaps could even make out the form of the professor, with his wavy hair and his own yellow utility uniform. But instead of heading toward the foppish man, La Nadie moved in the opposite direction, toward the smattering of late-night tourists strolling through the beautiful landscape of the trocadero. Toward the gardens, and the city lights beyond.

A beautiful city, in some ways even more impressive than Barcelona, where La Nadie had spent her childhood. Unfortunately, there would be no more time to play the tourist, no time to find another handsome young Frenchman to squire her about town.

Once again, she knew exactly where Hailey and Nick were headed. An ocean away—they would need to go to the airport, of course, but rather than accost them there, La Nadie would use the Family's resources to get to the destination first. This time, she would let them do the hard work for her.

Blinking her eyes, La Nadie could still see the two pages lying next to each other in the metal case. One, a blueprint—similar to what she had seen on the train, but different enough to raise questions she couldn't yet answer. And the other page, the canvas—not a blueprint, but a *painting*.

On their own, the two pages were more mystery than solution. But together—they were impossible to misinterpret.

Together, they were the sort of thing that could set the entire world on fire.

CHAPTER THIRTY-TWO

Twelve hours later, Adrian Jenson dodged a thick spray of salt water as he leaned over the steel railing encircling the second floor of a double-decker ferry, his eyes pinned to the frothy waves below. He knew he was being childish. But he refused to look up at the view that had just sprung up across the horizon, forcing gasps from the crowd of tourists that lined the railing on either side of him. Even above the waves, and the rumble of the ferry's engines, he could hear their cell phone cameras clicking, lenses up and aimed like the countless eyes of insects. To him, that was what these tourists were, mere insects flittering close to a bit of history that had been commercialized for a century and a half into something you wore on a T-shirt or a baseball hat, or dangled from a key chain.

But not to Adrian; to him history was sacrosanct, it was the struts and steps the present was built on, the framework for reality, for everything solid he had built his life around.

And now, here, that framework was shimmering and faltering and disappearing, like a mirage on a windy day. Everything he had believed, everything he had thought was solid and real—betrayed by what Hailey and Nick had discovered. The past few days of horrid fantasy and science fiction had come to a head with the biggest reveal of all, and it was something his mind just simply refused to accept.

323

The anger inside him was palpable. He had been barely able to stomach the idea that the Eiffel Tower, the greatest monument in Europe and perhaps the world, had not been just the work of a talented engineer and architect, but also a testing ground for a device invented by Benjamin Franklin, building from the work of Paul Revere, hidden and communicated forward in a manuscript by Mozart. But this—this was *too* far.

Head still down, he could *feel* his two traveling companions behind him, sitting together on the low bench that ran along the outer wall of the ferry. Behind them, picture windows framed the interior, with its rows of cushioned seats. But though thick clouds were gathering in the gray sky above New York Harbor, threatening rain, most of the tourists were outside along with Nick, Hailey, and Adrian, providing the cover of a crowd. Which was a good thing, because at the moment Nick and Hailey were entirely engrossed in the two pages laid out next to one another on Hailey's lap, barely shielded from the view of any of the tourists who might have wandered too close.

Adrian's entire body shook at the thought of those pages, found in the metal case beneath Eiffel's apartment at the top of the Eiffel Tower. Finally, despite himself, he lifted his head to stare at what everyone else at the railing was seeing. There, in the near distance, growing closer with every bounce of the ship over the white-crested waves—there *she* was. Rising more than three hundred feet, including its pedestal of pure granite, from a star-shaped base on the edge of Liberty Island. Spiked crown atop her head, huge, slablike tablet clutched in her left hand that sported the date of the Declaration of Independence in great Roman numerals, and that gold-tipped, fiery torch, held high above the harbor in her right.

Lady Liberty—a monument Adrian had visited countless times,

a monument he probably knew as well as any dozen park rangers who milled about the craggy island set at the mouth of the harbor where she made her home, guiding the cell phone–wielding tourists up and down its spiral stairs.

As an expert in Revolutionary War history, and specifically Paul Revere, Adrian could have gotten by with just a passing knowledge of the neoclassical copper sculpture that had been gifted to the American republic—dedicated on October 28, 1886—by the French. But since the statue's construction and dedication were closely tied to the alliance between the two countries during the war, he felt an urge to study its historical context.

He'd discovered, very quickly, that the statue had, in fact, very little to do with the Revolution, despite the Declaration she held in her hand. Adrian doubted that even a handful of the tourists at the railing around him realized the Statue of Liberty had been built to commemorate the end of slavery and the cessation of the Civil War, not of British rule, or that by one of her feet snaked an enormous broken chain, while her other foot was still in manacles.

And the deeper he'd studied the statue, the more he'd learned about the many levels of meaning beneath the obvious—from the crown, to the torch, even to the statue's face—every aspect of the copper monument opened doors to rabbit holes he'd always refused to climb down. Because he was a historian, not a fantasist like his dead Harvard colleague Charles Walker, who had started him on his current journey.

And yet here he was, about to tumble down the biggest, deepest rabbit hole of all.

He shifted his head, swiveling back to see Hailey and Nick— and the pages on Hailey's lap. He didn't need to focus his eyes, because the images were too striking to ever forget.

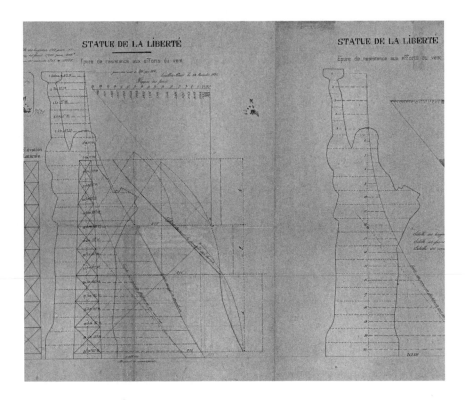

A blueprint and a painting. An interior sketch of the Statue of Liberty, presumably drawn by Gustav Eiffel—who, though it was lesser known than much of the history of the famous monument, had built the metal framework inside the copper exterior, which had been designed by French sculptor Frédéric Auguste Bartholdi—and the portrait of Benjamin Franklin, *Drawing Electricity from the Sky*, painted by artist Benjamin West circa 1805.

Side by side, the implication seemed undeniable. Eiffel's engineering blueprint of the structure inside the Eiffel Tower wasn't just a smaller-scale replica of the iconic tower he built, at approximately the same time, in Paris; it appeared to be visually almost identical to the shape and structure of Benjamin West's portrait of Franklin. That Hailey and Nick had found the two images next to

each other below Eiffel's apartment made it impossible to ignore. Eiffel's design—Mozart's design, Franklin's design—had been hidden in Benjamin West's painting all along.

It had always been a puzzle that West had painted such a strange painting so long after his friend's death, on his own deathbed; perhaps there had been a purpose to it beyond a eulogy. He had put to paint what Mozart had hidden in music, and Eiffel had then taken that paint and turned it three-dimensional, a work of architecture and engineering. His Eiffel Tower was supposed to be a temporary structure from the beginning, so he had used it as a test—but he had also turned the blueprints into something that was meant to be permanent. A Trojan horse, of sorts, a gift from France to America that contained a secret.

Hailey looked up from the bench, saw that Adrian was eyeing her and Nick. She handed Nick the pages and crossed to the railing.

"The exterior," she said, nodding at the statue, which seemed to grow larger the closer they got. "Copper plates, correct? But thin. Almost bizarrely so, less than the width of two pennies in most places. Not the most practical way to build a statue—but maybe the most *conductive*."

Adrian didn't respond, so Hailey continued. "The guidebooks say it gets struck by lightning more than any other building in the world. Over *six hundred* times a year."

Adrian didn't want to listen. But deep down, he knew the lightning strikes and odd depth of the copper were only the tip of the iceberg. The Statue of Liberty had always been the sort of monument that could inspire many a conspiracy theorist's wet dreams.

It wasn't just the connection to Gustav Eiffel, a known Freemason. Bartholdi, too, was a high-level mason, a member and leader of the Lodge Alsace Lorraine. There was a masonic cornerstone at the base of the statue, and numerous symbols throughout its design. The crown, for instance, sported seven spikes, which some thought represented the seven seas, or the seven continents—but more likely had to do with the Freemason notion of the sun, which was imagery shared by early alchemists. The torch, too, had numerous nods to the number seven, as did the number of steps leading up to the statue's viewing platform, and the height of the statue itself.

And Adrian knew—for the conspiracy minded—there was an even bigger, more obvious connection between the Statue of Liberty and alchemy. He only had to look up at Lady Liberty's countenance, beaming across the harbor to see it.

Bartholdi hadn't originally set out to build a monument to be gifted to America; in fact, it was after a visit to Egypt in 1855 that the artist conceived of building a giant statue—but not for the New York Harbor. He had planned a ninety-foot colossus to stand at the entrance to the Suez Canal. He had even designed his Egyptian statue's face—modeled on that of an unknown Egyptian woman.

When he ran into financial difficulties with his Egyptian project, he shifted gears, eventually coaxing the French and American governments to take up the funding of his colossus—and with the help of Eiffel, and his iron lattice work—the Statue of Liberty was born. But rather than craft an entirely new face for Lady Liberty, Bartholdi had simply repurposed his colossus—giving Lady Liberty the face of an Egyptian woman.

Egypt—the birthplace of alchemy—and a statue crafted by two Freemasons, filled with symbols having to do with masonry and alchemy—and now, an undeniable connection to Franklin and Revere's quest to invent the philosopher's stone.

"Copper," Hailey continued, "like the wires I found beneath Eiffel's apartment in the tower. Except here, it's not just running through the architecture—it *is* the architecture. The entire statue is wired to conduct those lightning strikes."

She paused and thought, her eyes focused on the statue's raised arm, which was touching clouds in the distance.

"Eiffel was an engineer and architect—but he wasn't an expert in electricity, and it's doubtful he could have handled the technical aspects of wiring his tower, let alone whatever is going on here. But we know he was close to Edison—who had conducted experiments in electricity and sound at the tower."

Adrian sighed. He didn't want to participate in her line of thought, but he couldn't help himself.

"Edison was also deeply connected to the Statue of Liberty. In fact, one of the original plans for the statue was for Edison to wire it for sound. He was planning to put a huge gramophone in the head, and have it 'speak' to visitors. Thankfully, the idea never gained much traction."

"Wire it for sound," Hailey repeated. "Edison could have easily done whatever wiring he needed to do for Franklin's device, under the cover of testing his gramophone plans. The question is, if indeed we're right, if Eiffel did build Franklin's device into the Statue of Liberty, is it still there? And if so, does it still function? Did it ever? If it's still functioning, you would have thought that someone would have noticed. Six hundred lightning strikes a year—at some point, the device would have been active."

When Hailey and Nick had first climbed down from the tower and told Adrian where they needed to go next, the idea had seemed ludicrous. Even if they could get back to the United States unaccosted, entering something as public as the Statue of Liberty—on an island, in New York Harbor, one of the most patrolled waterways in the world—would be a feat indeed. They didn't have the FBI agent's help anymore—as far as they knew, from what he'd told them on the way out of the police station in Paris, he had been recalled to Washington, which meant they were on their own, still wanted fugitives. Even Adrian himself had probably been added to the Boston PD's APB.

But Hailey had been certain the two images told her, in unmistakable terms, that their quarry was in the statue—and that was where they needed to go.

"The answer is there." She pointed over the ferry railing, but not at the statue's base, or its robes, or even its crown—she pointed at the statue's torch. "If Edison had used the copper as a conductive channel—fed from the exterior, through some sort of wiring, to Franklin's device somewhere in the statue's upper core, in alignment with the image from Mozart's music—then the starting point would be at the highest point. That's where the lightning strikes—that's where the electricity that powers the device, however it may work, enters the system. If it's not currently active, that's where we, too, need to start."

Adrian glanced from her to the torch, then shook his head. He didn't want to participate—but he knew, deep down, that he had no choice. Hailey was smart, Nick was resourceful, but they wouldn't succeed without his knowledge.

"If you think we need to start at the torch," he said, "then you're off by about three hundred feet."

CHAPTER THIRTY-THREE

One of the many things Nick had learned in the past few days was that it was much easier to go unnoticed staking out a national monument than it was a bank. Case in point, wandering the grounds of Liberty Island as the minutes ticked toward the late-afternoon closing time; the sun, mostly hidden by thickening rain clouds sweeping in from the direction of the open ocean, beginning its slow descent toward the choppy inlet waves; the ever-present crowd of tourists buffeting him, Hailey, and Adrian along the out-skirts of the base of the great statue, their cameras and cell phones pointed in every direction except his. The three of them had easily circumnavigated the small, twelve-acre island twice since they'd escaped the confines of the double-decker ferry, careful to avoid getting close enough to any of the island's park rangers, or the handful of New York state troopers, who were lazily patrolling between the two main attractions: the squat modern museum on the far end of the island, a mostly glass-and-steel building erected just a few years ago with picture windows facing the city, a pin-cushion of gray barely visible through the growing conglomerate of clouds, and the statue herself, dominating the view directly ahead of them.

The base of the statue alone was impressive; a massive 154-foot-tall cement pedestal with multiple levels, viewing balconies, and high walls. But to Nick, the pedestal wasn't the most intriguing part of the statue's base. The pedestal itself stood atop a star-shaped construction made primarily of granite. Adrian had explained that the star-shaped structure was actually the remains of a military fort that had existed on the island before the statue had been shipped over, in pieces, from Paris. Fort Wood—named for an American Army engineer who had been killed during the War of 1812—had been decommissioned in the 1930s, well after the statue had been dedicated. Star-shaped forts—such as Fort Wood, which sported eleven points, went back as far as Michelangelo, who had designed such a fort to protect Florence from invaders, and they had been popular in Europe for nearly three hundred years. Though the structure was no longer occupied, it had been repurposed as a fitting setting for the monument that rose, like a copper-plated jewel, from its center.

Up close, Lady Liberty was beyond impressive. From Nick's angle as he strolled around her base, she looked enormous, her sweeping cloak, though dull and green in color, seemed to shimmer in movement, as if swirling with the wind coming in off the harbor. Nick could only imagine what the statue had looked like when it had first been built—covered in bright, shiny copper, before the copper had oxidized to its current, protective state.

Beneath the cloak, he could clearly see the statue's feet—enormous, one stepping ahead of the other—and the stretch of broken chain by one of her ankles. He could also see the manacle still around the other ankle, chaining her to her roost. Shifting his head upward, he could just make out her crown, high above her noble Egyptian nose and cheekbones, but he couldn't see the torch at all, lifted upward into the darkening sky. He could only imagine the twists of plated gold that covered the flame leaping up from the torch, punching through the thickening clouds.

Nick shifted his gaze downward as they passed the entrance to the base, with its metal detectors and turnstiles. He counted at least three park rangers outside, along with a pair of state troopers, though at the moment there was no line to get in because of the late hour. The statue would be closing in minutes, and the larger crowds were moving away from the base toward the paths and gardens that led to the docked final ferry for the return to the city.

As they continued past the entrance to the base, the tourists began to thin. Nick touched Hailey's arm, then nodded toward one of the corners of the star-shaped granite former fort. If his plan was going to work, they were going to have to move fast, when the moment was right. He wasn't as concerned about Hailey as he was about Adrian, who had noticed his nod and had suddenly seemed to freeze up, his shoulders stiffening beneath his tweed jacket.

"You with us, Professor? We can try this without you. Just head back to the ferry, and wait for us back at the terminal."

Adrian shook his head, his hair bouncing with the motion.

"OK. When I give the signal, move. When we reach the trees, drop low and follow me."

He continued a few more feet until they were beyond the last few tourists, who had turned to head back toward the ferry. Then he grabbed Hailey's hand and jogged off the path, toward the trees. Beyond the first set of trees he saw a second, and then a low embankment ending in a low chain, a waist-high fence.

He didn't look back to see if Adrian was following. A moment later he was pulling Hailey through the trees, then he dropped into a crouch and continued forward, yard by yard. To his right, he saw a deep incline leading toward a sea wall that had been built around the lip of the island. Beyond that, he assumed, was dark water, at least fifty feet deep. But to his left, just a few yards away beyond the low fence, one of the granite walls, jutting out to one of the star's points.

He reached the fence in two steps, then heaved himself over and helped Hailey over after him. Adrian, struggling to follow, reached them a moment later. It took both Nick and Hailey to help pull the professor by his sleeves over the fence and onto the ground. Then the three of them rushed around the edge of the star's point, then into the indent before the next point.

They moved close to the granite wall and made their way farther from the path leading back around to the entrance to the base. The farther they walked, the less nervous Nick felt that they would be discovered. An added bonus—so close to the early-nineteenth-century ruins of the fort, Adrian's attention became focused on the history of the place, rather than their trespassing.

"A medieval design," he monologued, as they continued along the wall, "that wasn't particularly effective once cannons became part of every military's arsenal. Although the star points gave defenders many vantage points, the walls were notoriously weak farther from the center. Which didn't keep the American Republic from building them up and down the coast."

They reached another jag in the wall, followed it around to another indentation. Now they were near the rear of the statue, lost in Lady Liberty's long shadow. Nick could feel the breeze getting colder, as the sun continued to descend.

"Fort Wood had been one of a necklace of such forts on islands around the harbor that never actually saw any action during the War of 1812; but it was used to house prisoners during the early years of the Civil War, which made it a fitting location for the statue, as her original purpose was to commemorate the freeing of the slaves."

Nick was less concerned with the history of the fort than he was about something else Adrian had told them when they'd first arrived on Liberty Island. As they reached the innermost point of the next indent in the wall, Nick finally saw the dark outline of a large bay door, in front of a path that led down toward the sea wall.

He pointed, and Adrian finally looked up from the aging granite to their right and nodded. As the professor had described, though the fort had long ago been decommissioned as a military base and a prison, it had also served as makeshift housing for the many engineers, coppersmiths, and construction workers who had built the statue, back when this island was little more than a deposit of rock and sand. More important, the materials that had been used to build the statue—the iron for Eiffel's interior structure, the components for the cement, and the smelting of the copper—had come via the ocean and were warehoused within the fort until they were ready to be used.

Heavy materials, shipped in via the water—that meant an access point, out of sight from dignitaries who might have been brought by to see the construction in progress. Even after construction was finished and the fort cleared out, access to the interior would presumably still be maintained; a structure this large had to be constantly monitored by engineers, which meant there would always be a way inside.

As Nick led Adrian and Hailey toward the bay door, he heard a PA system cough to life in the distance. A monotoned park ranger announced that the last ferry's departure was imminent, and that the island would be closed to visitors in five more minutes. Nick didn't know what the protocol was for the island's closing, but he assumed there would soon be a sweep of the grounds, maybe even a flyover by helicopter. Which meant they would have to move fast.

He sprinted the last few yards to the bay door—and as soon as he was close enough to the dark outline to make out details, his lips turned down at the corners. Not only did the door appear bolted shut, but there was a keypad halfway above the bolts, sporting a blinking pair of lights. No doubt alarmed, and not something simple like he'd dealt with at the Royal Academy of Music.

As Adrian pulled up next to him, he shook his head.

"This isn't going to work. I can't get through this quickly—if at all."

"Then we need to head back," Adrian hissed. "Before the ferry leaves."

"Hey guys. Look up."

Hailey, who was behind them, pointed to a spot about two feet above the top of the bay doors. An indentation in the granite, in the shape of an arched window. The window had been sealed over by what looked like aging plaster.

Adrian raised an eyebrow. "Fortified Stars were built mainly for siege situations. Poorly designed for fights involving cannons—but before cannons, they could withstand many months of siege. The walls were difficult to breach, easy to defend. But often, attackers would set fires to try and smoke defenders out. Which meant there needed to be many ways in and out. My guess is, that's an original hatch—an escape route."

"It appears sealed," Nick said. "But worth a look." He eyed the frame of the bay door, then glanced at Adrian. "Give me a boost."

The professor looked like Nick had just asked him to dance. But he braced himself against the wall, and held out his hands, fingers linked. With his help, Nick managed to reach the ledge at the top of the bay door, then heaved himself up toward the arched hatch. The effort sent shards of pain through his chest—his rib hadn't healed much since the day before, and he had no choice but to ignore it—but he managed to get his feet onto the ledge, then extend himself until he was in front of the plaster sealing.

He tapped the sealing with his fingers. It didn't sound thick, and there was a hollowness to it. He quickly pulled his jacket off his shoulders, wrapping the denim around his right fist. Then he arched back, and punched at the center of the plaster as hard as he could.

The plaster shattered, and his hand hit wood planking, which seemed to bow inward. He brought his arm back again and slammed his fist into the wood. There was a loud splintering, then the wood clattered inward.

He could feel cool air coming from inside. He used both hands to widen the opening, until he could fit his shoulders through. The interior was dark, but he could see the floor just a few feet below the window, the entrance to a maintenance corridor.

He crawled inside and dropped his feet to the floor. Then he leaned back outside and beckoned for Adrian to send Hailey up.

It took a few minutes for all three of them to make it through the opening; most of that was Adrian making feeble attempts at jumping high enough for Nick to reach his outstretched hands—something he didn't accomplish until he heard the sound of helicopter blades in the distance, the first of many sweeps of the island that they nervously witnessed from the safety of the corridor, once they were all inside. Nick wasn't worried anyone in a chopper would see the open hatch—it was dark enough outside now that it would take a perfectly aimed spotlight to notice. But there was always the chance a guard on the ground had caught sight of them on their way in, so he held his breath until he felt confident they had made it inside unnoticed.

Stepping back from the opening, he glanced around the corridor. It was mostly cement, the ceiling lined with rusting, aging pipes, with a few shinier lengths in various places. Following the pipes, he saw another hatch a few yards ahead, with the end of a metal ladder just beyond the opening.

"Looks like plumbing," Nick said. "Probably a sprinkler system. Some of this has been added more recently."

Adrian nodded. "The statue has been evacuated more than once because of fire alarms; just last year there was an incident involving a shorted-out spotlight in the torch, and they added an entirely new emergency alarm system, as well as more sprinklers. They draw water right from the harbor."

Hailey was looking at the bottom of the ladder. "You think this runs all the way through to the pedestal?"

"Probably," Nick said. Irrigation systems like sprinklers had to be accessible for maintenance, and if the pipes ran all the way to the statue, then there had to be a way through for the plumbing work.

Which meant that it was possible they would be able to access the statue without ever going through the front entrance, which would assuredly be locked and monitored.

But Nick knew, from what Adrian had told them both as they'd disembarked the ferry onto the island—though the statue was their eventual destination, they had somewhere else they needed to go first.

He glanced back toward the hatch they had come through, watching and waiting for the air to continue to darken outside.

———

If Nick squinted his eyes just right, he could see it.

Looming over him, where he stood next to Adrian in the center of the glass-walled atrium on the first floor of the museum that had been erected in 2019 for this singular artifact. It was backlit by the glow on the other side of the glass, which was provided by small spotlights set around the edges of the craggy outcropping that separated this museum from the edge of the island not twenty yards below, and the dark waves crashing against the rocks. Three thousand pounds of copper, blown glass, and iron, chiseled and pressed over a century and a half ago, then rechiseled a half dozen times over the course of decades into something that looked both malformed and beautiful. From just the right angle, in the mist of awe inspired by both the artistry of the object itself and the knowledge that there may well have been an almost mystic purpose behind it—Nick could *see it*—the *living, undulating,* spitting flames of the massive torch rising up—if not to the heavens, then to the cantilevered ceiling above his head.

"The Torch of Enlightenment," Hailey murmured, from behind him. "A symbol of liberty, abolition, the American revolution. A nice cover story, anyway."

Nick took a step back. He had to admit, he was overwhelmed, seeing the torch up close. The actual, *original* torch of the Statue of Liberty, created in a factory in Paris and carted across the ocean. Nick hadn't known that the torch in all the pictures and postcards and TV shows and movies he had seen growing up was a replica, put in place in 1984 to replace the damaged, aging original torch. First moved to a museum in the pedestal beneath the statue, the original torch was then hoisted, in 2018, over to this spot—a new museum, built expressly to show off the iconic artifact in all its glory.

It hadn't been difficult for the three of them to make their way over to the modern, squat museum hanging over the edge of the far side of Liberty Island; once the helicopters had finished their patrols, and the clouds had blocked out what little moonlight remained, they'd gone back out through the hatch and scrambled from patch of tree to patch of tree. Twice, they'd seen flashlights along the paths winding up from the ferry dock, but they hadn't encountered anyone. There was some sort of security presence on the island, but it was doubtful they took their jobs too seriously. Patrolling an island in the middle of New York Harbor, with a storm on its way, wasn't the sort of gig that would end up high on anyone's résumé.

Thankfully, the lock on the delivery entrance on the first floor of the Torch Museum had been simple enough—a tumbler job set on a timer that had been easily shorted with the business end of a nail file Hailey had found at the bottom of her bag. Once inside, they'd been careful to avoid the cameras pointed toward anything that looked valuable; they'd moved quickly past exhibits filled with paintings and photos of the statue and torch in various states of construction, and skirted past a small theater showing a looped video of a flyover of the island.

Once they'd reached the torch itself, Nick had spotted three more cameras hanging from the ceiling; impossible to avoid, so he'd gone directly to the source, finding the wiring junction that connected the cameras to the closed-circuit system. He again used the nail file to cut through the plastic covering and sever the conductive links. Somewhere, he assumed, a security screen would have just gone dark, maybe followed by a blinking warning light— but he hoped that with the weather turning worse by the moment, they would assume that it had something to do with an electrical disturbance. Eventually, someone would be sent out to take a look, but that was unavoidable. Most of Nick's life had been lived with a clock ticking in the background.

It wasn't until Nick, Hailey, and Adrian had gotten close to the torch—stepping over a velvet rope that ringed the platform it had been set on top of—that he'd realized the flames of the original design looked very little like the replica on the statue itself. Instead of smooth, golden-hued flickers rising upward toward the sky, the original torch had a flame made up of numerous panes of colored glass. Around the panes, there were braces made of the same copper of the statue, but still much more brassy and shiny, having been kept indoors for the past few decades. On top of the flames was what appeared to be a small pyramid, plated in gold. The base of the torch seemed more familiar. Right beneath the flames, there was a balcony of sorts that could fit a few tourists, surrounded by a low railing. Around the balcony's edges stood a series of sculpted, triangular copper palm leaves on long stalks—maybe four feet tall. They seemed to spring right out of the torch's cylindrical base, which presumably had fit into the statue's raised right hand.

Adrian and Hailey walked around the edge of the torch as Hailey eyed the colored glass of its flame. "You used to be able to go inside," Adrian said. "When it was first constructed, a handful of VIPs would make the long climb up the statue's arm and spend time inside the flames, peering out at the city and the harbor. But on July 30, 1916, that all changed. An act of terrorism—the largest act of terrorism to ever hit our shores before 9/11—nearly blew the entire statue off its pedestal and closed the torch to tourism forever."

Nick raised his eyebrows. "Someone tried to blow up the Statue of Liberty?"

"Not exactly. At the start of World War I, a cabal of German spies planted a number of pencil bombs on the nearby island of Black Tom, which happened to contain a secret American munitions depot. The explosion was so large, it measured 5.5 on the Richter scale, shattered windows in Times Square, and shook buildings as far away as Baltimore. The Statue of Liberty was pummeled by shrapnel, and the torch was damaged so badly that it was closed to the public forever."

"Is that why the torch was replaced?" Nick asked. He noticed that Hailey had paused halfway around the torch and was staring curiously at one of the palm fronds rising along the side of the balcony.

"That was much later," Adrian said. "The torch was recon-structed numerous times after the blast. At one point, the idea was to turn the torch into some sort of lighthouse. Holes were drilled along the base, and a bunch of candle-powered spotlights were added—but it never looked right, so the holes were covered up with the colored glass you see here. That pyramid you see on top was originally supposed to be solid gold. But that was deemed too expensive and was replaced with glass. Then it was refitted with plated gold."

"A pyramid," Nick said. "Another nod to Egypt—maybe to alchemy as well. And those palm leaves? More alchemical symbolism?"

Hailey cleared her throat, then reached into her bag and retrieved one of the two pages they'd uncovered at the Eiffel Tower. To Nick's surprise, it wasn't the blueprint of the statue, but the print of the Benjamin West painting. She held it up and looked at the image, then showed it to Nick and Adrian.

"See anything that looks familiar?"

Nick squinted at the image. Franklin in his cape, surrounded by the half-naked cherubs. The strange, orb-like device in one cor-ner, the storm clouds above. And then he noticed that Hailey was pointing to an object directly above the main group of cherubs. A triangular object, white, that seemed almost disconnected from the rest of the painting.

"Franklin's kite," Nick said.

Oddly, the kite didn't seem to be attached to the string that ran above Franklin's head, from which the famous key dangled, directly above his outstretched hand. He focused on the kite itself, and immediately noted its oblong triangular shape. Then he looked upward, toward the torch's balcony, and focused on one of the palm leaves attached to one of the four-foot-long copper stems.

"Maybe," Hailey said, putting words to her thoughts, "these aren't supposed to be leaves—or not just leaves."

Adrian made a noise, but Hailey ignored him and turned her gaze toward the torch's cylindrical base. Then back to the painting.

"Look at Franklin's hand. His arm is raised, but his hand—it's not open, it's closed, as if he's holding on to something."

Nick had to admit she was right. Franklin's hand was almost closed into a fist, as if he were holding something aloft. In fact, Franklin's hand was in the exact same position as the hand of the statue standing tall on the other side of Liberty Island—except the shape of Lady Liberty's hand made sense, because it was wrapped around the cylindrical base of the torch.

If the painting had really led to the blueprint, which had led to the statue, then it made sense. Because Franklin's hand had, from the beginning, been designed to hold that torch.

The Torch of Enlightenment.

Hailey broke away from Adrian and headed toward the base of the torch.

"*Benjamin Franklin Drawing Electricity from the Sky,*" she said, as she moved. She reached the base and then was suddenly climbing up the side. It wasn't difficult—though the cylinder at the bottom was smooth, the balcony hung low enough so she could get a grip beneath the railing. A moment later she was hoisting herself between two of the palm stems onto the balcony's base.

"*Drawing* electricity," she said. "Not passive—not Franklin being struck by lightning, or discovering the power of electricity. West meant this painting to show Franklin *drawing* the electricity out of the sky."

"Hailey," Adrian hissed, but she ignored him.

She moved from palm leaf to palm leaf, putting her hands around each stem—testing them one at a time.

"What are you doing?" Adrian nearly shouted.

"Nick, come help me."

Nick didn't need to be asked twice. He pushed past Adrian and clambered up the side of the torch, sliding under the railing until he was next to Hailey. Together, they tried the next palm leaf. The copper felt cold and smooth against Nick's hand, and the stem didn't give at all. Then they moved to the next leaf.

This time, when they put their hands around the stem and twisted, together, there was a metallic click. The entire stem came loose, and Hailey pulled it free. As Nick had guessed, it was about four feet long from the triangular leaf to the other end—which, it turned out, was oddly shaped. Almost like a hexagon, with six sharp corners—except the entire bottom was covered in a soft, cloth-like material.

"Looks like a gear," Nick said. "But what's this around the end?"

Hailey's face was flushed as she looked from the end of the palm stem to Nick, then to Adrian.

"I think I know what this is," she said quietly. Then she glanced up through one of the glass windows that looked out onto the island. The air was so thick now from the coming storm, it was hard to see anything outside, but Nick had an idea what Hailey was looking toward.

"More important," she continued, "I know where this goes."

CHAPTER THIRTY-FOUR

Down on her hands and knees, cold aluminum pressing into the flesh of her palms and against the thin material of her slacks, she moved forward, halfway between a crawl and a crouch.

Hailey was following the dark shape of Nick's similarly bent body, as he led the way through the narrow service shaft. Large metal pipes snaked along the walls to Hailey's left and right, but she did her best to keep her focus directly ahead. She could feel Adrian's heavy breathing behind her, as he crawled along after them—thankfully, he'd stifled his bitter, self-cursing monologue when they'd first crawled up into the plumbing system from their hiding place in the remains of the fort, helping to keep their progress through the base of the great statue as quiet as possible. Still, it was obvious to Hailey what Adrian thought of their current situation—climbing their way upward, one level of service shaft at a time.

They reached another incline in the shaft, and Hailey knew they had to be near the top of the pedestal now. A tremble moved through her, as she caught sight of the long copper palm stem strapped to the center of Nick's back by a length of velvet rope they'd borrowed from the torch museum. Though it was too dark to see any of the palm leaf's details, she could picture the triangular frond and the strange, hexagonal knob at its bottom, covered in soft padding. She hadn't yet explained to Nick and Adrian what she was planning. *Part hunch, part science.* Mostly intuition.

Nick coughed, as he turned another corner, then continued upward on the incline. Hailey could tell he was in extreme pain. Though he hadn't complained about his rib since they'd reached the island, his breathing hadn't sounded right since he'd taken the blow from the woman on the top of the Eiffel Tower. The amount of abuse Nick's body had taken over the previous few days was frightening. Hailey could only pray that they were close to the end of their journey—

Nick stopped so suddenly that Hailey nearly crawled right into him. He had his burner phone out and was playing the light on the ceiling above his head. Hailey saw the panel immediately, similar to the one they had come through at the lowest level, no doubt another access hatch for the plumbing experts who maintained the monument's sprinkler system.

Nick braced his shoulder against the panel and used his legs to push it open. The noise echoed back through the tunnel behind Hailey, and cool air spilled in from above. A moment later, Nick was through, then reached down for her and Adrian.

Hailey rose to her feet in the back corner of the upper floor of the statue's pedestal. The space was dimly lit by various security bulbs strung along the low ceiling, and from the dull red glow from a pair of emergency exit signs in the far corner. She saw that the walls around her were a mix of cement and steel, while the floor beneath her feet was corrugated metal. To her direct left was a doorway leading out to the balcony that ringed the upper part of the pedestal. To her right, the glass entrance to a narrow set of metal stairs leading upward.

Looking across the submarine-like space, she could see that the metal stairs were actually one of two identical sets of stairs—one for the ascension through the statue, the second set designated for the way back down. The stairs were contained on either side by metal railings, and each step was little more than a wide shoulder-length in width.

She reached the glass entrance ahead of Nick and started upward. She knew it was going to be a long way—354 steps from the pedestal to the crown—high enough that tourists were warned to be in good physical condition before they were allowed to make the ascent. The toughness of the climb was amplified by the narrowness of the staircase and the way it wound in a tight spiral above her. It didn't help that the interior of the statue seemed cold and stark, like she was ascending through the skeleton of some ancient, iron dinosaur. Around her, open bars and staggered joints led off in every direction toward the statue's outer skin, which was as far as a dozen yards away in most places, a dark greenish hue that mimicked the tarnished copper of the exterior.

Faster and faster she climbed, her chest heaving as her thighs and calves went numb. She could hear Nick behind her, and Adrian behind Nick. Both of them sounded like they were struggling to keep up, but Hailey didn't slow her pace. Any fear she felt at being inside the statue in the middle of the night or of encountering the woman from the Eiffel Tower who might appear at any time, dissipated in the face of her anticipation.

Each footfall reverberated through the metal framework of the statue and echoed off the copper walls. Taking the steps two at a time, counting as she went, she finally saw a glow coming from the spiral above, a glow that got brighter with each step, until she burst out the top of another twist of stairs onto a small metal platform.

The first thing she saw were the windows. Twenty-five of them, arranged in a circular pattern around the base of what she realized immediately was the crown's interior. Each window was small—eighteen inches wide and two feet tall—and set about three feet above the floor. They looked to be thick glass, leaking what little moonlight there was outside against the curved walls and ceiling of the viewing area. The space was embraced by a high metal railing, and ended in the second set of stairs, which led back down into the statue.

Nick and Adrian finally came off the stairs behind her and joined her at the edge of the viewing platform. Both were breathing hard, and Adrian's hair looked damp with sweat.

"What, exactly, are we looking for?" Adrian said between breaths.

Hailey reached into her bag and pulled out the print of the painting again. Instead of Franklin's extended hand, or the triangular kite above the cherubs, this time she pointed to something to Franklin's left—a device tended to by a pair of cherubs, a metal sphere suspended by a string from a curved frame. Out of the bottom of the metal sphere, a swirl of electricity flowed toward a pair of glass bottles—Leyden jars.

"Franklin's device?" Nick asked. He looked around them, at the empty viewing platform. "I don't see anything that looks like that machine. I definitely don't see any naked cherubs."

"Look harder," Hailey said. And then she shifted her own eyes up, toward the ceiling.

The ceiling of the viewing platform was curved like the interior of a dome, a sphere that had been cut in half, crisscrossed by curved metal beams. Curved—in exactly the same shape as the frame of the device in the painting.

Nick exhaled. Adrian looked from the ceiling to Hailey.

"You're saying Franklin's device, his philosopher's stone—"

"We're standing in it."

Hailey spoke quickly now, her excitement growing. "When the

statue is struck by lightning, the electricity flows around the copper exterior, like a Faraday—or Franklin—cage. But instead of harmlessly flowing to the ground, internal wiring—Edison's copper wiring—funnels the electrical charge into those beams, which focuses it into the center of this platform."

"Christ," Adrian said. Then he shook his head. "Why wouldn't anyone know about this? As you said, the Statue of Liberty is hit by lightning more than any other object on Earth."

"By design," Hailey said, still putting the pieces of the puzzle together. "But it isn't enough. Not nearly enough."

She whirled toward Nick and pointed to the long copper palm leaf and stem tied to his back. He carefully undid the velvet rope and handed it to her.

"Revere's bell worked, briefly—but the chemical transformation wasn't permanent, because the sonic energy created by the ringing of the bell wasn't enough. Franklin's armonica wasn't any better—sound wasn't the answer. But electricity—lightning, Hellfire—Franklin knew it contained the power he was seeking. He just needed to find a way to harness that power. Not just to use it—to *draw* it, from the sky."

"The torch," Adrian said.

Hailey nodded. "The flame was originally lined in gold," she said. "Even more conductive than copper. It's naturally the part of the statue that is struck the most. But it's more complex than a simple lightning rod. It was built separately, placed in the statue's hand—"

"—and reconstructed and replaced," Adrian said. "The torch out there"—he gestured through one of the windows, in the direction of the statue's extended arm—"isn't even Eiffel and Bartholdi's design."

"Part of it has been reconstructed and redesigned," Hailey

countered. "But the base is still the same. Lady Liberty's hand—*Franklin*'s hand—still holds tight to the same, original design. I think that base is *complex*, as well."

She showed them both the painting again, and put her finger above Franklin's extended hand. Right there, unavoidable, impossible to ignore—the *key*. Spitting electricity down between Franklin's clenched fingers.

Nick was watching them both. Then he looked at Adrian.

"Is it still accessible?" he asked. "Since they closed it to the public?"

Adrian shrugged, then nodded. "A few turns down the other stairwell, there's a maintenance ladder that runs up the interior of the statue's arm. They've placed a series of high-powered spotlights within the torch, a tribute to the original idea of having the statue act as some sort of lighthouse."

Nick gestured for the palm leaf. Hailey shook her head.

"Someone needs to stay here. To see if it works. Only one of us needs to go up there—to see if I'm right."

Nick kept his hand out but Hailey stepped away, toward the stairway on the other side of the platform. This was her puzzle to solve.

"How will we know if it works?" Nick called after her.

"You'll know," Hailey said simply. Then she started down the steps.

Hailey had gone five turns of the spiral, maybe twenty feet down from the viewing platform of the crown, when she found the opening in the railing. A stretch of scaffolding beyond the opening led to the interior of the statue's copper wall, along which was affixed a fireman's ladder, leading at a slight angle up into a hollow, cylindrical tube of more scaffolding—no doubt the interior of the statue's uplifted arm.

Hailey stood at the opening in the railing for a good beat and gathered her strength. She couldn't see the top of the ladder from where she was standing but imagined it had to be another twenty to thirty feet up, into near darkness. But there was no turning back now.

She put the copper stem under her arm and hurried across the scaffolding to the bottom rung. Then she started up, willing herself not to look down as she went. The slight angle of the ladder made it an easier climb than she'd expected. Before she realized it, she'd gone more than halfway—and peering up through the cylinder above, she could make out a circular hatch planted in the metal ceiling at the top.

The cylinder grew narrower as she reached the top few rungs, becoming barely wider than her shoulders at the peak. The hatch had an extended handle, which turned easily, clicking as she opened it. Then it swung upward, and cold, wet air swept down through the opening, nearly causing her to lose her grip on the ladder. She steeled herself, then pulled her body up and through.

She stood on the circular metal balcony that ran around the base of the torch. It was about the same width as the balcony from the original torch in the museum, but out here, with the wind pulling at her from every side and the darkness closing in around her, it felt painfully narrow and open to the elements. The waist-high railing that ran around the outside seemed flimsy, and beyond that was a vertigo-inducing drop.

Hailey focused her attention in the opposite direction, to the surface of the torch to her left, which ran upward toward the dancing, gold-plated flame above. The torch was about eighteen feet high, blocking off her view of the other side. Whatever spotlights were inside were off—perhaps because of the stormy weather, or the thick cloud cover.

She started around the balcony, keeping her eyes on the inner wall, searching for an opening. What she was looking for would be inside protected from the elements. She moved carefully, one foot in front of the other, her face pelted by heavy raindrops as the clouds began to open up. The metal floor of the balcony reverberated with the rain, and her feet nearly slipped as she followed the circle, then reached the back of the torch. A few more steps, she thought to herself. A few more steps—

"I was getting worried, dear, that this was going to take all night."

Hailey froze. From around the curve in front of her stepped the woman from the Eiffel Tower and train. Her hair was down now, swimming with the wind in front of her rounded cheeks. A spray of rain splashed across the lenses of the pair of thick glasses she was wearing, so she removed them and tossed them over the railing, where they vanished without a sound.

"How did you . . . ?" Hailey started.

The woman shrugged. "The same way I'll be leaving when we're finished." She nodded at the railing, perhaps toward the water of the harbor far below. Had she scaled the exterior of the statue? Had she come by boat?

Then the woman noticed the palm leaf and stem in Hailey's hands. "Interesting souvenir."

Hailey took a step back, but the woman shook her head. Slowly, she removed a handgun from the belt of her slacks. "I know. I hate them, too. I almost never carry them. But my employer insisted. And in truth, they can be quite—persuasive."

The woman shifted so that Hailey could see past her—a few feet farther along the curve of the torch, a door leading inside.

The woman nodded again, then stepped aside so that Hailey could move past.

Hailey's mind spun. She thought about swinging the palm leaf—the four-foot length of copper was heavy enough to cause damage—but she'd seen this woman fight before. It would be a pointless exercise, even without the gun. Hailey had no choice but to play this out and hope that an opportunity arose.

She moved carefully past the woman and reached the hatch. Bending slightly, she slipped inside.

The space was small, like the cockpit of an airplane. There were transparent panels along the walls, looking out on the balcony and then farther out, on the harbor, which was mostly shrouded in clouds. The floor was thick metal, and the entire back curve was taken up by a series of large spotlights in steel casings, with wires running behind them. The lights were all off—but looking at them, Hailey had a sudden thought.

She heard the woman behind her, standing in the open hatch.

"I assume we're here for a reason," the woman said. The gun hung almost casually in her right hand, not pointed at Hailey, but not pointed away.

Hailey turned back to the interior of the torch, and began scanning the walls, the glass panels, the curved ceiling—and then the floor. The floor looked concave, and in the direct center she saw a drain. She didn't think the windows around the sides could open—and she knew that the original plans were for an opaque, golden flame, and no windows at all. Which meant the drain seemed—*superfluous.*

She bent low and crawled forward until she reached the center of the floor. She put her fingers into the drain. The metal looked old, like it was part of the original design. Rusted through between many of the holes in its center, and covered in dark crud along the edges. She got her fingers into three of the holes, and pulled as hard as she could.

There was a crack, and the top of the drain came loose. She put the rusted piece aside and peered down. Directly where the drain cover had been, she saw a perfectly round hole leading into the interior of the torch's base. Reaching a finger inside, she felt around the edges—there was something thick and almost glassy inside, running down through what appeared to be a narrow tube.

"Amber," she said quietly.

She could tell from touch alone, even before she saw the slight golden glow coming from the material. The interior of the tube was lined in amber.

"Made from fossilized tree resin," she continued, a little louder. "In ancient times, they actually believed it was a special material produced by the rays of the sun. Perhaps the most important material in humanity's early history, thought to have healing powers."

The woman was watching her carefully from the open hatch. Hailey leaned back from the opening and took the palm leaf in both hands. She turned it over, eyeing the long shaft. She could hear the wind from outside, sweeping in through the hatch around the woman, pulling at the free strands of her hair.

"It was the Egyptians who first realized amber had electrostatic properties. Drag something fibrous across its surface—cloth, hemp, felt—and it gives off sparks. But it wasn't until the mid-eighteenth century that anyone concluded the phenomenon was something other than magic."

She held up the leaf, showing the woman in the open hatch the butt of the long stem, wrapped in soft material.

"Lightly frayed hemp," Hailey commented.

The woman's eyes were widening, but Hailey ignored her.

"It was actually a Dutch physicist who first discovered what today we call static electricity," she said. "Rubbing lightly frayed hemp against amber. He was able to store the electricity in a device that he named after himself—a Leyden jar."

She paused. The woman looked at her. The barrel of the gun had drifted toward the floor as Hailey talked, but the woman didn't seem to care. She was intent on Hailey.

"Is that what this is? In there—some sort of huge Leyden jar? To store static electricity?"

Hailey shook her head. "A Leyden jar is basically a battery. This isn't a battery. It's something else."

She lifted the palm leaf in both hands, up into the air. She aimed the base, covered in the frayed hemp, toward the hole in the floor.

"As the story goes . . ." she said, her heart thudding in her chest. *Would this work? Was she right? Were the puzzle pieces lining up the way she believed they would?* "Benjamin Franklin flew his kite on a stormy night. Hanging from the kite was a key, that drew lightning out of the clouds. But not into a Leyden jar. Franklin wasn't charging a battery."

Hailey glanced at the woman—who was still in the doorway, the wind whipping in from behind her—and then focused on the hole in the floor.

"He was powering a generator," Hailey hissed.

And then she jammed the stem into the hole. She felt the frayed hemp slide in against the amber interior. With all her strength, she gripped the palm by the leaf, and twisted it in a tight spiral.

"The biggest generator on Earth."

There was a loud screeching sound as the hemp slid against the amber, and then she felt something tighten against the copper stem. Suddenly the palm leaf twisted out of her hands and started spinning, faster and faster, carried forward by the electromagnetic connection of the two materials. There was a groan of metal against metal. Hailey felt her skin tingle, as her hair rose above her head. She slid back—and then shielded her eyes with her hands.

The woman in the open hatch stared at her, was about to shout something—when suddenly the spotlights on the other side of the room flashed on. Several thousand lumens of light exploded directly into the woman's face. She screamed and stumbled back, clamping her hands over her eyes.

Hailey was ready. She leapt forward and yanked the palm leaf out of the hole in the center of the floor. The groaning stopped, and the spotlights flickered off—but Hailey was moving fast. Without thinking, she dove at the woman, the palm frond in her hands like a spear, the triangular leaf aimed directly ahead.

There was a sickening crunch. Hailey looked down and saw the leaf embedded two inches into the woman's chest, right below her collarbone. The woman gasped—but Hailey was still moving forward, her legs churning with all her strength. The woman lost her footing and skidded across the wet floor of the narrow balcony, then hit the railing hard. There was a brief, frozen pause—and then her body toppled backward over the top of the railing.

Hailey held on tight to the copper stem. There was another sickening sound as the triangular leaf tore free, and then the woman was gone, plummeting straight down into the darkness. Hailey looked over the edge just in time to see the woman hit the statue's outstretched arm. Her body jackknifed like a broken doll, then slid along the rippling copper robes, down, down—and then she was gone from view.

Hailey fell back from the railing, gasping for air. She felt a momentary pang of guilt; she had just sent a woman over the edge to her death. But she'd had no choice. And frankly, she could hardly believe it had worked. Her theory had been correct. The torch wasn't a lightning rod, it was a generator. Franklin's device wasn't powered by lightning strikes—it *drew* lightning from the sky, using the physics of electromagnetism. The static electricity caused by the spinning palm leaf against the amber interior of the torch's base amplified the electrical currents in the clouds, creating a feedback loop of electromagnetism.

And that same electromagnetism powered the spotlights. Just as the ambient electricity in the air had caused Hailey's skin to tingle and her hair to rise—it had excited the chemicals inside the spotlights, causing them to power on.

Franklin's device had saved Hailey's life. But at the moment, that was in the back of her mind—because she had been *right*. The Statue of Liberty didn't just house Franklin's invention—his philosopher's stone. The Statue of Liberty *was* his philosopher's stone.

She turned, still gripping the palm leaf, and crawled back through the hatch into the interior of the torch. She lifted the leaf above her head again, ignoring the rivulets of blood that dripped from its triangular peak. Then she jammed the long stem back into the hole in the center of the floor. With all her might, she twisted.

The groaning began again, as the leaf began to spin on its own. Hailey slid back, away from the twirling metal. She could *feel* the electricity spreading around her, could almost *hear* it sizzling through the air. She could imagine it rushing down from the clouds and touching the copper exterior of the statue, riding down the curves and angles of her cloak. Spreading into the wiring beneath the cloak, into the very structure of the monument.

The spotlights flashed on again, thousands of lumens turning the air as white as a star. She closed her eyes tightly and crawled backward toward the hatch. As she reached the opening, she heard one of the spotlights' bulbs burst—glass sprayed through the air and clattered against the curved walls of the torch. Then she was outside.

There was a great rumbling around her. She opened her eyes and saw the clouds had suddenly become thick around the top of the torch, darker than the night itself. There was a sudden crack and a huge bolt of lightning tore down, hitting the gold-plated flames above her. The entire torch shook, and there was an intense sizzling sound, the very air tightening around her. But she felt no heat, no pain. She realized the electricity was being pulled down through the torch, through the statue's uplifted hand, and into the base. A massive Van de Graaff generator and Faraday cage, funneling an immense amount of electricity—of pure, untethered power—toward one destination, one spot. For one purpose, thousands of years in the making.

CHAPTER THIRTY-FIVE

Adrian gasped as he stumbled backward, as far from the center of the viewing platform in the crown of the Statue of Liberty as he could, and nearly toppled down the spiral set of stairs behind him. Nick was only a few feet away, standing his ground, but the ex-con looked like a ghost. His hair was rising above his head, and his skin had turned nearly transparent. Adrian could feel his own hair was also rising, some of the strands nearly three inches above the top of his head.

The sound was immense—a metal groaning coming from somewhere above, followed by a strange sizzling that seemed to run along the crown's walls. Then he looked up at the ceiling—and he nearly fell down the stairs again. There were flickers of blue spreading across the curved metal bars, an almost liquid fire, running from one side of the curve to the other.

Nick snapped Adrian out of his terror with a shout. Adrian saw that Nick was pointing to a spot at the direct center of the platform ahead of them, right below the middle of the curved ceiling. As they watched, a tiny bolt of electricity—white, jagged lightning—ran down from the curved bars above to the floor. It hit, dissipating into the metal—and was followed by another bolt, then another. It was like watching a Van de Graaff generator—but from the *inside*.

"We need something lead," Nick shouted.

Adrian's eyes widened. Could this really be happening?

Nick didn't wait for Adrian to respond. He leapt forward, stopping a few inches from where the bolts of electricity were hitting the floor, and pulled something out from under his jacket. He placed the object on the ground, then slid back next to Adrian.

Adrian squinted toward the object—and realized instantly what it was. Something lead, and small, and utterly familiar.

A key. The skeleton key to the archive in the Royal Academy of Music, which Nick had lifted off the dean's neck.

Suddenly, another bolt of electricity jagged down from the ceiling like a disembodied, serrated knife blade, followed by another, then in quick succession, again and again, so many bolts they blurred into a steady stream. The key began to tremble. And as Adrian watched, it began to *change*.

Its surface lightened, going from dark gray, to light gray, to yellow—and then—

Gold.

"I don't believe it," Adrian whispered. "This can't be real."

There was a sound from the other side of the platform. Adrian looked up and saw Hailey coming up the opposite set of stairs. She was breathing hard, and there was sweat beading beneath her raised hair. Nick started toward her, but Adrian reached out and grabbed the man by his denim shirt.

"Wait," he started to say, trying to keep the fool from crossing through the bolts of electricity—

But then there was an awful sound, like a metallic cough, coming from above. Adrian smelled smoke and looked up. To his shock, the curved metal beams had turned bright orange, and he saw that the edges had begun to melt. Molten metal dripped from the corner—and then suddenly the entire center of one of the beams buckled inward.

"We need to get out of here," Nick shouted.

There was another metallic cough. Another of the beams twisted nearly concave. The entire platform shook beneath Adrian's feet. He looked across at Hailey, who had an anguished expression on her face. She had been right. They had found Franklin's device— his philosopher's stone. But now it was collapsing in front of them.

Adrian looked at the key, shining in the center of the platform. Pure gold, being struck again and again by the little bolts of electricity. Benjamin Franklin had completed what Paul Revere had begun—

"We've got to go!" Nick shouted again.

This seemed to wake Hailey from her stupor. She looked across at them, then at the ceiling, warping downward. She nodded, then turned toward the spiral steps behind her.

"Meet at the bottom!" she shouted.

Adrian gave one last look at the golden key, shook his head, then turned and leapt down the first two steps. He could feel Nick coming behind him.

———

By the time he burst out into the statue's pedestal, his mind was two self-destructive monologues deep.

History was wrong. The Statue of Liberty wasn't some gift from the French to commemorate the freeing of slaves—it was the culmination of a three-thousand-year-old pseudoscience. Paul Revere and Benjamin Franklin weren't simply Founding Fathers and revolutionaries—they were alchemists, part of a secret cabal that included Gustav Eiffel and Amadeus Mozart.

Everything he had believed was false.

There was no choice: History would have to be rewritten.

He skidded across the floor, then caught sight of Hailey ahead of him, rushing back to the hatch that led into the maintenance corridors. He rushed after her, and followed her into the darkness, barely ahead of Nick, who scrambled in after him. Around them, the entire statue still trembled—but they could no longer hear the groaning or the buckling from above. They could smell the smoke, though.

He crawled after Hailey, descending level by level.

History rewritten. He would be ridiculed. A fantastical, absurd, impossible story, but all of it was true. He had seen it himself.

Hailey reached the last corridor, then rushed to the hatch that opened out into the night. She was through just as Adrian felt the wet air of the outdoors himself, and then he had his legs over the ledge. The four-foot drop felt like a mile, and he hit the wet ground with a thud. Nick was right after him, landing in the dirt nearby.

Hailey rushed away from the statue until she'd reached the trees. Adrian ran next to her, then he looked back toward the star fort, and above that, the pedestal. Then the statue's feet, the length of broken chain above her ankle. Higher, higher, he could see the orange glow coming from the statue's crown.

The lightning seemed to have stopped. Whatever Hailey had done in the torch was over—the buckled beams of the crown's ceiling had destroyed whatever connection Eiffel had engineered into the statue's design. Franklin's device was quiet, maybe dead, forever. But it had been real. It had worked. Franklin, building on Revere, with the help of Mozart and Eiffel, had built a working philosopher's stone. It had collapsed—the energy from the bolts had simply been too much. Franklin was just too far ahead of his own time, handcuffed by the technology and materials of only a handful of decades beyond his lifespan. But he had, indeed, succeeded. For a brief moment, Adrian had stood witness to one of the greatest achievements in history.

Adrian couldn't see the flames, but he could imagine what the fire department helicopters would witness. Licks of fire leaping from the crown's windows, copper melting around its exterior, the ceiling collapsing down onto the viewing platform. It was going to be the headline in every paper in the world. Adrian could hear the sirens already, coming from every direction across the harbor, Coast Guard and fire department boats on their way. As he listened, he heard another noise—a hiss of water—and he guessed it was the sprinkler system finally going on inside the statue, echoing against the steps and beams and walls.

The sprinklers and the helicopters would be too late. There would be little, if any evidence left behind. Maybe the firefighters who picked through the wreckage would find the golden key, but it would mean nothing to them. Franklin's device would be melted and destroyed.

And yet, thinking of that wreckage, evidence lost and mangled and buried beneath melted copper and ash, Adrian didn't feel dismay. He felt elated.

He was a historian. He had built a career, an entire life, on his ability to resurrect the truth from ruins. Not fantasy, not science fiction, but real-life history, conjured out of dust and dirt and, more often than not, ash.

And here was history—but history that he had seen with his very own eyes.

"My god," Hailey said, interrupting his thoughts.

Adrian realized she wasn't looking up toward the statue's crown—but to a spot much lower, right beside one of the monument's feet. She was looking at the broken manacle, carved from the same copper as the rest.

There was something glowing against the copper. A smoldering sort of glow, lines of white and orange etched into the sheer side of the manacle.

"Edison's wiring," Hailey mumbled. Nick had moved next to her, looking as well. "Some of that wiring must have led all the way down to the feet. Carried the charge through."

Adrian watched as the glowing lines came together, then apart, then together. He realized the wiring had been placed in a specific design. It was—an image.

A message.

Adrian stumbled a step back. Hailey glanced at him.

"You know what this is," she said. It wasn't a question.

Adrian stared at the image—and suddenly, the lines began to fade. The white and orange dissipated, and then—the image was gone. Maybe because of the sprinkler system. Or maybe it had always been meant to come and go.

But it didn't matter. The image could have vanished a second after it had appeared. Adrian would have known exactly what it was.

The sirens were louder now, the Coast Guard and fire department boats coming closer. There were voices farther back on the island, too—security coming toward the statue, with walkie-talkies buzzing and boots pounding on the paths.

"We need to move," Nick said.

"Where?" Hailey asked. "We're on an island."

"In a minute this place will be swarming with firefighters," Nick responded. "Coast Guard, emergency personnel—we'll find a way to slip out. They won't be here looking for us. They'll be trying to save the statue."

He was pulling Hailey deeper into the trees. Adrian was still frozen in place.

Hailey looked back him. "Professor."

Adrian shivered, then turned away from the statue, trying to forget what he'd just seen.

"This isn't over, is it?" Hailey said, seeing the look on Adrian's face. And he saw that she was smiling.

She was right. They had found Franklin's philosopher's stone, had solved the mystery that had begun with Revere and the stolen art from the Gardner Museum. But the image on the side of the Statue of Liberty meant there was more to the story, if they had the will to continue looking. Revere's bell and Franklin's device, his kite and his key, were not the end of their journey.

She was going to keep going.

This wasn't over.

As Adrian turned to follow her, he realized—as much as he hated himself for the thought—she was *right*.

CHAPTER THIRTY-SIX

It was a true testimony to the craftsmanship that had gone into the fourteen-thousand-ton ship, the fine design of the nine parallel Rolls-Royce engines that powered its propulsion system, that the only sound Athena heard as she entered the hospital wing on the third level of the *Kratos* was the soft, rhythmic throb of a mechanical ventilator, emanating from beside the only bed in the concise, windowless cabin.

The hospital wing was forty feet long, consisting of a half dozen similar cabins; all had been decorated the same, white upon white upon white. The goal was for the wing to be as close a palate as possible to the Family compound on Arachne, a design throwback to the days when her father was still well enough to travel.

White on white on white, from the thick carpeting that silenced Athena's deck shoes as she moved through the cabin, to the curtains surrounding the single bed, even to the medical machinery itself, the boxy, shiny devices bristling with knobs and levers and tubes. The staff, too, currently two nurses in masks, gowns, and caps, and a renowned Greek surgeon and former head of trauma at one of the top hospitals in Europe, garbed in white upon white upon white.

Athena herself was wearing white; a sundress open a few inches at the top, her neck covered in an ivory-colored scarf. The weather along the eastern seaboard of the United States was dreadful compared to the Mediterranean—and she'd already spent more time here than she would ever have imagined.

Unfortunately, she now knew that she would be spending more time away from the sun, her father, and Arachne. Even now, despite their silence, the superyacht's engines were churning at top capacity, as the *Kratos* cut a path southward, away from its anchorage just beyond New York Harbor. In a few moments, Athena would return to the upper decks; she'd always enjoyed watching the ship pick up speed, and the squall that had formed so suddenly over the harbor was finally beginning to recede. Perhaps, by the time she was in the open air, the emergency choppers and news helicopters would have finished buzzing above the waters closer to the city— not that she was concerned about the attention the *Kratos* would no doubt receive. Her captain had filed all the necessary papers, and the Family's tendrils would ensure that nobody—not the press nor the emergency personnel—would ask the wrong questions. There would be nothing to link the *Kratos*, or the Family, to what had just happened on Liberty Island, which would be deemed either an act of terrorism or an accidental fire—depending on how inquisitive the responding officials intended to be.

She reached the curtains by the bed, and drew them back with one hand. The nurses quickly scurried out of her way, while the Greek surgeon moved next to her, his gloved hands holding a medical chart.

Athena didn't need to see the chart to understand the state of the patient in the bed in front of her; she could see the silhouette of the woman's broken and bruised body beneath the white sheets that covered her. The surgeon had already explained that so many bones were broken, it hadn't made sense to begin setting them.

Only the woman's face was visible above the sheets. Her rounded cheeks were red and raw, from where they had scraped along the electrified copper. Her hair was partially gone, and a section of her skull appeared to be missing, directly above her left eye.

It was amazing that she was alive at all. To survive, even if only temporarily, a fall from a monument of that height seemed impossible—though she was surprisingly not the first. A half dozen attempted suicides from the top of Lady Liberty had ended similarly, though an equal number had been successful. La Nadie hadn't just survived; she'd dragged her burned and broken body to the edge of the water, where Mr. Arthur had carried her aboard the waiting tender. Even so, she was so damaged now, she was barely recognizable.

But Athena didn't need the poor woman to recover—she had only needed La Nadie to be briefly revived. And to that end, the Greek surgeon had succeeded.

Moments after La Nadie had been brought aboard and transferred to the hospital wing, the woman had come awake. She had been in terrible pain, gasping, unable to talk. Instead, she had gestured for a writing utensil, and Athena had ordered one of the nurses to bring a pen and pad.

With broken fingers, La Nadie had begun sketching. It had been amazing to watch. Even to the end, the woman had been a true professional. It had taken her a few moments to fill the pad, her breathing becoming more strained by the second. Finally, she had collapsed back against the bed, her gnarled and burned hand opened, and the pen dropped to the carpeted floor without a sound.

Then the surgeon had moved in to place a trach tube and the ventilator.

Now, only a dozen minutes later, Athena listened to the rhythm of the woman's aided breaths, as she looked at the pad, which had been propped up on a stool parallel to the woman's disfigured head.

The pad was white, as was the stool; but the lines La Nadie had drawn on the paper were dark and strong, intersecting and converging into an image. In the moments after, Athena had raced upstairs to her computer center on one of the upper decks to match the image with her memory—and what she had discovered made up for all of the setbacks of the past few days.

The image wasn't just familiar; it was *historical*.

One of the most recognizable buildings in the world, though the image La Nadie had drawn—the image she had seen on the manacle at the base of the Statue of Liberty—was an early architectural version, perhaps from the original blueprint.

The White House, as it would have appeared at the turn of the nineteenth century, when it had first been constructed. Perhaps the most famous building in America, arguably in the world.

If Athena was right—if the image La Nadie had seen on the Statue of Liberty meant what Athena believed it meant—then the White House was more than the seat of the greatest political power on Earth. It was, itself, the most powerful *object* on Earth.

Athena felt the energy rising inside of her. She couldn't hear the *Kratos*' engines, but she could picture the massive turbines spinning, bursting with raw, incredible force.

She stared at the image next to the broken woman, as her heart pounded in her chest.

Her birthright. Her children's future. Her quest.

She turned away from the image, and the broken woman in the bed. As she passed the surgeon, she nodded, and then she let the curtain close behind her.

A moment later, as she crossed the thick carpeting toward the door of the cabin, the rhythmic sound of the mechanical ventilator paused, then went silent. And all that was left was the whisper of her deck shoes against the carpet.

White upon white upon white.

ACKNOWLEDGMENTS

First and foremost, I am immensely grateful for the wonderful community of readers who responded to the wild—and sometimes maniacal—twists and turns that played out in the pages of the *Boston Globe* when the first part of this story came to life as "The Mechanic," a serialized novella that ran daily over a period of two frantic weeks in 2021. It was one of the most exciting and terrifying writing experiences of my career, and it led to what I consider one of my favorite works, *The Midnight Ride*. It's because of those readers that I got to continue this story with *The Mistress and The Key,* and I am forever indebted to both the readers and to my hometown newspaper for giving me this opportunity. Special thanks to Linda Pizzuti Henry, without whom this story would not exist; and to Brian McGrory, Mark Morrow, and Heather Hopp-Bruce, who helped bring it to life in such spectacular fashion.

Likewise, immense thanks to my wonderful editor, Lyssa Keusch, a bright light showing me the way forward as I twisted the many threads of this epic, historical mystery together. Thanks also to my many advisors: my friends at the Paul Revere House in Boston, especially Dr. Robert Shimp, whose brilliance was vital to my research; my dad, for his scientific expertise; and many other experts in various fields who continually pointed me in the right directions.

As usual, immense thanks to my incredible agents, Eric Simonoff at WME and Matt Snyder at CAA. And to my family—Tonya, Asher, Arya, Bagel, and Cream Cheese—who were around every step of the way. I couldn't have done this without you.

ABOUT THE AUTHOR

Ben Mezrich is the *New York Times* bestselling author of *The Accidental Billionaires* (adapted by Aaron Sorkin into the David Fincher film *The Social Network*), *Bringing Down the House* (adapted into the #1 box office hit film *21*), *The Antisocial Network*, and many other bestselling books. His books have sold over six million copies worldwide.

PHOTO CREDITS

125, et alia: Philadelphia Museum of Art: Gift of Mr. and Mrs. Wharton Sinkler, 1958, 1958-132-1

195: Public domain via Wikimedia Commons

260: Alexandre Jaborska, Public Domain via Wikimedia Commons

295: Maurice Koechlin, Emile Nouguier, Public Domain via Wikimedia Commons

326: Barry Lawrence Ruderman Antique Maps Inc.

370: Courtesy of the Maryland Center for History and Culture, 1976.88.3